RYDER
a slater brothers novel

Stacey,
xoxo
—L.A.

NEW YORK TIMES & USA TODAY BESTSELLING AUTHOR
L. A. CASEY

Ryder
a slater brothers novel
Copyright © 2016 by L.A. Casey
Published by L.A. Casey
www.lacaseyauthor.com

Cover Design by Mayhem Cover Creations | Editing by JaVa Editing
Formatting by JT Formatting

This book is licensed for your personal enjoyment only. This book may not be re-sold or given away to other people. If you would like to share this book with another person, please purchase an additional copy for each recipient. If you're reading this book and did not purchase it, or it wasn't purchased for your use only, then please return to your favorite book retailer and purchase your own copy. Thank you for respecting the hard work of this author.

All rights reserved.

Except as permitted under S.I. No. 337/2011 – European Communities (Electronic Communications Networks and Services) (Universal Service and Users' Rights) Regulations 2011, no part of this publication may be reproduced, distributed, or transmitted in any form or by any means, or stored in a database or retrieval system, without prior written permission of the author. The scanning, uploading, and distribution of this book via the Internet or via other means without the permission of the publisher is illegal and punishable by law. Please purchase only authorized electronic editions and do not participate in or encourage electronic piracy of copyrighted materials. This is a work of fiction. Names, characters, places, brands, media, and incidents are either the product of the author's imagination or are used fictitiously. The author acknowledges the trademarked status and trademark owners of various products referenced in this work of fiction, which have been used without permission. The publication/use of these trademarks is not authorized, associated with, or sponsored by the trademark owners.

Ryder / L.A. Casey – 1st ed.
ISBN-13: 978-1519782038 | ISBN-10: 1519782039

Also by L.A. Casey

Slater Brothers series:

DOMINIC
BRONAGH
ALEC
KEELA
KANE
AIDEEN

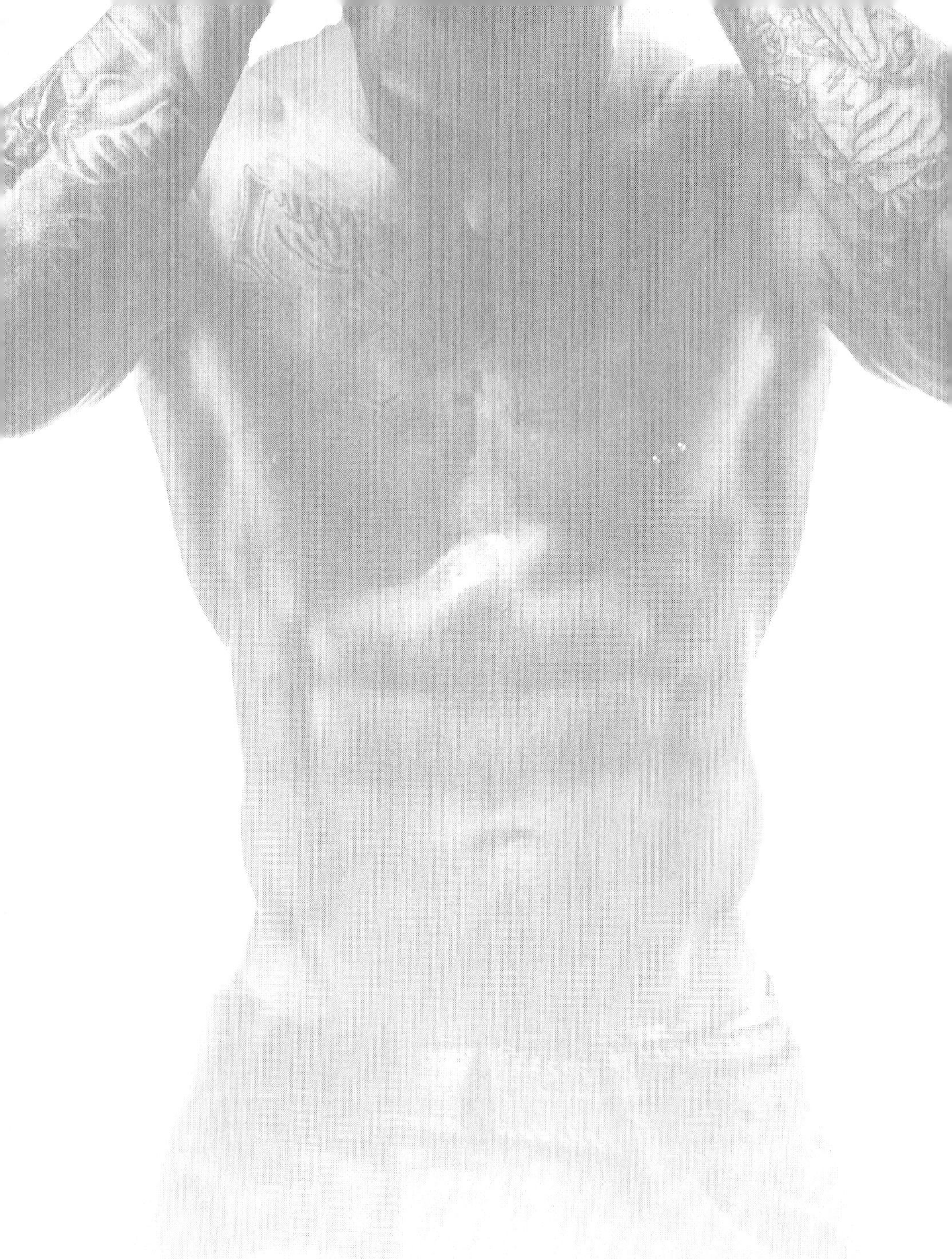

My readers – this is for you.

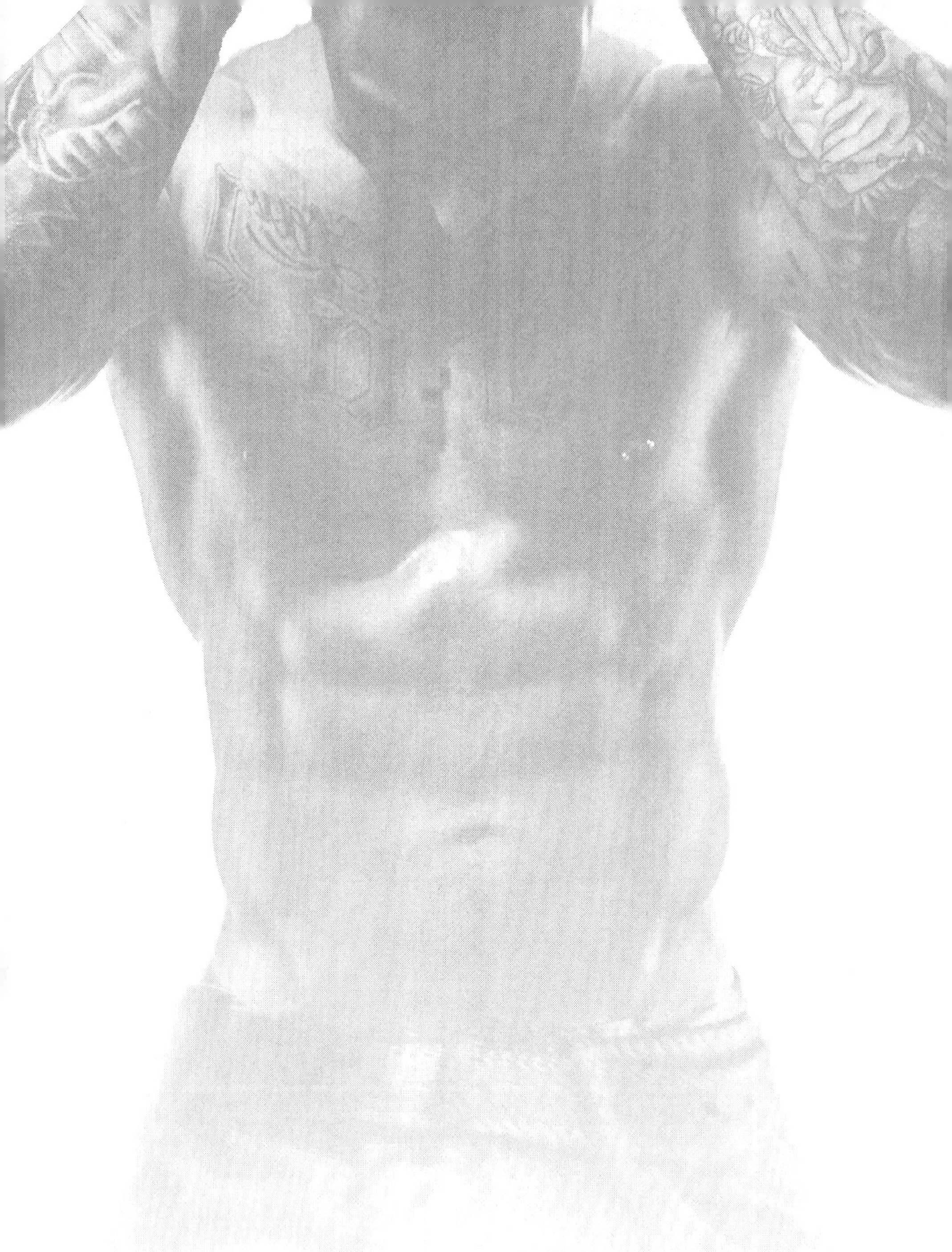

TABLE OF CONTENTS

Chapter One	1
Chapter Two	12
Chapter Three	30
Chapter Four	76
Chapter Five	87
Chapter Six	100
Chapter Seven	137
Chapter Eight	151
Chapter Nine	162
Chapter Ten	172
Chapter Eleven	177
Chapter Twelve	183
Chapter Thirteen	194
Chapter Fourteen	224
Chapter Fifteen	245

Chapter Sixteen	256
Chapter Seventeen	279
About the Author	304
Acknowledgements	305

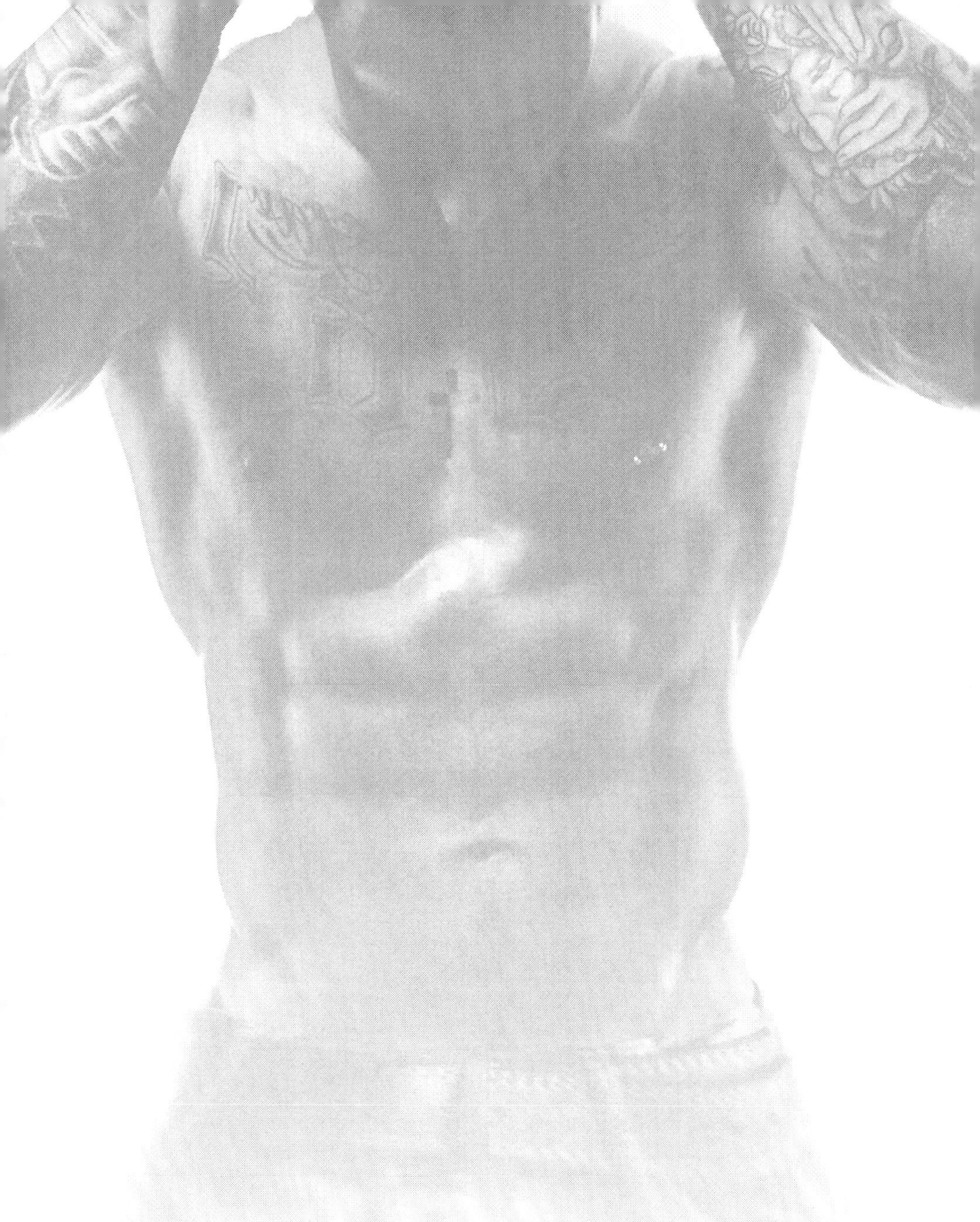

CHAPTER ONE

Don't cry.

I repeated the thought over and over as I sat in my best friend's apartment. Aideen Collins was wrapped up in the arms of her fiancé—Kane Slater—and they both focused their attention on their beautiful baby boy, Jax.

Those I loved surrounded me, and what should have been a happy time, wasn't. Not for me anyway. I watched my little sister, Bronagh, interact with *her* fiancé, Dominic Slater, who, like Kane, was *my* fiancé's brother, and I fought back tears as his hand absentmindedly stroked her abdomen where their baby girl was growing.

I gnawed on my inner cheek as I looked away from the happy couple and focused on the plasma screen TV on the wall facing me. My eyes watched the programme that was showing, but my brain had no clue what was happening because it was elsewhere. I straightened up and hoped I didn't appear to be so out of sorts, but I wouldn't have been surprised if I did, because I felt dreadful.

I was jealous.

I was green with envy every time I looked at Kane and Aideen with their sweet Jax, but my heart broke when I watched how Dominic interacted with Bronagh. She was my little sister. I was a whole decade older than her and she had surpassed me on the journey to motherhood. I had no doubt she would marry before me, too.

I hated that I felt so bitter towards my own blood. I was beyond happy for them, but I hated them a little at the same time. She and Dominic were solid. They suited each other so well, and their love, though sometimes extremely intense, was true and forever binding. The more I let myself think about them, the more depressed I felt when I looked at my own relationship.

I didn't think it could even be classed as a relationship anymore. Ryder and I, we both changed. Somewhere along the line, we stopped being nice to one another. To a point, we stopped being loving towards one another. It started out as normal bickering that grew into full blown screaming contests. We weren't even at that angry stage anymore; we were at the silent one.

We ignored one another, and when we did interact, it wasn't pleasant.

I didn't know where we went wrong, but Ryder and I, we fell out of love. It pained me to admit that, but it was the truth. I loved him dearly, but I wasn't *in* love with him anymore. Not with the version of Ryder I was living with. I was deeply in love with the man he *used* to be, the man who would give me the world if I asked. It broke my heart because I had no idea how we had gotten to the point we were at. I had no idea what I did wrong.

It was sorrowful.

I glanced to my left to where he was sitting on Aideen's sofa. He was, as usual, tapping away on the screen of his phone and paying me no mind. I almost snickered when I remembered, many months ago, that I used to feel hurt when he gave his phone more attention than me, but now I relished that the stupid device held his gaze, because I never wanted him to look at me and *really* see me like he used to, because he would see how weak I had become.

I didn't want him to see that I was broken.

I looked away from him and picked up the bottle of water I got from Aideen's fridge when I came over. I uncapped the bottle, took a swig and swallowed down the cool liquid. I widened my eyes when some of the water went down the wrong way and entered my lungs. I lowered my bottle and instantly began coughing as I lifted my hand and pressed it against my chest.

I jumped with fright when I felt a hand press against my back, and lightly tap away, helping me get the water up and regain my composure. I looked back to my left as Ryder retracted his hand away from me, without ever looking away from the screen of his phone.

I stared at him blankly, blinking.

I wasn't sure what to make of his kind gesture, which was terribly sad. He was my fiancé and I was surprised that he touched me. He never touched me anymore. Not if he could help it, anyway.

"Thank you," I said to him, my voice low.

He didn't look at me as he said, "Don't mention it."

Silence settled over us again and instantly my sadness returned.

I hated feeling so down.

I looked away from Ryder and glanced around the room, my eyes landing on Aideen as Bronagh and Keela moved away from her, smirks in place on both of their pretty faces.

What were they up to now? I wondered.

I smiled to myself and shook my head at the troublesome trio. I glanced down to my leg when it vibrated. I reached into my pocket and took out my phone, smiling when my co-worker's name flashed across the screen.

Ash Wade.

He joined our crew at the hospital about six months ago. He was a twenty-eight year old English man who moved over from London when he was twenty years old and loved it so much that he never went back home.

Ash was a hoot. He made me laugh on days that I thought I could do nothing but cry. He talked to me, and he listened to me talk. A *lot*. He became quite a good friend of mine, and I was very thankful to have met him at a point in my life when I needed a pick-me-up.

Ash was pure light; he would brighten up anyone's day.

I slid my finger across the green blob on the screen then brought the phone to my ear. "What do you want?" I asked, grinning.

Ash snorted through the receiver. "It's a good thing I didn't misdial a hotline number and ask for phone sex when you fired *that* loaded question my way."

I joyfully laughed, the sound surprising both me, and others around me. I looked forward when I felt many sets of eyes on me, but only one set that caused me to tense up.

His eyes.

We had grown apart, but I could never seem to shake the sensation that came over me when he looked at me. The moment his eyes locked onto my body, I became hyper aware of every movement I made.

"Branna?" Ash's voice called out. "You there, Angel?"

I playfully rolled my eyes.

Ash decided to label me with the nickname 'Angel' when the grandfather of one of our patients a few weeks back kept calling me it when he addressed me. I asked him to drop it, but he refused and called me it as often as possible, and it had seemed to stick.

"I'm here," I replied. "Sorry, just zoned out for a second."

"No worries," Ash chirped then lowered his voice. "You won't *believe* what happened on the ward today after you went home."

Ash worked the delivery ward with me, and bar a few extra hours here and there, we had an identical roster. Since he started, I hadn't been on a shift where he wasn't there with me. It was like the Health Board knew we would make a good team and lumped us together indefinitely.

"If you tell me the patient in room four that screamed feckin' murder all day randomly stopped when I walked off the ward, then I'm goin' to bloody curse her."

Ash's deep laughter filled my ear, and it warmed my hurt heart.

"No, she was *still* screaming when I left... even though she got her epidural and was numb from the waist down."

I giggled. "There's always one who goes *way* overboard."

Ash grunted. "You're telling me."

I chortled. "Go on, tell me what happened."

"The lady in room one, you know, the hot redhead with the *massive* tits?"

Ash was brilliant, I silently sighed, *but he was still such a man.*

I good-naturedly shook my head. "Yeah, what about 'er?"

"She shit herself as she pushed. Her husband freaked out not knowing what was happening and fainted. As he fell he knocked into the bed and caused shit to literally fly *everywhere*."

I leaned onto the arm of the sofa as laughter erupted out of me.

"I swear," Ash laughed with me. "It was both hilarious *and* disgusting."

I wiped under my eyes with my free hand when tears of laughter gathered and threatened to spill over the brim.

"Did she deliver fine? Is the baby okay?" I asked, automatically switching to midwife mode. "And the husband, is he okay?"

"All three are fine. The mother did well, and she had a healthy little boy, but I doubt the husband will step foot on the delivery ward ever again. He made his wife swear to bring her mother with her in the future."

I continued to laugh. "I bet you all had a right laugh about that."

"We did," Ash confirmed. "Sally almost wet herself from laughing after she got the baby cleaned up."

Sally was the fifty-seven year old mother of the delivery ward. I wasn't on shift with her very often, but when I was, she cracked me up with tales from her younger days.

I shook my head, smiling joyfully. "I can't say I'm sorry I missed it. I've fifty-three deliveries runnin' with nothin' other than regular bodily fluids and a baby poppin' out." I blessed myself before I said, "Thank God."

"You know your first patient on shift tomorrow will shit herself just for that comment?"

"Bite me!" I quipped.

Ash gleefully laughed. "I'll see you in the morning, but remember I can't pick you up, okay? I've to bring my sister to college on my way into work."

He usually picked me up on our way to work since I sold my car last year and Ryder always needed his Jeep.

"Yep, no problem, I'll see you at work."

I pocketed my phone and yawned before looking to Ryder who was still busy with his phone.

"Do you plan on being here long?" I asked, not looking at his hands in fear I'd take his phone just to see what was so captivating that he couldn't look away from it.

He glanced at me and shook his head. "You wanna leave now?"

I nodded. "I'm on shift at eight in the mornin' and wanna go to sleep early."

Ryder pocketed his phone. "I'll see if Damien wants a ride back."

I absentmindedly smiled as I thought about my boy. He helped bring some life back into me when he came home and moved back into the house. He made it—me—feel less empty.

I blinked when Ryder stood up from the chair. He offered me his hand and, for a moment, I was hesitant about putting my hand in his. I shook it off and slid my palm into his large calloused one. I licked my lips when he pulled me to my feet, but frowned when he immediately released my hand and moved past me, heading towards his brothers'. I tried not to let it get me down, but I couldn't help it. I missed him. I missed being close to him. I missed sex with him. I couldn't remember the last time we were intimate, and I hated it.

I said goodbye to the girls, the brothers, and winked at Kane as he brought Jax into his room to put him to bed. I congratulated my sister and Dominic on finding out the gender of their baby once more, and followed Ryder out of Aideen's apartment, down the hallway and into the elevator.

"Dame will be home later," Ryder said as he hit the button for the ground floor.

The doors closed shut, encasing us together. I felt him look at me, so I kept my eyes dead ahead, making sure my body was tense and non-moving, too.

"Who were you talking to on the phone?" he asked me, his voice so low I barely heard him.

I was a little annoyed that he asked me an invasive question when he never answered any of mine. I wanted to counter with multiple questions of my own, asking where he went every night when he thought I was asleep and why he was on his phone all the time, but I had no energy for a fight. He wouldn't answer me if I asked anyway; he never did.

"Just Ash who works the delivery ward with me."

Out of the corner of my eye, I saw Ryder nod. He had never met Ash, so I had no idea what was going through his mind with my response.

"Are you okay?" he randomly asked a moment later.

I was so surprised at the question that I looked at him with raised eyebrows and said, "Yeah, why wouldn't I be?"

He shrugged, staring down at me, his eyebrows raised. "You barely cracked a smile when Bronagh was announcing she was having a girl."

Because I did my happy dance back at the hospital when she found out.

I looked forward. "I had a long day at work, I'm just tired."

"Too tired to be happy for your sister?"

"I *am* happy for 'er." I snapped at the insult. "I don't need to be all up in her face to be happy for 'er, Ryder."

Silence.

"It seems to me like you're a little bit..."

"A little bit *what*?" I pressed.

The door of the elevator opened just as Ryder said, "Jealous."

I stepped out of the elevator, politely nodded to the security man that manned the lobby desk of Aideen's apartment building, and quickly walked in the direction of the main entrance.

"Branna?" Ryder called after me. "Look, wait a second."

I didn't. I picked up my pace and almost sprinted out of the apartment complex. When I got outside, I nodded to the security guards at the doors and headed straight for Ryder's Jeep that was parked in-between his brothers' cars.

I rushed to the passenger door and stared at the handle until I heard Ryder sigh and press on his car key, unlocking the doors. I gripped the handle, pulled the door open and got up into the car, slamming the door shut behind me.

"God dammit, Branna," Ryder complained when he got into the driver's seat. "Don't take your bad mood out on my car."

Fuck you and your stupid car, I inwardly growled.

"I wouldn't be in a bad mood had you not said somethin' so..."

"So what?"

"*Insensitive!*" I finished.

"Insensitive," Ryder repeated and turned his body to face me. "*How* is me saying you're jealous of Bronagh having a girl insensitive?"

I couldn't even look at him.

"You aren't stupid. Think about it and I'm sure you'll realise why."

Ryder didn't move a muscle as he continued to stare at me.

"You *are* jealous," he murmured then gasped. "You want a baby?"

I looked out the window, not answering him.

"Branna," he pressed. "You want a *baby?*"

Without looking at him I said, "I've wanted a baby for *years*, I just never said anythin' to push the issue with you because so much bullshit has happened to our families, and being the oldest pair we had to push everythin' aside and make sure everyone else was okay. We're the parental figures. We make sure everyone is doin' good before we even *consider* lookin' at our own needs."

Ryder was silent as I spoke so I pressed on.

"You *know* I love kids and I probably would have had a few before I met you, but havin' a life was put on hold when me parents died. I had to focus on Bronagh, not me, *her*. Bein' a midwife was me dream, it's the *one* thing I allowed meself to want. It's why I worked me arse off to become one in me late twenties whilst raisin' a bratty teenager."

I glanced at him as he continued to remain silent.

"Do you think we're at a point where we should have a kid?" he eventually asked, and I heard the doubt laced throughout his voice.

It killed me, but I agreed with him.

"No, we aren't in the position to raise a dog, let alone a child."

Ryder faced forward and jammed his key into the ignition and started up his car. He backed out of the parking spot, and pulled onto the road and began the journey of driving us home.

"Besides," he argued, "we'd actually have to *fuck* in order to get you pregnant."

I flattened my hands out on my thighs and resisted the urge to ball them into fists.

"We probably would if *you* didn't go off every single night to do God knows what."

The silent 'or who' was implied, but the words never left my lips because I was terrified it might turn out to be a 'who' that was the reason for him leaving every night. I didn't think I would be able to handle that, and decided I was better off not knowing. My sister, and the other girls, would smack me around for resorting to this way of thinking, but they didn't know what my home life or relationship with Ryder was like.

They thought they knew, but they didn't.

"Don't feed me that bullshit," Ryder growled as his hands tightened around the steering wheel. "I'm home a lot and you *still* never put out. You left our bed to sleep up in Dominic's old room, the farthest away from me that you can be in *our* house."

I felt disgusted.

"Me purpose on this Earth isn't to fuck you whenever you see fit, Ryder."

"No," he agreed, "but it'd be nice if I could hit it at least once a fucking week. I haven't touched you in months. I'd settle for fucking *spooning* at this point."

He spoke of me like I was nothing more than a sexual object.

"And whose fault is that?" I bellowed, throwing my hands in the air. "*You've* pulled away from me. We don't talk, we don't laugh, we don't do anythin' but fight with one another and it's *your* bloody fault. *You* have landed us in this rut, and the sad thing is I don't even know why! I don't know what you do when you leave the house every night or why you're always on your phone, and it's pathetic that I've just accepted it, but I'm too tired. I fight with you all the time, I'm too exhausted to do anythin' else."

I turned my head and looked out the window of the car, willing the tears in my eyes not to fall. I didn't want to cry. I was fucking *sick* of crying.

"I've *told* you I'm taking care of some things. That's all you need to know."

He had been 'taking care of some things' for a fucking *year* now; he needed to change up his response because it was getting old, and the more I heard it, the more it grated on my already worn nerves.

I closed my eyes, gutted he still wouldn't share his secrets with me.

"I don't believe you, Ryder," I said quietly.

"Then I don't know what to tell you, Branna," he replied with agitation though he tried to cover it up with a scowl.

"How about the truth for once?" I countered. "Just *tell me* where you go and what you do. Please."

His hands tightened around the steering wheel once more as we approached our street.

"I can't tell you, you wouldn't understand."

I looked down to my thighs. "I can't understand if you don't help me to."

Ryder grunted as he pulled into our driveway, and put the car in park. He took his keys from the ignition and said, "This is on me, okay? It's nothing for you to worry about, and you *will* worry if I tell you, and I don't want that to happen. We're all under a lot of pressure with Big Phil still out there, and my business doesn't need to be added to that."

He got out of the car, closed the door, then walked up the pathway and disappeared into our house, leaving me on my own with only my thoughts for company.

"I can't do this anymore," I said aloud, forcing myself to hear the words I've silently repeated over and over these last few months.

We couldn't continue on the path we were on. Something had to change, and in that moment I knew *exactly* what I had to do to start the healing process for the many wounds that had been cut open and exposed over the last few years. I had to make a change. I *had* to separate myself from the very being that wounded me so... even if he didn't mean to.

I squeezed my eyes shut as pain struck. The remaining fragments of my willowed heart shattered into a million pieces as I made a life changing decision. A decision that would affect not only me, but my family and friends too. I reached out and blindingly gripped onto the dashboard of the car to stop myself from collapsing forward as I realised what I needed to do to be free.

I had to break up with Ryder.

Don't cry.

CHAPTER TWO

When my alarm went off the next morning, I sat up from my temporary bed in Dominic's old bedroom and winced. I lifted my hands to my face and sucked in a deep breath as my fingertips ran over the tender flesh under my eyes. They were slightly swollen and stung like a bitch, no doubt from crying myself to sleep the previous night.

I wanted to weep all over again when realisation hit that the sleep I eventually managed to get did absolutely nothing to change my mind about the decision I came to about Ryder, and that hurt even worse. I was hoping I would wake up and completely disregard my thoughts from the night before, but I didn't. I was so tired of being sad, and I needed to say goodbye to Ryder to stop that hurt.

I knew leaving him would open a whole other kind of wound filled with a different hurt, but I couldn't see a way around our current situation. Talking to him didn't work, shouting at him didn't work, screaming and crying didn't work. *Nothing* bloody worked.

I didn't want to argue anymore, I didn't want to cry anymore, I didn't want to fight anymore. I was exhausted. I was *done*.

"How am I goin' to do this?" I whispered to the empty room.

I closed my eyes and wished for the billionth time that I had my mother to talk to. I desperately needed someone to guide me, and I couldn't ask Bronagh or my friends, because it was me they came to when things went wrong, not the other way around. I was the eldest. I was never meant to lose my way; I was supposed to help others find theirs.

I was on my own.

I opened my eyes after a few moments and took a deep calming breath.

Work, I reminded myself. *You have to go to work.*

I would figure out how to end things with Ryder later, but right now I needed to get showered, dressed and go to work. I loved my job, which wasn't something a lot of people could say. It wasn't easy, and there were times I shed a lot of tears when a delivery went wrong, but nine times out of ten, I got to aid a woman bringing life into this world, and that soothed my soul.

It was the only thing in my life that kept me sane.

When I exited Dominic's old room, I listened for any sign of movement downstairs, but I heard nothing, which told me that Ryder wasn't home yet, or that he was still in bed. I didn't dare venture towards our shared bedroom to check because I would be hurt either way. If he were there, I'd be reminded that I *had* to break up with him, and if he wasn't, it was another reminder of *why* I had to break up with him.

I didn't win either way.

I turned and went back into the room I slept in and headed for the attached en-suite. I had showered in it multiple times over the last few months, so I kept some of my products in there for times when I couldn't sleep with Ryder, or in our bed. It was so messed up, but lately I couldn't sleep in our bed *without* him because I felt lonely, and I couldn't sleep in it *with* him either because his refusal to tell me what he was up to hurt too much.

It was a royally fucked up situation that I found myself in, and unfortunately the only solution I could find would kill me as much as it would Ryder.

Don't think about it, I willed myself.

After I showered, I dressed and plated my hair back into a

French braid. I flattened my palms over the front of my uniform and made sure I attached my pocket watch and nametag to my shirt. In the bathroom, I filled in my brows to darken them and applied my favourite strawberry scented moisturiser.

I never put anything else on my face when I went to work. I did back when I first started, but I quickly found that I rubbed my face and eyes a lot during my shifts and thus ruined my carefully applied makeup. Not to mention it got it all over my hands, too. It wasn't worth the hassle so moisturising my face and filling in my brows were all I ever focused on.

I grabbed hold of my bag and put my phone and purse into it then headed downstairs, and made sure to keep all noise to a minimum. Whilst in the kitchen, I passed on breakfast and made a cup of tea instead. When I finished drinking my tea, I checked the time and cursed under my breath when I saw I was going to have to hustle to make it in time to catch the bus.

I scurried out of the kitchen, grabbed my coat from the rack in the hall, put it on then high tailed it out of the house. I shivered as the crisp October morning air surrounded me, nipping at my exposed skin. I made a mental note to buy a scarf and a pair of gloves as I walked out of the garden and closed the gate behind me. I turned and briskly walked in the direction of the bus stop.

I didn't know why, but I felt as if someone's eyes were on me so I glanced over my shoulder and when I saw no one was behind me, I looked at my house and swallowed. I locked my eyes on the window to my bedroom and saw Ryder was standing at it, shirtless, with his arms above his head. I knew he was gripping onto the curtain pole above him, but I wished he hadn't been because it showcased his rippling torso perfectly. I could see each sculpted muscle even at a distance.

He was looking at me, I *felt* his gaze trained on me, but I forced myself to shrug it off. I couldn't allow myself to become putty in his hands simply by him *looking* at me. I had to be strong. I had to focus on me. I turned away from my house, and Ryder, and broke out into a jog. I didn't stop moving until I reached the bus stop down the end of the street. I got there just as the bus pulled up.

Thirty minutes later I was off the bus and walked into the Coombe Maternity Hospital. I shook off the cramp in my behind from the hard bus seats and counted myself lucky that I managed to get a seat in the morning rush. I disliked public transport, and I missed car-pooling dearly. There was a time when Ryder drove me to work before he went off for the day, but that abruptly ended when things started going south between us. Most days Ash would collect me for work and Bronagh would pick me up when my shift ended. I had recently thought about getting myself a cheap car because I *hated* having to depend on others or have them go out of their way for me, but money was an issue.

Ryder, and his brothers, made a considerable amount of—blood—money from their past work, but I recently learned that a bad investment with Brandon Daley left Dominic, Alec and Ryder broke. I overheard something from the brothers months ago that I shouldn't have and brought it up to Ryder a few weeks after Aideen was hospitalised.

I found our joint account was dangerously low on funds but was quickly shut down when I asked Ryder about it. I asked where the money had gone, but he never gave me a direct answer, he just told me 'not to worry about it, and not to talk about it'. I asked if it was something to do with Brandon or his old life, but he ended each conversation with arguing. He never allowed any talk of Brandon or his old life in our house, and enforced it with foul words.

I never countered him because I never wanted to talk about it either; it brought back too many horrifying memories, but something was going on with Ryder, and I *knew* it had something to do with where he went every night. It was too much of a coincidence that the brothers lost a lot of money over the last few months then for Dominic to start working for Brandon to earn an income. I didn't know what Alec had his hand in, but I knew it wasn't legit.

Kane made his money legitimately. I wasn't supposed to know about it, but I overheard him and Aideen discussing expansions for his apartment complexes. I asked Ryder about it and he reluctantly filled me in on what Kane wanted to be kept private. I kept my mouth shut and pretended to be in the dark on his business ventures, but what I really wanted to do was congratulate and hug the hell out of him. He had managed to stay off the trail that Dominic, and possibly Ryder and Alec, had fallen back onto.

"Branna," Taylor Carey beamed when I walked onto the delivery ward.

Taylor was cool. She wasn't the type of friend I would confide in or tell my secrets to, because I didn't know her that well, but she made the job interesting when we were on shift together. I liked her.

I lifted my head and wiggled my fingers. "Hey, Tay."

Taylor lifted her arms over her head as she stretched and yawned.

My lip twitched. "Long shift?"

She nodded. "Busy night. There have been eight births in the last twelve hours since I came on shift at eight last night."

I whistled. "Good for the mammies, babies and the staff. Quick labours benefit everyone."

Taylor yawned, again. "They benefit the time passin' for me. I can't believe me shift is over already. I *love* when that happens."

I grunted. "I can't believe me shift is *just* startin', I feel like I've gone twelve rounds with Mike Tyson."

Taylor winced. "I noticed your eyes were a little puffy but I didn't want to say anythin'. Are you okay?"

I nodded. "Just a touch of the sniffles."

Lie.

Taylor frowned. "You shouldn't have a busy mornin' so you can be miserable here in peace. Rooms one and two are occupied and the women are only three and four centimetres dilated. I already noted their bloody pressure, temperature and pulse ten minutes ago so you're solid on that for another hour before you have to check them again. Both are teenagers, so they should keep occupied with chattin' until the others get here."

I grinned. "I bet in an hour five or six women from the holdin' wards will go into active labour and I'll have me hands full."

Taylor stood up and bumped her hip with mine. "That's the job."

"Aye," I agreed.

"Is Ash on shift with you today?" she casually asked as she gathered her belongings.

I took her place on the chair behind the nurses station.

"Yeah, he should be here now," I said as I seated myself. "We're always on together, I can't remember the last time I was workin' and he wasn't here."

Taylor sighed, dreamingly. "I'm so jealous, he is gorgeous and *so* bloody funny."

"Who is gorgeous and *so* bloody funny?"

I looked up when Ash spoke from behind Taylor and laughed when she spun around and almost knocked him out when her bag went airborne. Ash reacted faster than what seemed humanly possible and grabbed hold of Taylor's bag before it hit the floor. He straightened himself then handed it back to her with a bright smile. I could see the tip of Taylor's ears were red, so I could only imagine how flushed her cheeks were.

"We were talkin' about Ryan Reynolds," I said to Ash. "You know the actor who is the star of the new Deadpool film?"

Ash looked from Taylor to me and he nodded. "I know him, good actor."

My lips twitched. "He's gorgeous, and *so* bloody funny."

Taylor turned to face me and her eyes were bugged out making me laugh. Ash looked between us, confusion marring his handsome face, but he shook his head and decided against saying whatever question was on his mind. He was a smart cookie.

"I'm gonna head off," Taylor mumbled, avoiding eye contact with Ash who went into the break room to put his things away in his locker.

I grinned. "That amused me greatly."

"I'm so feckin' mortified," she whispered, her cheeks still flushed. "Do you think he knew I was talkin' about 'im?"

I shook my head. "Nah, he wasn't payin' attention I'm sure."

Taylor exhaled a relieved breath. "Okay, I'm gonna go before I say somethin' else that makes me want the ground to open up and swallow me whole."

I laughed. "See you."

Taylor pulled a face then scurried off the ward. I got up and brought my bag and coat into the break room and placed them into my locker. I attached my phone to the clip on my trousers then I glanced at Ash who was leaning against the small kitchen counter with his arms folded across his chest and a smug grin on his face.

I raised my brows. "What're you lookin' at me like that for?"

"I know Taylor was talking about me, I *was* paying attention."

I feigned annoyance. "You eavesdropper!"

Ash devilishly smirked. "So I'm gorgeous and *so* bloody funny, huh?"

I shrugged. "*She* thinks so."

"And you?" he pressed. "Do you agree?"

I pretended to think about it and it caused Ash to scowl which only made me laugh louder than before. "I think you're funny... *so* bloody funny," I teased.

Ash gripped his chest. "And not gorgeous?"

I playfully rolled my eyes. "You're alright."

He sobered up and waggled his brows. "I'm a bit of alright?"

"Yeah," I snorted. "You're a bit of alright."

"I'll take it!" He cheered.

I cringed. "You're too energetic for this hour of the mornin'."

Ash pointed at the kettle. "You want a cuppa to wake you up?"

I nodded. "Yes, please."

He got to work and made me a cup of tea that had me humming as I swallowed it down. We settled behind the nurses station and greeted three other co-workers who would be working the day shift with us. Shannon, Katie, and Jada. I relaxed as they checked on the two patients that were currently on the ward.

"Anything exciting going on this month for you?" Ash asked as we flipped through the files of the two patients on the ward.

I shrugged. "Bronagh turns twenty-three on the tenth, I'm sure we'll be doin' somethin' for that. You, of course, are invited to come along."

Ash chuckled. "Thanks, but I haven't met Ryder *or* his brothers yet, and from the sounds of things, I'd want to do that when everyone is sober."

My lips twitched. "They're all harmless. Most of the time. To us girls... maybe you shouldn't come now that I think of it."

Ash belly laughed, and it caused me to smile, but the smile was instantly wiped from my face when an unholy scream came from down the hallway and the buzzer for *code red* sounded. Both Ash and I jumped to our feet. He took off in the direction of the room that signalled the emergency along with our other colleagues while I dove for the phone.

"OR," a male voice answered on the second ring.

"Clear an OR, stat!" I breathed. "Code red on the delivery ward. Get Doctor Harris or the actin' chief on shift prepared for an emergency C-section. *Now*."

"Damn," the man on the phone hissed. "I'm on it."

The line went dead so I hung up the phone and rushed down to room two, the room that the red light was flashing above. I instantly felt sick and scared. In my four years at the hospital, I'd been on shift for seven code reds, and it never got easier. A code red on the delivery ward in my hospital meant a baby or mother flat lined—there was no trace of a heartbeat. The mother gets hooked up to a machine that tracks her and her baby's heartbeat, a code red meant the machine triggered the alarm attached to the machine.

When either mother or baby flat line we had only a matter of minutes to perform a C-section to get the baby out before we could work on either of them. I knew it was the baby who flat lined as I neared the room because I could hear the mother's screams and pleas for help. I entered the room and found who I guessed to be the father with his hands on the sides of his head and tears in his eyes, while Ash and another midwife, Jada, were holding down the mother-to-be.

I muscled my way into her view and grabbed hold of her cheeks. I had memorised her personal information from when I read her file at the nurses' station and roughly said, "Samantha, listen to me right *now*!"

She could barely contain herself, but her eyes locked on mine and I knew I had her attention for a just a few moments before she went off the hinges again.

"We're movin' you down to the OR for an emergency caesarean section. We're goin' to get your son out and into the world within the next few minutes to try and save 'im, and we *can't* do that without you, okay? We need you to be strong for us. Can you do that for me, honey?"

"Okay," she cried. "Just please save 'im. Promise me you will. *Please*."

I nodded, because I couldn't say the words aloud in case they turned out to be a devastating lie.

Everything passed by in a blur as myself, Ash and the father of the baby rushed Samantha down to floor two of the hospital and checked her into the OR where Doctor Harris and his team were ready and waiting.

"Ninety-one seconds since code red was activated. Well done, Branna," Doctor Harris said and patted my shoulder. "Good time from you and your team."

I nodded and released Samantha into their care. I stood like a statue and watched as the double doors to the OR swung shut. I heard Doctor Harris bark orders for a catheter and IV lines to be placed on Samantha, and for her abdomen to be cleaned with disinfectant. I held my breath seconds later as he announced he was administrating anaesthesia. As it was an emergency, Samantha would be out under general anaesthesia in a matter of seconds and would not be awake to witness the birth of her son.

I jumped when an arm hooked around my neck and pulled me into a firm chest. I knew it was Ash without having to look up. I closed my eyes and wrapped my arms around his waist and squeezed. He kissed the crown of my head and said, "We got her down here fast and Doc Harris is already making the incisions for the section. If anyone can save the baby, it's him and his team."

I knew that, but it didn't take away the fear I felt.

"I always get so invested," I whispered. "How can I help patients when I let me emotions take over?"

Ash held me out at arms length so I opened my eyes and looked up at him. "Listen to me," he said firmly. "When Sally isn't on shift with us, *you* are the mother of the ward. You're in charge, and that responsibility doesn't fall on your shoulders because you're sweet and kind, it's because you're a damn good midwife. You heard Doc Harris, we got her down here in ninety-one seconds and that is thanks to *you*."

I felt my lower lip wobble. "Thanks, Ash."

He winked. "No thanks necessary, kid."

Kid.

I managed a snort. "I'm four years older than you."

"Age is just a number, baby."

I chuckled, but closed my mouth when I heard commotion in the OR. I gripped onto Ash's arm when I heard a cheer. The doors opened slightly, and the beautiful sound of a newborn's cry filled the hallway.

"Yes!" I squealed and jumped onto Ash who was laughing as he caught me mid-air.

He swung me around then set me on the ground and gave me a tight squeeze. We waited ten minutes for Samantha's incision to be stitched closed and for the baby to be checked over. We both turned to a smiling Doctor Harris who rid himself of his surgical scrubs when he exited the OR. He gave me a hug and bumped fists with

Ash, which caused me to smile wide. Doctor Harris was fifty-five, and watching him bump fists with someone never failed to amuse me.

"This is on you, and your team," he told us both. "You did great. The baby is breathin' on his own, and the mother's vitals are steady, too. We'll admit him into ICU for observation, but he looks good. Well done."

A fresh surge of relief hit me.

"Thank God," I breathed.

Ash and I left the OR and headed back up to the delivery ward with an extra spring to our step. After we informed our colleagues that both Samantha and her baby were okay, we settled back behind the nurses station.

"It's hard to believe it's not even nine am yet," Ash said with a shake of his head.

I nodded in agreement. "It's goin' to be a long day."

"Thank God for tea," Ash mused making me laugh.

Thank God for *him*. I wholeheartedly knew I wouldn't be able to do this job without him. He was my partner in crime and we fed off each other in our field of work. I was lucky to have him in my life. Having good friends made even the darkest of times seem bright.

"Was it scary?" Dominic asked, his eyes wide.

I had just finished telling him about the code red on the ward that morning while Bronagh was upstairs in the bathroom.

I nodded and said, "It's always scary. I *hate* code reds."

Dominic nodded in understanding then glanced towards the kitchen door when we heard Bronagh descend the stairs. I reached over and touched his arm. "Don't mention it to 'er. I never tell 'er about them because it upsets 'er, but now that she is pregnant I don't want 'er to be scared that somethin' like that might happen to *her*."

Dominic nodded once, then turned his attention to Bronagh

when she entered the room. She placed her hands on her hips and sighed, deeply. "I'm so fat." She frowned. "It took me a whole sixty seconds to get meself off the toilet."

I snickered while Dominic tilted his head to the side.

"Fat?" he questioned. "And here I thought you were pregnant. Man, you had me fooled."

Bronagh gave him the finger. "Bite me, Fuckface. *You* did this to me."

"You bet your phat ass I did," he grinned, unfazed by the insult.

To be fair, Fuckface had made the transition from an insult to a term of endearment years ago, and I figured that was why Dominic never minded it.

I smiled while Bronagh moved to the end of the kitchen counter. She—stupidly—tried to jump up and sit on the counter like she had always done in the past, but now that she was pregnant it was dangerous, and hilarious, because she could never get up onto the counter without help.

"Dominic," I mused. "Give her a hand."

He got up, moved to Bronagh and carefully lifted her up on the counter. My sister watched him and smiled which caused him to smile too.

"Why're you looking at me like that?" he asked, amused.

"You didn't struggle liftin' me, that means I'm not *that* fat yet."

Dominic snorted. "I can bench press my own weight without breaking a sweat, and even halfway through pregnancy you're *still* fifty pounds or so lighter than me."

Bronagh clapped her hands together. "I hope it stays that way."

"It won't," I evilly grinned. "You'll put on another twenty pounds by the time you have 'er with the way you eat. Dominic has been orderin' pizza for you *at least* five times a week he said."

Bronagh scowled at me while Dominic laughed.

"You know," he began as I stirred the spoon in my cup of tea. "It bugs me that you haven't come around to calling me Nico like the other girls."

I grinned. "I knew you as Dominic long before you were the Nico who was hasslin' Bee in school."

His lip twitched. "Hassling? *Please*, she loved every second of my focus on her."

"Yeah," Bronagh said with a playful roll of her eyes. "Interaction with your annoyin' self was what I lived for back then."

Dominic gestured to his body. "You can't blame yourself. You have incredible taste, sweetheart."

Bronagh lazily swung for him, and he easily ducked out of the way, laughing softly. He got in her face before she could jump down from the kitchen counter and start a mess fight with him.

"And now," he murmured, resting his hands on her swollen abdomen. "We're having a baby together."

Bronagh leaned her head forward, and nuzzled her nose against his. I smiled at the pair of them, adoring the love they had for one another. They were still opposites in so many ways, but one thing no one could deny was how hard they loved each other. It was dangerous, the dependency they had on one another, but I understood it.

I understood what it was like to love someone so deeply that you invested your soul in theirs. I had that with Ryder, and it's why I was so broken now that it was fading away. I was slowly dying without his unconditional love, and I only had myself to blame.

You should have guarded your heart better, my mind sneered.

I looked away from Dominic and my sister and looked down to my phone when it pinged. It was a text message from Ash. I read it and snickered. I thumbed out a reply, hit send then pocketed my phone. I looked up to find the two love birds staring at me.

"Who was that?" Dominic asked, his eyebrow raised.

Nosey git.

"A co-worker," I responded then flicked my eyes to Bronagh. "He is pickin' me up to head back to work, are you still collectin' me at four?"

"Four?" she questioned. "Why not eight?"

I shrugged. "It's trainin' day for fourth year midwives from the university, I opted out of being part of it so I get to come home earlier. I'm exhausted and need to get some mental rest. I'm gettin' old, it appears."

That was a bullshit lie if I ever told one. What I wasn't saying was that I needed some me time to figure out how I was going to break up with Ryder. I was going to do it sooner rather than later. I wanted to do it like ripping off a plaster, quick and painless. Or just quick.

Dominic waved my concerns off. "You're still the hottest thirty-something year old I know."

No one was allowed say my real age, thirty-something was as close as they could get.

My lip quirked. "Thanks, that makes me feel *so* much better."

"He's right," Bronagh grinned. "You have a bangin' body, *and* your boobs are still perky."

Dominic's eye flicked down to my chest and it made me laugh.

"He is so predictable," I said to Bronagh.

My sister looked at him and gave him a nudge, regaining his attention.

"I'm sittin' *right* here," she scowled.

Dominic scratched his neck. "*You* were the one who was talking about her tits, not me."

Bronagh shook her head, grinning. "How dare I."

I smiled then stood up when I heard a horn beep outside. "That's for me," I said as I picked up my bag, and hooked the strap over my shoulder before pointing at my sister. "Four o'clock. Don't forget, I don't want to have to get the bus."

Bronagh saluted me. "I'll be there."

I gave her a hug and poked Dominic in the sides before I left their house. I smiled when Ash came into view as I approached his car. I carefully opened the passenger door and slid into the passenger seat. When I was buckled up I turned my attention to Ash and smiled, "Hello, loser."

He feigned hurt and his facial expression caused me to laugh, loudly.

"How was your break?" he asked as he pulled away from the kerb.

I yawned. "Not long enough, I could sleep for a year."

"Me too," Ash agreed, looking as tired as I felt. "I'm probably just going to hit the deli in the hospital for lunch in the future, being at home is too tempting because my bed is there."

I chuckled. "I agree, next time we can stay on site and shoot the shit in the café."

"Sounds like a plan, buddy."

We got to talking, and before I knew it we arrived at the hospital and were back on the delivery ward within half an hour.

"What are you doing?"

I looked up at Ash when he spoke. He placed his elbows on the desk of the nurse's station I was sitting behind, his blond hair falling into his sky blue eyes.

I pointed to the stack of paperwork next to me. "Signin' off on discharges, admittance forms and fillin' out the supply list that needs to be filed by the end of the day. It's nearly four and I want this done before I go home."

Ash gripped onto the counter, then heaved himself up until he was sitting on it and looking down at me. I shook my head at him.

"Sally will wipe the floor with you if she catches you sittin' up there." I commented. "She is on shift today, she came in after lunch."

Ash smirked. "*Please*, Sally loves me."

My lips quirked. "It's 'cause you flirt with 'er all the time."

"I flirt with *everyone*," he corrected.

I chuckled. "You're such a flirt slut."

Ash didn't deny the charges, instead, he embraced them. "A man's gotta do, what a man's gotta do."

I shook my head good-naturedly and looked back down to the

form I was filling out, but once again my thoughts shifted to Ryder and it caused me to sigh.

"Hey," Ash murmured. "You okay?"

I glanced up at him and nodded. "Huh? Oh, yeah, I'm great."

He deadpanned, "You wanna try telling me the truth this time?"

His awareness of me caused me to smile as I looked back down to the form I was filling out. "You don't want to hear about me silly drama, Ash," I assured him.

I looked up just as he raised an eyebrow and said, "I wouldn't have asked if I didn't want to know."

I thought about that for a second then said, "I... I just had a fight with Ryder last night."

He winced. "*Another* one?"

Ash was the only person in the world who I talked to about Ryder because he was outside of my family circle. He didn't go and tell the brothers or girls about my worries, he kept them between us, and I really liked that. It was kind of therapeutic to be able to vent to someone and not worry if they would tell Ryder or one of his brothers.

I nodded solemnly. "It was a bad one. He was so insensitive about me feelin's with Bronagh's baby. He called me jealous and told me it was me own fault I wasn't pregnant because we never have sex."

I left out the crude things Ryder said because Ash didn't need to know how he spoke to me.

"What a fucking prick," my friend grumbled, surprising the hell out of me.

I widened my eyes at him and he shrugged his shoulders unapologetically. "I'm not sorry," he stated. "Your fiancé becomes a bigger dick every time you tell me about him. Does he not realise how good he has it with you?"

I felt my cheeks heat up. "I don't think I'm anythin' to fuss over, Ash."

"You bloody well are," he countered. "Don't allow him to make you feel less than perfect, you're all of that and more. Own it."

I was mortified.

"Stop, Ash," I whispered to avoid hearing the tremor in my voice. "You always embarrass me when you talk about me like that."

He chuckled. "I know, but I'm hoping the more I go on about how fabulous you are, the sooner you'll realise it's the truth."

I waved him off. "Your sugar sweet words will get you nowhere with me, cowboy."

Ash winked. "I know, because you're loyal to the core. You're a good woman, and fuck Ryder if he can't see that."

He had a very odd way with words.

I smiled, appreciatively. "Thanks, Ash."

"You got it, Angel," he replied.

I lost my smile and growled. "If you 'Angel' me one more time—"

"I'm going to bring up a patient from Peter's ward, catch you in a few." He laughed and jumped off the counter before I could catch him and whack him upside the head.

"I'll be here when you get back." I wickedly grinned and wiggled my slapping hand at him. "Waitin'."

He only smirked at me, the challenge I set clearly amusing him. I shook my head, smiling when he went out of view. He was great and I knew if Ryder wasn't in my life I would be fawning over him and doing almost anything to be with him because not only was he gorgeous, he was so sweet and caring, but having him as just my friend meant so much to me.

I knew he would help me get through my break up with Ryder when I eventually ended things. I knew he would be there for me. That was just the kind of person he was. He was a sweetheart.

Thinking of how sweet Ash was brought on thoughts of how different he was compared to Ryder. My fiancé wasn't horrible... he was just different now. For the first several years, he was so sweet and caring and put me at the centre of his world. Everything between us was so incredible. Things had certainly changed between us over the last year and a half.

    Every time I saw him I felt just like the first night he entered my life, and that was both comforting and soul shattering because I had to break up with him knowing that he breathed life into me from the darkness.

CHAPTER THREE

Five years ago...

"I'm not feelin' Darkness tonight, Ado," I sighed into the speaker of my phone as I twisted my waist length brown hair around my fingers. "Bee had a bad day at school today, I think she got into an argument with someone. She won't tell me what happened, but she is *really* out of sorts, she hasn't picked up her Kindle at all today and that isn't like her."

Aideen, my life-long best friend, groaned. "She is a big girl, Bran. If she won't tell you what's up then maybe she just wants to deal with it herself *without* her big sister pokin' her nose in."

That hurt my feelings.

"I don't poke me nose into her business... I just worry."

"Aye, mama bear, I know," my friend agreed, "but she isn't a kid anymore. She's a teenager and they keep a *lot* of shit bottled up."

I knew that and I knew Bronagh was almost eighteen and wasn't considered a child anymore, but I couldn't help but stress over her. It had been my job to worry about her for the last nine years, and I couldn't just switch the instinct off. She was very much my little sister and baby wrapped into one.

I sat on my bed and frowned, deeply. "I suck at this parentin' thing."

Aideen chortled. "Don't even go there, you're a better parent to Bee than most people are to their biological children."

I appreciated her saying so.

"I try very hard with her," I sighed, "but the older she gets, the harder it gets. I'm worried sick that she will get cabin fever and go insane because she is always indoors. She hardly ever socialises, her teachers at school tell me durin' parent teacher meetin's that they've never met a girl so closed off."

"Listen to me," Aideen began. "There is *nothin'* wrong with that girl, she is perfectly fine, she just deals with things—and others—differently."

I glanced up at the picture of my parents on my bedroom wall and looked away when tears threatened to fill my eyes. "I don't know of she'll ever fully accept that they're gone, Aideen," I swallowed. "She doesn't even like seein' pictures of them, never mind talkin' about them. I'm very concerned for 'er mental health."

Aideen grumbled to herself then said, "She'll accept it eventually, it just takes longer for some people. Trust me, her hormones are goin' to kick in eventually and she will have boy fever, you mark me words. These conversations will be replaced by typical big sister complaints like, 'I have to re-stock the condoms in the bathroom because Bee is shaggin' too much."

"Aideen!" I shouted with unexpected laughter.

She cackled through the receiver of the phone, snorting every now and then.

I shook my head. "You can seriously tell you were raised with all lads, Ado. You do *not* speak like a lady."

"Darlin'," she chuckled. "I'm perfectly okay with not being a lady, a lady wouldn't land herself a man like Skull, would she?"

I still couldn't believe she dated someone that went by the name Skull. Even more, I couldn't believe that before she dated him, *I* had a very brief fling with him. It was the tattoos that drew me to him; he had a mean as fuck tattoo on the side of his head that travelled down his neck and ended at his hip bone. If the tattoos and his incredible good looks didn't sway me, his manners would have. Skull might look like a menacing man, but he was most definitely a sweetheart.

"His nickname still gives me the creeps," I shivered. "Can't you just call him Trevor when we speak about him?"

Aideen cackled. "Nah, I like how freaked out you get when I say it."

"Bitch," I grumbled.

She wasn't bother by my insult.

"Can you let your sister sulk on her own for a few hours and come dancin' with me? We haven't had a night out in *forever*."

Guilt settled in my chest. "Aideen—"

"Please, Branna," she cut me off. "*Please*."

I groaned. "You're makin' turnin' you down very hard."

"That's what she said."

I laughed. "Okay, loser, I'll come out."

Aideen whooped. "Brilliant. Wear somethin' sexy, I want you to *at least* kiss some hot piece of man flesh tonight."

I grimaced. "You're vile, Aideen Collins."

"I know," she laughed. "Do you want to meet at Darkness or at me apartment?"

"Is Skull pickin' you up?" I quizzed.

"No, he is on shift at the club tonight. He is on at ten, but we won't be goin' 'til half eleven or so."

I gnawed on my inner cheek then said, "I'll meet you at the club. It's already half nine and I need to shower and get ready. I'll have more time if I just meet you there."

"'Kay, bitch." Aideen cheered. "I can already taste the Vodka."

I snorted. "See you later."

"Byeeee."

I lowered my phone from my ear when the beep signalling Aideen hung up sounded. I plugged my charger into the base of my phone then headed out of my room and went down the hallway to my sister's bedroom. I knocked on the closed door and waited.

"Come in, Branna," Bronagh called out.

I opened the door, and the sight I was greeted with caused me to smile. My sister was tucked up in bed with her covers pulled up to her chin. I glanced at her television and chuckled when I saw she was watching *Supernatural*. It was quite possibly her favourite television show. She watched it religiously.

"Are you okay?" I asked Bronagh when I climbed up onto her bed and settled in next to her.

She nodded. "I'm good, school was just a little... hectic today."

I wanted to press her for information, but I knew it would just lead to an argument. Aideen was right; she would talk to me about whatever was bothering her when she was ready to.

"Okay, well, if you want to talk to me. I'm here."

Bronagh's lips twitched as she watched her program with focused eyes. "Thanks."

I played with her hair for a minute or two then said, "So Aideen asked me to go out with her for a few drinks tonight, do you mind?"

Bronagh shook her head. "I'm goin' to sleep after this, so nope."

I knew she wouldn't mind, but it relaxed me hearing her saying it.

I loosened up. "Okay, great. I've already locked the house up before I came up here, but before I leave I'll check once more and set the alarm."

Bronagh lifted her arms out of the covers and gave me two thumbs up. I leaned over and kissed her forehead and said, "I'll see you tomorrow after school. I've to head to class in the mornin' then I've to go to the hospital in the afternoon."

My sister nodded. "Can you leave some money out for me? I'm going to the deli on my lunch hour tomorrow."

I kissed her head and stood up. "Okay, I'll put it on the kitchen counter for you."

Bronagh looked at me then and grinned. "Be good."

I raised my eyebrow. "I'm always good."

"You're right," my sister smirked. "Maybe you should be very *bad* then."

"Bronagh!" I gasped making her laugh.

I folded my arms across my chest. "I'm still not used to you makin' jokes like that."

"Get used to it then," Bronagh snorted. "I'm sure when I see you tomorrow I'll take the piss out of you again."

"You're a bitch," I grumbled.

"And proud." My sister smirked.

I playfully rolled my eyes. "I'll see you tomorrow."

I walked out of her bedroom and closed her door just as she shouted, "Have fuuuuunnn!"

I grunted to myself as I headed in the direction of the bathroom. After I showered, dried and styled my hair I glanced at the clock on my bedroom wall and groaned. It was twenty to eleven, and I hadn't even decided on what to wear yet. I groaned and slumped back onto my bed, and stared up at the ceiling.

"This night is goin' to be a *disaster*."

"Where are you?" I impatiently asked Aideen. "I just pulled up outside in a taxi and I don't wanna wait around on me own."

"I just got here, too. I'm over with Skull at the entrance to the club."

I relaxed. "Okay, see you in a sec."

I paid the taxi driver then got out of the car and brisk walked past the lengthy queue of people and made my way to the top of the queue. Aideen's face lit up when she saw me. She let go of Skull's arm and hugged me when I reached her.

"You look gorgeous!" She gushed.

I looked down at my black tube dress that stuck to me like a second skin and pushed my boobs up, then switched my gaze to Aideen.

"Me?" I quizzed and brushed the compliment off. "Have you *seen* your boobs in that dress?"

"But of course," my friend wickedly grinned. "They're me best asset."

I raised my eyebrow. "That'd be your brain."

Aideen snorted at my correction and took hold of my hand as we moved over to Skull who greeted us with a bright smile. "Well if it isn't me fantasy threesome partners," he teased.

I playfully rolled my eyes while Aideen cracked up with laughter, which caused Skull to smile. He flicked his gaze to me and winked.

"How is Branna this evenin'?" he asked.

I teasingly fanned my face. "I'm great, how is Skull keepin'?"

"Grand," he said and jabbed his thumb at Aideen. "I've this one on me arm, I couldn't be better."

Aideen snorted. "You're already gettin' laid later, there's no need to sweet talk me."

"Maybe I *like* sweet talkin' you." He grinned.

I pretended to heave. "You're both too cute, stop or I'll be sick."

They laughed and Skull moved us inside the club's entrance and instructed us to go down the stairs. He promised to meet up with us later after the door was clear of punters. I thanked him then took Aideen's hand as she led us down the flight of stairs. At the bottom of the stairs a bouncer who guarded the main entrance to the club greeted us.

"Heya John," I said with a wave.

His face brightened up. "Branna, how are you, babe? Haven't seen you in a while."

"I'm good, this one dragged me out tonight."

"I expect nothin' less from Miss. Collins," John teased.

I smiled as he stamped *Free* on my left wrist, and *Darkness* on my right in thick black ink.

"Thank you," I smiled warmly as he did the same for Aideen.

"You got it, darlin'." John winked. "Have a good night."

I thanked him again and followed Aideen through the double doors that lead into the nightclub. I needed a moment to allow my vision to adjust to the club's next to no lighting. The strobe lights were already forming an ache in my temples. I followed Aideen over to the crowed bar, and I hung back while she ordered us some drinks.

I tapped my hand against my thigh and bobbed my head along to the song that was pouring through the speakers. I took the drink that Aideen offered me and took a sip. I hummed as the liquid slid down my throat.

Vodka and Coke.

"Me favourite," I grinned.

Aideen clanked her glass against mine and downed her drink in just a few gulps. I blinked, and didn't even attempt to do the same with my drink because I knew it'd be back up my throat just as quick. I drank mine at a regular pace, which was not what Aideen did. By the time I finished my first drink she was on her third.

"Let's dance!" she shouted when her glass was empty.

I put my empty glass on the bar, took hold of Aideen's hand and allowed her to lead me to the dance floor. We danced, laughed and danced some more. I was just about to request we take a little break, when the sea of people parted on the dance floor and opened up the view of the booths across the club.

My eyes locked on the corner booth, or rather on the man in the booth.

Oh, Christ.

"Branna?" Aideen laughed. "Will you blink?"

I knew I was staring, and for the life of me I couldn't make myself stop, or at the very least look away. My libido sprung to life and had taken over full control of my body.

Pulse. Pulse. *Pulse.*

"Who is *that*?" I asked Aideen without taking my eyes away from the Greek God that was sat in the corner booth gulping down Budweiser like it was water.

"*That*," Aideen wickedly grinned as she nudged me to the edge of the dance floor, "is Ryder Slater. Skull says he is from New York and that he just moved here with his younger brothers, one of his brothers—who is an identical *twin* by the way—is a fighter. He has fought here almost every weekend for the past few weeks, he is lethal and is only Bronagh's age."

I heard everything Aideen said, but my mind, and vagina, only focused on one crucial detail of her Intel. *Ryder Slater.*

"He is gorgeous," I gushed, unable to look away from him.

Aideen whooped over the music. "Go get him, mama."

I felt molten heat creep up my neck. "I can't."

"Can't or won't?" Aideen asked, clicking her tongue.

I looked at my friend and frowned. "How does a woman like *me* talk to someone who looks like *him*? Because I honestly have *no* idea, I'll make a tit out of meself."

Aideen rolled her eyes and over the music she said, "Branna, will you *listen* to yourself? You sound like you've already been rejected by him, but you haven't and you *won't*, if you just be yourself. You're stunnin', babe, and you're a hell of a girl, too. Lads *dig* that."

I hated that my eyes welled up. "You're so sweet to me," I said and quickly dabbed under my eyes, careful not to ruin my eye makeup.

"We have *got* to get you laid," Aideen grumbled. "And Ryder Slater will be the one to work out all of your kinks. Come with me."

Everything happened rapidly when Aideen grabbed hold of my hand and quite literally tugged me along behind her as she briskly walked off the dance floor, not caring that body after drunken body was in our way. I shouted for her to slow down, but either she couldn't hear me over the music, or she flat out ignored me. I only shouted once because I became very self-aware that I was shite at walking in heels, and brisk walking in them could very well cause my immediate death.

When we made it through the crowd and across the dance floor I silently thanked God that I survived, but then quickly asked him to take my life when I realised where Aideen brought us to a stop. We were no more than a metre away from the very booth that the stunning Ryder Slater was sat at. He was looking down at his phone, but when he noticed we were standing next to his table staring at him, he pocketed his phone and gave us his full attention.

I stepped behind Aideen out of sheer mortification.

"Hiya," she shouted over the music. "I'm Aideen, and this is Branna, we thought you might like some company. You look a little lost sittin' over here on your own."

How can she speak to him, or any man, with such confidence? I wondered. *I would never be able to do that, not without looking like an utter fool in the process.*

I was jolted from my thoughts when Aideen turned to me, and roughly pulled me out from my hiding spot behind her. I stumbled to her side and knocked my knee against hers causing me to hiss. I resisted the urge to rub the sting away, because my attention was now on the grey eyes that were trained on me.

Oh, hell.

"Hello," Ryder said at the exact same time the song playing changed. It allowed me to hear how deep his voice was, and how wicked his accent sounded.

I waved at him—like an idiot—and said, "Hey."

His lips twitched and I wondered if he already thought I wasn't worth the trouble of talking to.

"Would you like to join me?" he asked, raising his voice to be heard over the now thumping sound that filled the club.

I swallowed, and stared at him with shock.

Aideen jabbed her elbow in my side and answered for me. "She'd *love* to," she gushed.

She put her small hand on the base of my spine and pushed me to the side of the booth Ryder was sitting on, and I didn't know why, but I resisted. I suddenly felt like I was being fed to the sharks. I brought my face to Aideen's and said, "I can't do this, I feel too idiotic to sit next to him. I don't trust meself not to say somethin' stupid."

Aideen *completely* ignored me and turned me around to face Ryder—who hadn't moved an inch since we arrived at the table—and nudged me forward with both of her hands. To avoid falling on top of Ryder, I had to turn on my side and drop into a sitting position next to him. I didn't look at him out of fear I'd see amusement on his face, so instead I looked to my friend—I use that term *very* loosely—and tapped the empty spot next to me, but she shook her head, grinning.

I widened my eyes, and pleaded with Aideen not to leave me through my skull drilling stare.

"I'm goin' to go and get us some drinks," she stated. "You two get to know each other, I won't be long."

I gasped when she turned and almost instantly got lost in the crowd. I sat up straight and searched for her in hopes I would see her, but I only saw strangers move their bodies to the playing music.

"Oh, my God," I whispered.

I sat very still for a few seconds before I plucked up the courage to take a glimpse at Ryder. I froze when I found his eyes were on me, and a smile had taken over his face. The sigh that left my body was one of need, because if I thought Ryder was incredible looking before, seeing him smile almost had me proposing to him. Almost.

"Are you okay?" he asked, a hint of concern in his tone.

I knew I couldn't get away with lying, Aideen and Bronagh told me enough times that my face told everything I kept inside, so I decided to be honest. I shook my head to Ryder's question and said, "I didn't know she was goin' to abandon me like that. I'm so sorry, it was *her* idea to come over here, not mine."

Ryder's lips quirked as he said, "I'm glad she thought of it."

I blinked, dumbly. "You are?"

"Of course," he nodded. "I probably would have never seen you otherwise. I've found over the last few weeks that this club is always wall-to-wall full. You're such a tiny thing; it'd be easy to miss you in the sea of bodies. And *that* would be a true tragedy."

Branna, breathe, my mind, and lungs, urged.

I sucked in a breath and exhaled it almost immediately, and it made Ryder chuckle.

"Darling, you look like I'm going to eat you up." His eyes held a glint of mischief as he spoke. "I won't bite you, I promise. Not yet anyway."

Fuck.

I cleared my throat and said, "I'm sorry."

This caused him to raise an eyebrow. "Why're you sorry?"

I lifted my arm and scratched my neck. "For being so awkward."

He smiled again, and really tempted *me* to bite a chuck out of *him*.

"It's not awkward," he said. "It's nervousness, which is the part I don't get."

I felt my cheeks heat up. "What don't you get?"

He lifted his arm and stretched it out on the booth seat behind me before he leaned in closer. I felt his breath on my face and I resisted the urge to roll my eyes back as it invaded my senses.

I want to taste him, my mind wickedly whispered.

I blinked my eyes when Ryder's voice gained my full attention. "I don't get why a woman who looks as edible as you is so shy."

I didn't know whether to run away with embarrassment, or fuck him where he sat.

"I don't usually do this," I swallowed. I'm not one to walk up to men and talk to them which is why me friend physically pulled me over to you."

Ryder's eyebrows rose with surprise. "Usually I'd call bullshit, but I think I believe you."

I didn't know what to say to that, so I said nothing. This decision prompted him to lean even closer to me which had my heart slam into my chest. "What is your name?" he asked me, his eyes scanning my face with an intensity that caused me to suck in another very large breath. "I didn't hear your friend very well when she introduced you both."

His. Voice.

I could hear it very clearly now that he was so close. A man's voice had never caused an ache to rapidly pulse between my thighs, but Ryder's voice was doing exactly that. It was a little unsettling because my body was reacting to him in such a way that scared me.

"Branna," I whispered.

He dipped his head even *closer* to mine and said, "One more time, beautiful, I didn't catch that."

Sweet Jesus, my mind gushed. *Did he really mean that?*

Aideen and my sister had told me enough times that I was beautiful, and some boys I dated over the years mentioned it here and there; but never a man, and that was exactly what Ryder was. A knicker dropping, fuck me hard as you can, *man*.

I cleared my throat and tried my best to ignore the sinful thoughts that had invaded my mind, but Ryder's closeness allowed his delicious scent to surround me, and I had trouble concentrating because of it.

"Branna," I said louder, licking my dry lips. "Me name is Branna."

Ryder's heated eyes returned to mine, and a smirk curved his mouth. "Branna," his voice was low and husky when he spoke.

Shit. Fuck.

"Yeah," I rasped, refraining from throwing myself at him and begging him to take away the aching pain between my thighs that he so brutally, and unknowingly, caused.

"I'm Ryder," he said and held his hand out to me.

I swallowed, and with a trembling limb, I lifted my arm and placed my tiny palm in his very large one. "It's nice to meet you, Ryder."

He gripped my hand and tugged me closer to him until our chests touch. He gazed down at me, a grin playing on his plump lips as he said, "The pleasure is all *mine*, Branna."

If he said my name in that low, husky seductive tone one more time, I was going to jump him in front of all of these people. Fuck my pride and dignity.

"Feel free to jump me at any given time, *Branna*," he said and licked his plump lips. "I'm *more* than ready."

I widened my eyes. "I beg your pardon?" I asked as my stomach churned a little.

He grinned at me. "You said you would jump me if I said your—"

"Omigod." I gasped and pulled my hand free from his so I could cover my face with it.

I said that out loud? I cringed. *How bloody mortifying.*

"I'm *so* sorry," I began, "I didn't mean to... not out loud... this is awful."

I was blowing this; I was single handedly fucking up *speaking* to someone. I was grateful for the loud music because I didn't want to hear Ryder laughing at me. I jumped and dropped my hands from my face when I felt a hand on my bare thigh. I looked up and found Ryder was grinning down at me.

"Hi," he said, smiling wide. "Branna was it?"

He knew good and bloody well what my name was, he was teasing now.

I cleared my throat. "Hi back... Ryder was it?"

"Yeah," he smirked. "I'm Ryder."

Yes. He. Was.

"Ryder," I repeated.

He lowered his head back to mine and said, "You're beautiful."

I blinked, dumbly. "You're beautifuler."

I cringed the second the words left my mouth.

He snorted and asked, "Who's sweet talking who here?"

Not me, I knew that much, I was talking out of my arse.

I shuddered. "You can sweet talk me, I'll be quiet."

There was less chance of me making a complete arse of myself if I kept my big mouth shut.

"I don't know," he mused. "I like this. You saying what you want to say then getting embarrassed over it. It's very cute."

I flinched.

Ryder blinked at my reaction. "Did I say something wrong?"

I shook my head. "No, it's just, I call me sister cute all the time and because we look similar it just weirded me out for a second."

"How old is your sister?" he asked, the corners of his eyes creasing.

"She turns eighteen next month," I said, and then found myself frowning. "She's growin' up very fast on me."

Ryder raised a brow. "On *you*?"

I nodded. "Yeah, our parents died when she was nine. I was nineteen at the time and refused to let anyone raise 'er but me, so I put everythin' on hold and brought 'er up. She's a good kid, too. I think I've done a good job with 'er."

Ryder was staring at me with his mouth agape, and what we were just conversing about hit me like a cold shower.

Fuck.

I think we had been flirting and I somehow managed to fit in the fact that I was a mother figure to my kid sister and that I've spent most of my life raising her. What I should have spoken about was sex related things, not baggage related things. I was *really* fucking this up. I felt my cheeks heat up.

Talk about a mood killer.

"I'm so-sorry," I stuttered. "I didn't mean to take a huge turn in the conversation."

Ryder shook his head. "No, don't apologise, I was just a little caught off guard. So, you've raised your sister?"

He was interested in the information that much was obvious. I just didn't get *why*. I bit down on my lower lip and nodded.

"All on your own?" he questioned. "No boyfriend?"

I shook my head. "No one serious, I brought a man home once for dinner but me sister—who was eleven at the time—didn't like him because he couldn't say her name right. He was from Spain and his English wasn't the best. She ran him out of the house while I was cookin' and we never saw him again. I stopped datin' after that."

When I finished speaking, Ryder had his head tilted back with the soothing sound of his laughter tangling up with the music. It was alarming how relaxed his laughter, and overall presence, made me feel. He was a stranger, but I felt very comfortable next to him. It was odd, but in a really nice way.

"Your sister sounds incredible," Ryder said with a big smile on his face after his laughter subsided.

I nodded. "Yeah, she's me world."

Ryder used the arm that was over the back of the booth to drape over my shoulders. I went as still as a statue as he pulled me closer until the side of my body moulded against his.

"Where is she tonight?" he asked, his lips almost pressed against my ear.

I swallowed. "At home. She's probably sleepin' now, she had a long week at school."

Ryder hummed. "I'll have to bring you to my place then, I wouldn't want to wake her up. She might do *more* than kick me out."

I felt my eyes widen and my heart come to a complete stop.

"Branna?" Ryder murmured.

I snapped out of my momentary shut down and turned my head to him and said, "Look, you're gorgeous, and trust me when I say that I really, *really* want to go back to your place with you..."

"But?" Ryder offered.

"But," I swallowed. "I've never had a one night stand before, and to be honest, the prospect of it kind of scares me."

Ryder's eyes scanned over my face when I finished speaking. "Would you believe me if I said we wouldn't have to have sex?"

I blinked. "Why else would you want me to come back to your place?"

He laughed and shook his head. "This is going to sound like bullshit, but I like talking to you, and listening to you speak. From what I've heard, you sound like an incredible friend and sister. You're independent and that's *hot*, but you know what's downright sexy?" he asked and I shook my head, not being able to verbally speak yet. "Your shyness and nervousness. It makes my dick hurt. You're beautiful and have a sense of humour. I haven't come across all that goodness in a woman in... ever."

I had to look away when blood rushed to my cheeks. Ryder laughed and placed his hand under my chin, forcing me to look back at him. "Yeah," he grinned. "That shyness is *definitely* hurting my dick."

The pulse between my thighs throbbed so hard I had to rub my legs together to try and soothe the ache. Ryder's eyes dropped down to my thighs and caught the motion, he kept his eyes lowered, and a smirk slowly curved his mouth. He knew I was aching.

"It's only fair," he murmured when his gaze returned to me. "If my dick hurts, I want your pussy throbbing."

Oh, Christ.

"Ryder," I breathed and squeezed my thighs tightly together. "Don't talk like that."

He growled at that and brought his mouth to my ear, breathing into it. "Why not?" he asked. "Your clit hurts so good right now, doesn't it? It's *begging* to be rubbed, licked, and sucked."

I lifted my hand to his thigh and squeezed in warning. "I'm serious," I panted. "I will do somethin' *insane* if you don't stop."

"Yeah?" he said as his teeth nipped my earlobe. "Like what?"

I lost a little bit of my control when I said, "Like fuck you where you sit."

I heard Ryder's quick intake of breath, and felt his leg muscle tense under my palm. "How would you fuck me, sweetness?" he asked after swiping his tongue over my skin. "Would you ride me slow and deep? Or fuck me fast and hard?"

Screw being in control.

"Let's find out," I almost snarled.

Ryder pulled back and looked at me with wide eyes, but before I lost my nerve, I let the pulse between my thighs urge my movements. I turned, bent my knees and crawled onto the seat. I cocked one leg over Ryder and sat on him, not being able to resist rocking my pelvis forward.

I groaned out loud when I felt the thick hardened length of Ryder's cock press against me, causing a shiver to spread throughout my body. I looked down to Ryder when I felt his hands clamp down on my arse. He squeezed my flesh between his hands and lifted his head up to mine. I lowered my mouth to his, and let it hover a hair away.

"You're coming home with me," Ryder growled. "I don't fuck in public, but darling, you're making me rethink that."

I groaned and rocked my pelvis against him once more. "I think I can come from doin' this alone," I said into his ear and then pulled back and snaked my tongue across his lower lip.

Ryder's hips bucked up into me. "Prove it."

Was he challenging me? I thought, my inner vixen smirking.

It was very rare that I let her out to play, but Ryder was coaxing her out into the open. Shy Branna was taking a backseat to Naughty Branna, and, for once, I did so willingly.

I covered his mouth with mine and squeezed his shoulders with my hands when I heard him groan at the contact. He plunged his warm, wet tongue into my mouth and growled as I rolled my pelvis against him. I continued to rock against him, panting as the added friction of our clothes roughly rubbed against my throbbing clit.

I pulled away from Ryder's mouth to try and catch my breath, but he wouldn't allow it. As soon I detached my lips from his, he lifted a hand from my behind and fisted it in my hair and roughly pulled my head back towards his and covered his mouth with mine once more. He bit down on my lower lip before sucking it into his mouth.

Fuck.

I moaned as he bucked his hips up and pushed his hardened length against me. I hissed and rolled my hips back and forth until my breathing became laboured. I could feel the sensation that was building up in my core. At first it was little licks of pleasure I felt, but the harder and faster I bucked against Ryder, the more intense the licks became until suddenly it was excruciating pleasure. I sucked in a breath and held it as I was thrown over the edge into bliss.

I felt kisses and a tongue trail along my jaw line, but I was only pulled back into reality when teeth bit into my neck causing me to cry out. The mixture of pleasure and pain was so intense I let go of Ryder's shoulders and started to involuntary lean to the right. Before I had a chance to fall, Ryder gripped onto me and pulled my chest against his. He held me against him until the cloud of ecstasy lifted from me and I blinked reality back into focus.

Heaven, my mind purred, *that was exactly what I experienced.*

"Holy Christ," I panted.

"You were right," Ryder growled. "You *could* come from just grinding on me."

I allowed his words to sink in, and the realisation of what I just did became very clear.

"Omigod," I whispered and squeezed against Ryder, hiding my face in the crook of his neck. "What did I just do? Oh, God, you must think I'm some little—"

"Don't finish that sentence," Ryder cut me off, bringing his mouth to my ear. "You used my body to give yours pleasure, it was the sexiest thing I have *ever* seen. That was for me alone, no one else saw. I dimmed the light in our booth. Only you and I know that you just came apart."

I widened my eyes to the point of pain, pulled back from Ryder and darted my eyes around the club. Shock hit me. I had just gotten off on a stranger in the middle of a populated nightclub.

"I just turned into the girl me parents warned me to avoid hangin' around with when I was younger."

Ryder's chuckle helped me relax.

"You amuse me, sweetness."

I looked down at him. "Sweetness?"

He nodded. "Your mouth tastes so sweet."

"You're *so* gorgeous," I breathed, overwhelmed that someone as perfect as him seemed to like me, or at the very least liked kissing me.

Ryder grinned. "Sweet talker."

I felt my cheeks flush, and I was about to tease him back when I heard sudden wolf whistles and catcalls. "Big brother is *getting some*," an unfamiliar male voice whooped as the light in our booth—which I didn't notice had turned off—came back on. "Damn, is her front as nice as her back?"

I pulled back from Ryder and looked over my shoulder to find four males staring at Ryder and myself. Mainly me. I could tell straight off the bat that they were the brothers Aideen had mentioned. They were all the same height, a few inches over six feet—easily. From the left to the right I scanned each male and saw similarities and differences. The main difference out of all the brothers was the kid on the far left who had hair as white as snow. He was younger than Ryder too, *a lot* younger.

The kid was standing next to *another* kid, just one with dark hair. Everything else about them was similar, and I remembered something else that Aideen said, she said they were twins. It was obvious that they were identical. I could see from the smirks they shot my way that they both rocked deep dimples in their cheeks, and it was a Godly sight if I ever saw one.

The dark haired kid had a red swollen eye that would be discoloured in a few hours as a bruise set in. He had a small cut on his lips, and the white hand wraps around his fingers and knuckles were stained with red. He was shirtless and I was surprised for a kid his age to have such defined abs and a prominent set of oblique muscles. His arms were big with muscle, and even his thighs were ripped. He was definitely the fighter.

Fuck.

I flicked my eyes to the right and they landed on an absolute beauty. He had shoulder length dark hair, big eyes, big shoulders, and a killer grin. I saw dimples, like his younger brothers, dented his cheeks when he grinned, and my insides did summersaults at the visual. He wore a black buttoned up shirt that was rolled up to the elbows, and I saw a partial of a very colourful tattoo that wrapped around his forearm and snuck under the shirt, hiding it away. I could only imagine the rest of the tattoo he was rocking.

Shit.

To avoid openly drooling, I flicked my eyes to the last brother, and I barely managed to hide the gasp I sucked in. I openly stared at the other three males with awe, but I couldn't *not* stare at the last brother even if I tried. He had supple tan skin like his brothers, and his hair was thick and dark, too. His jaw line was out of this world, and he was big with muscle all over... but his face and neck. They were scarred. Badly. I was terrified to think, let alone ask, what could have caused such damaged. He looked vicious, and unlike his brothers, he wasn't grinning or smiling at me. He just stared at me... or maybe glared?

Bollocks.

"Fuck," the brother that had longish hair grunted. "*Definitely* as nice as the back. You're hot, baby."

I blinked at him then looked down to Ryder when he growled. "Don't even *think* about it, Alec," he warned his brother.

Alec. Damn, his name was hot, just like him.

I glanced back to Alec and saw he frowned at his brother. "I can't play?"

"Not with this one," Ryder stated. "She's *mine.*"

And fuck me if that declaration didn't stop my heart.

Alec groaned out loud. "You're no fun."

The brother who I was nervous to look at said to Alec in a deep voice, "You fucked that black haired chick with the big tits in the bathroom, why are you complaining?"

Alec looked at his brother with a raised brow. "That was a whole hour ago. I'm bored now that Dominic isn't fighting."

Dominic. Shit, their names suited them to a tee.

Dominic lifted his hand to his swollen eye and rubbed his tender flesh before he dropped it and grinned at Alec. "I heard her screaming 'Elec' from outside the bathroom. You didn't correct her?"

Alec snorted. "I was balls deep, she could have called me Barney the Dinosaur and I'd have answered her."

I laughed at that, and it drew everyone's attention. The white haired brother tilted his head as he stared at me, his eyes raking over me leisurely. "What's your name?" he asked when his gaze locked on mine.

Shit, he sounded eerily like his twin.

"Branna," I said lowly.

All four brothers leaned in trying to hear me, but when I didn't repeat it they looked to Ryder who said, "Branna."

The white haired brother smiled, and the hands on Ryder's shoulder instinctively flexed. No one should possess a smile that alluring. No. One.

"Nice to meet you, Branna," he said, bowing his head. "I'm Damien."

He jabbed his finger to his left. "This is Dominic, the perv is Alec, and that guy glaring at you is Kane."

Kane. I flicked my eyes to the menacing looking Slater brother and bit down on my lower lip. Oh, yeah, he looked like a Kane. Sexy, mysterious and downright terrifying.

"Am I glaring at her?" Kane asked Alec, his brows furrowed.

Alec nodded. "Just a little bit."

Kane sighed and looked back to me. "I don't like crowds."

I didn't know why he said that, so I just continued to stare at him. He sighed, again, deeply. "If I glare, stare or seem pissed at you, I'm not, I'm pissed at everyone else. I don't like crowds," he repeated.

Oh, he was explaining his tenseness.

I nodded. "It's cool, I won't hold it against you."

I could have sworn his lips twitched, but I wasn't sure. "Thanks," he said and glanced to Alec who was grinning at me.

Ryder sighed from underneath me. "Can you four go away now?"

"No," Kane almost growled. "You said we could leave after Dominic fought. He fought and won so can we leave now?"

Damn, he wasn't lying; he really didn't look like he enjoyed being here.

Ryder looked to Dominic. "You fought?"

"And won." He nodded.

I looked down to Ryder and caught his frown. "I didn't hear the bells, or cheering. I actually didn't hear a damn thing."

Damien snorted. "I wouldn't hear anything other than the beat of my own cock if Branna was on my lap either."

I don't know why, but I dramatically gasped.

"You dirty little bastard," I said, shocked.

I wasn't prepared for the burst of male laughter that followed my insult, nor was I fully ready to see the five brothers smile. What I *really* wasn't ready for was to see Kane smile. My God, I didn't know who was better looking of the five of them—well, I was sitting on my preference—but Kane won the award for best smile. It was stunning, and transformed his entire face.

"I apologise," Damien said to me, still chuckling.

I eyed him. "You shouldn't say stuff like that around women... or girls. How old are you?"

He didn't break eye contact with me as he said, "Eighteen."

He was a baby!

"My baby *sister* is almost eighteen." I gulped.

Dominic grinned at me. "Is she as hot as you?"

I blinked. "She's beautiful."

Dominic's eyes gleamed. "Maybe I'll get to meet her if Ry lets you stick around."

Let's me stick around, I silently repeated. *What did that mean?*

"Not if I meet her first," Damien said, nudging Dominic with his shoulder. "I call dibs."

Dominic glared at his twin. "You don't even know what she looks like, you can't call dibs unless we see her at the same time. That's the deal."

They had a deal about dibs?

Damien jabbed his thumb in my direction. "If she looks like her, I'm calling an early dibs."

Dominic narrowed his eyes. "Fine, whatever. She's probably not even *that* hot."

I glared at the pair of them. "She is beautiful, and hot, and everything in-between you little shites. Don't talk about me sister like that unless you wanna go a few rounds with *me*. I'll put you on your back before you could blink."

Dominic's jaw dropped while Alec and Damien cracked up laughing. I looked at them, then to Kane who was smirking at me before looking down to Ryder. I felt my cheeks stain with heat, but I refused to let them get away with that kind of talk about my blood.

"I'm not sorry," I defended. "They shouldn't talk about girls like that."

"You're right, they shouldn't." He looked at his brothers and shot them a glare that would have frightened the knickers off of me. "Apologise."

The twins did almost immediately, but Dominic had a grin on his face that told me he wasn't all that sorry.

"It's a shame you said what you did," I said with a shake of my head. "I thought you were cute, too."

I yelped when hands squeezed my behind. "I'm still here," Ryder said, amused.

It was then I realised that I was still sitting on his body, and a flush attacked my cheeks. I made a motion to get of Ryder, but he blocked all of my efforts. "I *have* to get off you," I whispered.

He didn't let me go. "Why?" he asked.

I looked at his brothers, then to the rest of the people dancing and walking around the club. "Because *I'm* in control now," I murmured, "*not* me vagina."

Ryder smirked up at me and said, "Give me your mouth and I'll switch the roles back."

I surprisingly laughed.

I heard a growl from our left. "Five minutes, Ryder."

Ryder nodded to Kane who spoke and said, "I'll only need one."

Cocky fucker.

I glanced back to the brothers and saw they had moved off, when I looked back down at Ryder I smiled. "You're all gorgeous, especially Damien. He looks like the real life version of the animated Jack Frost, and I have a *huge* crush on that character."

Ryder licked his lower lip. "You think my baby brother, and other brothers, are hot? My ego would be shot if it wasn't me you were sitting on."

I giggled. "I like you best."

He grinned. "Prove it."

I raised an eyebrow. "I think I did that before they showed up."

He hummed. "I think I need a reminder."

I lowered my head to his. "A reminder, huh?"

"Just a little one," he murmured.

I pressed my lips against his and intended to grind against him once more, but shock tore through at the same time molten pleasure did. Ryder removed his right hand from my behind and instead of bringing it to my hair like he did before; he slid it up the front of my bare thigh. He pushed my dress up to my hips along the way then snaked his finger under my knickers and glided his fingertips up my wet slit until they came into contact with my throbbing clit.

"So wet, Branna," he rumbled against my mouth. "Damn, baby, you're *so* ready."

He swirled his fingers over my hardening bud before he pulled his hand away and brought his fingers up to his lips where he sucked them into his mouth, and fluttered his eyes shut as he tasted me. The wave of need that slammed into me in that moment was greater than anything I had ever experienced.

"You're *definitely* my favourite kind of sweetness," he smirked at me when he pulled his fingers from his mouth.

"Ryder," I rasped, the pulse between my legs now unbearable.

He flicked his mysterious eyes to mine, and I think he *saw* what I was thinking, what I needed, because he set his jaw. "Say it," he growled. "Say the words and it's done."

Oh, God.

"Fuck me." I begged.

Things quickly became a blur of activity. One-second I was on top of Ryder and the next he had a death grip on my hand as I was pulled behind him pulling my dress back down my thighs. He weaved around body after body and hauled us up the stairs and out of the club.

"Branna?" I heard Aideen's voice laugh.

"Aideen?" I called out, looking around for her while trying to keep up with Ryder.

"Have fun, babe!" She whooped from behind me earning chuckles from who I think was Skull. "Take care of her, Ryder!"

"I intend to!" Ryder shouted earning more male chuckles.

We came to a stop next to a large Jeep. Ryder dug out keys from his pocket, pressed a button that unlocked the doors then threw them behind me and said, "You drive."

I didn't get to see who he was talking to because he hustled me into the backseat, pulling me onto his lap and pressing his mouth against mine in a frenzy.

"Oh, Jesus," I heard Dominic grumble. "I'll give you one-hundred Euros if you swap seats with me?"

"Not on your life, kid," Kane's deep voice replied.

I heard Dominic curse under his breath as he climbed into the car and settled next to Ryder and me. Kane slid in next to him and slammed the back door shut while two doors up front closed. I didn't want to have my legs draped over the kid so I turned and straddled

Ryder. It certainly wasn't the safest seat in the car, but it was definitely the hottest.

"Don't fuck around, Alec," Dominic warned. "He's about to tear her clothes off back here. Put your foot down."

I was mortified so I pulled back from kissing Ryder, breathing heavily.

"Your brothers can see and hear us," I said, trying to get him to see reason.

He growled and tried to kiss me once more but I shook my head and said, "I'll let you do *anything* you want to me in private but I'm not puttin' on some live sex show in the back seat of a car for your little brothers, I don't care how hot you are. I won't do it."

"I like her," Damien's voice chuckled.

Ryder pressed his face against my shoulder and growled, "Alec. Drive faster. *Please.*"

I didn't move my eyes away from him as he leaned back with his eyes closed and began to count out loud making me feel a little giddy inside. He was trying to calm himself down, and the vixen within me didn't want that to happen just yet so I leaned into him, and brought my mouth to his ear. I closed my eyes before I spoke, and sucked up every ounce of and act out the naughty dreams I've had all my adult life.

"I can't wait to fuck you with me mouth," I whispered in his ear, making sure only he could hear me. "I can almost taste you on me tongue."

"Oh, Christ," Ryder breathed.

"I want your hands all over me," I murmured. "I want your cock or tongue inside me as I scream your name."

"Branna," he growled in warning. "I'm *this* close to traumatising my brothers so please shut that hot little mouth of yours. They don't want to see my dick any more than I want to pull it out in front of them, but if you keep talking like that, we'll all be in for a big fucking shock."

This prompted three of Ryder's brother to say in unison, "Alec, drive fucking faster!" making me laugh out loud.

"You think you're funny?" Ryder growled and dug his fingers into the flesh of my behind. "You think you'll be laughing when I have you all alone?"

That shut me up, and I felt a flush crawl up my neck and spread out over my cheeks.

"Seeing you blush hurts *more* than hearing you say you want me to tongue fuck you," Ryder groaned.

"Damn," Dominic whispered. "I should have found a chick to bring home if I knew I'd have to listen to live porn."

"You and me both," Kane growled.

"I have phone numbers," Alec rasped from up front. "I'll call a few women who I know will come by just for sex. They're all hot, and have *very* willing friends."

That instantly sobered me up and my face burned when I realised that I had lumped myself into the same category as those women who Alec would be calling when he got home. I was easy.

"Maybe this is a bad idea," I murmured.

Ryder's hold on me tightened. "This is a great idea. The fucking *best* idea."

I smiled, lightly. "Your brother just made me realise I'm acting like a... like a... slut."

Alec winced up front. "I didn't mean *you* Branna."

"But I'm going to have sex with Ryder and I've only known him half an hour. I'm no better than the girls who you're goin' to ring up for sex."

"First of all," Kane chimed in, his voice very gruff. "There is *nothing* wrong with no strings attached sex whether you're a man or a woman. If you want to fuck everyone in sight that is *your* business, no one else's. Second of all, it's quite obvious you don't do this often so you don't need to feel ashamed or embarrassed. Sex is a part of life, deal with it."

I stared at Kane, unblinking, but shifted my gaze to Dominic when he snapped his fingers in Z formation and said, "You sure told her, Oprah."

Kane thumped Dominic's shoulder making him snicker as he rubbed the spot with his hand. I looked to Ryder who lifted his hand and rubbed his thumb over my lip. I held onto him as Alec took a few sharp turns.

"We can just talk," Ryder murmured even though it looked like it pained him to say it. "If you don't want to do anything else, we won't."

He became instantly hotter in that moment.

"We'll see," I whispered making him grin.

I yelped when the car came to a sudden halt.

"Welcome to *casa* Slater!" Alec announced, proudly.

Nerves settled in as I climbed out off of Ryder's lap and out of the Jeep. I stood on trembling legs and gasped when an arm came around my waist and tugged me back into a hard, warm body. I glanced over my shoulder to Ryder when he nudged me forward, and I smiled up at him. His breath caught and he mumbled something to himself.

"What was that?" I asked as we walked in the garden of a huge, four story house.

"I said," he murmured, "you're so beautiful."

I chuckled. "You're *definitely* the sweet talker out of the pair of us."

He grinned as I glanced at my surroundings before walking through the front door Alec opened and entered the beautiful house.

"You live in Upton," I commented.

"Yes," Ryder said. "Where do you live?"

"On Old Isle Green, it's just ten minutes from here."

Dominic halted next to me then. "Old Isle Green did you say?"

I nodded.

He blinked. "What's your sister's name, can I ask?"

I wondered why he asked, but I didn't get a chance to reply because I was suddenly turned, picked up and thrown over a large shoulder.

"Omigod!" I breathed and gripped onto Ryder's shirt as I hung upside down. He headed for the stairs and ran up them two at a time, with me bouncing and grunting against his back along the way.

"Have fun!" Alec shouted followed by Damien's yelling, "Don't break her!"

The last thing I heard was from Dominic as he stated, "I want to be like Ryder when I grow up."

Ryder heard him, too, and it caused him to rumble with laughter.

"Thank God," I breathed when I was placed upright on the ground.

I closed my eyes and inhaled deeply and stayed that way for a few moments until the dizziness I was experiencing passed. Ryder's hands were on my shoulders, gripping me tightly reminding me of his presence. "Sorry," he chuckled when I opened my eyes and looked up at him. "They would have started a conversation with you and I didn't want that."

I grinned. "I could tell."

He reached behind me and flicked on the light to his room. He stepped past me and it gave me view to his humble abode. I stared around with wide eyes. The room was huge, and brilliantly decorated. A massive king-sized bed was in the middle of the room, the furniture was all dark oak, and the theme was black and white. It looked incredible.

"Wow," I breathed. "This looks like it belongs on an episode of cribs."

Ryder snorted as he rid himself of his shirt. "Thanks, I like it."

His room, and how well it was decorated, was forgotten the moment Ryder removed his shirt. I swallowed as I took in his heavily tattooed torso. His oblique muscles were so defined that I audibly groaned. I allowed my eyes to roam over his hardened chest, large, wide shoulders, thick arms and, of course, his incredibly cut abs.

He had six of them. And they were mouth-watering.

"*Damn*," I whispered.

"You'll need to worry about *me* jumping *you* if you keep looking at me like that."

The sweet spot between my thighs pulsed back to life.

I licked my lips and looked up to Ryder. "That doesn't sound bad to me."

Ryder took a step towards me. "Are you sure?"

I frantically nodded my head, even though I felt heat spread out over my cheeks at my obvious need.

"Last chance to run, darling," he warned as he gripped his belt. "Once you allow me to touch you, you won't leave this room until I fuck the shyness right out of you."

My legs trembled as he undid his belt and slid it through the hoops of his jeans. The throb between my thighs kicked into overdrive and took full control of me.

"I need you," I pleaded. "Right here. Right now."

Ryder invaded my space at a rapid speed and backed me up against his bedroom door.

"I'm going to make you scream, beautiful."

I licked my dry lips and whispered, "I can't wait."

He lowered his head and took possession of my mouth with his and kissed me with a hunger that almost hurt. Almost. I lifted my hands to his thick arms and gently scraped my nails against his skin. A low growl rumbled deep in Ryder's throat, and I swear it felt like a physical stroke against my clit. It provoked my hips to rock forward and knock against his pelvis which caused him to tear his mouth from mine and press his talented lips against my ear as he whispered, "One more bump like that, darling, and I'll forget about easing you into *my* way of fucking."

His way of fucking, I mentally repeated.

My eyes rolled back at both his words and the sensation of his hot breath on my ear. "I can take it," I replied, huskily.

I hissed when Ryder sucked my earlobe into his mouth and lowered his right hand to my thigh. He raised said hand farther and farther up my thigh while sucking on my earlobe. It was probably the most basic thing a man had ever done to me, but it garnered top results with Ryder, and I knew I'd never let another man do it to me again.

It was something just for him.

Just Ryder.

"How long do you think you can take of my cock pounding this sweet pussy of yours before you scream my name?" he asked, his tone laced with desire.

I couldn't focus on his question as he brushed his fingers over the soaked wet lace material of my underwear. The brief contact caused a loud groan to tear from my throat.

"Answer me," he growled in my ear before sticking his tongue inside it.

I cried out, "Ryder, *please.*"

His low chuckle was the sexiest sound I had ever heard. "You cried out my name before we even got started," he murmured, moving his lips to my cheek. "Oh, darling, I'm going to have *so* much fun with you."

Yes, I silently pleaded.

He took my hand and led me over to his bed; his gaze on me like I was his next meal.

"You look stunning, but I want you naked. Now."

Oh, fuck.

I swallowed. "O... Okay."

Ryder bit down on his lower lip as I gripped the hem of my dress and slowly shimmied it up to my waist, exposing my bare stomach, hips and thighs. Ryder set his jaw and balled his hands into fists by his sides, like he was forcing himself to remain still as I undressed for him. It gave me a spurt of confidence and urged me to remove my dress completely.

I dropped the fabric on the floor next to me and stood before Ryder in my matching lace black strapless bra and underwear. I still had my heels on, which oddly make me feel sexier, not that I needed them when I had Ryder's burning eyes locked on every inch of me.

"I'm going to ruin you," he whispered when his eyes flicked up to mine.

I sucked in a deep breath and said, "Yes, please."

With a growl he came at me and practically tackled me back onto his huge, soft bed. I instantly opened my thighs for him allowing him to invade my personal space with ease. He covered my mouth with his, and forced his tongue between my lips as he roughly kissed me. I groaned in delight and matched the fierceness of his heated kiss.

"What can I do to you?" Ryder breathlessly asked when he pulled his mouth from mine. "I want to know now so nothing I do surprises you."

I gripped onto his thick arms. "I want you to do everythin' to me, Ryder. Every. Fuckin'. Thing. Don't hold back, *please*."

"Not in my nature, darling," he said, his voice low and gruff.

He sat me up and before I knew it, he unsnapped the clasp of my bra and the material was instantly pulled away from me by Ryder's hands.

"Damn," he breathed. "Your nipples are mouth-watering. Dusty pink is my *favourite*."

It was just words he was speaking, but the impact they had on my body was like throwing petrol on a fire. I ignited and burned for him.

"Ryder," I whispered. "Please, I'm hurtin'."

His eyes dropped to between my thighs and his lip curled upwards. "We can't have that, can we?"

I quickly shook my head.

"So what will I do about it?" he asked, looking up at me as he grazed his index finger over my underwear, making contact with my throbbing clit.

I groaned. "Please."

"You have to tell me," he teased. "I know what you *want* me to do, darling, but I want to hear you *say* it."

Again, he rubbed his finger over my clit, but this time he took it a step further and pushed my underwear aside then pressed his thumb against my swollen bud, slowly rotating it around in circles. It was sweet torture and it caused me to moan out in pleasure.

"I can smell you, darling," Ryder growled. "If you want me to have a taste, tell me."

I heard him, but I was too focused on his thumb on my clit.

"Branna," Ryder prompted. "Tell me or I stop."

I looked down at him, my eyes holding a silent threat of what I would do to him if he dared stop, and it only caused him to smirk. He was playing with me, and the bastard was enjoying it.

"Tongue fuck me," I said through clenched teeth as the pleasure Ryder's thumb was giving me began to build. "Lick me, suck me, then fuck me with your mouth."

I couldn't believe I had said the words as soon as I had spoken them. It was so brass and direct, two things I was *not* when it came to men and sex.

I whimpered when Ryder literally tore the fabric of my knickers as he pulled them away and tossed them over his shoulder, but screamed when his warm, wet tongue flattened against my clit and began to unravel me. He flicked his tongue over the tiny bundle of nerves, and each swipe sent a shockwave of delight throughout my body. I reached down and fisted my hand in his hair as he feasted on me, his groans indicating he was enjoying it just as much as I was.

"Ryder," I whimpered as my legs began to shake.

He lifted his arms from under my thighs, moved them around my hips and flattened them above my mound, locking his hands together to keep my lower half on the bed. I found out why he did this when a delicious pressure throbbed at my core and my hips involuntarily began to buck into Ryder's face.

"Yes!" I cried out. "RYDER!"

My body exploded into sensation. Pure pleasure struck me and spread to my every nerve ending. My back arched off the bed, my hands balled into fists and my breath caught in my throat. My hips continued to lightly buck into Ryder's face, and I came back down to Earth just as he released my clit from his mouth and placed a gentle kiss against it before he untangled his hands from around me and climbed up my body.

"I could eat you forever," Ryder growled.

My eyes, that were closed, fluttered open at his words. My chest was rapidly rising and falling, but again, my breath caught in my throat when I gazed up at him and saw the hunger in his eyes. The hunger for me. The *need*.

"That was... wow."

Ryder's lip twitched. "I couldn't tell if you were enjoying it over all your screaming."

I found myself grinning. "That was all just a big act for your ego."

Chuckling, Ryder stood up off me, undid the buttons on his jeans and pushed them down his thighs. It was then that I noticed he wasn't wearing boxers, and I was staring at his very large, and very erect, cock.

"Is that wide eyed look of yours for my ego too?" Ryder questioned.

I swallowed as I looked up to his face and nodded. "Of course, I'm not impressed in the slightest. In fact, not only is your cock size lackin', but your tongue skills need some *serious* work."

Ryder was smiling at me now as he stepped out of his jeans, leaving him fully naked before me, and what a sight he was to behold.

"Would you mind being my practice partner?" he asked. "I definitely don't want to be a *fucking* disappointment."

"Fine," I dramatically sighed. "Have your way with me, but don't be surprised if I fall asleep half way through."

Ryder pounced on me then, and it had me roaring with laughter. My laughter was quickly replaced by moaning when Ryder zoned in on my neck and locked his lips on my sweet spot.

"Fuck," I hissed and bucked under him.

He allowed me to move under him until I switched our positions and I was on top of him. I shimmied down until I was sitting on his knees and then I looked up at him.

"My turn."

Ryder's his cock jumped as he clasped his hands behind his head and winked. "Go right ahead, sweetness."

I looked down to his shaft and gripped him tightly in my hand, giving it a good squeeze that made Ryder hiss. I kept my firm grip on it as I moved my hand up and down. The movement wasn't as slick as I'd have liked so I let go of him and moved my hand between my thighs where I coated my fingers in my juices before grabbing hold of him once more.

"There," I murmured as my hand slid freely up and down his hardened length. "Does that feel better?"

I looked up and saw Ryder staring at me with wide eyes.

"Holy shit," he breathed out. "That was sexy as *fuck*!" He stared at me like he was going to eat me alive.

I shuddered at the same time he did.

His eyes never left mine as his face contorted with pleasure. I could tell he wanted to roll his eyes back with the sensations that filled him, but he fought it and kept his eyes on mine. His mouth dropped open and a groan like I'd never heard from a man before escaped him when I bent down and sucked on the throbbing head.

"Brannaaaaaa," he moaned and reached down and tangled his fingers in my hair. "Christ. Fuck. You suck *so* good, babygirl."

I hummed around his shaft. His grip on my hair became painful when he threw his head back and groaned louder, longer.

"I won't last," he panted. "I need to come to take the edge off."

I went to work then and bobbed my head up and down, applying heavy suction each time I let Ryder's cock almost fully withdraw from my mouth only to deep throat him at the last moment. It was a method I had on constant repeat.

"Fuck!" He roared. "Yes, sweetness. Fuck me with that sexy mouth—oh *shit*!"

He suddenly tapped the back of my head with his hand, and for a moment I didn't know why, then the first hot jet of his release coated my tongue and I realised why he did it. He was warning me that he was about to come in case I wanted to pull away. I didn't. I swallowed the liquid down and hummed when the contractions of my throat drew out more spurts of the salty goodness.

Ryder was talking to God—loudly—and, using a few choice words, he thanked him for gracing me with the ability to suck cock so well. I refrained from laughing as I slowly released him from my mouth.

"Sinful," he breathed as he looked down at me. "You're down right fucking *sinful*."

I did nothing but smile up at him. He growled and pulled me on top of him before rolling my body under his. He appeared over me and he nudged his way between my thighs.

"I may lock you up now that I know how good you are at—"

"Suckin' your cock?" I cut him off, snickering.

He nodded. "Darling, you should add it to your resume because *damn*."

That cracked me up.

"Hush," he mused. "I don't want my brothers thinking you're laughing at the size of my dick or some shit like that."

I covered my mouth with my hands to muffle the sounds, but I didn't have to worry about my laughter becoming a problem when Ryder zeroed in on my sweet spot on my neck for a third time and sucked.

"Oh, fuck," I rasped and bucked under him.

Ryder applied some of his weight on me, and I felt him getting hard between my thighs.

"Already?" I asked when he pulled back.

He looked down to his once again hard and erect cock and grinned at me.

"What can I say?" he smirked. "You bring it out in me."

"Lucky me," I said and licked my lips.

Ryder cursed under this breath then leaned over to the locker next to his bed. He dug around the drawer for a few seconds before he pulled his hand back with a square packet between his fingers. He sat back on his heels and tore the condom wrapper open with his teeth. I watched him roll a condom down his pulsing cock, and the urge to suck on it some more overwhelmed me. I licked my lips.

"Fucking hell," Ryder groaned. "You want to blow me again, don't you?"

I flicked my eyes up to his and nodded.

"You'll be the death of me, woman."

I devilishly grinned. "Death by head, that'd be a good way to go."

"You have *no* idea," Ryder said before he moved between my legs.

He placed his left hand next to my chest and used it to hold his body up. He used his right hand to fist his dick and rub it against my aching clit.

"Ryder," I breathed. "Please. Fuck me. *Please.*"

"You don't need to beg me darling, but I'd be lying if I said I don't like how it sounds."

I balled my hands into fists as he continued to torture me with little licks of pleasure. When I thought I'd beg him some more he lined himself up with my entrance. Before he moved though, he looked at me with a grin and said, "You ready?"

Was that a legit question? I wondered.

"Hell. Yes."

With a grin he thrust forward, and I watched as the cocky expression was wiped from his face and replaced with tortured pleasure. His lips curled up as if he was about to snarl and his eyes fluttered closed as he inched his way into my body until he buried to the hilt.

I bit down on my lower lip as my walls stretched around him, making it a snug fit. The feeling of fullness I experienced was one I wouldn't quickly forget. I lifted my arms and glided my hands over his skin.

"Why so quiet?" I murmured, barely controlling my groans. "Nothing to say now?"

"You... I... *Fuuuuuuucccccccckkkkkkk.*"

I smiled as I tangled my hands in Ryder's hair and pulled his face down to mine. He placed his elbows on either side of my head and held himself up as I covered his mouth with mine. As I kissed him, I slid my hands from his hair, down his rippled back and straight to his meaty arse. I dug my nails into his flesh and it caused him to growl into my mouth. His body reacted by pulling out of my body and thrusting back in.

"Your pussy is like a vice around my dick," he snarled against my mouth and used his right hand to dig his fingers into the flesh on my hip. "Fuck me. You feel like heaven, sweetness."

Breathe, Branna, my mind screamed. *Fucking breathe!*

I greedily sucked air into my lungs and lifted my hand to his shoulder where I dug my nails as he thrust in and out of me, causing a sensation I had never felt during sex before to awaken.

"Holy fuck!" I cried out.

Ryder growled. "That's it, baby. Let me hear you."

I couldn't control my vocals even if I wanted to. With every thrust from Ryder, a delicious fire licked at my core. Burning me with pleasure.

"Oh, my God," I moaned.

"God can't help you now, babygirl," Ryder said. "No one can."

Good thing I didn't want anyone's help, I silently purred.

I held onto him as he fucked me, kissed me and sucked on my neck. I screamed out when he thrust into my body and hit a spot that caused my eyes to see stars.

Ryder leaned his head down and pressed his ear against my chest before he brought his mouth to my ear and said, "Your heart is beating so fast."

"Just for you, darlin'," I replied on a moan.

I felt Ryder smile as he kissed my neck.

"Such a sweet talker," he purred.

"Oh, *there*!" I panted seconds later. "Right. There."

"Here?" Ryder murmured and thrust at the angle he did just seconds before, hitting a spot inside my body that caused my body to hum.

"Yes, yes, yes!" I cried out.

Ryder kept his hips positioned at that very angle and hit my core with his thrust.

"This is *my* pussy," he rumbled as he drove in and out of me.

I scraped my nails against his back. "Yes, yours."

He bit my neck, catching me off guard, and when it should have been pain I felt, the bite oddly drew a moan from me as my nerves misinterpreted it for pleasure. I dug my nails into his shoulder blades in response and the actions caused Ryder to hiss and pump into me faster. He fucked me so hard I knew it would leave bruises.

That bit of knowledge caused me to gasp just as pleasure tore through me and a scream left my body that was so loud Ryder had to bury his face in my neck and press his ear against my skin to block it out.

He slammed into me once, twice, thrice. Four deep strokes. His movements became jerky and quick then as he came. He bit down on my shoulder once more as his pleasure consumed him. His hips still pumped into me as he came down from his high, the movements becoming less and less as the seconds ticked on. When he was spent, he all but collapsed on me.

I didn't complain because his weight felt *so* good on me.

"That. Was. Amazin'!" I panted. "It's *never* been like that before."

Ryder rolled off me after a moment, but kept his arm draped over my chest, his hand covering my left breast. He gave a gentle squeeze and said, "You were never fucked by me before, that's why."

My automatic response to that would normally be to put him in his place, but I couldn't argue with him. What he said was fact. Sex had *never* been like that before him, and by God I knew it wouldn't be like that after him either. He had ruined me for any other man, and I didn't have a single fuck to give about it.

"Can we do it again?" I asked, my breathing still rapid.

Ryder muffled his laughter as he turned his head into his pillow. "Give me a few minutes," he mumbled. "I'm not a machine."

I hummed. "You sure about that? You have a *serious* amount of stamina."

Again, Ryder laughed, and this time, he gave my breast another squeeze.

I fully expected us to have sex again straight away, but we didn't. Instead we got to talking. Ryder asked questions about my parents, my job, Aideen, and my life in general. He gave me some of his background and I learned his parents died a few years ago and that he and his two brothers were raising the twins. They moved to Ireland for business, but he didn't tell me what business that was. When I asked about it, he kissed me and that paved the way for us to have sex for the second time. When we were finished, I was too tired to breathe, let alone ask any more questions.

I fell asleep listening to Ryder chuckle and tease me about my *lack* of stamina, but I didn't care because he quite literally fucked me to sleep, and let me just say, it was a hell of a way to be knocked out.

I tensed when I heard the vibrations of my phone. Someone was calling me because it was vibrating too long for it to be a text message. I groaned when the person didn't hang up. I sat up on my bed and worried who would be ringing me during the middle of the night.

I groggily pushed my covers from my body and walked in the direction of the vibrations. I hissed and opened my eyes when my knee knocked into something hard. I reached down and rubbed the pain away before standing upright.

It didn't take me long to realise I wasn't in my bedroom, and it also didn't take long for the memories of last night's events to slam into me with the impact of a train. I gasped and flung my hand over my mouth. I spun around and widened my eyes when they landed on the sleeping form of Ryder Slater. My heart slammed into my chest as I took him in. His tanned, scuttled body was only half covered by his bed sheets and I had only God to thank for that.

I had sex with him, I told myself. *Twice.*

I let a huge smile over take my face, and barely contained myself from doing a happy dance. I had sex with a Greek fucking God. Two bloody times! Aideen was going to piss herself when I gave her a play by play of how well Ryder turned me out. The soreness I felt between my legs, and on other parts of my body, was a delicious reminder of just how well he fucked me.

I reluctantly tore my eyes away from him when I realised my phone was still vibrating.

"Shit," I whispered and looked around for my clutch.

I found it near my discarded dress, and quickly picked it up. I retrieved my phone and almost passed out when I saw it wasn't a phone call that had my phone vibrating, it was my alarm to wake me up for school. I checked the time and saw it was quarter past seven which meant I had forty-five minutes to get to class otherwise I was so fucked.

Bollocks.

I was about to put my phone away when I saw I had two text messages. One message was from Aideen, and the other from my sister. Aideen, unsurprisingly, wanted to meet up later to hear every detail of my night with Ryder, while Bronagh was letting me know something else.

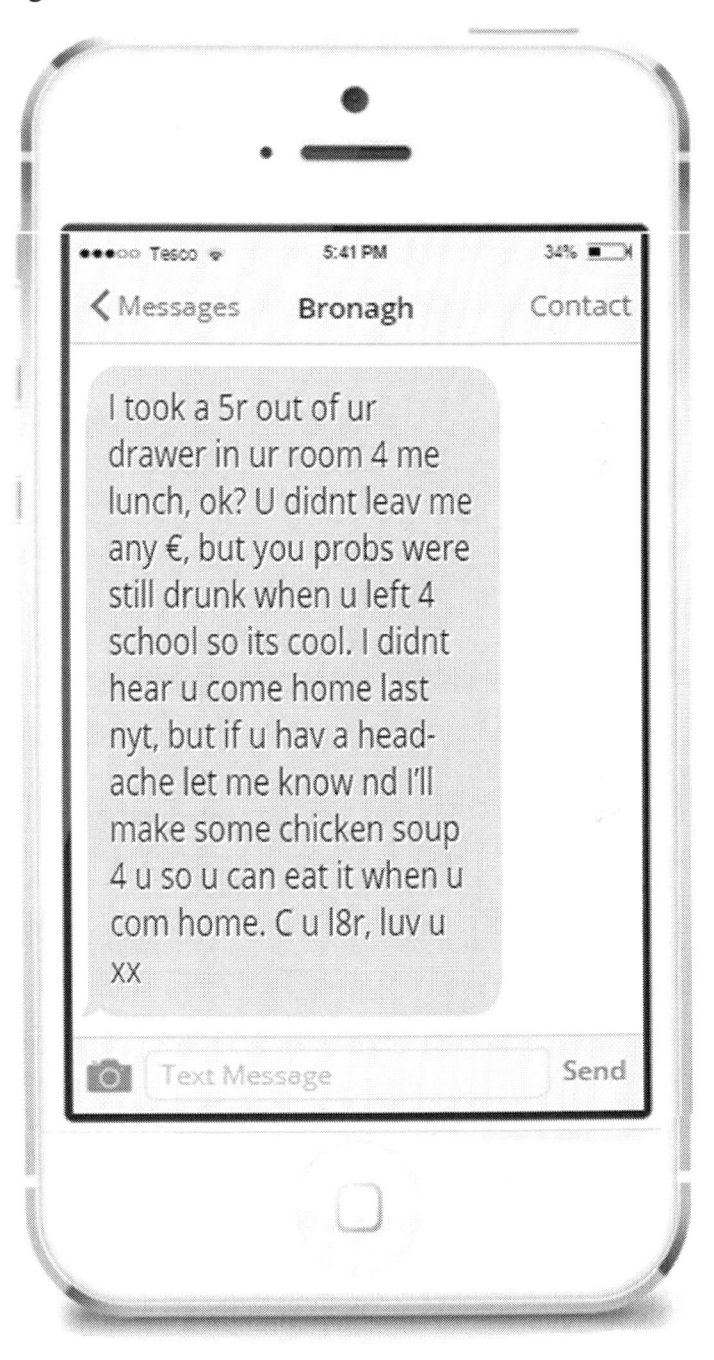

> I took a 5r out of ur drawer in ur room 4 me lunch, ok? U didnt leav me any €, but you probs were still drunk when u left 4 school so its cool. I didnt hear u come home last nyt, but if u hav a headache let me know nd I'll make some chicken soup 4 u so u can eat it when u com home. C u l8r, luv u xx

I smiled as I read my sister's message and wanted to give her a big hug. She was a darling girl and had a beautiful heart that I wished she would open up and share. It wasn't right that only I got to see how brilliant she was.

I thumbed out a reply that I was okay—which wasn't a lie, I was *so* okay—and told her I forgot about her lunch money. I apologised and told her I'd see her later when she came home from school. I didn't let on that I stayed out all night, if she thought I came home then that's exactly what I was going to let her think.

I didn't know how she would receive my night with Ryder, so I figured it'd be best to keep it—*him*—to myself.

I put my phone back in my clutch, and silently scrambled around Ryder's room. I found my bra that Ryder aimlessly flung behind him, put it on then got my dress back on. I picked up my heels, gripped my clutch and stared at Ryder for a few moments.

I wanted to wake him up and say goodbye, but I couldn't because I was afraid I would cry. I wasn't a fool; I knew it was a one-night stand. Not only was the sex off the charts amazing, but also his company made me smile. I was pissed for allowing myself to form a slight attachment but I couldn't help it. He was really great, and my night with him was incredible and I would remember it forever.

Leave before you cry and he wakes up and freaks out, my mind sneered.

I sighed as I looked at him once more before turning and tip toeing over to his bedroom door. I opened the door and without looking back, I stepped out into the hall and closed the door behind me. I exhaled a deep breath and walked over to the stairs and began to walk down them. I stopped when a door on the floor above opened and closed. I looked up and froze when one of Ryder's brothers leaned over the banister and smiled when he saw me. I remembered his name and cleared my throat.

"Hey, Alec."

He winked. "Morning, beautiful."

I felt my cheeks flush. "I have to leave and go to school, will you tell Ryder goodbye for me? Tell him I had *so* much fun."

Alec's laughter was low and rumbling. "You got it."

I wiggled my fingers at him, gave him a smile then continued my descent of the stairs. I blew out a breath when I reached the bottom of the stairs and moved towards the front door but gasped when I heard movement upstairs.

"Shit," I heard Ryder's voice shout. "Shit, shit, *shit!*"

Oh, fuck. I thought. *He was coming downstairs.*

I told myself to run, but I couldn't, I was frozen to the spot as Ryder ran down the stairs, only coming to a stop when he saw me. He was wearing boxer shorts now, and I sort of wished he were fully naked again.

"There you are," he breathed, his shoulders sagging with what looked like relief. "Where are you going, sweetness?"

I swallowed. "I didn't think I'd be good at sayin' goodbye so I figured it'd be best if I left quietly."

I didn't know what to do so I turned and made a motion to move towards the door, but arms came around my waist, a hard body moulded into my back and hot breath tickled my neck, bringing me to a halt.

"Why would you say goodbye to me?" Ryder murmured as he causally trailed his tongue over my skin, causing me to shudder.

"Because, um, it was a one-night stand and—*oh.*"

I lifted my hands and covered his, squeezing as he began to suck on my neck, directly on my sweet spot. My eyes fluttered shut and a moan escaped me.

"Sounds like you don't want to say goodbye to me at all," Ryder murmured, his amusement obvious in his tone.

I licked my lower lip. "I have to go to school."

Ryder hummed. "At the university in town, right?"

I nodded, barely containing another moan. "That's right."

"Can you not call in sick?" he asked, sucking on my neck once more.

I gasped. "I've never called in sick."

His hold tightened on me. "There's a first time for everything."

I swallowed. "I don't know..."

"Come on, beautiful," Ryder murmured. "Spend some more time with me, please?"

He was *killing* me.

"Why?" I asked a little breathlessly.

"I'm not ready to let you leave," he replied, surprising the hell out of me.

I turned in his arms and looked up at him. "It's because I'm a sex goddess, isn't it?"

Ryder smiled and it made me smile too.

"You've figured me out," he mused. "I want to keep you here to avail of your wickedly naughty pussy, *and* your talented mouth."

I playfully slapped his arm. "Ryder!"

He rubbed my cheeks when they stained with heat.

"It amazes me how shy you are during normal conversation," he smirked, "but in bed you're a naughty siren."

I covered my face with my hands.

"Shut *up*!"

Ryder laughed and pulled me against his chest, hugging me tightly.

"Stay with me," he said and kissed the crown of my head. "I want to bring you out for a few hours. Just me and you."

I pulled back and looked up at him.

"Are... are you askin' me out on a date?" I asked, my heart slamming into my chest.

Ryder smiled and brushed my hair out of my face and tucked it behind my ear.

"Yeah," he murmured. "I have a gut feeling that I want to get to know you better, and I *always* listen to my gut."

My legs began to tremble.

"I thought this was just a one-night stand," I whispered.

"I thought it was, too," Ryder said, his eyes scanning my face, "but it's more than that. I don't know *what* it is, but one night with you isn't enough."

My stomach fluttered with butterflies.

"Yes," I whispered. "I'd *love* to go out on a date with you."

"Good." Ryder teasingly grinned. "I wasn't taking no for an answer anyway."

"Is that so?" I laughed, merrily. "Do you think you can get what you want from me so easily?"

"I do," he replied, smugly. "And if all else fails, I've other methods at my disposal to persuade you into doing things my way."

"Yeah?" I asked, my breathing picking up in pace. "What other methods would that be?"

Ryder pressed his front against mine and lowered his head, brushing his lips tenderly against me. I gasped when he bent down and his hands suddenly gripped my behind. I wrapped my arms around his neck and my legs around his waist when he lifted me into the air. He turned and walked over to the stairs.

"I can show you a lot better than I can tell you," he said, grinning.

My laughter and his tangled together as he climbed the stairs, and soon after, so did our bodies in the most delicious of ways. I lay in Ryder's bed long after we had sex for the third time and when I caught myself watching him sleep I knew I was royally screwed because I could see myself falling in love with him very easily if I wasn't careful.

Guard your heart, my mind whispered as my eyes drifted shut. *Don't give him the power to break you.*

I didn't realise it then, but Ryder had the power to break me from the moment he locked his eyes on mine in Darkness, and there wasn't a damn thing that I could do about it.

CHAPTER FOUR

Present day...

I yelped with fright when a pink folder was dropped on the desk of the nurses station. I was reliving a moment from my past, and was completely blindsided by the sudden movement and noise.

"Sorry," Ash's voice quickly apologised. "I thought you heard me."

I placed my hand over my chest, feeling my heart rapidly pound against my chest.

"I'm fine," I breathed. "I was in a world of me own."

I looked up and caught Ash frowning at me, so I waved his concerns off.

"I'm okay, just daydreamin'."

He was hesitant for a moment and then nodded.

"It's quiet on the ward, you can daydream if you want to."

I snorted. "I wish I had that luxury. I want to keep a close eye on the patient in room one."

"I just checked on her," Ash said. "She got her epidural and is sleeping. Her husband is too. Everything is progressing well with her, a few more hours at most then she'll deliver and be moved downstairs."

My shoulders sagged with relief.

"Thank God," I breathed. "I couldn't take any more of her screamin'. I try me hardest to be considerate and never open me mouth about how the women deal with their pain, but *damn*, she hasn't shut her mouth since she was brought on the ward."

Ash snickered. "I could hear her, too. Sally said she was going to jam the gas and air down her throat if she didn't give it a rest soon."

As if summoned, Sally strolled down the hallway with two pink folders in her arms. The site of the folders caused me to groan, it meant two new patients were about to be admitted to the delivery ward and put into our care.

Sally was what we called the mother of the ward, and not because she was the eldest member of our staff, but because she was the most experienced. She had been at the hospital since it opened nearly thirty-five years ago and had the most deliveries under her belt. She was a delivery ward veteran, and everyone knew it. She was married to Doctor Hector Harris that ran the OR.

"Hey Sally," I said when she looked up.

She stopped in front of the nurses station and gave me a bright smile. "Hello, Branna darlin'. Great job on your delivery time to the OR with the patient this mornin', I read the report you and Ash submitted and Hector told me about it. Ninety-one seconds, that's very fast. I've only capped at one zero two at the earliest, so be proud of yourself."

I felt heat stain my cheeks with Sally's praise, and my blush spread even further when I felt Ash's approving gaze on me.

"Thanks, Sally," I said but quickly added, "but I wouldn't have been able to do it without Ash and the others. It was a team effort."

Sally winked. "That, right there, is why you're such a good midwife, you act as a team and never a lone wolf."

It was something she taught me when I used to volunteer at the hospital many years ago, and something that stayed with me. You aren't better than your fellow midwife, and together in numbers you're stronger.

"Well, I work with the best." I smiled then looked to Ash and bumped him with my leg.

He snorted. "Sweet talker."

Who is sweet talking who here?

I blinked away Ryder's voice in my head and refocused on Sally who was talking to me and Ash.

"—should be a busy day, and we'll have to keep a tight ship."

Ash saluted Sally. "You got it, beautiful."

Sally fanned herself. "If I wasn't married and old enough to be your mother I'd—"

"Sally!" I cut her off with a laugh.

She waved me off. "What I'd do to him if I was *your* age is public knowledge, I always tell him."

Ash grinned. "She does."

"You're both as bad as each other," I chuckled.

Sally giggled as she ventured off to do her duties; I glanced at Ash who got to work evaluating the new patients' folders. I shook my head at him and grabbed the second folder Sally brought us.

"Why're you shaking your head?" he asked, not looking up from the folder.

I shrugged. "You amuse me."

"Of course I do, I'm hilarious."

Cocky shite, my mind teased.

"Hey Branna."

I looked up at Yolanda, a lovely African lady who had been working the delivery ward as a cleaner since it first opened.

"Hey Yolanda," I smiled. "How are you today?"

She gave me her trademark beaming smile, and it only caused me to mirror the action.

"I'm great, hon. Jesus woke me up this morning so I can't complain."

I felt the corners of my eyes crease as my smile deepened. "I'm glad to hear it, how are your grandkids? Are they over their dose of the flu?"

Yolanda blessed herself. "Yes, thank Jesus, I prayed every morning and night for them." She frowned. "I hate seeing them so unwell, but I know Jesus will look after them."

Yolanda was *very* religious, everything out of her mouth was 'Jesus this and Jesus that'.

I nodded. "I can imagine. When Bronagh was sick growin' up, I worried meself silly about every cold or stomach bug."

Yolanda winked. "That's what we do, we worry about our babies no matter how old they are. Jesus, help us."

Ain't that the truth, I thought.

"I hear you," I said as she pushed her mop bucket down the hall in the direction of the supply room.

I looked over my shoulder to Ash when he exited the break room with two cups of tea in his hands. I groaned out loud and reached for my pink cup. "I could kiss you," I said as I took the cup and sipped on the addictive sugary liquid.

Tea was—quite literally—my life; I could *not* function without it.

"You can't go and do a thing like that," Ash said. "You'd break Sally's heart, she loves me, you know?"

I cocked a brow. "She loves the attention from you, that's all."

Ash grabbed his chest. "You heartless wench, how *dare* you dismiss what Sally and I have!"

It took everything in me not to laugh, or crack a smile.

"Just tellin' you like it is," I smirked. "*Kid.*"

Ash growled. "You have five-seconds."

Oh, shit.

I stood up and quickly scurried around to the other side of our work counter, and placed my hands in front of my chest.

"Ash," I warned, my voice low. "Don't even *think* about it."

He rounded the station and advanced on me, a smirk playing on his lips.

"Don't!" I said firmly, hoping my no-bullshit-demeanour would give him reason to stop.

It didn't, if anything, it only fuelled the freak to come at me faster.

"No!" I shrieked and made a move to dive behind the counter but Ash was too fast, and caught me mid-air.

He set me down, and full on assaulted my sides with his fingertips as he tickled me. I laughed, shrieked some more, and did the strangest moves known to man as I made my bid to escape the terror.

"Mercy!" I laughed. "For the love of God, *mercy!*"

Ash pulled back on his tickling but kept hold of me as I steadied myself and came down from my laughing high. I was about to playfully sucker punch him and make a run for the break room when I heard my name being... bellowed.

I turned and looked down the hallway and raised my brows.

"Dominic?" I said aloud, hearing the confusion in my own voice. "What are you doin' here?"

He was glaring as he walked up the hallway towards me.

"Bronagh can't collect you today." He said, or rather, growled. "She's not feeling good, her morning sickness is still lasting most of the day, so I said I would come get you instead since I was on my way home from using the gym at your place. Who is he?"

I blinked, and glanced to my right when Ash moved to my side.

"Me?" he questioned, and pointed his finger at his chest.

"Yeah, you." Dominic narrowed his eyes. "I'm looking at you, aren't I?"

He wasn't happy.

Ash cleared his throat and extended his hand. "My name is Ash Wade. I'm Branna's co-worker... who are *you?*"

Dominic didn't even glance at Ash's hand as he said, "I'm her *brother-in-law.*"

Ash furrowed his eyebrows in confusion and lowered his hand back to his side when it was evident Dominic wasn't going to shake it.

"Branna isn't married."

Thanks for the reminder, I silently grumbled.

"That's a technicality," Dominic's eye twitched. "She's dating my brother, and has been for a long ass time. They're engaged."

Ash nodded. "Ah, I see. Nice to meet you."

"I wish I could say likewise, but I can't." Dominic quipped. "Take a couple of steps back from my brother's fiancée."

Oh, for the love of God.

"Stop it, Dominic." I chastised. "You're being rude."

Dominic's eyes never left Ash's. "I'm about to get real rude if this guy doesn't back up away from you."

Ash held his hands up in front of his chest and took a hesitant step away from me. "We were only joking around, man."

Dominic's eyes blazed with anger. "You don't 'joke around' with another man's woman. Ever."

Ash lifted his hand and scratched his neck. "We're friends."

Dominic took a threatening step forward. "Let's see how long that lasts, shall we?"

I stared at him. "What the hell does *that* mean?"

Dominic flicked his eyes to me. "It means he might have trouble breathing when Ryder finds out he was touching you like that."

"Touching her like *what*, man?" Ash asked, his tone firm, as he grew impatient. "We've been on shift the last eight hours and for once we have ten minutes where a woman isn't giving birth. We were just joking around. I was tickling her, not dry humping her."

I nodded in agreement. "He's tellin' the truth and I don't appreciate you insinuatin' somethin' other than harmless fun was goin' on because I would *never* betray Ryder." I frowned then. "He probably won't even care anyway, he never does."

I felt Ash take a step closer to me and Dominic quickly closed the distance between us, putting his body in the way of us.

"What?" Ash taunted. "Are you gonna hit me for seeing if my *friend* is okay?"

"*I'll* see to her," Dominic growled. "You go stare at a massacred pussy."

He did *not*!

"Dominic!" I growled.

He held up his hand to shut me up. "I was there when Jax was born, don't you try to convince me all births aren't as horror filled as that. Bronagh makes me watch *One Born Every Minute*. I know what I'm talking about."

"And the trained midwives don't?" I questioned.

Ash shook his head and turned to me and asked, "Is he always this pigheaded?"

"Hey!" Dominic snapped, clearly offended.

"Yeah," I replied to Ash. "He is."

Dominic turned to face me and stared down at me, his expression displeased.

"Can we leave?" he asked me. "I don't want to hurt your friend, but I will."

I held his gaze. "You wouldn't dare."

He turned to his side and with his eyes on me, he lifted his arm and in the blink of an eye, he reached out and jabbed Ash in the shoulder with his left hand.

"Ow!" Ash gasped and grabbed hold of his shoulder. "That hurt, you arsehole."

I blinked at Dominic as he shifted his gaze to Ash. "You bastard."

"You challenged me," he said to me without looking away from my friend.

I wanted to smack Dominic who leisurely dropped his hand to his side and laughed at Ash who was behaving like he was shot in his arm, instead of just being punched.

"It's on fire!" He hissed and gripped it tightly, furiously rubbing the aching spot. "What the fuck is your hand made of? Steel?"

Dominic looked at Ash with distaste. "I barely touched you."

"*Barely...*" Ash repeated, his eye-wide. "My future fucking grandchildren felt it."

Dominic snorted, but said nothing further.

I shook my head in annoyance. "You're being very immature

and irrational right now, Dominic."

He blinked. "I'll apologize later."

He was as stubborn as Ryder, if not worse.

"Get your stuff," he continued. "It's four, your shift here is over."

I think what he meant to say was my time with Ash was over.

"Okay, I'll get me coat and bag." I pointed my index finger at Dominic and gestured to Ash with my head. "Leave him *alone*."

"No promises," he muttered.

I rolled my eyes and quickly scurried into the break room where I got my coat and bag from my locker. I put my coat on, hooked my bag over my shoulder and rushed back out front where I found Dominic and Ash staring at one another. Well, Ash was staring while Dominic was glaring.

"Stop it," I hissed to Dominic and pinched his arm.

He grunted and rubbed the spot once before taking my arm and tugging me to his side. I resisted fighting him because I was in my place of work, I'd save the arse whooping I had in mind for him when I got home.

"I'll see you tomorrow, Bran," Ash said as he backed away, his eyes on Dominic.

I sighed. "Bye, sweetie. I'm sorry about *him*."

Ash waved me off like it was no big deal, and I hoped it was no big deal because I didn't want Dominic's rudeness to make him uncomfortable around me. I thought this over as I left the hospital and power walked ahead of Dominic all the way to his car.

"Why're you running away from me?" he asked when he unlocked his car and we climbed inside.

I punched him on the shoulder when he was settled. "Because I can't bash you outside, but in here I can." I spat and punched him again.

"Are you supposed to be hurting me?" Dominic asked, grinning as he easily dodged my swinging hands. "Because you aren't."

I growled in frustration as I buckled my seatbelt and folded my arms across my chest.

"You're bloody maddenin'!"

"Bronagh tells me that all the time," he mused, not seeming bothered one bit.

"She's not lyin', you can be a real prick. How *dare* you behave like that on me ward? That's me job, and co-worker, Dominic!"

He backed out of the hospital car park and pulled onto the main road.

"I didn't like what I saw, so I acted on an impulse. Sue me."

"I'd *never* cheat on Ryder." I bit out. "Never fuckin' *ever*."

"I'm sorry if I implied you would." He frowned. "I *know* you wouldn't do that. I don't know Ash but I *do* know that he likes you. It's obvious."

I widened my eyes. "We were jokin' around! Ash is me friend. He flirts with everyone. Literally *everyone*."

"If he knows you have a man, he shouldn't flirt with you. Period."

"You can't just treat people like that though, Dominic. He was only messin' around," I scowled.

He grunted. "Sorry for making sure some stranger wasn't groping you."

I scoffed. "You could tell that we were jokin' around. I was *laughin'*!"

"You can laugh *without* him touching you," Dominic countered.

I glared at him then looked out the window of his Jeep, contemplating on whether or not to murder him.

"You might want to square shit with Ash because when I tell Ryder about this, he might end up in a body bag."

I exploded.

"What the fuck are you goin' to tell 'im?" I angrily asked. "That me *friend* was ticklin' me. *Really*?"

"*Yeah*," Dominic countered. "*Really*."

He was un-fucking-believable.

"I can't talk to you anymore, I'll go crazy!"

With that said, I focused my attention out of the car window until we pulled up outside my house some twenty minutes later.

"Thanks for the lift," I said politely as I unbuckled my seatbelt and grabbed my bag, making sure not to look at Dominic for fear I'd bite his over-reacting head off his shoulders.

He grunted. "Remember what I said, tell Ash to back off."

I set my jaw as I exited his Jeep and slammed the door behind me.

"Rude little bastard," I muttered as I walked up the driveway of my garden.

I didn't look back as I unlocked my front door and stepped inside my house, closing it firmly behind me. I hooked my keys up on the key rack and then headed into the kitchen, turning on the hallway light along the way. I hated the winter months; it got dark out way too bloody early. It was only nearing four pm and the sun was already set.

"Damien?" I called out; making sure my voice was loud enough to carry up the never-ending staircase.

I heard movement from upstairs then, "Yeah, Bran?"

"I'm makin' cottage pie for dinner, do you want some?"

"Yeah, please."

"Okay, hon."

I took off my jacket, hung it up under the stairs along with my bag. I grabbed my phone from my bag then headed into the kitchen and got a start on dinner. Twenty minutes later I was mid-way through my prep when the front door of my house opened and slammed shut.

"Branna?" Ryder's voice roared and echoed throughout the house.

Uh-oh.

"I'm in the kitchen," I called out.

I heard his footsteps pound against the floorboards as he stormed down the hallway and into the kitchen, shoving the door open in the process.

"Who the *fuck* is Ash Wade?"

I was going to *murder* Dominic Slater.

CHAPTER FIVE

Present day...

I glanced away from peeling potatoes and looked over my shoulder to Ryder when he stormed into the kitchen, dropping his coat and keys on the kitchen counter. I stared at his coat until he growled and snatched it from the counter and hung it up in the hallway under the stairs where all of the other coats and jackets went.

"Ash is me co-worker, he works the delivery ward with me." I replied calmly and went back to peeling potatoes.

Things were silent for a moment until I felt a firm hand take hold of my upper arm. The surprise of him touching me caused me to drop the potato and peeler from my hands and into the sink. When I was spun around I gasped to find how close Ryder was to me.

His body was a hair away from pressing against me and his face was dangerously close to mine. I licked my dry lips and looked up at him; momentarily staring at the face and eyes I've come to miss so dearly.

Instead of saying something emotionally stupid, I said, "I don't have time for games, Ryder. I'm preparin' dinner. Damien is hungry."

His lip curled a little, and I could feel his anger radiate from his body as I frowned at him.

"Why're you so mad at me?" I questioned.

"Are you cheatin' on me?" He asked, his voice shockingly low.

I blinked with surprise, shock... and hurt.

"I... what?" I asked when nothing else would come out.

"Are. You. Cheating. On. Me?" he snarled.

He unknowingly just stabbed me in the heart with a knife.

I swallowed down the lump that formed in my throat and blinked back the tears that wanted to be shed. "If you have to even ask me that, then you're truly lost to me." I whispered, my heart pounding against my chest as pain surged through it.

"Answer the fucking question," he bit out.

I shook my head. "No, I'm not cheatin' on you."

The muscles in his jaw rolled back and forth. "Do you *want* to cheat on me?"

Cue the twisting of said knife in my heart.

"No," I answered. "I don't want to cheat on you."

"Then why," he rumbled, "are you fooling around with a co-worker of yours? Who, by the way, will have one of his limbs broken by morning."

Panic filled me.

"Don't you *dare* hurt Ash!" I warned. "He is me friend, *just* me friend, and fuck Dominic for tellin' you otherwise."

"How do you know Dominic—"

"Because he picked me up from work and saw Ash ticklin' me and, as usual, he jumped to conclusions!"

Ryder got in my face and pressed his body against mine using his hips to pin me against the kitchen counter. I knew he wouldn't physically hurt me, even if I ever *did* cheat on him I knew he would never raise his hand to me, but that knowledge didn't calm my spiked nerves.

"He had his hands on you?" he asked, his voice dangerously low.

I cleared my throat. "It was playful, Ryder. Harmless. Ash is me friend, and nothin' more. He flirts with everyone on the ward—"

"Everyone on the ward isn't *my* fianceé, are they?" he cut me off, his voice a growl.

My shoulders sagged. "No, they aren't."

"They why would you think it'd ever be okay to playfully mess around with some guy?"

I sent my jaw. "I do it with the girls all the time, but just because Ash has a dick you're gettin' bent out of shape."

I gasped when Ryder lowered his face to mine. "The only dick that should ever be near you in any way is *mine,* do you understand me?"

I turned my head to the side. "You don't own me, and you certainly don't tell me who I can and cannot be friends with. Do *you* understand *me*?"

Ryder's entire body tensed. He pushed away from the counter and began to pace back in forth in front of me like a caged lion.

"What do I have to do?" he hissed. "Piss on you to mark my territory?"

I clutched my chest. "How romantic."

My sarcasm was met with Ryder's rage.

"Cut the bullshit, Branna."

"Says the man who constantly spews it."

We stared at each other for a long moment until his beeping phone broke the silence. He angrily dug the device out of his pocket, pressed on the screen, read whatever message he received and set his jaw.

"Put the fuckin' phone down for one second and focus on me!" I snapped.

"I am focused on you, and *this* isn't over." He growled at me whilst shoving his phone back in his pocket. "We'll continue this *later*."

With that said he turned around and stormed out of the kitchen, his heavy footsteps echoing throughout the house.

"Where are you goin' *now*?" I bellowed, throwing my hands up in the air.

"You don't need to fucking worry about it!" He shouted back.

When the front door slammed shut I screamed with frustration. Without thinking I turned, picked up the plate containing the potatoes I already peeled for dinner and threw it against the cupboards. I watched as it smashed into pieces and flew in all directions.

I stood staring at the mess I just caused and crumbled to my knees. Everything was a mess. My kitchen. My relationship. My fucking life. I squeezed my eyes shut and tried to regulate my breathing, but it was no use, I was close to my breaking point.

"Bran," I heard a voice murmur.

I looked up, and when I saw the grey eyes of Damien, I burst into tears.

"He's being a dick, Bran," Damien said as he bent down and put his arms around me. "I didn't mean to eavesdrop, but you both weren't exactly being quiet. I heard what was said, and Dominic *clearly* fed Ry some bullshit and he just lost it."

I hugged Damien back and let all my built up sorrow come out.

"Branna," Damien sighed and swayed me from side to side. "Don't cry, Mama Bear. It'll be okay."

That only caused me to cry harder because I knew how false that statement truly was.

"It won't, Dame," I sniffled.

He pulled back from our hug and frowned at me. "What do you mean?"

"I'm breakin' up with him," I whispered.

Telling another person, especially Ryder's brother, about my plan made it feel much more real, and much more harrowing.

Damien swallowed. "You both just had a stupid fight, you don't need to jump to—"

"I've been plannin' on breakin' up with him," I cut Damien off. "I just haven't found the right moment to do it."

Damien stared at me with wide eyes.

I nodded. "You look how I feel."

He blinked his eyes a couple of times, opened his mouth then snapped it shut. I felt like another dam was about to break within me when an expression of pain flashed across Damien's eyes.

"Don't look at me like that," I pleaded.

He cleared his throat. "Like what?"

"Like I'm goin' to take your entire world away."

The muscles in Damien's jaw rolled back and forth.

"You're my big sister, Branna," he murmured. "Not having you here, or by Ryder's side, will change everything... just *everything*."

My heart hurt.

"I know, sweetie, and trust me," I whispered, "I didn't want it to turn out like this, but I've been puttin' up with Ryder's shite for a long time. He has pushed me to this, and left me no choice."

"I'll help fix whatever he has done. Just tell me what he did and I'll make it better, I promise." Damien said in an almost desperate attempt to try and change my mind.

"Honey, I won't leave your life, not when I've just gotten you back. I love you to death, you're me family and that will *never* change whether I'm with Ryder or not."

"Tell me what he did," Damien bit out, ignoring me. "I can't help if I don't know what he did. Just tell me, please."

"He's done a lot of things," I replied, my shoulders sagging. "While you've been away, things changed between us and they're just goin' from bad to worse."

"But... why?"

I managed a snort. "Sweetie, I've been askin' meself that question for months."

"I don't understand, Branna," Damien grunted, furrowing his brows. "I *need* to understand, help me to. Please."

He took my hands in his and carefully pulled me to my feet then we sat at the kitchen table across from one another.

"It started off small," I began. "He'd go out for a late night run or to grab some food, but instead of being gone only a little while, he'd be gone most of the night. Honestly, I didn't notice a pattern until a few months after it first occurred. Workin' at the hospital wipes me out so I paid no mind to when he left the room at night because I'd fall into a dead sleep, but when I started to mention it, that's when the fightin' started. He refused to tell me anythin' when I asked so he resorted to blockin' me out and ignorin' me. It got worse when nothin' was resolved so we've just been growin' apart from one another ever since, and I'm at a point now where I want to detach meself completely from 'im so I can start to move on from 'im."

Damien's brows were drawn together. "My brothers, do *they* know what he is up to?"

"I'm confident that they do." I swallowed. "Keep what I'm about to say between you and me, okay?"

Damien nodded.

"All of Ryder's money—our money—is gone."

Damien's jaw dropped open. "I don't understand. *How?*"

"I've *no* idea," I said with frustration at my situation. "I asked about it, but Ryder threw up his wall and blocked me out so eventually I stopped askin' and just started payin' the bills and for food out of me own wages."

Damien looked more confused than I felt.

"It gets *more* mind bogglin'," I frowned.

"Jesus, *how?*"

I gnawed on my inner cheek.

"Dominic's money is gone too, and so is Alec's. Ryder told me about a bad investment they made with Brandon Daley. It's why Dominic started to fight again, he needed money and he knew fightin' got 'im good money and that bein' a personal trainer didn't. He tried the 'normal' side of workin' and it's obvious he finds fightin' is best suited for 'im. I'm sure me sister is in the dark as to what happened to his money, too, she'd tell me otherwise."

I hated not telling Bronagh the real reason I thought Dominic was back fighting, but I couldn't do it. Not now. Not while she was pregnant for him.

I turned my attention from my thought back to Damien and noticed he was processing everything I told him, I could see the wheels turning in his mind as he thought.

"How could I not know any of this?" he whispered after a few moments of silence.

I frowned. "You're the baby of the family. From the start, the deal was to keep you out of the life they were roped into, and I guess they're still tryin' to protect you."

Damien growled. "I don't need any fucking protection. I'm not a damn child, Dominic is only four minutes older than me!"

I sighed. "I know that, sweetie, it's just that you're precious to them. They risked everythin' to see you safe, it's a trait that's instilled in them. You can't blame them for wantin' to keep you safe from harm, can you?"

"No," he agreed, "but I'm not in danger anymore. Marco and Trent, they're dead."

"And thank God for that," I said and blessed myself.

"I don't see why they couldn't fill me in on their problem. I'm a brother, too."

"Of course you're a brother, too. You're my *favourite* Slater brother, if I'm being honest... don't tell Alec that though."

Damien managed a snort. "You say I'm a Slater brother, but since that day back in New York with Trent when he baited me into a fight about my dad, I've felt like nothing but an outsider to my own flesh and blood."

"Damien," I whispered.

He sighed. "I'm cool, it's cool. Don't worry about me, you've got enough going on."

I wanted to argue that I'd always worry about him no matter what I had going on, but he didn't give me a chance.

"You stay here in case Ryder comes back, I'm going to see Dominic. I'm bringing all this to him. He may be silent with you, but let's see him give *me* the run around."

I blinked. "You look a little scary right now, Dame."

His lips quirked. "Well, hell, I *might* be a Slater after all."

"Smartarse."

He kissed the crown of my head then walked out of the kitchen, and a few steps later, out of the house, closing the front door behind him. I didn't like the silence, so I got my phone and dialled my sister's number. I put my phone to my ear and waited for her to answer.

"Hello?" a cheery male answered.

Dominic Slater.

"You word twistin', weight liftin', fight pickin', cock suckin', son of a *bitch*!"

My future brother-in-law gasped. "I have never, and will *never*, suck someone's cock you misinformed wench!"

I gripped my phone tighter. "I'm goin' to *end* you when I see you, Dominic."

He was silent for a moment then he said, "Ryder spoke to you then?"

"Oh, Ryder spoke to me all right!" I snapped. "He came home and accused me of *cheatin'* on 'im, and he said he is goin' to break one of Ash's limbs and it's all *your* fuckin' fault!"

"What the hell is that screamin' about?" I heard my sister's voice. "Who are you talkin' to, babe?"

"Bronagh!" I shouted.

"Is that Branna?"

"Yes, but—no, give that back to me *now*!"

"What's goin' on?" Bronagh asked me.

Her voice was clear now, a sign she took her phone from Dominic without much of a fight.

"Dominic told Ryder I was cheatin' on 'im!" I stated to my sister. "I told the lyin' prick that Ash was me friend when he mistook us jokin' around for somethin' more than friendship, but he *still* called Ryder and told 'im his views. Ryder thinks I'm *cheatin'* on 'im, Bronagh."

"This has to be a joke," my sister said. "It's a joke, right?"

"No," I growled. "And if that bastard you call a fiancé comes near me house again, I'll gut 'im!"

"Tell me she is lyin'!" I heard Bronagh growl.

"This dude had his hands on her *hips*—" I heard Dominic's voice in the background.

"Did you tell Ryder you thought she was cheatin' on 'im?" Bronagh snapped, cutting Dominic off.

"I told him what I saw, and what it looked like to me, but he came to his own conclusions."

"You didn't tell 'im that Branna told you he was harmless?" she pressed.

"No, I didn't because—"

"Get out!" She snapped. "Get the hell out of this bedroom. You have *no* idea the trouble you have just caused them!"

"Pretty girl—"

"No, Dominic!" Bronagh spat. "Get. Out. Go find Ryder and make this right or I swear to God I'll make you miserable!"

Things were silent for a moment then Dominic said, "How miserable?"

He was *such* an arsehole!

"*Very* miserable!" My sister warned. "You think you have blue balls now? You have no idea of the term, but unless you fix this you will. I *promise* you!"

I think I heard a door slam then came my sister's tired sigh.

"I'm so sorry, Branna," she said, and I heard the sincerity in her voice. "I can't believe Dominic would do somethin' like this. I don't know why he didn't believe you when you set him straight."

My lower lip wobbled. "Me either."

"Don't cry," my sister pleaded. "Not over that prick I call me other half, he isn't worth it."

I rubbed my eyes with the back of my hand. "Ryder said he was goin' to hurt Ash, do you think he will?"

Bronagh was silent for a second then she said, "I don't know, Bran. Maybe you should call Kane and Alec, they could help find 'im? He'd listen to them quicker than the twins."

I nodded. "That's a good idea, I'll do that now."

"I'm goin' to get showered and dressed then I'll come over to see you, okay?"

"Okay," I said to my sister. "I love you."

"I love you, too."

When the phone line went dead I opened up my messenger app, and sent a message to both Kane and Alec to come to my house as soon as they could because I needed to speak to them about Ryder. I added to the message that he was okay just so they wouldn't worry. Thirty-seconds after I sent the message I got two messages back saying they were on their way to my house.

I didn't know how long I was sitting at my kitchen table, staring at the floor, but I snapped out of it when I heard the sound of a key in a lock. The noise of the front door opening sounded and my heart jumped up to my throat.

"Branna?" Alec called out.

My stomach churned on the diminished hope of it being Ryder coming home.

"In the kitchen," I called out as I quickly grabbed the sweeping brush and began to sweep up the mess I made earlier.

Alec and Kane entered the kitchen, and they both greeted me with a kiss on the cheek, and tight hug. When he stepped back, Kane frowned at my cleaning bits of potato off the cupboards.

"What happened?" he asked.

"Me and Ryder, we had a big fight." I sighed. "I lost me temper and smashed a plate so be careful you don't step on any bits I may have missed when sweepin'."

Alec whistled. "Did you hit *him* with the plate?"

I shook my head. "I threw it at the cupboard when he stormed out mid-argument. His poxy phone beeped, and as usual, he left the house to do God knows what or God knows *who*."

Alec's gaze hardened. "Ryder isn't cheating on you Branna."

"How am I supposed to know that?" I snapped. "How am I supposed to know *anythin'* anymore? He leaves the house for hours on end every day, he is gone every night and he *never* tells me where he is goin' or who he is goin' with. I can't take the lies and secrets anymore. I can't fuckin' do it!"

Kane and Alec's mouths were agape when I finished shouting, and it did nothing to settle my burning temper.

"I *know* you both know what he is up to, but don't worry, I won't pester you both with questions because Ryder should be the one to tell me what he is fuckin' around with. I deserve to know."

Alec scratched his neck. "Things are very complicated, Branna."

"Me life is complicated, Alec, and it's why I'm settin' out to *un*complicate it."

Kane stepped forward. "What does that mean?"

"It means," I said with my head held high, "that I'm breakin' up with Ryder. I've been plannin' on doin' it but haven't found the right time. I'm realisin' now that there is no right time, so the next time I see 'im, I'm just doin' it."

"Are... are you serious, Bran?" Alec asked, his eyes wide.

I nodded. "I'm sad, Alec. I've been sad for *months*. We either fight or ignore one another, there is no in-between and I refuse to live like this anymore. I don't love this version of Ryder. I love the man he used to be, but I am *through* waitin' around for him to reappear. I deserve to be happy, and Ryder, as he is now, doesn't make me happy."

Kane scrubbed his face with his hands. "This will change..."

"Everythin'." I finished for him. "Yeah, it will change everythin', and that's the point. I can't live like this anymore so I'm gettin' out."

"Have you talked to the girls about this?" Alec asked. "Keela hasn't mentioned anything about you wanting to leave Ryder to me."

"Neither has Aideen." Kane chimed in.

"Aideen is busy with Jax, Keela is busy with her writin', Bronagh is pregnant, and Alannah is swamped with work. They're all under enough stress as it is. I didn't want to burden them with problems that don't concern them so I kept this to meself."

"Nothing about you is a burden, Bran," Alec frowned.

I managed a small smile. "Thanks Alec, I appreciate you sayin' so."

"It's the damn truth," Kane firmly stated. "You're family, and family isn't a burden. Understand?"

I nodded, and my mind wondered if they would still consider me family after I broke up with their big brother.

"When you find Ryder, please, don't tell 'im any of this. I have to talk to him about this meself, okay?"

Both of the brothers glumly nodded.

"What set him off anyway?" Alec asked a moment later. "What was the big fight about?"

I filled them in on what went down with Ash at work earlier in the day, and what Dominic said to Ryder about it.

"I'll *kill* him!" Kane growled, talking about his younger brother.

Alec grunted. "Not if I get my hands on him first."

I chewed on my nails. "You don't think Ryder would hurt Ash, do you? He really *is* me friend, and I'd never forgive Ryder if he hurt him."

Kane and Alec shared at look.

"What does that look mean?" I questioned.

Alec sighed and looked at me. "I'm not going to lie to you, Bran. Ryder, when he is pissed and pushed to the edge… he can be, well, terrifying. He hasn't been that angry in a long time, I honestly don't think you've ever seen him lose it before, and I don't want you to either. We'll find him and bring him home to you."

I swallowed down bile. "Thank you."

They both nodded and stood. "Let us know if he comes home in the meantime."

"I will."

When they left I was on my own with just my thoughts for company, and that didn't bode well for me because, like earlier in the day, my mind drifted to happier times with Ryder. It was like I was hurting myself on purpose by remembering how incredible things were with us, but I couldn't help it.

Ryder, the way he used to be, was my addiction, and like any addict I had to have him in any way possible, even if that way was just a memory.

CHAPTER SIX

Five years ago...

"Just sit her down and *tell* her about Ryder." Aideen demanded. "She won't go crazy like you think she will."

"But she *will*." I groaned and adjusted my phone against my ear. "Bee doesn't like people, and she especially doesn't like *me* bein' with people. Men in particular."

Aideen clicked her tongue. "She's goin' to have to take the stick out of her arse and get *over* it. She can't stay closed off forever, and she can't expect you never to have a relationship. You've been datin' Ryder over eleven weeks now, Branna, the longer you leave it the worse it will be when you do eventually tell her. You *love* 'im so it's time to introduce them."

"Shhhh!" I hissed. "Don't say that out loud!"

Aideen laughed. "No one can hear me, you freak."

I relaxed. "Just don't say it out loud, I'm still overwhelmed that I have feelin's like *that* for 'im. We've only been together a few months."

"You're spendin' a shit load of time with 'im on the sly, what did you *expect* to feel for 'im?"

I frowned. "I don't know, but love definitely wasn't it."

"Well, you love 'im," Aideen said firmly, "and that's not just goin' to go away because you're scared. It will only grow and develop into an even deeper lover the longer you're with him."

"I know," I groaned. "I *know* that it's time for Bee to meet 'im but just don't know if *now* is the right time. That Nico kid in school has been a huge bother for her, then she was jumped by that girl a couple of weeks ago and I just don't know if I should throw this curve ball at her. She is stressed as it is, Ado."

"Bring her to Darkness to cheer 'er up," Aideen suggested. "She's eighteen now. Bring her out for her first official drink and have some fun. Slip Ryder being your boyfriend into the conversation somewhere after her fifth or sixth drink. She'll take the news much easier then."

I blinked. "That's actually a good idea."

"I've been known to have them," she grinned.

I smirked. "They're few and far between."

"You're such a bitch," Aideen quipped and laughed.

"But of course," I teased then sobered. "What time will you be at the club?"

"Sorry, babe, I can't make it tonight," Aideen grumbled. "I'm in work at seven tomorrow mornin' which means I'll have to be up at six to shower. Me class is going on an outin' and we leave at eight."

I groaned. "You mentioned that, but I didn't think it was *this* week. Shite."

How can I do this without my partner in crime?

"I'll be there in spirit," Aideen quickly said. "Don't back out of it."

"I won't," I sighed, "but I'll be more nervous without you there."

"You got this, Bran."

I bloody well hoped so.

After I got off the phone with Aideen, I ventured out of my room and went down the hall to Bronagh's. I knocked on her door and entered her space when she shouted out for me to do so. I was glad to find she wasn't watching television, but was reading a book on her Kindle instead.

"What are you readin'?" I asked as I approached her.

"*Life Interrupted* by Yessi Smith," she replied, not glancing away from the screen.

I smiled at how engrossed she was. "Is it good?"

Bronagh nodded enthusiastically. "Yeah, but I really want to physically harm this one character, he defines the word psychopath."

I chuckled. "Sounds intense."

"It is," she agreed, "but I like intense."

I stood idle by her bed for a few moments and it made my sister smile as she switched her attention to me.

"Ask whatever it is you want to ask me," she said, her eyes laughing at me.

I licked my lips. "Do you want to come out with me tonight?"

Bronagh blinked. "Like, to the cinema?"

I shook my head. "Clubbin'."

She widened her eyes. "You want to bring *me* clubbin'?"

"Yep," I chirped. "You're eighteen now, you're legal. I want to have some fun with you. I want to cheer you up to after all that's happened with that Nico shite and the fight you were in."

"Thanks, but I'm not exactly a social person, sis, do you think a club is the best place for me?"

"You've gotta start somewhere, kid."

Bronagh mulled it over and I saw in her eyes that she wanted to reject my invitation, but she took one look at me and sighed in defeat. "Fine."

Thank you, Jesus.

I whooped. "Atta girl."

"What will I wear?" she asked and pushed her bed covers from her body.

"Go and get showered," I encouraged. "I'll go and to pick out somethin' for us to wear, okay?"

My sister reluctantly nodded before she left the room and headed for the bathroom. When I heard the door closed, I snuck down the hallway and re-entered my room and grabbed my phone. I dialled Ryder's number and pressed the phone to my ear.

"Hey sweetness," he answered on the second ring.

"Hey sweetness," I heard his brothers mimic him in the background.

Amusement filled me.

"Your brothers are children."

"I'm aware of it, and so are they," Ryder said then cursed at his brothers to keep it down.

"What are you doin' tonight?" I asked on a chuckle.

"Darkness," Ryder replied. "Dominic has a fight."

Oh, I inwardly squealed, *this was perfect.*

"Brilliant," I gushed. "I'm goin' there tonight, too."

"With who?" Ryder questioned, his voice was deep and it had me rubbing my thighs together.

I licked my suddenly dry lips and answered, "Me sister."

Silence.

"You're going to introduce us?" he asked after a few moments.

I gnawed on my lower lip. "Yeah, I want 'er to meet you."

"Shit," he breathed. "I'm nervous now, thanks."

I unexpectedly laughed. "Think about how *I* feel! I'm scared shitless, I've never done this with 'er before."

"We've got this," Ryder assured me. "I'll be extra sweet and won't invade her space like you said, I'll let her warm up to me in her own way."

I let out a relieved breath. "That will help."

"Don't worry, Bran, she'll love me."

I hoped so, because I loved him, and it would kill me if Bronagh didn't accept him.

Dominic Slater is Nico. The little bastard who had been hassling my little sister in school, and had caused nothing but problems for her over the last few months was my boyfriend's little brother. I had an atrocious moment were I let my raging emotions take over my body and I did something really bad. Deplorable really. I punched Dominic in the face, in front of his other brothers, and Ryder broke up with me because of it.

I wasn't proud of my actions, but I didn't exactly regret them either, which didn't help my situation in the slightest.

It was *not* how I expected my night to go. I shook my head as recapped what happened and before I could feel real emotion, I downed the remainder on my Vodka and Coke. I swayed a little and laughed at myself, wondering how many drinks I had consumed but couldn't think of a number.

I was pretty sure it was close to double digits though.

"Are you okay?" I asked Bronagh as the lights of the club came on signalling everyone to get the hell out and go home.

She nodded and laughed for no reason.

"You're drruuunnnkkkkk," I sang, giggling.

She placed a hand on her forehead. "It's *so* warm in here, I'm roastin'."

I took her hand in mine and tugged her towards the exit of the club. We laughed as we stumbled up the stairs. I felt good until the cool fresh air hit me. One-second I remember talking to The Destroyer kid that Dominic/Nico fought on the platform in Darkness then the next I was heaving and slumping down with my eyes closed. I groaned when I felt myself being lifted into the air.

"Bee?" I mumbled.

"Not Bee."

I forced my eyes open and looked up.

I curled my lips upward in disgust. "Put. Me. Down."

Ryder glanced down at me and said, "Make me."

I tried to lift my hand to do just that, but I couldn't, I could only lean my head back against his arm and moan as my head spun.

"You drank too fucking much," my *ex*-boyfriend growled. "I've been watching you all night, you knocked back glass after glass."

I humourlessly laughed. "I had an eventful night, I needed to take the edge off."

"Fucking *hell*, Branna," he angrily replied, his grip on me tightening.

"Why do you even care?" I hissed and tried to swat at him again, but failed. "You broke up with me, *remember*?"

"I remember," he replied on a grunt. "And I didn't mean it."

"Sounded to me like you meant it." I countered.

I was met with silence as Ryder walked, holding me against his chest like I weighed nothing. I grunted and groaned when a car door was opened and I was placed in the back seat.

"Alec," Ryder grumbled. "You drive."

"This is becoming a pattern," Alec muttered.

"Just do it," Ryder hissed.

"Jesus, okay. Should I find something for the backseat in case she gets sick?" Alec asked, and I felt like his wary eyes were on me.

"No," Ryder replied to his brother as he got into the car and pulled me onto his lap. "We don't live far away, I'll hold her on my lap. Dominic has Bronagh."

I heard male grumbling then a quick, "I call shot gun."

It was Kane who spoke.

"The fuck?" Damien snapped. "Why do *I* have to sit between lover boys and the drunken sisters?"

"Because *I* called shot gun," Kane quipped. "Are you deaf, little brother?"

"Fuck you," Damien growled to Kane, making him laugh.

Reluctantly, Damien climbed into the middle of the backseat and adjusted himself when Dominic climbed in on the other side of him with my sister against his chest.

"If *either* of them puke on me, I'm dishing out dick shots." Damien warned his brothers.

I laughed on Ryder's lap and said, "Dick shots. I want to *drink* one of those."

This caused all of the brothers to rumble with laughter.

"Dirty girl," Ryder's sexy voice murmured in my ear. "You can drink *my* dick shot anytime you like."

I growled. "I'll bite your dick *off* if you don't get away from me."

He snorted. "You're lying on me, sweetness, not much I can do about getting away from you right now while we're driving, is there?"

I tried to sit up but light-headedness prevented me from doing so.

"You shouldn't have drank so much," Ryder grumbled as he pressed his palm flat against my back and began to stroke up and down. The action soothed me instantly.

I closed my eyes as I leaned back against him. "You shouldn't have broken up with me. It hurt, you know?"

I felt his lips on my bare shoulder.

"I didn't mean it," he murmured. "I take it back."

"Too late," I stated. "I'm already over you and lookin' forward to me first single night out. I'll be on the rebound so it's sure to be a *fun* night."

Ryder's hold on me tightened. "I'll spank your ass red and raw if you even dare."

I hissed. "You'd like that, you perverted bastard."

"You'd like it too, you perverted bastard."

My temper flared when Ryder's brothers laughed, *again*.

"Stop listenin' to what we're sayin'!" I snapped.

"What do you want us to do?" Dominic sarcastically asked. "Plug our ears?"

"Don't *you* speak to me you little prick," I growled like a predator. "You've been makin' me sister's life hell in school for *no* fuckin' reason. She is a good kid, she never does anythin' to hurt anyone and yet *you* targeted her! If you think the punch I gave you was bad, just wait until I get me hands on you now, you little wanker!"

"Well, fuck me," Kane whistled from the front of the car. "I'd be scared if I were you, little brother. She's going to kick your ass *back* to New York from the sound of things."

"I can deal," Dominic snorted, clearly not giving a damn that I was furious with him.

I screeched and extended my hands to grab him, but Damien being in the way made it difficult. I tried to push his head down so I could reach Dominic, but it only caused him to yelp and shout for me to stop.

"You sound like a little bitch," Alec laughed from the driver's seat.

Damien sat upright, lifted a hand to his head and rubbed where I shoved at him.

"Fuck you, asshole," he growled. "Her nails were out."

Ryder's arms clamped around mine, pinning them to my body.

"Let. Go."

"No," came his immediate response. "I'm not letting you hurt my little brothers."

"I don't want to hurt both of them," I spat. "Just *one* of them, the one that is about to be dick*less*."

"Ryder," Dominic snickered. "Control your woman."

Oh, *hell* no.

"Oh, shit," Ryder grumbled and applied more pressure to his hold on me when I went, what can only be described as, batshit crazy.

"I'm goin' to *kill* you!" I bellowed.

Damien practically lay against Dominic and Bronagh as he watched me with widened eyes.

"This is both insanely hot and terrifying at the same time," he muttered to his bully of a twin.

Dominic snickered, but I saw him nod in agreement. I was about to dish out some more insults his way, but I froze when I watched his focus turn from me, Damien and everyone else to Bronagh, and her alone. It shocked me how he looked at her; it was like she was his whole world. He lifted his hand and gently brushed her hair back out of her face. She lightly snored and it caused him to smile as he stared down at her, his eyes only blinking here and there, like he was trying to savour what she looked like when she was in his arms. I blinked when he leaned down and pressed his lips to her forehead.

He likes her.

I continued to stare at him, but jumped when Ryder spoke in my ear.

"Yeah," he whispered, loosening his hold on me. "He cares about her. He has a funny way of showing it, but he's trying, Branna. He doesn't understand what he's feeling and it's taking him longer than he would like to express to her that he likes her. She fights him tooth and nail at every turn, and it's bred into him to push back when he is backed into a corner. When she is hostile, he becomes hostile, too. I think it's a bad match, but he likes her, and he can't help that."

"He needs to back off of her."

"I agree, and we can talk about it tomorrow. She'll be sober, and in my home so we'll lump them together and figure it all out, okay?"

I reluctantly nodded.

"Thank you, darling."

I tensed. "I'm not your darlin', Ryder."

"Yeah, *darling*, you are."

I hated that I wanted to smile.

Alec pulled to a stop in front of his house and said, "Welcome to *casa*—"

"Slater," his brothers finished. "We know."

"Assholes." Alec grumbled.

I snorted and it made Ryder smile as we exited the car. He kept a firm hold on me because even though I was coherent, my legs were quite unsteady.

Bloody Vodka, my mind grumbled.

"'Bout time you showed up!" A male voice shouted, followed by laughter and cars screeching to a stop.

I looked around and when I took in all the people that were ambling up the driveway to Ryder's house, I pressed back against his chest. His arms came around me, and his face nuzzled against my neck.

"Don't be frightened," he said into my ear. "We're throwing a party to celebrate Dominic's win at Darkness."

A house party?

I went rigid. "Maybe me and me sister should leave—"

"Dominic is already inside with your sister."

I broke out of Ryder's hold and pushed through the crowd of people waiting to gain entry into his house. I heard him shout after me then curse when I didn't turn and wait for him. I stumbled through the front door and shouted, "Bronagh!"

"I'm here!" I heard her call out.

I followed her voice over to the bottom of the stairs where she was now awake and standing up, but was still in Dominic's hold. He kept his eyes on me as I neared them, and I saw annoyance flash across his face as I reached for my sister and took hold of her hand.

"We're goin' home, Bronagh." I said firmly.

"She wants to stay here," Dominic argued.

I cut my eyes to him and narrowed them. "I don't give a flyin' fuck what she wants, if I say she is goin' home then she is goin' *home*, you got that?"

Dominic set his jaw and nodded once so I turned my attention from him to my sister. She was giggling and turning into Dominic's chest, which prompted me to release her from my hold. I was about to grab her again when hands grabbed hold of me.

"When I tell you to wait for me, you fucking *wait*." Ryder's voice growled as he wrapped his arms around me. "I don't want to lose sight of you in a crowd of strangers."

I struggled against him. "You shouldn't have invited them to your house then, you bloody eejit!"

"I didn't," he countered. "Alec did."

As if on cue, Alec shouted, "Paarrtttyyyyyy," from somewhere down the hall followed by loud, pulsing beats of music. The strangers in the house cheered.

Dominic laughed at his brother, but quickly turned his attention to Bronagh when she spoke to him. "I want to sleep with you," she purred.

The lad's entire body went rigid.

"Dominic," my sister slurred. "Did you he-hear me? I wanna cuddle with you. *Now.*"

A switch flipped inside his head because without hesitation he hooked his arm around Bronagh's waist, then bent down and slid his arm under her knees and lifted her. My sister squeaked the moment she became airborne and wrapped her arms around Dominic's neck as he protectively tucked her into his chest. He turned then and hauled arse up the stairs.

"Dominic!" I growled after him, but he ignored me and took the stairs two at a time, with my laughing sister in his arms.

I made a move to shoot up the stairs after them, but hands clamped down on my hips.

I tensed. "Get away from me, Ryder."

I felt his hot breath on my neck.

"Not a chance, sweetness," he murmured into my neck and squeezed my flesh. "You'll kill him if you get the chance, and I can't allow that. It goes against the bro code."

"Yeah, well, lettin' some stranger haul me sister off to an isolated part of a big house is against the *big sister* code!"

"He. Won't. Hurt. Her."

I huffed. "He has done nothin' *but* hurt 'er since the moment he met 'er!"

Ryder hissed when I dug my nails into the arms that were wrapped around my waist.

"That's *it*," he snapped.

He let go of me and for a spilt second I thought he backed off until I was swung around, picked up, and tossed over his shoulder like a bag of potatoes.

"Ryder Slater!" I snapped. "Put. Me. Down."

"Destiny," I heard Damien's voice chuckle. "Dominic is *busy* right now, but I'm not. Why don't you keep *me* company for a little while?"

These brothers were something fucking else!

I heard Ryder chuckle as he jogged up the stairs with me hanging upside down on his back. I screeched and used both of my hands to keep my boobs from spilling out of my top and I failed miserably because I heard some hooting from younger males who were situated at the bottom of the stairs.

I gave them the finger until they were out of sight.

One-second I was hanging upside down, then the next I was upright on my feet and inside Ryder's bedroom. I steadied myself and backed away from him, keeping my gaze locked on his as he kicked the door closed with his foot.

"I'm not in a confined car space with you now. You can't whisper in my ear and make me forget what happened tonight. We're *done*," I bit out. "I remember how you spat those words *and* how you pushed me off you in Darkness like I was nothing more than a piece of dirt."

The muscles in Ryder's jaw rolled back and forth.

"You punched my brother in the face," he said, exasperated. "What was I *supposed* to do?"

I almost growled. "*Your* brother has made *my* sister's life hell over the past few weeks!"

Ryder blinked. "He is the one who has been in *two* fights for her, and suspended from school *over* her. *He* isn't the only guilty party here, Branna."

I balled my hands into fists. "None of that would have happened if he had just left 'er alone when she asked 'im to the first fifty times!"

"I *told* you he doesn't know how to handle her!" He snapped back. "He has never liked a girl before, not for longer than a few hours, anyway, but he likes Bronagh and he doesn't know what to do about it. He has no clue how to approach her or how to behave around her, and it's not his fault, it's our upbringing."

"What does how you were brought up have to do with how

Dominic treats me sister?" I asked.

I saw the moment that Ryder closed up, and it pissed me off.

"Fine," I growled. "Don't talk, I didn't want to hear your bullshit anyway."

I made a move for the door, but froze when I realised Ryder firmly maintained his position in front of it and stared me down like a predator ready to pounce on its prey.

"What's the matter, Branna?" he asked as he studied me from across the room. "Cat got your tongue."

I nervously swallowed. "Fu... Fuck you."

Ryder shot across space between us and got in my face.

"I intend to, sweetness," he all but snarled. "I intend to fuck you until you can't remember your own name."

"No!" I spat and shoved at his firm chest. "We're *done*, remember? D-O-N-E. Done!"

"You can say it, spell it, and write it across your damn forehead for all I care, because it's not fucking true. We're *not* done. We will never be done do you understand me? *Never*."

My legs began to tremble.

"Ryder—"

"Branna." He cut me off. "This isn't up for debate, we aren't done. Get over it."

I balled my hands into fists. "You don't just get to decide that we aren't done after you already said we are. You'll give me whiplash with your indecisiveness!"

He sighed, loudly. "We. Are. Not. Done. You're my woman, and I'm your man. We're boyfriend and girlfriend. We're a couple. How many different ways do I have to say it for you to get it into that beautiful head of yours? We're together. End. Of. Discussion."

I growled. "I hate how... domineerin' you are."

Ryder grinned at me and I glared at him. I didn't mean sexually, because we both knew how dominant he was during sex, I meant in every other aspect of his persona.

"You *know* what I mean," I angrily stated. "You're quiet around your brothers, and you never voice a problem if we have one. You wait till we're alone to go all cave man on me."

"I'm a private person," Ryder shrugged, not allowing his eyes to stray from mine. "Anything between us will always be private so if I have to cuss your sexy ass out, or spank it and kiss it better, it will all be in private. I'm a patient person, you can piss me off all day and I'll smile and nod... until we're alone, then your ass is *mine*."

I shuddered. "I don't doubt you."

"Good, never doubt me."

I frowned. "I never have."

"I'm sorry about tonight, okay? I regretted what I said the instant it was out of my mouth. I knew it, and so did my brothers. It was Dominic who told me to go and kiss your ass until you forgave me and took me back, you know?"

The brother I physically whacked?

I blinked. "*Dominic*? Really?"

Ryder nodded. "You impressed him tonight, and not many people do that often."

That pleased me because I wanted Ryder's brothers to accept me, but I didn't want him to know that so I shrugged it off like it meant nothing to me.

"I impressed 'im by punchin' 'im in the face?"

Ryder grinned. "Yes."

"You're all *so* weird."

"Trust me," Ryder chuckled. "I know."

I thought about my sister and said, "She'll really be okay?"

Ryder nodded. "He'll tuck her into bed and they'll go to sleep, I'd put my life on it. Dominic would never hurt a woman. He'd never hurt *anyone* unless he had no choice. He isn't a bad person, Branna, he just has to do bad things."

Has to? That wording worried me.

"Tell me what you mean about him," I pressed. "So he likes me sister, big deal, millions of people like other people and—"

"She is the first person he has *ever* taken a liking to." Ryder cut me off.

I blinked. "How can that be possible? He is gorgeous. Surely out of all the girls throwin' themselves at 'im one would have ignited these feelin's within 'im."

Ryder shook his head. "Dominic is focused, and he believes women are a... distraction. To a point, he is right. He fights, and he *cannot* afford a distraction when he fights, so he distances himself from women until he... needs one."

Disgust must have shown on my face, because Ryder sighed and rubbed his face with both hands.

"He has sex with women, *lots* of women, and don't let his age fool you. He has fucked women older than you."

I swallowed. "That's disgustin', he is only a baby!"

"It is what it is," said Ryder with a shrug of his shoulders. "When he wants to have sex, he finds a willing woman, and he has sex, but that's the extent of things."

"So what's his deal with me sister then?" I questioned. "She isn't willin'. She doesn't even *like* 'im so I know she won't have sex with 'im."

Ryder snapped his fingers at me. "That's exactly *it*. He took an instant attraction to her, and *she* instantly shut him down. That's never happened before. I don't mean to sound conceited, but me and my brothers, it's never been a task to hook up with someone we set our sights on."

I grunted. "Yeah, you're all genetically blessed, I get it."

Ryder's lips quirked. "You think we're genetically blessed?"

I rolled my eyes. "You're all gorgeous, and you all bloody well know it."

Ryder had the decency to slightly blush. "Yeah, well, genetics didn't help Dominic with your sister."

I shrugged. "From what she has told me, he is an arsehole. Why would she want to hook up with an arsehole?"

"You'd be surprised how many women dig the asshole vibe, most think they can be the ones to finally straighten out the bad boy."

I frowned. "That's not me or Bronagh. If you're an arsehole, then that's it. No matter how good lookin' you are, nothin' will shine brighter than your dickhead personality."

"It's why Dominic is struggling with Bronagh. He is demanding by nature, so when he orders her about, or his hard on her, she comes out swinging and he has no fucking clue how to deal with a female like that. It's why he screws up so much with her, he just doesn't know what to do when sex isn't involved."

I frowned. "That's kind of sad, Ryder."

He nodded. "I know it is, but it is…"

"What it is," I finished.

His lips twitched and he took a step towards me. "You don't think I'm an asshole, do you?"

My own lips twitched in reply. "The jury is still out on that one."

Another step.

"Branna," he murmured, his eyes locked on mine.

I locked my knees together to avoid them buckling from under me and quickly lifted my hand and held is out in front of me. "Stop lookin' at me like that, we aren't finished talkin'."

His hands went to his belt buckle, and so did my eyes.

"Aren't we?" he asked as he popped the buckle.

The sound sent a shiver up my spine and—*No, Branna, be strong*!

I cleared my throat and lifted my eyes back to Ryder and narrowed them. "No, we aren't."

Ryder sighed when he saw I wasn't backing down. He let go of his now undone belt and placed his hands on his hips. "Okay, talking it is," he said. "What else do you want to talk about?"

"You said before that all of Dominic's behaviour isn't his fault, you said it was your upbringin'. I want to know what you meant by that."

Ryder set his jaw so I pointed my index finger at him. "This isn't up for debate, I want to know *exactly* what you meant by that or I'm leavin'."

"Don't threaten me," Ryder said, his voice low.

Shit.

"I'm not threatenin' you, I'm promisin' you. Talk or I walk."

Ryder stared at me for a long moment, and I *knew* he was thinking about whether I was worth telling the information that he was purposely trying to keep private. That told me it was a secret, a very *important* secret.

"Last chance, Ryder," I warned. "Talk, or I'm gettin' me sister and neither you *or* your brother will have anythin' to do with us ever again."

He curled his lips up in frustration. "I'm trying to think of a way to explain it to you *without* scaring you."

I blinked. "Why would it scare me?"

"Because," he began, "my life is a world away from yours. You have no idea the things I've done, or that I'm still doing."

I took a hesitant step back and it made Ryder grin.

"Does it scare you to know I'm not straight laced like you think I am?"

What the hell did that mean?

My heart began to beat faster as I recalled the many conversations we've had about his job. I never got any information when I asked questions about it, Ryder would seduce me and all would be forgotten.

"You don't scare me, Ryder," I replied honestly.

An emotion flashed across his eyes, and his shoulders sagged, his tough demeanour vanishing.

"I know, sweetness, and that's why I want to word what I have to say correctly. You're *very* important to me, and I don't want you to be scared of me. Not ever."

I tilted my head to the side. "So ease me into it."

He snorted. "This isn't a conversation you can ease someone into, all of it is… heavy."

I sat down on his bed, and patted the empty spot next to me.

"I've got all night."

Ryder came to my side and settled down on the bed next to me. He reached over and took my hands in his. "Before I say anything, please know that I don't want to do what I do, I just have no choice."

I didn't like the sound of that, but I nodded in understanding.

"Back in New York, my brothers and I, we were raised on a compound run by gangsters."

I was waiting for a laugh, or a 'gotcha' to follow that bizarre statement, but nothing followed.

I blinked. "Wow."

Ryder gauged my reaction for some indication of what I was thinking, but I knew he would draw a blank because *I* didn't even know what I was thinking.

"My father was one of those gangsters," he continued. "And he was co-boss along with a friend of his called Marco Miles. Both of them built up their empire from scratch, and by the time I was twenty they had a hand in everything from prostitution to drugs and weapons. You wouldn't think it, but it was a *very* secure business they had going as nearly all law enforcement was on their payroll. The Feds were the only ones not under their thumbs, and when there were a few runs in with honest cops, a payoff to the chief of the NYPD cleared that up quickly. It was a surprisingly safe environment to grow up in, but it was in no way normal. A prime example would be for the twins' thirteenth birthday me and my brothers gifted them escorts because we felt bad about them having to jerk off all the time."

I felt my mouth fall open, and Ryder winced.

"I know, and honestly, it's as bad as it sounds, but that was the norm for us. Girls, girls and more girls. Guns, drugs, violence, verbal abuse... it was all we ever knew because we were exposed to it twenty-four-seven."

I blinked. "You've done drugs?"

Ryder didn't look proud of it, but he nodded. "Yeah, I've dabbled in a lot of different ones... probably any major one you can think of, but I never hit up enough to form an addiction. I only did it once in a while at parties or some shit like that. I gave it up after a while and was a hard ass about it with all of my brothers to make sure they never touched the stuff, and they didn't. Thank God."

I knew the relief he felt, because for years I prayed that I raised Bronagh right so she would know never to touch drugs, and I was blessed that she was a good kid who steered cleared of that mess.

"While I was using, I was *very* careful about what I consumed, that natural paranoia was instilled in me from an early age. I was aware of everything around me, and I noticed everything... it's why Marco picked me for my job after my parents... died."

I knew his parents died, I just didn't know how, it was something Ryder was also mute about. I didn't want to pry because I knew from personal experience how that felt.

"You don't have to talk about them if you don't want to."

"I do, it's just hard talking about all of this shit." Ryder rubbed his face with his hand. "Right, okay. There's no casual way to say this, but they were murdered by Marco."

I stared at Ryder again, not being able to believe what he was saying was truth, but I saw in his eyes that he wasn't joking. A family fucking friend *murdered* his parents! I couldn't begin to imagine what that must have been like to go through.

"Oh, my God!" I gasped and instantly reached out and pressed my hand on his arm. "I'm so sorry, sweetheart."

Ryder looked at my hand then back up to me. "It's okay, don't feel sorry for me... my parents—let's just say they weren't like yours."

I furrowed my brows in confusion and it caused him to sigh.

"My mother cared more about materialistic things than she did her sons', and my father's only interest in us was when it was to talk about us joining the 'family business'."

I shook my head in shock. "I am so sorry, I can't imagine what that must have been like for you and your brothers'."

Ryder shrugged seemingly like it was no big deal. "We leaned on one another when things got tough," he explained. "It's why we're so close, Branna. We aren't a normal family, we would die for one another without hesitation."

I blinked. "I'd die for Bronagh without hesitation so I'd say it's normal."

Ryder's lips quirked. "Not many people feel that strongly about their siblings, but mine are all I have and I'd do anything to protect them. Any. Thing."

I understood that.

I nodded. "I would, too."

"Keep that in mind for what I have to say next, okay?"

Oh, shit.

"Okay," I said warily.

"I never thought I'd have to explain this to someone," he murmured before training his gaze on me. "My parents were murdered by Marco for crossing him. They got greedy and wanted more money than they already had, so they double-crossed their business partner and friend. Understand that in our life, loyalty is everything. Every. Thing. In the compound, we were a family, and you *never* betray your family. If you weren't loyal, you were nothing."

It seemed a little over the top, but I didn't live his life, so I nodded in understanding.

"When they died, it wasn't like me and my brothers didn't feel anything." He admitted, rubbing his fingertips over his knuckles. "No matter how they treated us, they were still our parents'. That being said, we accepted their death pretty easily considering what they did, and I know that sounds inhumane, but it was what it was. Damien though, he took their death hard. He always held out hope that they would both change and become affectionate towards us. It's my fault he is so soft hearted, I coddled him and Dominic too much to make up for what our parent's never showed I guess."

I couldn't imagine what it was like to yearn for affection from your parents, but that was probably because I freely basked in it from mine.

I frowned as sadness hit me. "Poor Damien."

Poor *all* of them.

Ryder kept his face expressionless as he nodded. "He had a cute girlfriend at the time called Nala, her dad was involved in the business too, but she was like the twins. She hated what he did, but accepted it because she had no other choice. Marco's nephews, Trent and Carter, were kind of close to the twins because they were the only ones around the compound in the same age bracket. Dominic and Carter never took great interest in Nala, but Trent did."

"What happened to Carter and Trent's father?" I asked, wondering why their uncle seemed to be the one in that position.

"I don't know, I don't even know if they have the same father, I just remember Marco always being the dad figure for them since they were babies. Marco's little sister was their mother, but she died from a drug overdose shortly after Carter was born so Marco stepped up and raised them."

I whistled. "That's pretty admirable."

Ryder humourlessly chortled. "Not when you come to realise Marco raised those boys to be *exactly* like himself. They were evil little bastards, and I argued with my brothers to stay away from them, but the twins got bored easily and Trent and Carter provided a distraction to that boredom."

Ryder sounded like he instantly became the parental figure to his youngest brothers, like I did with Bronagh when our parents died.

"How old were the twins when your parents' died?" I quizzed.

"It happened a couple of weeks after their fourteenth birthday."

I gasped. "Oh, my God!"

Ryder nodded. "I know, it was shitty timing."

Very shitty.

"Don't get me wrong." I stressed." I'm glad you're here and that I've met you, but if you're so loyal to your compound family, then why are you here in Ireland?"

Ryder's eyes averted from mine for a moment. "We're here on a job. Dominic's last job, actually."

I levelled him with a stare. "Explain."

"I'm trying to," he assured me. "Marco's nephews have to be explained before we get to *why* we're here, they're directly involved in why. I promise."

I nodded, and closed my mouth so he could continue speaking.

"A very long story short—Trent got a little too close to Nala and my brother called him out on it. My brother was only a kid, but we were raised around the mentality that no other person touches what is ours, and that included chicks. Damien was already on the edge from our parents' murder, so when Trent moved in on his girl, he snapped."

I hugged myself with my arms knowing this story was going to go from bad to worse real fast.

"I don't like where this is goin'," I mumbled.

Ryder tensed as he continued telling me what happened.

"Trent snapped, too, and he threw my father's betrayal in Damien's face, and he said he deserved what he got. As you can imagine, fighting ensued. Damien can handle himself *very* well, but Dominic lost it when he saw Trent hit him. As brothers, we're very close, but naturally Dominic and Damien's bond is unbreakable, and Dominic beat the shit out of Trent for laying a hand on him. The beating prompted Trent to pull out a gun he stole from his uncle, and he trained it on Damien."

I gasped so Ryder reached over, took my hands back in his and stroked his thumb over my knuckles, which instantly relaxed me.

"Nala came to Damien's rescue, she jumped on Trent's back and knocked the gun from his hand. Damien picked up the gun and pointed it at Trent when he had already pushed Nala away. My brother ignored Dominic's pleas for him to put the gun down, he focused on Trent and when that little prick brought our father back up, Damien didn't hesitate. He shot him."

My eyes almost popped out of my head.

"Damien *shot* someone?" I asked, my shock evident.

"Yes," Ryder said as he watched my face as if trying to grasp what I was thinking.

I knew, again, he wouldn't be able to guess what was going through my mind, because I *still* had no idea what to think. The information he just fed to me seemed too impossible to be real. I knew Damien, and he was sweet, caring, and his only bad trait was his womanising. He never *ever* came across as the kind of person who could shoot another human being.

"What happened then?" I hesitantly asked.

Ryder cringed. "A *lot* of bad shit."

"I'm listenin'."

"You're so persistent," he mumbled.

I shrugged. "If I'm goin' to be with you, I need to know all of this. I can't be with you and be blind to your history."

Ryder gave me one sharp nod before he said, "Trent died."

Oh, my God.

"And Marco was pissed. He wasn't sad that his nephew was dead, just pissed off because it was a mess he had to clean up."

I felt my insides churn.

"The heartless fuckin' bastard."

Ryder sadistically grinned. "Yeah, that describes Marco perfectly."

"What did he do to Damien?" I asked, almost scared to know the answer.

"Nothing," Ryder said firmly. "I made sure of that, and so did my brothers'."

I furrowed my eyebrows in confusion, and Ryder saw this.

"Marco knew I was planning on moving my family out of the compound and away from the life we had been living. Once my parents were gone, there was nothing keeping us there. Once Damien killed Trent that changed. Marco gave us an ultimatum, either Damien died in payment for Trent's murder, or we worked off the debt."

I blinked. "A *life* debt?"

Ryder nodded. "Marco sorted us into different jobs based on our individual skill set."

I stared at him in horror. "This sounds unreal."

"Trust me, darling, it's more real than you can ever imagine."

I moved closer to him and gripped his hands more firmly, letting him know that I was there for him if he needed me.

Ryder gave my hands a reassuring squeeze then said, "My attentiveness, and knack of moving around unnoticed, pushed me into drugs and weapons. It turns out I am very good at moving shipments and making deals for Marco. Kane became his enforcer, Dominic his fighter, and Alec his... buffer."

"His buffer?" I questioned, my mind reeling.

Ryder laughed a little then. "Alec, as you know, is very friendly. With *both* sexes."

He flicked his eyes to mine and waited for a reaction from me, and he raised his brows when he got one.

I laughed. "If you're tryin' to tell me he is bi-sexual, you don't have to, I already know. I saw him kiss a lad, and a girl, a few weeks ago in Darkness, and he constantly goes on about attractive male and female celebrities. It wasn't as if he was tryin' to hide that he bats for both teams."

Ryder smiled wide at me. "It doesn't bother you then?"

I cocked a brow. "Why would it bother me?"

"Because some people aren't accepting of it."

"I'm not some people."

"Yeah," he murmured. "You're pretty incredible."

I grinned. "Nice try, but finish what you were sayin' before you seduce me."

Ryder's smile faltered. "Yeah, okay, so Alec is basically an escort to anyone Marco gives him to."

Anger surged through me.

I growled. "He isn't a piece of fuckin' meat!"

"To Marco he is, to Marco we *all* are."

That infuriated me.

"So you all work these jobs to keep Damien safe, what does he do?"

"Nothing," Ryder instantly replied. "It was part of the agreement that he doesn't have a job."

I nodded. "Okay, so why is this Dominic's last job? And more importantly, when is *your* last job?"

"Mine was a few weeks back, so was Alec and Kane's. We've been around the world doing jobs for Marco for a long time. We knew he never cared about Trent like an uncle should; he was just a pawn and his death at Damien's hand worked out perfectly for him. He could control us, and make a lot of money off us, but we're done. After Dominic's last fight, we're out."

"Just like that?" I quizzed, not believing it could be that easy.

Ryder nodded. "He can't force us to stay, we've done what he wants of us for years. The debt is re-paid. We've made him more money than Trent ever could have."

I swallowed. "What if he tries to make you all stay workin' for 'im?"

The thought of Ryder leaving the country, leaving me, was too scary to think about.

"It won't work out in his favour." He stated. "We're done, Branna. We want a life away from being under his thumb."

That relieved me greatly.

"I'm glad," I smiled, hoping I didn't look as relieved as I felt. I didn't want to freak him out by how devastated I would be if he *ever* left me.

Ryder took my face in his hands. "You are? After everything I just told you, you're glad?"

I nodded. "I'm still tryin' to wrap me head around it, but I understand you and your brothers' so much better now, and I am so glad you're gettin' out of that life, because I don't think I could take part in it if you didn't."

Ryder stood up and pulled me to my feet, then into his arms as he hugged me.

"I'm out," he assured me. "And you're mine. I told you my mentality is to protect what's mine, and I can be *very* possessive."

I hummed as he lowered his head and trailed kisses along my neck.

"How possessive?" I rasped.

He nipped at my skin. "Let me show you."

"Ryder," I breathed when he sucked on the spot below my ear.

His hold on my hips tightened.

"Wait, this isn't fair," I panted. "That's a sensitive spot and—oh God."

While I was speaking Ryder unzipped my dress and tugged on it until it fell to my ankles. He wasted no time in nudging my legs apart and putting his hands down my knickers where he instantly zeroed in on my pulsing clit.

"You were saying?" he rumbled as he lazily drew circles around the sensitive bud.

I gripped onto his shoulders and recited the Lord's Prayer, but when he pinched my clit, my pleas to Heaven became audible.

"Jesus!" I cried out as I shamelessly rocked my hips and stroked my clit back and forth over Ryder's fingers.

"Why do you talk to God so much when I touch you?" he mused, his fingers rubbing me to ecstasy faster. "He's not going to save you from me, no one can stop me from making you scream when you come."

His wicked words blended with the action of his fingers and sent me flying into ecstasy. I heard myself scream, and I heard Ryder's name spill from my mouth, but it all sounded like background noise. My body was focused on the delicious pulses of bliss that filled me.

"I *love* your facial expressions when you come," Ryder murmured in my ear before nipping at my earlobe with his teeth. "It's sexy as *fuck*."

I groaned when he removed his fingertips from my clit. I opened my eyes as he brought said fingers to his mouth, but before he could suck my juices from them, I grabbed hold of his hand and brought them to my mouth instead. Ryder's eyes were wide as he watched my lips wrapped around his fingers. He hissed when I sucked, and used my tongue to lick them clean.

I hummed and released his fingers from my mouth with a pop.

"You're right," I smiled. "I do taste sweet."

"Oh. My. Fucking. God." Ryder whispered.

I tilted my head to the side.

"Why do you talk to God so much when I touch you?" I asked, mimicking his earlier tone.

"Because," Ryder growled as he pressed against me. "He needs praise for creating a *fine* specimen such as yourself."

My lips quirked. "Always the sweet talker."

"You know me." Ryder grinned.

Warmth surrounded me. "Yeah, I do know you."

Ryder lost his grin and stared into my eyes before he lowered his head and covered my mouth with his. We kissed one another with a hunger, and before I knew it, I was lying naked on his bed, with his naked body hovering over mine. When he entered me, it felt like heaven, but quickly turned to torture when he ceased to move.

"Relax for me, sweetness," Ryder murmured, his voice caressing me like physical touch. "I'll take care of you."

"I can't," I said breathlessly, opening my thighs wider for him. "You *need* to move."

"I'll move when I'm good and ready," he rumbled.

His firm tone only teased my body further.

"You're killin' me, Slater," I hissed. "Fuckin'. Killin'. Me."

Ryder pulled back, withdrawing from my body, but before he could slip out of me completely, he drove his hips forward and slammed into me with a resounding *slap*. My breath caught in my throat along with a scream of pleasure.

"Watch your mouth or I'll fill it with something else to shut you up."

Chills spread out over my body, and I found myself *loving* how domineering Ryder was during sex. A command, warning or even a little bit of a threat from him had me quivering with need for him. I never thought of myself as having a small submissive side, but my eagerness to please Ryder when he dished out his commands, and my need to *hear* those commands during sex was like wildfire.

Unstoppable.

"You'd like me forcing my cock into your mouth, wouldn't you?" Ryder growled.

He sounded pained as he withdrew from my body, before thrusting back into my heat.

I moaned as sensation overcame me. "Yes."

"Such a dirty girl." Ryder rasped as he lowered himself down to his forearms that were on either side of my head.

He brought his lips to mine, and gave me chaste kiss before sucking my lower lip into his mouth. He hummed as he suckled before releasing my lip with a pop.

"I love how you taste," he panted. "Your mouth, your pussy, your skin. I'll never get enough. Never."

I moaned in response, raking my nails gently up and down his back, watching him tense when I dug them into him every so often. I smiled when he caught me staring.

"Keep it up and I'll dish out some pain of my own on this sexy ass of yours," he warned.

My eyes lit up with wonder at the same time my pussy walls clenched around Ryder, making him groan as he drove in and out of me.

"That turns you on?" he moaned. "*Damn*, baby, I've hit the fucking jackpot with you!"

I allowed my eyes to roll back as licks of pleasure fill me. My mouth dropped open when Ryder's hot breath blew into my ear in puffs followed by his warm tongue.

"Ah!" I cried out and tried to escape the sensation, but didn't make it very far.

Ryder bit down on the nape of my neck and flicked his tongue over the flesh between his teeth. He bit down harder and slammed into me with such a force, my back arched up off the bed. I cried out as the first unexpected spasm of pleasure shot through me.

"Fuck!" I screamed.

Ryder released my neck and took my mouth in a passionate kiss as I rode out my toe curling orgasm. When I came back to reality, it was to the skin slapping sound of Ryder driving into me like the Devil himself was on his heels. My inner walls clenched around Ryder and it prompted him to shift the angle of his hips, allowing him to brush up against a part of my body that had my breath catching.

"One more, sweetness," Ryder panted, sweat coating his skin in a thin layer. "Give me one more."

He thrusted into me harder, faster, rougher.

I screamed when it all became too much and a second orgasm suddenly slammed into me with as much intensity as the first. I cried out Ryder's name and I heard him growl mine. His hips slowed to jerked motions. Seconds later he slipped out of me, and moved to the left where he face planted into the mattress. He slung his arm over my waist, an action that caused my lips to quirk as I tried to catch my breath.

"I've decided that I'm keeping you," Ryder said, and while the mattress muffled some of his speech, I got the gist of what he said and it made me giggle.

"You only want me for me body," I playfully dismissed.

"No," Ryder protested. "I'm all about your brain, your mind is a serious turn on for me. I've watched you figure things out almost instantly, and *that* gives me wood, *not* your body, I just put up with that because it's attached to your head. I'll get over the disappointment of it in time, don't worry."

I was laughing so hard that I snorted. Ryder lifted his head up, and turned it to the side. He watched me laugh with a smile, and after a few moments, the intensity of his gaze gave me butterflies in my stomach.

"You look like you've got somethin' to say," I mused.

He blinked. "I do."

"Spit it out, I'm *this* close to fallin' asleep in me *double* orgasm aftermath."

"You're welcome," Ryder grinned.

"Out with it," I laughed, again. "What did you want to say to me?"

He lifted his hand from my waist and brought it to my face where he cupped my cheek. He stared into my eyes for a few seconds, and then the smile I loved stretched across his face.

"I love you, Branna."

I stared at Ryder, my eyes wide and unblinking.

He WHAT?

"Please," I whispered after a few seconds of silence. "*Please* don't say that unless you mean it."

He turned on his side and pressed his naked body to mine.

"I. Love. You."

My heart was slamming into my chest, chills ran up and down my spine, and tears threatened to fall at any given moment.

"How do you know?" I hesitantly whispered. "Maybe you're just comin' down with somethin', I heard the flu is goin' around."

Ryder's lips twitched. "I know I love you because I *think* about you all the time, I want to be *with* you all the time and fuck me, but your smile makes my whole day. Your laughter is my favourite sound. I could listen to you laugh all day. I love it. I love *you*. Everything about you blends perfectly with me, and I know that if I didn't have you around me all the time, I'd go crazy. You're my one, I know you are."

His one, I thought. *I was Ryder's one.*

"Omigod," I whispered as my palms became sticky with sweat.

He leaned his face down to mine. "Don't feel pressured to say it back, I didn't intend to have this conversation right now, but after everything I told you, I wanted you to know that I'm *very* serious about you."

Screw that.

"I love you, too." I blurted. "I've been terrified of how deeply I feel for you because it has happened so fast, but I feel how I feel, and I love you."

Ryder brought his face to mine and I swear the smile that was in place on his face was bigger than I've ever seen before.

"You know I'm never going to let you go, right?" he murmured.

Good, my heart countered, *because I'm never letting you go either.*

I rubbed my nose against his. "I'm countin' on it, sweetheart."

He kissed me deeply and once more, I was lost in him.

I awoke when I heard a scream, a scream that belonged to my little sister.

"Bronagh!" I shouted and scrambled out of Ryder's bed, kicking his bed covers off my body.

"Branna, she is fine," Ryder's raspy voice—which told me he had just woken up, too—assured me. "Dominic would *never* hurt her, I promise you."

I rushed around the room as I pulled my clothes on.

"I want to see that for meself, Ry!"

Ryder reached out and grabbed hold of my arm. "I *know* your sister, she has done this before. She is probably just arguing with my brother, that's all."

He knew Bronagh?

I turned and stared at Ryder. "You knew Bronagh was me sister?"

Ryder blinked. "No, wait a second—"

"You knew who she was and you let me date you while knowin' what your brother was doin' to her? Did Dominic know, too? Did all your brothers' know? Were you all laughin' at me behind me back because I was too clueless to see what was right in front of me?"

"What? Fuck, no, baby—"

"Don't baby me, arsehole!" I spat.

I turned and ran out of the bedroom with Ryder cursing as he got out of bed and hurriedly dressed himself. I ran up to the top floor of the house, and banged on the bedroom door that I knew belonged to Dominic.

"Bronagh!" I shouted, wrapping my fists against the door just as Ryder jogged up the stairs and came to a stop behind me. He sighed and placed his hands on my hips, but backed off when I slapped his hands.

I heard a pained groan from inside the bedroom then Dominic shouted, "We're busy!"

Busy? I gasped. *Fucking busy!*

I heard Ryder laugh from behind me, so I jabbed my elbow into his gut causing him to yelp.

"Get away from me sister you pervy little fucker or I'll end you!" I bellowed.

It took a few seconds, but eventually the door to Dominic's room opened wide revealing my eighteen-year-old sister who looked hung-over as hell, and a half naked Slater brother lingering across the room with his eyes glued to her arse.

Typical man.

"I can't remember anythin' or how I got up here, but I didn't do anythin' with him. I swear!" Bronagh gushed to me.

I let my eyes roam over her looking for any sign of injury, and luckily I saw none, but what couldn't be missed were the love bites scattered over her neck. I felt heat crawl up my neck and spread out over my face.

"You *better* not have touched her without permission—"

"I didn't!" Dominic cut me off, his anger evident. "I'm not a fucking rapist!"

I growled. "You better not be because I'll fuckin' rape *you* if you harmed her in any way!"

Dominic's smirk put an instant scowl on my sister's face, but his reply had her flat out glaring at him.

"You can rape me anytime you want, gorgeous."

He was a Slater brother, I thought, *there was no denying it.*

"You're a prick!" My sister snapped at him.

Dominic flicked his eyes to my sister and rolled them. "I'm kidding, don't be mad at me for that. Even though your sister *is* smoking hot, you're hotter."

Did he really think that was a smart thing to say? I wondered, *because it really wasn't.*

Bronagh set her jaw and said, "Piss off, Dominic!" before turning to me, and grabbing hold of my hand. "We're leavin'!" She stated.

I nodded my head, wholeheartedly agreeing with her decision. With my sister's hand in mine, I turned and narrowed my eyes at Ryder.

"Move."

He didn't move.

"I'm not letting you leave here until you hear me out!" He demanded, the firmness in his voice giving me chills.

Bronagh scoffed from behind me, and before I could stop her she said, "You can't keep her here, arsehole."

I felt Bronagh's hand tense in mine when Ryder switched his soul-shuttering glare from me to her, and I *felt* how scared she became of him. She shifted behind me a little bit, blocking most of her body from Ryder's stare. I had to turn so she wouldn't twist my arm off at the angle she was tugging it at.

"Don't look at me sister like that, do you hear me?" I snapped at Ryder. "You're scarin' her!"

He scrubbed his face with his hands. "Bran, baby, I didn't know Bronagh was your sister. You called her Bee when you talked about her. If I had known who she was I would have told you so you didn't look at me like you did last night."

I knew what way I looked at him last night, like I did just a few minutes ago. I looked at him like he played me.

"Hold up, rewind and freeze. Branna... are you seein' him?" my sister asked, blatant shock laced in her tone.

Shit. Fuck.

"I wasn't keepin' it from you, sweetie." I assured her. "I met 'im at Darkness a few weeks ago when I was there with Aideen. We hit it off and went on some dates since then. I wasn't goin' to tell you about 'im until I was sure about 'im. I know how you feel about people, and I didn't want to bring 'im around unless I was sure he was goin' to *stick* around." I cut my eyes to Ryder then, and found he was looking at me with a deep intensity.

I was beginning to gather that he was always intense, but had a special intense gaze about him whenever he looked at me, and I'd be damned if I didn't love it.

"What is your deal with people, Bronagh?" Dominic's voice asked from behind me, making my sister tense up. I felt her hand squeeze mine to the point of pain.

"It's *none* of your business," I snapped at Dominic then looked back to Ryder. "I'm not doin' this to 'er. She doesn't like you, and that means it won't work between us."

The pain of Bronagh's death-like grip on my hand had nothing on the agonising pain that encircled my chest when I spoke those words to Ryder.

Bronagh comes first, I reminded myself. *Bronagh always comes first.*

Ryder's face was the picture of rage, and something else, as he reached for my free hand, and tugged me away from Bronagh. He wanted to converse in private, but his raised voice meant Bronagh and Dominic could hear everything he was saying.

"You can't just dump me because your sister doesn't like getting close to people, Branna. I really like you, and I *care* about you a *lot*," he said, his eyes drilling into mine.

I knew what the look was. He was telling me that he loved me, but didn't want to freak Bronagh out more than she already was so he lessened the intensity by changing the word love to care. I greatly appreciated it, and it tore me apart that I might have to let him go.

"I *know* you feel the same way about me. I don't want this to end. I want you to be my girl. We can take things slow. I won't press Bronagh out of her comfort zone but please don't give up on me, on us."

Well, fuck him anyway, I thought as I forced the dam in my eyes to stay strong.

I loved this man, and he loved me, but I loved my sister, too, and I couldn't risk her becoming more withdrawn just so I could be happy. I mentally slapped myself when I realised how unfair that was on me, but Bronagh came first in my life, and she always would. Ryder got that too, which made this harder.

"Branna," my sister mumbled, pulling me from my thoughts and gaining my attention.

"Don't break up with 'im," she murmured. "I'll... I'll try harder for you. I promise."

I couldn't hold my tears back at that vow.

"Baby, you don't have to try for *me*." I cried. "Try for yourself, this outlook you have isn't healthy. I want you to let other people in; you can't only have me in your life. If anythin' ever happened to me, you would be all alone, and that terrifies me, Bee, more than anythin'."

Bronagh was silent for a few moments as she mulled things over in her mind, but when she looked at me, she nodded and said, "Okay, I'll try harder. I promise."

She switched her gaze from me to Ryder and she lightly blushed.

"Sorry for causin' trouble for you, Ryder."

He smiled at her. "I think you just *saved* me a lot of trouble, Bronagh."

She smiled at him then to me she said, "I can't believe you didn't tell me about 'im. You usually can't keep shite to yourself, so how you didn't let on about 'im is beyond me."

I laughed, sniffled, and then rubbed under her nose. "It was horrible. I wanted to tell you so many times but had to bite me lip or talk about somethin' random."

Bronagh chuckled. "So, you're both like a real couple? Boyfriend and girlfriend?"

Ryder and I looked at each other, smiled, and nodded.

"This should be interestin'." My sister grumbled

Ryder looked to her. "Why is that?"

"Because she is a freak," she stressed, "and you will soon learn things about 'er that will have you runnin' for the hills. For example, she is an OCD cleaner and has multiple personalities. I'm not even jokin', she could be me sister one minute then me ma and da the next."

I playfully slapped Bronagh's arm while Ryder laughed.

"Why would she be your mom or dad?" Dominic asked my sister.

I had forgotten he was there, and from the look of shock on my sister's face, so did she.

"Our parents' died nine years ago, Dominic," I explained. "I've been 'er guardian since I turned nineteen. I took over raisin' 'er when our parents passed away, so she considers me her sister, her ma, and da all wrapped into one. 'er memories with them are limited, because she was so young when they passed. She doesn't talk about them at all."

I frowned at my sister as the wheels turned in her mind, and in that moment, I'd have given my left arm to know what she was thinking. She blinked her eyes after a few moments of silence just as Dominic said, "Is that why you have people issues, you won't get close to anyone in school, or people in general, because you're afraid you could lose them like you did your parents?"

Bronagh widened her eyes.

"Dominic," Ryder snapped. "Show some compassion!"

"I was just asking a question." He defended. "When our parents were killed you took over the mother and father role like Branna did, but I didn't push everyone away from me because I was afraid they might die. That's a pretty shitty way to live."

I wanted to skin the little shite alive for being so blunt.

"I want to go home," Bronagh said as tears filled her eyes.

"Bronagh," I whispered and quickly followed her as she pushed past Ryder and ran for the stairs. I heard Ryder shouting at Dominic, and Dominic shouting to Bronagh that he was sorry.

The next few minutes that followed included more arguing and me trying to beat the crap out of Dominic for him being a complete dickhead to my sister. My sister, however, had enough of him and pushed him into the gym room so they could talk in private.

While they spoke I turned to Ryder and said, "It'll be hard, but we can't interfere with them, they'll only argue with us and tell us to mind our own business. Unless we have no other choice, we're keepin' our noses *out* of their relationship or their not relationship or whatever it bloody is they have goin' on."

Ryder grinned as he put his arm around me and lowered his head to mine, "Yes, sweetie."

"Oh, my God." I laughed at the same time Alec and Kane said, "So it begins."

Alec proceeded to make whipping noises, which only amused Ryder further. I could feel his smile as he kissed me, and it made me smile, too. I had a feeling about us. I didn't know whether it was good or bad, but it was a very strong feeling and I decided then that Ryder was stuck with me too.

Maybe falling in love with him would be the best thing I ever did... at least I *hoped* it would.

CHAPTER SEVEN

Present day...

"Branna?"

I blinked as I was pulled from a memory and thrust back into my sombre reality.

On a sigh, I called out, "In the kitchen, Bee."

I stood up as my pregnant sister barrelled into the room, her eyes wild until they landed on me. When she saw me, a breath of what sounded, and looked, like relief left her.

"You're okay."

I raised my brows. "Why wouldn't I be okay?"

My sister crossed the room and hugged me, which caused me to smile as I felt her bump brush against me.

"I was scared you'd do somethin' stupid."

I frowned when we pulled apart.

"Because of Dominic?" I quizzed.

"Because you're goin' to break up with Ryder."

Oh.

I swallowed. "How do you—"

"Damien showed up at our house before Dominic could go lookin' for Ryder and he started askin' 'im a bunch of *crazy* questions. Dominic got mad and tried to move to a different room so they could speak in private, but Damien literally grabbed Dominic and pinned him against the sittin' room wall." Bronagh said, her eyes wide and she recited what happened. "Branna, I nearly wet meself I was so scared. Damien was bloody furious with Dominic, he said you filled 'im in on things that Dominic and the other brothers should have told him about long ago."

My sister took my hands in hers.

"Dominic wouldn't speak on it when I asked, but Damien told me to talk to you to clear up some of me questions."

Thanks a lot, Damien!

I groaned in annoyance. "I barely know anythin' though! It's one of the main reasons *why* I'm breakin' up with Ryder!"

"Just start from the beginnin'," my sister pleaded. "I'm so blindsided by your decision, and the shite Damien was talkin' about. I knew you were havin' troubles with Ryder, but damn, sis, you're really goin' to walk away from him? You're *really* goin' to walk away from Ryder?"

I swallowed down the bile that threatened to shoot up my throat.

"Yes, I'm really goin' to walk away from Ryder." I admitted. "I have no choice, Bee… *he* has left me no choice."

"I don't understand."

"Join the club," I mumbled.

"Bran," my sister pressed.

I sighed. "Okay, I'll start with Dominic. You know the way he announced on the day Keela and Alec moved into their house that he was back fightin', and this time he would be fightin' for Brandon Daley?"

"I'll never forget it," my sister grumbled.

I felt sorry for her. I knew it killed her that Dominic turned back to fighting, but he kept his promise to her. It wasn't like his old life; he just fought in a circle and got paid.

"And do you remember how he announced his money—*your* money—was dried up?"

Bronagh nodded.

"Well, he wasn't the *only* brother who suddenly lost his money. Alec and Ryder did, too, with some sort of investment with Brandon Daley. They should have known better since he is the only sleaze ball that they're friendly with."

My sister stared at me. "I asked Dominic last year about where the money went and he said he made a very bad investment."

"Do you know what *kind* of investment?" I quizzed.

"I've no idea. He apologised to me, and swore his fightin' at Darkness was to earn quick money to get us comfortable again. It's been a year since he started back fightin' and recently I told him I'd get a job to help out, but he doesn't want me to work, he wants me at home with the baby when she is born."

I stared at my sister as she spoke.

"I didn't want to fight with 'im about it, you know?" she continued. "I've done me anger management classes, and I've matured so much mentally that I didn't want to start somethin' out of nothin' while we're at such a good place in our relationship. As far as I'm concerned, the money Dominic had was blood money, and I was glad it was gone so I didn't question where it went. I just accepted it and moved on."

I nodded in understanding.

"*Now* I'm wonderin' though," she frowned.

I cringed. "I'm sorry, I should have kept me mouth shut to Damien."

"No," Bronagh stated. "You're right. We should know where their—our—money went, we *are* their fianceés after all, and what's theirs is ours, right?"

I humourlessly laughed. "After tonight, I'll just be an ex."

My sister tilted her head. "Tell me what's goin' on between you and Ryder, sis."

"I don't *know* what's goin' on with us, Bee, that's the problem. I don't know anythin'."

Bronagh blinked, so I sighed and told her the same shortened version of my relationship's downhill spiral that I gave to Damien.

By the time I was finished speaking, she was crying and I wanted to thump myself.

"Bee," I crooned. "Don't cry, sweetie. It'll all be okay, I promise."

"It won't," she sniffled. "Our family is goin' to be divided."

I couldn't say anything to make her feel better because she was right, once Ryder and I broke up, our family would be divided. Forever. I would make *damn* sure that it was an easy transition for her, though.

"It *will* be okay," I repeated, firmer. "Trust me, I'll never let me life affect yours. I'll work it out with Ryder so things are as normal as possible for you."

Bronagh wiped her tears away and said, "Stop that."

"Stop what?" I asked.

She didn't answer me instead she said, "How can you live like this?"

"Like *what*?"

"You brush everythin' about yourself under the carpet. Why?"

I looked down to my hands. "I don't know. I just do it."

"Well, stop, you can't continue livin' like this."

"Existin'." I absentmindedly murmured.

"What?"

"I'm existin', not livin', there's a difference between the two."

My sister went still. "You don't feel like you're livin'?"

"Bronagh, I barely feel like I'm existin'," I admitted. "I'm here, but I'm not at the same time. I just don't care anymore."

"I think you're depressed, Branna."

"I think it's worse than that," I frowned. "You have to *feel* somethin' to be depressed, right? I don't feel anythin' anymore."

Tears gathered in my sister's eyes. "Bran."

I smiled and patted her hand. "I'll be fine, don't you worry."

"Stop that," Bronagh cried. "Stop puttin' yourself at the bottom on the list of priorities, you've done it all me life and I'm sick of it. Your mental health matters. *You* fuckin' matter!"

I reared back as if she slapped me.

"I can't just turn off me instincts to protect you, Bronagh," I said defensively.

She cried harder. "I know you can't, but I'm not askin' you to stop protectin' me, I'm just askin' you not to not put me before yourself!"

I couldn't accept that.

I shook my head. "You *always* come first."

"Maybe when I was younger, Bran, but I'm an adult now."

I raised a brow. "That doesn't change anythin', you'll *always* be me little sister. I know I didn't birth you, but I raised you. You're mine, too."

No matter what, Bronagh would always be mine.

"Yeah," she agreed, "I am, but even little sisters have to grow up and learn responsibility. I know you'll always worry, but everythin' else you freak out about falls on Dominic's shoulders now. I'm his, too, so it's only right he shares some of the responsibility for me. It's what he signed up for."

I swallowed down the sob that wanted to break free.

"I love you, but I *need* you to stop puttin' me before yourself." My sister pressed on. "You're the most important person in your life, and that's how it should always be."

I blinked. "It's easy for you to say that now, but wait till you have the baby, she'll be the most important person in your life."

"She's me child though."

"You're practically *my* child." I countered.

Bronagh's shoulders slumped. "Touché."

"I hear what you're sayin', and I love you for it. I'll work on it, okay? I know you're now a beautiful butterfly who needs space to flap her wings, and that you don't need me all the time." I smiled her way even though I wanted to cry my eyes out.

"I'll always need you, but I don't want any of my problems to trump yours."

I nodded.

Bronagh released my hand and rubbed her nose with the back of her hand. "I'm tellin' Dominic 'I'm a beautiful butterfly who needs her space to flap her wings' whenever he pisses me off."

I laughed and it felt good.

Bronagh leaned back into the chair, and rested her hands on her round stomach.

"When are you goin' to do it?" she asked when she stopped sniffling. "You mentioned tonight, but will you *really* do it then?"

I nodded, glumly. "Yeah, I need to get it over with now that me mind is made up. If I don't, it will fester and I'll probably never get the guts to do it."

"What will you do if he reacts badly?"

I snorted. "He *will* react badly. He blew up at me because he thought I was cheatin' on him. Endin' things will only fuel that anger, but he'll get over it."

"Will *you* be okay with it?" Bronagh asked.

"With what?" I questioned. "The break up?"

My sister nodded.

I shrugged. "In time. In time I'll be okay with it."

"Really?" my sister asked with a raised brow. "You'll be okay comin' to family dinners and watchin' another woman kiss him, holdin' his hand, and be the one puttin' a smile on his face?"

I glared at Bronagh as my stomach churned with the images she put in my head.

"Yes," I almost growled.

She shook her head. "You're a shitty liar, you look ready to tear me head off for just suggestin' Ryder being with another woman."

I looked away. "It's because I haven't had time to live me life without 'im, but I'm sure I'll get over 'im just fine. Time heals all wounds."

"Bran?"

"What?"

"I wasn't jokin', you're *really* a shitty liar."

I laughed then, but only to cover up the tears that were suddenly falling onto my cheeks.

"Hey," my sister murmured. "Come here."

I turned to her and leaned into her embrace.

"I'll be fine," I sniffled. "It can't be any worse than how things are right now. Being with 'im, but not havin' 'im is worse than not being with 'im at all."

"Oh, Bran," my sister whispered. "I hate meself for not realisin' how bad things were between you both."

I pulled back.

"How could you know?" I asked as I wiped my face. "I've hidden it from everyone, I didn't want to burden anyone."

"How could you *ever* think anythin' about you is a burden? We're sisters, that means everythin' about you, even your bullshit, is important to me."

I felt my lower lip wobble. "Thanks, honey."

"Don't thank me, dipshit," my sister stated. "I love you, and that means I get to protect you, too."

I nodded. "I'll be more open with you in the future."

"Good," Bronagh said, firmly. "That's exactly what I want. We will both be the other's ear to vent to when things get tough, and shoulder to cry on when things get tougher."

I nodded in agreement. "Deal."

Bronagh sat back on a sigh. "What are we goin' to do about the knowledge we have about the investment the lads made?"

I shrugged. "I'll probably bring it up to Ryder, and you can mention it to Dominic."

"Or we could just have a big family meetin' where we get all the lads, us and the girls in one room and get it all out into the open. If we don't know, you can bet your arse that Keela and Aideen don't."

"Sounds good to me, but it will have to be at your house. Ryder might break a lot of things here tonight... which reminds me, can I stay with you and Dominic until I get meself together and find an apartment?"

Bronagh stared at me blankly, blinking.

"The fact that you even have to ask that question pisses me off. Of fuckin' *course*, it's still your home, too. It always will be."

I smiled. "Thank you."

"Can I tell you a secret?" my sister asked.

I smiled. "Always."

"Me, Keela and Aideen planned an intervention with you and Ryder."

I sat back and blinked. "I don't understand."

Bronagh scratched her neck. "We've all noticed how weird Ryder was being with you, but I just didn't know how bad things were. You've gotten *very* good at keepin' things to yourself."

"What kind of intervention were you three plannin'?" I pressed.

Bronagh's lips twitched. "Last night in Aideen and Kane's apartment we decided that we'd use Ash Wade... as a pawn of sorts. I know you're good friends with him, and I was goin' to ask 'im to be really flirty with you whenever a brother was around so it'd get back to Ryder. We thought it would snap 'im out of whatever is wrong with 'im and his Slater instinct would kick in and he'd reclaim you."

I stared at my sister for a long moment, and then burst into laughter.

"*Slater instinct?*" I repeated. "What are they? Animals?"

Bronagh laughed, too. "They might as well be, they're all very possessive over us and I wanted to use it to our advantage in this situation, but it kind of backfired. I never spoke to Ash about it, and when Dominic thought you were flirty earlier today he went and told Ryder an arse backwards story and Ry flipped out."

I shook my head, still chuckling.

"I'll give you points for formin' a plan in the first place." I mused. "I *knew* the three of you were up to somethin' when I saw you all smirkin' last night. Me bullshit sense was tinglin'."

Bronagh held her side as she laughed, but she stopped almost instantly when the front door to my house opened and shut.

"Branna?"

Oh, fuck.

"Shit," I whispered and jumped to my feet at the same time my sister did.

"Don't interfere when I'm speakin' to 'im," Bronagh said to me, and glared at the kitchen doorway until Ryder appeared.

"You're a fuckin' prick!" My sister bellowed as soon as she saw him. "I *hate* you for what you've done to 'er. You've broken me sister's heart you son of a bitch!"

Double fuck.

Ryder looked at my sister and I saw the pain in his eyes. "Bee—"

"Don't!' She cut him off, her body shaking. "Don't you *dare* call me that, Ryder."

Ryder looked distressed as he took a step towards her.

"Kid, please, I'm going to fix everything. I swear on my life."

Bronagh growled, her face getting red with anger. "I *told* you that day Aideen was in hospital after the attack that she was goin' to leave you because of the way you treated her, and I was right."

"I know." Ryder replied almost instantly.

"Do you remember what else I said?" she questioned.

Without hesitation Ryder said, "You told me that when she got the courage to leave me I'd finally realise how incredible she is."

I couldn't take them talking as if I wasn't in the room.

"Bronagh, calm yourself down right now," I demanded. "This isn't good for you, or the baby. Relax, dammit."

My sister turned away from Ryder, and looked at me.

"I'm goin' home so he can fix this."

She knew nothing between Ryder and myself was fixable, especially after the conversation we just had, but to avoid piling more stress on her, and to remove her from Ryder's presence, I didn't protest to her leaving.

"Bee," Ryder said. "I'll make this right."

She ignored him and to me she said, "I'll call you later, but if you need me for *anythin'* before you hear from me, pick up the phone and I'll be here."

She turned and stalked—or waddled—out of the room, then out of the house, slamming the door behind her.

"She hates me." Ryder said with his shoulders slumped.

Comforting him was the last thing I should have thought about doing, but breaking up or not, this man meant everything to me, and I couldn't stand to see him hurting. That knowledge hurt *me* because as much as I told myself I didn't love this version of him, I knew it wasn't true. I was in love with Ryder in any way I could have him, that was how deeply I felt for him.

"She doesn't hate you," I murmured. "'er hormones are all over the place, and she's just upset because I'm upset. Don't worry about it, she'll be speakin' to you by tomorrow."

"Why do you do that?" Ryder asked, looking at me with an expression I couldn't read.

I was stumped.

"Do what?" I asked.

"You're trying to make me feel better about Bronagh because I said she hates me. You're trying to save me from being hurt when you're furious with me."

I gnawed on my inner cheek. "Bronagh says I do it to 'er because I'm protectin' 'er. Maybe I'm doin' the same for you, too."

Ryder stepped towards me. "I'm sorry for what I said to you earlier."

I straightened.

"You hurt me," I said. "Accusin' me of cheatin' on you was somethin' I never thought you would ever say to me."

Another step.

"I'm sorry, I didn't mean it. I just pictured this Ash person touching you, and I got so angry that I lashed out at you."

I shrugged. "I'm used to you lashin' out at me."

Ryder looked like I slapped him across the face.

"Please, don't say that," his voice low.

I licked my dry lips.

"I bruise you and you bruise me. That's how things are between us now."

Ryder's eyes searched mine, and what he saw caused his head to drop.

"I don't know how we've gotten here, Branna."

My heart began to pound against my chest.

"Me either."

Ryder swallowed. "I think... I think we should talk."

I did too, and it killed me because I didn't want to say what needed to be said, but I had to. For both of our sakes, I *had* to.

"Yeah, we do."

Ryder leaned his shoulder against the wall. "I have a feeling the outcome is going to break me, am I right?"

Break him? I thought. *Him?*

I stared. "I don't know, it depends on how you take what I have to say."

He set his jaw. "Say it."

This was it.

"I think you know what I'm goin' to say."

He nodded. "I think I do, too, but I want to *hear* you say it."

My palms became sticky with sweat.

"I can't do this anymore, Ryder."

"Say it, Branna."

I was always Branna or Bran now, never Sweetness, and it was pathetic how much I missed that term of endearment. The tears that sat on the brim of my eyes finally spilled over and splashed onto my cheeks. Pain pulsed in my chest. This was really it. This was the end of us.

"You feel the same way I do, I know you do." I sniffled, quickly wiping away my tears. "We don't make each other happy anymore."

He pushed away from the wall and stepped towards me.

"Say. It."

I began to sob. "I don't know what else you want me to say!"

"Say the fucking words." He demanded. "If you're going to

break up with me you have to say it out loud, I want to *hear* you say it."

I swallowed and looked down at the floor, then with a heavy heart I said, "Ryder... I'm... I'm breakin' up with you."

"*No.*"

I looked up at him and blinked with confusion. "What do you me-mean no?"

"We aren't breaking up," he stated, his face red. "We aren't giving up just because shit has gotten hard, we're going to fight."

He was *killing* me.

"We *have* been fighting—"

"*With* one another, not *for* one another."

I met Ryder with silence so he pressed on.

"We're going to start over. I don't know where we lost one another, but if we go back to the start we can find our way back to each other. I *know* we can."

I felt hopeless.

"So we're thrustin' ourselves back into the beginnin' stages of dating?" I quizzed, shaking my head.

"Yeah." Ryder replied, firmly. "That's *exactly* what we'll do."

I wiped my cheeks with the back of my hands when more tears fell.

"Why?"

"Because I'm going to make you fall in love with me all over again."

"Don't say things like that to me!" I shouted. "You can't say things like that and expect me to believe you. You promised me the world when we first got together, promised to always take care of me, to always be there for me, to always show me love. You swore up and down that we'd grow old together but the only thing we've done is grow apart."

"I don't believe that," Ryder replied, the veins on his arms bulged as he tensed his body.

"Then I don't know what to tell you!" I snapped. "If you can't see what's been happenin' over the last year then me simply explainin' it won't penetrate your bloody mind!"

"You have to trust me, Branna." Ryder said, shocking the hell out of me.

"Trust you?" I repeated. "Trust fuckin' *you*! What about *you* trustin' *me*? Where did that trust fly off to when I *begged* you tell me where you go every night or why you're always on your phone or why you shower as soon as you get home? What happened to poxy trust when *those* questions where asked?"

"You will have the answers to those question in forty-eight more hours, just give me that time and when it's up, I'll explain *everything*. I'll answer every question you throw at me fifty times over. Please."

The confusion I felt hurt my head to the point where I had to close my eyes and flatten my palm over my forehead in an attempt to soothe it somehow.

"I don't understand." I whispered, lowering my hand to my side, and reopening my eyes. "Why forty-eight more hours? Why not now?"

"Because in forty-eight more hours I can freely tell you."

I tilted my head to the side. "Meanin' now you freely can't?"

Ryder nodded his head. Once.

"The only thing I can think is why? Why? Why? Fuckin' *why*?" My voice climbed an octave with each question asked.

"Branna," he said, firmly. "Trust. Me."

Exhaustion hit me at that point.

"I can't do this, Ryder. You're killin' me."

"Just listen to me, carefully," he said as he stepped closer to me, pressing his chest against mine, reintroducing me to the sensation of what it felt like for my body to be moulded against his. "I love you. I *know* things are up in the air with us right now, and that I haven't shown jack shit over the last year that would make you believe me when I say it, but I *do* love you. I've never said those words to any other woman in my life. Remember that, and remember that in forty-eight hours we're going to hash *all* of this out."

Slowly, I nodded, because I wanted him to just stop talking.

"I know you love me, or the man who I fell in love with loves me, but I just don't know if that's enough anymore, Ry."

"It will always be enough, and I'm going to prove that to you."

I wanted to believe him, God knew how much, but I couldn't let myself hope for us anymore. The heartache that I felt when things fell apart was too great.

I somehow stood strong.

"We're *over*, Ryder."

"No, Branna, we aren't. I told you five years ago that we'd never be over, and I fuckin' *meant* it. You're my world, and I refuse to watch it, *you*, crumble around me. Just. Fucking. No. I'm going to fix this, I swear it."

He turned and without another word, stalked out of the house. When I heard the front door slam shut, I dropped to my knees and let out the sob that desperately wanted to break free. I wrapped my arms around my waist, hugging myself as I rocked back and forth.

I did it, I meekly thought. *I broke up with Ryder, but he refused to let me go.*

A huge part of me clung onto that as a sign that something might be salvageable between us, but fear shut out that ray of light with overwhelming darkness. I couldn't allow myself to grasp at straws like that. I couldn't allow myself to think of what happened as anything other than a break up because if I let my mind stray, I would think of scenarios where things could end differently, and that frightened me. I was terrified that if I let Ryder back in and he closed me out again then I would cease to function altogether.

I was afraid he'd ruin me all over again.

CHAPTER EIGHT

Five years ago...

"**D**ominic and Bee, they're either datin' or they're *about* to be datin'."

Ryder's foot slipped from the clutch of his car, and the gearbox made an unholy sound that caused me to cringe. He quickly shifted gears until the car was purring nicely once more.

"You want to explain that to me?" he asked, flicking his eyes from the road to me then back to the road. "'Cause we're on the way to the *hospital* to see your sister who got injured while beating on my *brother* because *he* was beating on her *date*."

I didn't need a reminder; I had just gotten off a phone call to Aideen explaining to her that I would take care of Dominic for jumping Gavin—her little brother. She had to call off her other brothers from finding Dominic and beating the shite out of him. I had to convince her not to end his life, too. The latter was proven the most difficult, but I managed to persuade her that I would make him pay, and I would. Somehow.

"You heard Kane's twenty-second recap of what happened when he called me after Bronagh called you," Ryder continued, regaining my attention, "so how did you come to the conclusion that they're dating or *almost* dating?"

Do all men have such small brains? I wondered. *Or is my man just lucky?*

"I'm not disputin' that Bee likes Gavin Collins, because if they got the chance, I'm sure they'd actually be great together. I'd love to see her date the brother of me best friend."

"I'm sensing a very big *but* here," Ryder sighed.

"But," I grinned, "even though she went on a date with Gavin tonight, she likes Dominic even though he has been the king of all arseholes from the moment they met. Goin' on a date with Gavin is her way of tryin' to force Dominic out of her mind, but it'll take more than that. Somethin' about the lad draws her to 'im, just like somethin' about *her* draws 'im to 'er. You understand?"

"No, not at all." Ryder exhaled. "You say the word 'him' and 'her' so messed up, do you know that? The letter H is just completely disregarded."

I folded my arms across my chest. "Now is not the time for the pronunciation game, *what* are we goin' to do about our siblin's?"

"Pray they don't get arrested?"

I growled. "Be serious."

"I am," Ryder stressed. "Dominic is on *very* fucking thin ice, he could have been arrested for fighting with Gavin in school, but he got away with it. He could have gotten arrested when he fought that Jason kid too, or McDonald's security could have retained him until the cops arrived tonight. He's messing up and all because he doesn't know how to handle your sister."

I scrubbed my face with my hands.

"Can you not talk to 'im about it?" I asked. "Maybe give 'im some pointers on how to approach me sister? He still has the compound mentality that when he says jump, women will ask how high? That doesn't fly here, that's the backlash he is gettin' for tryin' to be bossy and intimidatin' with Bee."

Ryder snorted. "Tell me something I *don't* know. I've been all around the world and I've never met women like you, your sister, or Aideen. Irish women can be terrifying. I'm glad my brothers haven't met Ado yet, she'd horrify them."

That amused me greatly.

"Tell your brother that."

"After tonight?" Ryder snorted. "He definitely knows."

I looked away as my lips turned up in a smirk.

"I love you," Ryder said, catching me off guard.

I turned and looked at him with adoring eyes.

"I love you too, sweetheart."

His lip twitched as he watched the road.

"Not that I don't love hearin' you tell me that you love me, but why say it now?"

Ryder shrugged. "When we're around Dominic and Bronagh, we end up fighting because *they're* fighting and we feel the need to defend our little siblings. I just wanted to say I love you once more today, in case we're at each other's throats in an hour."

I couldn't help but smile.

"That's really sweet, you know that?"

Ryder glanced at me and smiled before returning his eyes to the road.

"I have my moments," he mused.

"They're few and far between," I countered, grinning.

"Which is why when my moments come along, I make them known."

I chuckled.

"We'll be fine," I assured him. "I mean, what's the worst that could happen?"

"Do you understand that if the kid you attacked presses charges, you will be arrested for assault, ma'am?"

The worst happened.

When Ryder and I showed up in A&E I was calm. So. Bloody. Calm. When my sister rang me and told me what happened, I was ready to *end* Dominic Slater, but on the car journey to the hospital

Ryder relaxed me, and I reached a point where I was willing to see him and behave like a normal human being... then I walked up to the triage nurse's office and saw Bronagh clutching her hand to her chest, and Dominic in her personal space. There is no other way to describe what happened—I just lost it.

I jumped on him, and while I wasn't a strong person, and didn't exactly know how to fight, I pulled his hair, ripped his t-shirt, slapped at his head, and managed to get in one solid punch to his face before Ryder wrestled me away.

Things got serious then, hospital security retained me and called the Gardai. I was furious at Dominic, but even more so at myself for behaving so irrationally. If I got arrested, I was screwed. I didn't know if the Health Board at the maternity hospital would allow me to keep my volunteer job or offer me a permanent job once I graduated college in a few months if they found out about this. I didn't know if they would hold an assault on my record against me either, but I *really* didn't want to find out.

"So let me get this straight," the male Garda questioning me said on a tired sigh. "The man you attacked is your partner's younger brother, and also your younger sister's boyfriend. Am I gettin' that right?"

Both Ryder and I nodded in unison.

The Garda sighed, *again*. "I don't get paid enough for this."

Ryder snorted, but covered it up with a fake cough.

"Okay, so why did you attack..."

"Dominic," I said, filling in the blank.

"Dominic," the Garda nodded. "Why did you attack Dominic?"

"Well, you see, since he moved here a few months ago he has been nothin' but a bother for me sister. He hassles 'er at school, and is *very* forward with 'er because he really likes 'er, but doesn't know how to handle a feisty introvert like 'er. They're the polar opposites of one another, but for some unknown reason, she likes 'im too, but she doesn't want to. She went on a date tonight with a cute lad in 'er class to play the field a little, you know? But Dominic showed up, ruined 'er night out by *fightin'* with her date. That forced 'er to defend 'er date which led to 'er hittin' Dominic, and hurtin' 'er hand. That's how she ended up here. She called me, told me what happened, and obviously I was furious, I mean, she's me *little sister*, and when I saw Dominic, the urge to smack the shite out of 'im consumed me, and then you and your partner were called and, well, yeah. That's what happened."

When I finished speaking, the Garda stared at me for a few moments, unblinking. When he came back to the land of the living, after another ten-seconds of silent staring, he shook his head and said, "I *definitely* don't get paid enough for this."

"If you think it sounds bad," I cringed, "you should try *livin'* with us."

The Garda quickly shook his head. "No, thank you."

His instant reply made Ryder laugh, and my lips twitch.

When the man finished writing down whatever he was writing on his notepad, he looked at me then to Ryder and said, "The lad won't be pressin' charges against your missus, will he?"

"My missus?" Ryder questioned, clearly confused if his facial expression was anything to go on.

The Garda sighed. "Your *girlfriend*, Ms Murphy."

I smiled and linked my arm through Ryder's. "He is still gettin' used to how we talk, he is gettin' much better at understandin' slang so please, don't hold it against 'im."

"I wouldn't dream of it," the Garda mumbled. "As I was sayin', your brother won't press charges against *Ms Murphy*, will he?"

"No, he won't." Ryder answered almost immediately. "I guarantee he will be telling your partner that there is nothing to report."

The Garda sighed for what seemed to be the twentieth time. "I figured as much, Mr Slater, but until me partner comes back and tells me that for 'erself, I have to ask these questions and write down what you say, Ms Murphy. Okay?"

I nodded in understanding. The Garda then ran through a few more standard questions, and when he was finished, he pocketed his notepad and pen.

"I'm goin' to have a smoke outside while we wait, I'm not supposed to leave me post—which right now is *you*—but I agree Mr Slater won't press charges therefore when me partner comes back, we can leave. However, that doesn't change the face that you have to wait until you're dismissed," he said then levelled me with a glare. "You stay here. If I have to come lookin' for you, I'll arrest you and leave you in the cells back at the station until tomorrow mornin', we clear?"

"We're clear," I nodded, firmly.

Ten-seconds after the Garda went outside and lit up his cigarette, I turned and headed for the double doors that led into the back where Bronagh, and Dominic, were.

"Branna," Ryder hissed. "Damn it, the cop said wait *here*."

"I heard 'im," I replied, still walking.

"So *why* are you heading for those doors?" Ryder asked, sounding like he was going to strangle me.

"I want to check on me sister."

"Branna—"

"I'll be back out before he comes back. Promise."

"Oh, my *God*!" He snapped. "You're unbelievable, woman."

I passed through the double doors, and after only a couple of seconds I felt a presence behind me.

"This is entirely on *you* if we get arrested."

At least we'd go down together.

I smiled. "Noted."

"So where are we going?" Ryder asked on a sigh as he fell in stride next to me.

I shrugged. "Look for an examination room, I heard the nurse say she was takin' Dominic there for stitches then bringin' Bee to one after her X-ray. I have a feelin' your brother will make sure he is in the same room as me sister."

"She's becoming a weakness of his and they aren't even a couple."

"Yet." I said. "Not a couple *yet*."

"We'll see," Ryder mused as we peeked into each examination room we passed.

When we came to the end of the corner I peeked in the final room and froze when I saw that both Dominic and Bronagh were in a room like I thought they would be, but I wasn't expecting to find them both kissing. *Really* kissing. I grabbed hold of Ryder's arm when I gently shut the door and pulled him back down the corridor with me.

"You're pinching my arm, you know?"

"They were in that room together!" I said, and let go of his arm. "*Kissin'*!"

"Dominic and Bronagh?" Ryder asked, surprised.

"No, Adam and Eve," I said, sarcastically. "Yes, Dominic and Bronagh! Who bloody else?"

Ryder eyed me. "Are you *sure* it was my brother and your sister?"

"Yeah," I quipped. "I'm a million percent sure."

"And they were kissing? On the lips?"

"What part of that aren't you gettin'?" I questioned as we turned and walked back out to the reception area of the A&E department that was Garda free. "Dominic and Bronagh, *your* brother and *my* sister, were in a full on lip lock. His hands were on her arse, too!"

Ryder grinned. "Well done, little brother. He finally climbed over the defensive wall your sister had built up."

I slapped his arm. "Be serious! How are we goin' to deal with the pair of them being in a relationship? They've already caused nothin' but problems and they weren't a couple then!"

Ryder lost his grin, and invaded my personal space.

"Listen to me clearly, you said that we weren't going to get involved in their relationship unless we had no other choice. So unless one of them in about to kill the other, we're Switzerland, okay?"

"But—"

"No buts," Ryder cut me off. "Dominic and Bronagh's bullshit is their own, we don't need to make it ours. Okay?"

I sighed and nodded. "Okay."

"I know it will be tough for you because you're involved in every aspect of Bronagh's life, but this will be good for you. She'll enter this relationship and learn how things are just like everyone else, and you can be a proud mama bear watching her grow."

I narrowed my eyes. "I'll eat your brother alive if he hurts her in any way."

"And I'll be the one to pin Dominic down while you beat on him, deal?"

I laughed. "Deal, honey."

Ryder smiled and leaned his head down and brushed his lips against mine. We pulled apart when a throat cleared. I blinked when the male Garda who questioned me stood next to the female Garda who I knew questioned Dominic and my sister.

"Hello." I said, curtly.

Both Gardai nodded in response.

"You were right," the male Garda said to Ryder. "Your brother won't be pressin' charges." His eyes switched to me then and he said, "I'm lettin' you off with a warnin' Ms. Murphy. If anythin' like this happens again, you will be booked and an investigation will ensue, am I clear?"

"Crystal, sir," I replied.

The man nodded and so did his partner.

"Have a good evenin'," the female Garda said, and while she looked pissed, she sounded sincere.

When Ryder and myself were free from questioning and the Gardai left the hospital, I sat down in the waiting area that was directly in front of the double doors that led back to the treatment area. We waited for Dominic and Bronagh there and when the doors opened, and the pair of them walked out into the reception area I relaxed because they both looked okay as could be considering the circumstances.

"Why're they looking at one another like that?" Ryder murmured to me.

"I reckon Dominic wants to be open about them, but Bee is reluctant and wants to keep it under wraps until she is okay with us knowin'. You see the way she is tryin' to keep 'er distance from 'im and not make it obvious?"

"You got all that from how they are looking at each other?" Ryder questioned.

I glanced at him. "You *didn't* get that from how they're lookin' at each other?"

He rubbed his temples. "This is a woman thing."

"A woman thing?"

"Yeah," Ryder said. "You all have a sixth sense about shit like this so I'm just rolling with it."

I snorted. "That's the smartest thing you've said all day."

When my sister's eyes landed on us, I jumped to my feet and rushed over to her. Her hand had a bandage on it, and the sight of it made me feel ill.

"Is it broken?" I asked, worried to hear her reply.

"No, just sprained it. I've to rest it for a couple of weeks. If the muscles don't strengthen in two weeks, then I've to come back but until then, I'm grand," Bronagh explained.

Ryder looked at Dominic after she spoke, shook his head at his bare chest and then focused on the cut above his eye. "How many stitches?" he asked.

"Eight," Dominic replied and cut his eyes to me.

I held up my hands. "I'm not apologisin' to you; me sister was hurt because of you tonight in *more* ways than one!"

Bronagh's cheeks flushed. "Branna, it's over and done with so just forget it."

My earlier conversation with Ryder repeated in my head, and I decided to start letting Bronagh make her own decisions in life by keeping my mouth shut—for once.

"Come on," I said. "I'm bringin' you home in *my* car. Ryder is goin' with Dominic in theirs."

I saw Dominic's hand to go to Bronagh's back, and I knew he wanted to bring her home instead, and Bronagh noticed it too. "Talk to you tomorrow, okay?" she murmured to him.

He wasn't happy about it, but he nodded and let her go without a fight—for once. He walked her to our car and I hung back for a few moments to let them say goodnight, and sneak a kiss if they wanted to. I leaned into Ryder when he blocked my view of the new couple by standing in front of me.

"I *told* you they were datin'," I said, my voice low. "You can sense the change in them too, can't you?

He nodded then shuddered, "It's scary how you're always right."

He had *no* idea.

"I kept me mouth shut." I smiled. "Did you see? I wanted to go on about what Dominic did, but Bronagh shut me down and I didn't ignore that."

"You done good, mama bear."

I beamed. "Thanks, babe."

"Can I ask you a question that has been on the tip of my tongue all day?"

I leaned back and nodded. "Shoot."

"Will you marry me?"

I squinted my eyes after a few moments of silence. "I'm sorry, can you repeat that. I've misheard you."

Ryder's lips twitched. "I said—will you marry me?"

I rapidly blinked my eyes before I lifted my fingers to my ears and wiggled them about inside my ear canals before lowering my hands and saying, "Sorry, say it one more time."

Ryder laughed. "Will. You. Marry. Me?"

I opened my mouth to speak, but Ryder cut me off and said, "You aren't mishearing me. I'm *really* asking you to marry me. I'd get down on my knee and do it the traditional way, but those two our there will probably have a heart attack if I do that."

"Ryder," I whispered. "What the fuck?"

He laughed, again. "Is that a no?"

"No it's not a no," I instantly replied. "If you're serious it's a hell fucking yes."

A smile similar to the one he gave me the first time I told him I loved him stretched across his face.

"I'm serious as a heart attack, I want you to be my wife."

"Oh, my God."

"So you'll marry me?" he asked, his voice low.

"Yes," I gushed, lowering my voice too. "Yes, I'll marry you."

We kissed then and broke apart when I began to jump up and down.

"I'm going to buy a ring tomorrow. I didn't plan on doing this, it just happened. I was thinking about how much I love you, and I imagined you not being in my life and I couldn't."

"Sweetheart," I breathed. "I love you so much."

"I love you, too."

I quickly snuck a glance at Bronagh and Dominic and saw they were too wrapped up in one another to spare us a moment.

"We'll tell them when we have a ring, Bronagh won't believe me otherwise."

Ryder nodded. "It's going to work out, darling."

I smiled. "We'll get there."

"Yeah, sweetness, we will." Ryder smiled as I wrapped my arms around him. "We're a family, we can make it through anything."

We're a family, we can make it through anything.

If I had known then that over the next few years our families were going to be tested to the limit to see what we could survive, I'd have hugged Ryder a little longer and loved him a lot harder. As a matter of fact, I probably would have never let him go.

CHAPTER NINE

Present day...

"And he just walked out of the house? Just like that?"

I nodded even though my sister couldn't see me.

"Yep," I sighed, and adjusted my phone against my ear. "He told me that we weren't broken up, and that we'd *never* be done."

"Damn," Bronagh murmured. "Ryder's more possessive that I thought he was."

You have no idea, little sister.

I grunted. "Lucky me."

"Maybe this could be good," my sister said, her voice raising an octave with her excitement. "He said he'd answer all of your questions in two days, right? Once he does that you can both work through everythin'."

I felt my shoulders slump.

"It's not that easy, Bee, he has ripped out me heart over and over. I'm a ghost of the person I used to be, and it's because of my and Ryder's relationship over the last year and a half. I don't think I have the strength to try and piece back together what's been broken. I'm tired."

My sister was silent for a moment, and then she said, "If you think leavin' 'im is best for you, then I'm fully behind you. No questions asked."

I licked my lower lip when it wobbled.

"Thanks, Bee."

"No thanks necessary. You're me sister and I always have your back."

And I thanked God for that every single day.

"I'm so antsy sittin' here," I admitted. "I wish he would just come home so I can get this over and done with. It's drivin' me up the wall, I just want to get it out of the way so I can start the process of movin' on."

"It's goin' to be bad, Bran. You know that, right?"

I nodded again even though Bronagh still couldn't see me.

"I know, Bee, but it's somethin' I *have* to do."

"I understand."

"Is Damien still at your house?" I asked.

It was after seven in the evening and was pitch black outside.

"He and Dominic left the house about twenty minutes ago," my sister said. "Kane rang them and told them that he and Alec had spoken to you so they went out to help find Ryder."

For some reason, I was worried about him when I should have remained angry with him for storming out on such an important conversation.

I swallowed. "I hope he is okay."

"He'll be fine," Bronagh assured me. "Oh, Dominic told me he agrees with me idea of all of us sittin' down and gettin' this shit out into the open."

"He did?" I asked, surprised.

"Yeah, he said all of the brothers would force Ryder to tell you what he does every night and why he has changed so much over the last sixteen months if he refuses."

That caused me to furrow my brows.

"They *know* what he does every night and why he has changed?"

Bronagh said, "Yeah."

"And they never told me?" I asked, my voice barely a whisper.

"Trust me, I can't believe it either. Dominic never let on to me that he knew what Ryder's problem was and why he was being so weird. I couldn't even look at 'im when he told me."

"I can't believe it," I said, my voice tight.

I felt betrayed by a group of men who I considered my brothers.

"Me either, I'm surprised at Aideen though."

My heart stopped. "What do you mean?"

"Dominic said that she knew Kane would be gone off with Ryder and called 'im out on it at the end of her pregnancy. He didn't go into detail, but that's the gist of what he said."

"Are you sure?" I asked, as a feeling of shock, dread and anger swirled in my stomach.

"Yeah, I'm sure."

A different form of betrayal shot through me like a bolt of lightening.

"I'll call you back," I rasped then without waiting for a reply, I hung up on my sister, and instantly dialled Aideen's number into my phone. She answered after the fifth ring.

"Hey, Bran."

"You knew Kane was goin' somewhere with Ryder behind me back when you were pregnant and you never fuckin' told me?" I snapped.

Aideen was silent for a moment then she said, "I'm sorry."

I wanted to scream.

"Sorry?" I hissed. "You're sorry? You knew he was goin' somewhere with Ry and you never talked to me about it! Kane knows where he goes, Dominic and Alec know, too, and none of them talked to me about it!"

"I don't know though," Aideen stressed. "I only knew Kane was off with 'im, but I never actually knew what they were doin', and I didn't even cop it until the end of me pregnancy. I was so caught up with fear after the attack and I didn't even think to talk to you about it. I'm so sorry."

I swallowed down bile and my sudden rage when I heard the truth in my friend's words. I remained quiet for a few moments then closed my eyes and said, "I broke up with Ryder."

There were several beats of silence.

"What?" Aideen almost shouted when she found her voice. "Are you shittin' me?"

"No," I replied and reopened my eyes. "I broke up with 'im, but he refused to accept it, and surprise fuckin' surprise, he stormed out of the house and I don't know where he has gone off to. The lads are out lookin' for 'im because he won't answer any of our calls."

"I can't believe this."

I heard the shock in her tone.

I humourlessly laughed. "Welcome to the club."

"But why?" Aideen asked after a pregnant pause. "Why did you break up with 'im?"

Wasn't that the question of the day? I wondered. *Why? Why? Why?*

"Because I can't deal with how me life is with 'im now. I'm on the verge of a break down. I'm so unhappy."

"Branna," Aideen breathed. "I had no idea things were *this* bad. I knew you were havin' some problems, but I never imagined it was to this extent."

"Bronagh and Damien said the same thing," I mumbled.

"Why haven't you talked to me?" she asked, her tone changing to one of annoyance. "Why the fuck have you been dealin' with this by yourself? This isn't healthy!"

"When things started going really bad, you were dealin' with your surprise pregnancy and Kane, then with Big Phil attackin' you and your stint in the hospital to recover from that. I wasn't goin' to pester you with me problems, and especially not when you birthed that beautiful baby boy of yours."

"I could fuckin' *smack* you!" Aideen shouted. "You're me best friend which means you're a fuckin' priority to me! You bloody well know that, Branna!"

My shoulders sagged.

"I just didn't want to bother anyone with it," I said, my voice tight with emotion. "I guess I felt like if I didn't talk about it, it wasn't real, you know? I mean, it's *Ryder*, and I don't want to leave 'im if I can help it. I love 'im, but I can't live the way I have been. It's killin' me, Ado."

"Honey," she breathed. "I'm so sorry. Look, give me half an hour. I'm gettin' Kane home then I'm comin' over."

I wiped away the stray tears that fell from my eyes.

"Don't you dare, I'm fine." I lied and rubbed my nose with the back of my hand. "I just had a stressful day at work. We had a code red on the ward and Dominic gave Ash a hard time when he picked me up, then my break up talk with Ryder went *completely* wrong. I just want to go to bed and deal with all of this tomorrow."

"I'm comin' over even if it's just to sleep with you. I'm not leavin' you alone when you're goin' through this, not a bleedin' chance!"

I decided not to object because she was right—I needed her. Being on my own wasn't something that was going to help me, having someone I loved just being there for me would.

"Okay," I said, holding back more tears that wanted to break free. "You have your key so just come up to Dominic's old room when you get here. I've been sleepin' in there the last few months."

Aideen cursed under her breath.

"Okay, as soon as Kane gets here, I'm comin' over. He'll probably pack up stuff for Jax and come with me; he won't let me be alone after everythin' that's happened. Dante is in the sittin' room right now on babysittin' duty until Kane comes home."

Aideen and Jax were Kane's life; of course he was going to make sure they were protected after a twisted human being tried to take them away from him. And there was no one better to watch over them than one of her brothers' when he couldn't do it himself.

"I don't blame 'im," I said with a firm nod. "There's more than enough room here, his room is *still* his room. We haven't changed it."

"Good. Go and get to bed, I'll be there before you know it. I love you."

"I love you too, and I'm sorry for shoutin' at you, I'm just out of sorts right now."

"You have every reason to be pissed, I flaked and that's not cool. Don't think about it until we can talk, okay?"

"I'll try not to, see you soon."

"See you, hon."

I leaned back against the chair I was sitting on, tilted my head back and stared up at the ceiling of my kitchen. The silence in my house was deafening, but my thoughts seemed to be on full blast because I couldn't escape from them.

I jumped when I heard the noise of car doors closing and without hesitation; I jumped to me feet, zoomed out of the kitchen, down the hallway and straight to the front door. My heart slammed against my chest as I looked through the peephole. I hoped it was Ryder with his brothers. I could try breaking up with him again and with them here they could help me get it into his head that he didn't have a say in my decision.

It wasn't Ryder though... it was his twin brothers.

I quickly locked the door from the inside and put the latch on, too. When one of the twins tried his key in the door and found it wouldn't open so they both rapped their fists against the door.

"Go away!"

"Branna?" Damien called out. "What are you doing? Let us in."

"I'll let *you* in, but not *him*!"

Another round of knocking.

"We have to talk, Branna." Dominic stated.

"Stay away from me!"

I heard him sigh. "Branna, please—"

"No!" I snapped. "I'm not listenin' to anythin' you have to say. You're a manipulative little pox and I never want to be in your presence again. You're dead to me."

Through the door I heard his sharp intake of breath.

"Take that back, Branna."

My heart hurt because even when I was furious with the little prick, I still loved him to death, just like I would a brother. I didn't mean what I said, but I was too angry to acknowledge that.

"No." I said firmly. "I won't."

"You don't mean it so take it back. Now."

I slapped my palm against the door, ignoring the sting.

"Don't tell me what to do when you've instilled a lie in Ryder's head. He thinks I'm cheatin' on 'im because of *you*!"

"I fucked up, okay?" he said. "I wanted him to go and beat on Ash to ensure he stays away from you, I thought if *he* thought another man was stepping up to you, he'd snap out of his bullshit and react like any of us would, but he didn't, and I'm so sorry."

I was furious with him, but a part of me also understood him. Dominic's logic was different to mine. He and his brothers' were raised differently in a diverse environment and things that seemed crazy to me were normal for them. I knew in Dominic's head that what he did was the only way he knew of to gauge a reaction from Ryder.

He thought he was helping.

On a sigh, I unlocked the door, opened it wide, and stepped to the side so the twins could enter the house. Damien kissed my cheek as he passed me by and Dominic stood in front of me.

"I'm so sorry," he repeated, his eyes trained on mine. "It was dumb of me to bait Ryder when I know how much stress he is under."

I saw the truth in his grey orbs, and I had to fight with myself not to hug him because I didn't want to break down and cry. I had done enough of that.

Instead, I gave him an affectionate smile and said, "I know, kid."

He stared down at me, unmoving and unblinking.

"What?" I quizzed.

Dominic nervously shifted from foot to foot, and after exhaling a shaky breath he said, "Take back what you said... please."

I hated that I said what I did because I saw fear in him. He believed I truly meant the vile words I spewed and unless I said otherwise, he would continue to think that way.

A lump formed in my throat as I said, "I take it back. I didn't mean a word of it, I swear. I'm sorry, sweetheart. You're me brother, and I love you dearly, just like I do Bronagh. Nothin' will ever change that, okay?"

He exhaled a relieved breath. "Thank you."

As he spoke, he hugged me tightly and kissed the crown of my head.

"It's going to be okay," he murmured. "We'll fix everything."

You can't fix what's already been smashed to pieces.

I hugged him back then closed the front door of the house when we separated. I watched as Dominic dropped his car keys on the table in the hall, then I followed both of the lads down to the kitchen and automatically filled the kettle with water and popped it on to make tea.

Tea was necessary.

"I know this is a stupid question," Damien began, "but are you okay?"

"No," I replied while I took out cups from the cupboard. "I'm not okay. I'm tired and I just want to go to bed and deal with all of this tomorrow."

"That's a good idea," Dominic said rapidly. "Why don't you go on up to bed and we can have tea later?"

I hesitated. "Bronagh told me you went to help Kane and Alec find Ryder. Why are you here and not out with them?"

"They know where he is," Damien said. "They just have to wait for him to be done with something."

I stared at Damien when he finished speaking. "You're being vague, *really*? A few hours ago you were in me shoes, you didn't know a fuckin' thing, but now you do and you aren't tellin' me?"

He swallowed. "This is something that has to come from Ryder, Bran."

I couldn't look at him.

"You're all keepin' things from me, and it's hurtin' me so much." I turned away as I spoke. "I'm goin' to bed, Aideen will be here soon with Jax and Kane."

"Branna—"

"Good night," I cut Damien off and walked out of the kitchen, closing the door behind me.

I walked down the hallway, and just as I was about to turn for the stairs, I heard a jiggle of keys in the lock of the hall door. For some unknown reason, I ran through the open door and into the gym room where I hovered next to the doorway.

I knew it was Ryder, I could sense him, but he confirmed it when he spoke in hushed whispers.

"No, I can't... because I just got fucking home and need to fix shit with my girl, you *know* that... for fuck's sake, why? I'm done with this bullshit after tonight. Damn it, *fine.* I'll be right fucking there."

I heard a bit of movement then a soft click. I peeked out of the gym room and found the hallway empty and the front door shut. I heard the ignition of a car starting up a few moments later and my heart jumped to my throat.

Ryder was leaving again, and in a split second I made a decision with that knowledge.

He asked me to trust him, to give him forty-eight hours before he could tell me everything that he was hiding from me, but I couldn't. In that moment, I simply couldn't. I waited over a year to find out what he was up to, and I couldn't wait another minute longer. Before I realised what I was doing, I grabbed Dominic's car keys from the table in the hall, quietly exited my house, jumped in his car, and began to follow Ryder at a safe distance. I was doing what I should have done a long time ago, I was going to find out for myself what he was up to, and I only prayed it wasn't as bad as what I imagined it to be.

Please, God, I silently begged. *Don't let this break me.*

CHAPTER TEN

Three years ago...

"I'm going to grow old with you."

My lips twitched, but I kept my eyes shut.

"You *do* realise it's incredibly weird when you stare at me while I'm sleepin', and say things like that to me unconscious form, right?"

I felt the heat of Ryder's palm press against my bare stomach as he moved closer to me.

"You say weird," he murmured, and I could hear the smile in his tone, "others would say romantic."

I giggled. "Sorry, it was weirdly romantic. How's that?"

"It's an improvement."

I blinked my eyes open, squinting until they adjusted to the light of our bedroom. I lifted my arms above my head and stretched. When I made sounds that resembled a baby dinosaur, Ryder laughed and poked at my sides causing me to squirm.

"You always sound like you really enjoy your morning stretch."

"I do," I nodded. "It wakes me up and feels good."

I looked at Ryder when he turned on his side and leaned his head down to mine, brushing his lips against my cheek. He parted his lips and gently flicked his tongue over my skin, causing goosebumps to break out over my flesh.

"Do you know what else feels good in the morning?" he murmured, trailing gentle kisses down my neck then to my sweet spot below my earlobe.

I licked my lips. "A foot massage?"

"How about a clit massage?" Ryder asked, his hot breath fanning my face before he brought his talented lips back to mine.

I burst into a fit of giggles when he pulled his mouth away and rubbed his nose against mine.

"We can't," I stressed, trying to sound firm. "I heard you shuttin' me alarm off. I have to get showered and dressed for work."

"I'll get you to work on time," he said softly. "I promise."

Well, maybe, if we were quick and—no! Don't be weak, Branna. You can't be late for work.

I groaned. "Don't make this harder than it needs to be. You rocked me world twice yesterday, can you not wait until I'm home lat—"

"No," Ryder cut me off. "I need to be inside of you. Now."

I knew talking to him was going to get me nowhere, so I needed to physically move away from him. I pushed the bed sheets from my body and shivered when a cool draft spread out over my naked body. I made an attempt to sit up, but as soon as my body was exposed, Ryder pounced on me like a teenager with a raging hard on; only he was a *grown man* with a raging hard on.

"You can't say no and then expose this masterpiece to me. No. Not fair. You aren't allowed to do that."

I laughed as he wrapped his arms around my body, rolled over, and pulled me on top of him. I adjusted myself until I was straddling his stomach. I looked down at him and shook my head when I found his eyes were locked on my breasts.

"You're *such* a man."

Ryder didn't bat an eyelid. "Thank you."

I rolled my eyes. "I'm goin' to be late for work."

"You won't," my sex crazed fiancé assured me. "Your alarm

doesn't go off for another hour and a half, the alarm you heard me shut off was mine. I'm going for a run with Dominic in twenty-five minutes."

I let what Ryder said sink in for a few moments, and then I flat out glared down at him.

"It's half five in the mornin'?"

Ryder nodded, *still* not looking away from my breasts. I glanced away from him, and looked over at the window where sunshine streamed in through the opened curtains. Summer time in Ireland meant sunlight was shining bright at unholy hours of the night. I considered five a.m. night-time. I gritted my teeth and looked back down at Ryder, annoyed at finding him licking his lips as his eyes feasted on me.

I reached down and pinched his nipple, gaining his attention.

"*Ow.*"

"Don't 'ow' me," I quipped. "What the hell did you speak to me for if I didn't have to get up yet?"

He grinned. "Scoot your ass down a little and you'll feel why."

I growled. "Sleep wins over sex *every* time, I thought I told you that already!"

His lips quirked. "Huh, mustn't have been listening to you when you said that."

Shocker.

I climbed off Ryder, and fell onto my side of the bed, facing away from him.

"I'm goin' back to sleep, keep your dick and hands away from me."

He was silent for a few moments and I thought that he accepted what I said as law, but that was until I felt something press against my hip.

"What did I just say?" I asked, trying my best to keep my voice even.

"You said," Ryder murmured, "to keep my dick and hands away from you, you said nothing about my tongue."

Said tongue slid over the curve of my hip and up the side of my body causing me to suck in a sharp breath.

Be strong, woman.

"Ryder Slater," I managed to say. "Back away."

He did almost instantly, but I practically felt his frown.

"Damn," he murmured. "You really aren't in the mood?"

I shook my head. "I'm tired. We have sex every single day, most days more than once. I'm only a woman, not a machine."

"Are you *complaining*?"

"No." I laughed because he sounded so disgusted. "I'm definitely not, but I need time to rest or I'm never goin' to be able to keep up with you."

I thought we were straying away from the topic of sex until Ryder opened his mouth and caused my eyes to roll towards the heavens.

"Can we swap you stroking my ego for stroking my cock instead?" he asked, and then laughed when I blindly kicked back at him.

"Goodnight, Ryder."

I felt lips press against my shoulder.

"Goodnight, baby."

I smiled when he settled behind me and hooked his arm around my body then covered our naked bodies with our bed cover. I snuggled into my pillow and sighed when my body started to relax once more. I blinked my eyes open a few minutes later when my mind refused to follow suit. I turned to face Ryder, glaring at him when I found he was looking at me with his shining grey eyes.

"I can't go back asleep now, you bastard."

He smiled. "So talk to me since we've got nothing else to do."

"What about your run?" I questioned.

Ryder shrugged. "It takes me two seconds to get dressed, which gives *you* twenty minutes to do what you keep yapping on about."

I grunted. "What do I keep yappin' on about?"

"You always say we don't talk enough, so let's talk."

I glared at him. "You're puttin' me on the spot."

"So?"

"So I don't have a topic in mind."

"I do."

"Shoot."

"When can we get married?"

I felt my mouth drop open, and it made Ryder laugh.

"What?" he asked. "You look like you didn't know that we'd eventually move on from being engaged to actually *getting* hitched."

My mouth went very dry, so I licked my lips.

"No, I know that, *obviously*, I just didn't think *you* would be thinkin' of that."

Ryder's lips quirked. "I knew what I was doing when I asked you to marry me outside of the hospital that night two years ago, Branna. I imagined my life without you and I couldn't, but more than that, I didn't want to. I love you, baby."

Without thinking, I got to my hands and knees then straddled his body with mine. I leaned my face down to his and said, "I love you too, and we can get married whenever you want to. I'm *so* ready."

Ryder smiled. "We'll figure it out."

"We always do… and since we're figurin' that out, I'm gonna figure your problem out."

"What do you—*oh*!"

I suppressed a giggled.

"Yeah," Ryder breathed when I shimmied down his body, and took him by surprise by taking his hardened length in my mouth. "I'm *definitely* going to grow old with you."

CHAPTER ELEVEN

Present day...

"Where are you goin', Ry?" I mumbled aloud to myself when a couple hundred metres ahead of me Ryder took a right turn that would lead into a secluded part of the mountain side where there were no street lights, no houses, no people.

Hell, there was barely a road to drive on.

I had been following him for only ten minutes, but I sensed we were near his destination. For the tenth time, I ignored the vibration of my phone from my pocket because I knew it was the twins who were calling me.

I switched my headlights off and took the same turn behind him but made sure to drive extra slow so I didn't wreck Dominic's car and also so he wouldn't see me. I didn't worry about losing Ryder because his car was the only car on the trail, and his taillights still shone brightly like a beacon.

I jumped when I drove over a pothole that caused the car to lurch. I gripped the steering wheel tightly and blew out a nervous breath. I was wired and couldn't control much of my body because I had a sudden case of the shakes. My entire body trembled with fear and anticipation of what was going to be the outcome of my mission.

I didn't have to wait long to find out as Ryder stopped his car up ahead and parked it in front of a white Range Rover. I could see the colour and make of the car because when Ryder got out of his car, he left his keys in the ignition and his headlights switched on. I stopped driving, put Dominic's car in park and switched off the ignition. I exited the car, closed the door quietly and thanked God for the dark of the night as cover.

I said a little prayer, and on unsteady legs, I made my move.

I ducked down and crept forward until I was not too far away from where Ryder stood. I hunkered down behind a hedge only a mere twenty meters or so from him and the white Ranger Rover. I was close but not close enough because I couldn't hear what was being said. I could only hear the tone of Ryder's voice and that of another voice.

A *female* voice.

My blood ran cold knowing it was a woman Ryder drove out here to meet. All kinds of things were running through my mind, but I couldn't settle on one thought. I felt like my eyes were deceiving me, and what I was witnessing wasn't really happening.

"You liar." I whispered as I watched Ryder lean into the window of the white Range Rover.

My chest squeezed when I heard laughter from the female in the driver's seat. I didn't know what she was laughing at, or what Ryder was doing to make her laugh, but what I did know is that he kept his head, shoulders and arms inside the driver's window of her car and was making her laugh.

I felt sick. I felt weak. I felt numb.

I didn't want to stick around and find out what he was doing *to* make her laugh because I feared I'd do something that would hurt me more in the long run. I lowered myself back down to my hunkered position, reached out and gripped onto the bush that I was hiding behind and inhaled and exhaled deeps breaths.

I'm going to pass out.

I squeezed my eyes shut and forced myself to continue taking deep breaths. When the urge to faint passed, I focused on not vomiting. My stomach was churning and rolling, and there was a pain in my chest that I had never felt before in my life. It was a similar pain I felt when my parents died, but for some reason, it was *much* worse.

Ryder... he was *cheating* on me.

He was betraying me, and I had the proof, but I still couldn't believe what was unfolding before my eyes. I didn't understand it, and I didn't want to. I just wanted to erase the image and sound of Ryder and the woman's laughter. I didn't want to think of him smiling because it reminded me so much of the smile he used to show me whenever he saw me.

Home, I told myself. *I need to go home.*

A strong woman would have confronted Ryder, and possibly run him over with his beloved car while the bitch he cheated with watched, but I wasn't a strong woman. I was a shell of the woman I used to be, and what I just witnessed would stay with me forever.

I was broken.

I numbly retraced my steps back to Dominic's car and when I got back inside the vehicle everything felt wrong. The silence was unbearable, but I didn't want to hear anything else. My heart was slamming into my chest, and the pain I felt with each beat was the only reminder that I was still living, but surely there was more to living than feeling so dead inside?

The taste of sickening infidelity in my mouth urged me to start Dominic's car. I quickly reversed until I came back to the main road where I switched my headlights back on and safely pulled onto it. I hated how I felt. I was numb to what I was experiencing, but yet my chest hurt. I couldn't cry, but I knew that's what the hurt I felt wanted me to do.

My body knew something was wrong, but my brain hadn't reached the point where it was on the same wavelength. I understood what I saw and what it meant, but I didn't feel any kind of way over it. I just couldn't believe it was real.

I found myself laughing hysterically like a crazy person when I realised only hours before that Ryder asked me if I was cheating on him, when it fact, *he* was the cheater.

Him.

I drove Dominic's car back to his and Bronagh's house. I didn't know why, but I completely bypassed my house and just went to theirs. I parked behind Kane and Alec's cars and I was glad to see that they were there. I didn't want anyone around me right now, and when I went back to my house, I wanted to be there on my own.

I quietly made my way up the pathway to Dominic and Bronagh's front door. I heard the cry of a baby and chatter of men. I distinctively heard Damien saying Dominic's name, too, which meant they were no longer at my house. When they realised I was gone with Dominic's car, this was obviously the first place they checked for me.

Before any of them could come outside and catch me, I quietly put the car keys inside their letterbox without them knowing. In a daze I walked back to my house and was fully aware that the numbness I felt would soon fade and agonising pain would fill me, but until that happened, I intended to go home and pack my belongings together.

I needed to get out before Ryder came back. I wasn't strong enjoy to face him, and I feared I'd do something dangerous if he lied to my face when I saw with my own eyes that he was with another woman.

Ryder is cheating on me.

I unlocked my front door and stepped into my house. I closed the door behind me and looked down to my pocket when my phone vibrated, and as if someone else controlled me, I slipped my hand into my pocket, and without looking at who was calling me, I answered the phone and placed it against my ear.

"Hello?"

"Branna?" Ash chirped. "Hey Angel, do you have a minute? I'm telling my sister about the code red we had today and I forget what our response time was. Was it ninety-one seconds, or ninety-five?"

"Ninety-one," I replied without hesitation, my tone flat.

"Bran?" Ash said. "Are you okay, hon?"

"No, Ash."

"What's wrong?" Ash asked and I heard him moving about.

"Ryder," I blinked. "He's cheatin' on me."

"Oh, fuck," Ash hissed. "I'll *kill* him!"

I didn't reply, instead I walked down the hallway and into the kitchen.

"Where are you?" Ash demanded. "I'll be right there!"

"I'm in me house, I just walked in—"

"Hello, Branna."

I swirled around at the unknown voice that cut me off and stared into the dark room. I was too far away from reaching the light switch without moving, and I couldn't move even if I tried. My legs had locked when I heard the voice of a strange man and fear broke through my numbness and shot through me.

"Branna?" Ash said from my phone. "Who was that?"

"Someone… someone is in me house," I replied and felt oddly calm, but that feeling fled a moment later.

I heard movement over by the back door, and screeched when the shadow of a tall man came out of the shadows and surged toward me. I dropped my phone and tried to run out of the kitchen, but the man was on me before I even had a chance to move. We hit the floor with a thud, and almost instantly I felt blunt pain rack up and down my body. It caused a shrill scream to rise up my throat and break free.

"BRANNA?!" I heard Ash scream through the phone lying by my head.

I had fallen to the ground first and the body of the man's added extra weight on top of mine when I hit the ground only caused the impact to hurt that much more. He used my sudden stillness to his advantage and quickly pinned my arms above my head with one hand, while he used the weight of his body to pin my legs and body to the ground. I forgot about fighting him off when fighting to breathe became my number one priority.

"Shhhh, sweetheart." The man crooned with a Southern American accent. "It's going to be okay, Branna. Don't you worry about a thing, honey. I'm going to take real good care of you."

I wheezed as I desperately tried to suck air into my lungs, but suddenly felt my body go lax as something pinched my neck. One second I was in pain and a blind panic, and the next I was slipping into unconsciousness.

My last thought was of Ryder and the woman from the white Range Rover, and how my life had already ended before this stranger had chance take it from me.

CHAPTER TWELVE

One year ago...

I was tired.

Not physically, but mentally.

I felt as if I was on a merry go round with Ryder. Our stupid arguing had amplified and instead of happening once or twice a week, it was happening once or twice a *day*. We either fought with one another, or ignored each other. It was becoming tiresome.

It all started six months ago, just after Dominic started fighting at Darkness under Brandon Daley. Ryder would disappear for a few hours, and when I asked where he was, he'd blow up at me. I forgot about it after a while because my long hours at the hospital had me overlooking his nightly absences. I could have probably dealt with him being evasive, but while he was in my presence his arsehole behaviour and snippy remarks picked away at me until a fight was ignited.

This was the beginning of our downward spiral, and now, six months later, I was at a stand still. I didn't know what to do about the situation, and I refused to bring my problems to my friends or Ryder's brothers because they had their own shit to work through. They didn't need my drama added to theirs.

The only thing I could do was turn a blind eye to the situation, which meant ignoring Ryder. I knew it was wrong to brush our problems under the carpet, but knowing any attempt to deal with it would turn into a screaming contest kept my mouth shut.

It was hurting me though. I didn't know what had gone wrong in order for Ryder not to talk to me or trust me anymore, but whatever happened, it was enough to change him. He wasn't the man I once knew, and it broke my heart.

I shook my head clear and grabbed my shower bag. I had been sleeping in Dominic's old room once or twice a week when fighting got bad between Ryder and myself, and last night was once of those nights. Usually, I'd shower in any of the bathrooms in the house when I couldn't use another one, but I preferred the shower in my and Ryder's master bathroom. It was bigger and the showerhead was made so it was like a waterfall raining water onto your head instead of a little spray.

I made my way down the stairs and headed into my room. It was empty, as expected. I didn't know where Ryder was; he probably didn't come home last night. He sometimes did that. Since I had two hours until I needed to leave for work, I would enjoy my shower and wash away my latest fight with Ryder, and try and relax.

It was something I hadn't done it a while.

I headed into the bathroom, and was surprised when steam puffed into my face. I dismissed it and closed the door behind me and turned towards the shower. I walked head first into a hard, wet chest.

I gasped and looked up. When my eyes landed on him, I swallowed.

"I'm sorry, I didn't know you were in here."

I didn't know you were home at all.

Ryder looked down at me and raised an eyebrow. "It's your bathroom too, don't be sorry."

I slowly nodded.

"Are you still giving me the silent treatment?" he asked on a sigh.

"I don't know. Are you still being an arsehole who can't answer a few simple questions?" I countered.

"Yeah," he quipped. "Seems I am."

I lifted my hand and wiggled my fingers for him to move out of my way, giving him my reply. Silently.

"Only you could give a huge 'fuck you' with a singlehanded gesture and silence."

I rolled my eyes, and tried to push by him.

Ryder didn't move, he just continued to stare down at me. I didn't like how he was openly raking his eyes over my body like I was a piece of meat, so I returned the favour. Only that backfired very quickly because I adored the view on display.

I found my eyes slowly, *very* slowly, scanning their way down Ryder's chiselled, tattooed body and fuck me if it didn't stir something lower in my abdomen. I licked my lips as I watched a droplet of water run from his chest, down to the beautiful defined oblique muscles at the base of his torso.

Fuck.

He was hotter than ever, all the extra hours of workouts he had been putting in over the last few months were clearly working and my eyes reaped the rewards. I badly wanted to run my hands, and tongue, all over him, but I remembered how things were between us and it dampened down the rise in my temperature.

"Enjoying the view?" he asked, his voice so low it hardened my nipples.

I snapped my eyes up to Ryder's and found him smirking down at me.

"So what if I am?" I challenged and broke my vow of silence by speaking.

I gasped when he suddenly grabbed hold of my forearms and forced me to step back until my back hit the bathroom door. I almost groaned out loud when his pelvis pressed against mine and I felt the hardened length of his cock press into me.

Shit.

"Careful, Branna," he said, his voice low and husky. "I might think you actually want me with the fire in those pretty eyes of yours."

I narrowed my eyes. "It's not like you'll fuckin' *do* anythin' about it."

Ryder's grip on my arms tightened.

"*Excuse* me?" he asked through clenched teeth.

I cleared my throat. "We haven't had sex in months. Somethin' about me has put you off wantin' to have sex with me so I doubt you'll do anythin' to me no matter how much heat is in my eyes... *or* knickers."

Fuck it.

If he thought he was going to intimidate me with his manhandling ways then he had another thing coming. He hadn't put his hands on me in such a way in the longest time, and I was savouring his touch because I knew when I left the bathroom, it probably wouldn't happen again for *another* few months.

"You think I'm not attracted to you?" Ryder asked, shock evident in his tone.

I shrugged. "What else am I supposed to think? There was a time when you couldn't keep your hands off me, now you can barely stand to be close to me."

Ryder growled, lowered his head, and thrust his hips against me. I shuddered.

"Does it *feel* like I'm not attracted to you?" he almost snarled.

I looked away and remained mute.

"Branna," he rumbled. "Look at me when I'm speaking to you."

An electric jolt of pure pleasure shot straight to my clit and pulsed at his demanding tone. I licked my lips, turned my head and looked up at him, my mouth hanging open as I began to pant. Ryder lowered his head and surprised me when he snaked his tongue out and ran it over my bottom lip. I closed my eyes and almost hummed when he closed his lips around it and sucked it into his mouth.

Whatever control I had snapped because one second I was allowing Ryder to suck and nibble on my lower lip, and the next I was climbing him like a fucking tree. My hands were all over him, and his all over me. It's like we were animals and roughly feeling one another to make sure what was happening was real, and not a figment of our imagination.

"Ryder," I breathed against his mouth and tried to take a step backwards, but his hold on me was solid and kept me in place.

He lowered his lips from my mouth to my neck and growled. "I'm going to fuck you, Branna."

My body practically sang with delight, but my heart frowned because it knew there would be no intimacy. This was purely primal. I momentarily thought about rejecting Ryder's advances, but I was only a woman, and I missed him so much that I wanted to grasp at any chance to be close to him, especially since I knew it would probably be the last time I *would* be close to him for a long while.

I licked my lips. "So fuck me then."

"Be careful," he warned through clenched teeth. "I haven't had you in a *long* time, if you give me the green light, I won't stop until we're both satisfied. That means you'll be very sore for the rest of the day, you understand?"

My lips quirked. "Promises, promises."

Ryder's grip on me tightened. "You doubt me, darling?"

I shrugged out of his hold.

"I thought I told you *never* to doubt me."

I frowned. "That was a long time ago."

"It had no time limit when I said it, it *still* doesn't."

I sighed. "Yeah, whatever."

"Who do you think you're talking to?" Ryder almost growled.

I blinked. "You."

"Are you sure you *know* it's me because when I say I'm going to fuck you into soreness, I mean it. You're acting like it's someone else who is promising this to you. You know I follow through with what's mine."

I tilted my head to the side. "It's been a few months, maybe I forget."

"You forget what it's like to me fucked by me, or you forget what it's like to be mine?"

Without hesitation I said, "Both."

Fire flashed in Ryder's eyes and it caused me to back away from him, but like an animal, he followed.

"I thought I made it clear that you were mine, Branna."

I nervously swallowed as I continued to back away from Ryder, who was still advancing on me, slowly, like a predator stalking its prey.

"Turn around, and bend over," he ordered. "Now."

My pulse spiked as excitement flowed through my veins.

"Wh-why?" I asked, not being able to hide the tremor in my voice.

"Because," he growled as he undid his belt buckle, "I'm going to give you a hell of a reminder who you belong to, and when I'm finished, you won't question it again. Now turn around. And. Bend. Over."

Holy. Shit.

I spun around so fast the rush of air against my face caused my breath to catch.

"Hmmm," Ryder hummed. "Are you *sure* you don't remember the feel of me inside your sweet pussy?"

"I'm sure," I breathed.

My clit pulsed so hard it caused me pain.

I felt his hand grab hold of the hem of my pyjamas shorts and knickers. He slowly pulled them down and I hissed when his nails scraped against my skin only to be replaced by his warm, wet tongue, soothing the sting away with tender flicks.

I opened my eyes when I felt a tug on my hair. I reached forward and rubbed away the steam from the bathroom mirror and stared at Ryder who was positioned behind me, his eyes trained on mine. My hair fell down around my shoulders a second later, and I realised the tug on my hair was Ryder removing my hair tie.

"You have *no* idea what I would do to you if you had no work today." He murmured, his eyes burning with heat. "You wouldn't be able to sit down."

I couldn't help it when my eyes widened and it caused Ryder to grin.

"Branna. Branna. Branna." He mused. "What will I do to you?"

I swallowed. "Make me scream."

"That," he smirked, "I can do."

I jumped when he pressed against me and carefully kicked my legs apart as far as they would go with my knickers and shorts acting as binds around my ankles. When he was happy when how far apart I was spread, with his eyes locked on mine, Ryder reached around with his hand, and slipped it between my thighs.

"You're so wet," he whispered, his pupils dilating as he coated his fingers with my essence.

I couldn't help but roll my eyes shut as I relished in his touch. I gripped onto the counter when Ryder brought his fingers to my throbbing clit and I cried out when they made contact.

He chuckled in my ear. "One touch and you scream."

I didn't care about his teasing; I just cared about his fingers and what they would do to me.

"Do you rub this pretty clit at night and think of me, Branna?"

What the hell?

"Ryder—"

"Answer or I stop," he said and picked up his speed, causing me to cry out again.

"Yes!" I shouted. "I pretend it's you touchin' me."

"Good," he growled.

I felt my jaw drop open when his rubbing on my clit caused my breath to hitch, my back to arch and my heart to briefly stop as I tumbled into bliss.

"Your face when you come is my favourite thing," Ryder gruff voice cut through my dream like haze, "but *feeling* you come when you're wrapped around me is even better."

He bent me forward then and without warning, he entered me in one fluid motion. He moaned as I cried out, the feeling of fullness and delight consuming me.

This, I thought, *this is everything.*

Ryder withdrew from me slowly, hissing as he did so, before driving straight back in to the hilt.

"Omigod," I screamed and arched my back.

Ryder's hands dug into the flesh on my hips as he began a steady rhythm of fucking me. That's what he was doing—he was fucking me, not making love.

He growled, "*Fuck*! I've missed pounding this pussy." I moaned when he pumped harder. "So"—thrust—"fucking"—thrust—"much."

I couldn't think, let alone form a reply to that crude remark.

I gripped onto the bathroom counter and tried to form a coherent thought, but it was impossible to do with the mind-blowing sensations that my body was experiencing. If possible, this was definitely the best sex we had ever had, and it gutted me a little because it was just a primal frenzy between our bodies, there were no loving or comforting touches.

I accepted it for what it was though. It was sex, and toe curling sex at that.

"Branna," Ryder groaned. "You feel fucking incredible."

"Ditto," I moaned as I bucked my hips back only for Ryder's pelvis to slam into my behind causing vibrations to race up and down my spine.

Yes.

I yelped when a sting spread out over my behind. I heard the sound of the smack, I felt the bite of pain, but it took me a few seconds to release Ryder actually spanked me.

"Are you serious?" I rasped, pushing my behind back against him.

He laughed, and slapped my behind again.

"Ryder!" I shouted.

I wanted my voice to be firm, but it fell apart into a moan when he rotated his hips and hit a spot deep inside me that caused me to see stars.

"Right there," I moaned.

Once I spoke the words of encouragement, Ryder became as still as a statue.

"No," I cried out and tried to buck back to chase down my own release, but Ryder's powerful hold on my hips prevented that from happening.

"Who is fucking you?" he asked, his voice gruff.

"What are you—"

"Who is fucking you?" he cut me off, his voice raised.

"You are," I answered, shocked that his pissed off tone was making me hotter.

He rewarded me with a deep thrust.

I groaned.

"Whose pussy is this?" Ryder then asked, his tone stern.

"Please, just—"

He cut me off with a stinging slap to my behind that caused me to cry out with surprise.

"If you don't answer me, I'll hurt you so good."

Part of me wanted to know what that entailed, but the sting I felt on my behind as Ryder's hand caressed the sore flesh kept me from asking.

"It's yours," I said, trying to keep my voice even.

Another deep thrust.

I moaned. "Yes."

"Last question," he murmured and leaned forward, placing his lips against my ear. "Who do you belong to?"

That was the easiest thing he had ever asked me.

"You, Ryder," I replied, envisioning I was speaking to the man I first met in Darkness. "I belong to you. Always."

"Damn. Fucking. Right."

He proved his point then. He fucked me so hard he reminded me that he did, in fact, own me. Body, heart and soul. It was just a pity that he had no idea that he was shattering two out of the three.

Once he repeatedly drove into me, and didn't stop, he made good on his promise and brought me intense satisfaction. Without warning, I was lost in bliss for a second time, and if it wasn't for the counter under my upper body, or Ryder's grip on my hips, I would have fallen to the floor in a satisfied heap.

"You okay?" he asked when I came down from my high.

I nodded against the marble my head rested on. "Yeah, I needed that."

He snickered as he withdrew from me, but said nothing further as I heard him bin the condom I didn't even know he put on. When he stepped away from me, a draft spread out over my behind and legs causing me to shiver. I straightened myself up and pulled my knickers and shorts up whilst doing so. I made sure not to look up into the mirror because I didn't want to see what Ryder was doing, but I mainly didn't want him to see the tears that filled my eyes.

I hated that I was getting upset. I didn't want to cry anymore.

"I've to head out for the day," he hesitantly said, "but can we do this again tonight?"

I blinked as I turned on the taps and pumped some soap onto my hands, washing them just to give me something to do.

"Where are you goin'?" I asked, although I knew I wouldn't receive an honest answer.

Ryder cleared his throat and moved behind me, snaking his hands around my waist, and lowering his lips to my bare shoulder. "Just out, nowhere important."

I tried not to focus on his touch, because it was about to open the dam in my eyes.

"Oh, I see." I murmured.

Ryder moved his face to the side of my neck and rubbed his nose against the tender flesh of my sweet spot, then placed a kiss beneath my ear, directly on said spot. The action caused my tears to splash onto my cheeks, and a sob to get suck in my throat. He used to always kiss me there right before he told me he loved me.

The 'I love you' never came.

"So," Ryder prompted, gaining my attention. "Can we have sex again tonight? I want to touch you some more."

Or you want to come some more.

"Yeah, we can have sex again," I replied, my voice as emotionless as a robot's.

Having sex with him only hurt me more, but any form of touching him was better than nothing. Even though we were having serious problems, I still craved him.

Ryder gave me a squeeze. "Great, I'll be counting down the hours until I'm home."

My lower lip quivered. "Me too, Ry."

He kissed the back of head, gave my behind a little tap then he practically skipped out of the bathroom and headed into our bedroom to dress.

"I'm getting a shower now," I called out as tears streamed down my cheeks.

"Okay, babe, I'll be gone by the time you're out." He shouted back.

I covered my nose and mouth with my hand to lessen the noise of my sniffles. I turned on the shower and after a moment, I stripped bare and stepped under the hot stream. I pressed my back against the cool tiles, and slowly slid down the wall until I was crumbled mess on the shower floor.

This is what I had become. This was what Ryder had unknowingly done to me.

He broke my heart.

He broke *me*.

CHAPTER THIRTEEN

Present day...

You know the feeling of when you just wake up, before your eyes open, and you're aware of everything happening around you whilst still being in a barely conscious state? That was what I was currently experiencing.

For a few moments, I didn't try to move or open my eyes. I couldn't think rationally yet, but there was a distinct pain in my chest and a churn in my gut that told me something wasn't right. It was a feeling I couldn't quite explain.

When my limbs involuntarily twitched, a sharp physical pain rocked through me, and out of nowhere, my head began to pound as if someone was using it as a drum. I made a small whining sound that drew entirely too much energy from me.

Slowly, I opened my eyes and was surprised to find everything was still pitch black. I blinked my lids a couple of times, but nothing changed. For a second, I thought it was the middle of the night, but when I lifted my head from where my chin was resting on my chest and felt the strain of fabric covering my eyes, I knew it wasn't. I figured it was my bed cover over my face even though, logically, I knew I would feel the cover on every part of my face if that were the case instead of just on my eyes.

I knew then that something was definitely wrong, but I didn't know what it was as my memory didn't have any recollection of anything for me to be scared of. My worries were pushed to the side when a fierce pain in my neck suddenly took focus. I slowly rolled my head onto my shoulders and winced when it cracked. I didn't like how restricted and tight my muscles felt. My head was very heavy, like a weight that I didn't have the strength to hold up.

I rolled my neck around in a circle to soothe the pain and it was then that I noticed I could do it easily without a pillow stopping me. Almost instantly I knew that I wasn't lying down on my bed. In fact, I wasn't lying down *at all*. I was in an upright sitting position on a hard chair if the ache in my legs and behind were anything to go by.

There was an unholy creak in my neck from when my head hung downwards in my sleep. I didn't understand it. Never in my life had I fallen asleep sitting upright, and I didn't have any reminiscence of sitting on a chair and dozing off in the first place.

What the hell did I do last night?

I was momentarily annoyed with myself for falling asleep the way I did, but when I tried to arch my back and lift my arms into a stretch, I found that I couldn't. Panic set in. I tried to move my arms once more and was shocked to find that they weren't at my sides, instead they were behind my back, and something was wrapped tightly around my wrists, binding them together.

I struggled against the bond that held my hands in place, and this caused me to move my legs too. I whimpered when I couldn't move them either. I felt the pressure of something around each ankle as I tried to tug them free. Whatever it was, it was hard, and secured my limbs to the legs of the chair I was sitting upon.

What is happening? Where am I?

I didn't have answers to the questions that surged through my mind, and the not knowing was terrifying me. It didn't stop me from trying to get loose, though. I searched my mind for answers, just as I searched for a way to wriggle free from the bindings that took away my free will.

"You're going to chafe your skin if you keep struggling like that."

I yelped with fright and swung my head from side to side in a desperate attempt to remove the cover from my eyes, but it was no use. Whatever the material was, it was tied securely around my head and completely obscured my vision.

My already pounding heart kicked into overdrive, and the fear that flowed through me was so strong I felt like I was going to vomit. I struggled to breathe steadily, and to remain calm, but it was immensely difficult not to let my fear take over.

Any plan formed to keep myself tranquil went straight out the window when I closed my eyes and thought hard about how I came to be tied to a chair, with a stranger who obviously had me held captive. For a few seconds, my mind was blank, then like the snap of my fingers, images came rushing back one by one.

Ryder was cheating on me.

His brothers' knew what he was up to and never told me.

A man attacked me in my kitchen and somehow knocked me out.

The strange man who was *still* in my presence while I was blindfolded, tied to a chair and completely at his mercy... remaining calm was no longer on my fucking agenda.

"Who's there?" I asked, my breathing laboured.

This has to be a nightmare.

"A friend of the family," the man replied on a guffaw.

His accent was semi-similar to Ryder's and his brothers', and that scared me greatly. The only Americans I knew were either bright light, or pure evil. There was no in-between.

I felt like I was going to wet myself as I asked, "What do you want?"

The man hummed. "I have a debt to fulfil."

What kind of debt?

"This is a mistake," I blurted. "This *has* to be some sort of mistake. My family has no debts, I swear. You've got the wrong person!"

My captor sighed. "I'll explain all *that* in good time, but first, I need you to confirm something for me. You're Branna Murphy, right?"

A fresh surge of panic set in. This *wasn't* some kind of mistake, this man knew my name, which meant he purposely was in the right house and came after me for a reason.

"Ye-Yes." I stuttered.

"Then there is no mistake, you *are* the right person," the deep voice responded. "I've been waiting a few months to get you on your own"

"Why?" I swallowed down bile. "Who are you? What do you want from me?"

"Which question do you want me to answer first?" he asked, sounding bored.

A sheen of dread settled over me.

"The second," I whispered.

"Well, Branna," he began, "my name is Philip, but I believe you know me as Big Phil. It's a pleasure to meet you."

My world stop spinning, and it hit me that every moment throughout my life where I had ever felt scared or alone didn't come close to the emotions I felt during *that* moment. I was absolutely terrified, and almost instantly began whimpering and trying my hardest to get free because this man... he tried to kill my best friend and her son, and once upon a time he tried to kill Kane too... and now... now he was going to kill *me*.

"Oh, my God." I cried. "*Please*, don't kill me."

I heard movement, and every muscle in my body tensed as I felt the monster approach.

"Why would I kill you?" Big Phil asked me and I could hear the smile in his tone.

The sick bastard liked that I was petrified.

"Why else would you abduct me?" I asked, now hiccupping from crying so hard.

"To draw out Kane," he replied. "Why else?"

I swallowed down my fear, which was no small feat, and asked, "Wh-why would I draw out Kane? I'm n-not with him... I'm not even with his br-brother anymore. Ryder and I br-broke up."

"How devastating for you," Big Phil said, sounding like he couldn't care less.

I was shaking as my fear amplified.

"So you see," I sniffled, "I won't draw Kane out be-because—"

"If you *don't* draw Kane out then there will definitely be no use for you so I suggest you stop talking."

I clamped my mouth shut.

"I like you." He chortled. "You're obedient, not like that fucking Aideen bitch. She had a mouth on her."

I couldn't begin to imagine how Aideen could backtalk him when he had her, I was almost too scared to breathe in fear he would hurt me.

"I made a mistake with her. I wanted her to suffer, like my boy suffered, when what I should have done is put a bullet in her head and stomach. That would have *really* killed Kane."

"You bastard!"

It was out of my mouth before I realised I said it.

Big Phil laughed. "Ain't that the truth."

I continued to cry, and it grated on his nerves.

"Stop your blubbering, I haven't got the patience for it. I've worn out every ounce of tolerance I have for your *fucking* family."

I closed my mouth and tried my hardest to control my sobs, but it was difficult. It was like every ounce of strength I had up and left me, and I just accepted my fate like a coward. I wanted to be strong, but my body hurt, my head hurt, and my heart did, too—I honestly didn't know how it was still beating.

After what I saw with Ryder and his... *friend*, I was positive it would never work right again. I thought for sure the shock alone would kill me.

I wasn't stupid, in the back of my mind I knew we were all in constant danger from Big Phil. A man didn't attempt to murder a pregnant mother for revenge then just disappear because he failed. No, Big Phil had an agenda, and it was obvious it was one he was going to fulfil no matter what—or who—it cost.

It was unbelievable, but the threat of him and what he was capable of faded to the very back of my mind when my relationship problems took centre stage.

To be honest, I just didn't care about Big Phil, or the threat he posed to me when I thought about what my so-called partner did to me. I didn't care about anything because I was so focused on Ryder and how much he, and our relationship, had changed.

It was then that I wondered *why* I was so scared. When I thought hard about it, Big Phil kidnapping me was kind of—in a twisted way—a favour to me. If he killed me, I would be at peace. No more sadness, no more bleeding for Ryder and the love we once shared, no more of anything. If he beat on me, maybe he would hit me so hard that it would erase my witnessing Ryder with another women. Maybe one solid knock to my head and he could wipe out all the heartache I carried and I could start over on a clean slate.

It suddenly became very tempting to anger him just to see if he would do it.

"You aren't shaking anymore," Big Phil commented, gaining my attention.

He was right. I wasn't shaking anymore. If I was being completely honest, I didn't really feel fear anymore either, what I felt was curiosity. This man could take all my suffering away, what the hell was there to fear about *that*?

"'Cause I'm not scared anymore," I replied, my voice firm.

This made him laugh before he asked, "Where are we, Branna?"

How in the Hell was I supposed to know? I wondered. *I had a blindfold covering my eyes for God's sake.*

"Darkness?" I guessed.

"Why would I take you to a nightclub?" he curiously asked.

I managed to shrug. "It's where me sister and friends were taken to when they were kidnapped, so I figured since you American arseholes and wanna-be gangsters are all alike, you would take me there, too. It's unoriginal which makes it the best bet."

Big Phil laughed loudly as I winced when I felt the sting of his slap as it tore through the side of my face.

Bastard.

"One of those American assholes you speak of was my friend, so watch what you say about him or I'll make you bleed."

There was a bro code between criminal scumbags, who'd have thought it? My mind sneered. *Not me.*

I wanted to make my thoughts know, but instead I grunted and kept my mouth shut because bleeding didn't sound appealing in the slightest.

"We're in my rented apartment." He eventually said.

That surprised me.

"You took me to your place?" I questioned. "Why?"

I heard him move around.

"Because I want to spend time with you in a comfortable environment."

Did that mean he wasn't going to kill me? I wondered and was surprised that the thought saddened me.

"How long do you plan to keep me here?" I asked, hoping the fear I felt didn't show in my tone. He would probably link it to fear of *being* killed if he did pick up on it anyway.

He hummed. "As long as it takes."

I furrowed my brows. *As long as what takes?*

"What are you talkin' about?" I asked in frustration.

I froze when I heard more movement close by and felt him approach me. The floorboards creaked under his weight as he stepped on them. I flinched then tensed up when I felt a rough pat on the crown of my head.

"You ask a lot of questions for a captive."

I actually grinned as I said, "If you wanted peace then you should've kidnapped a mute."

Things were silent for a few moments then Big Phil guffawed. I lost my grin, drew my brows together and glared at him through my blindfold. He was maddening.

"You're amusing me greatly."

I set my jaw. "Glad I can entertain you."

Another chortle.

"Are you going to be silent enough for me to answer your earlier questions?"

I hesitated. "I kind of forget what they were."

"You asked why you were here and if I was going to kill you, and I'm prepared to answer them."

It was twisted that I got a tad bit excited at the prospect of knowing my fate. Would it end in freedom or death—in a perfect world, the latter would win.

"Oh, right," I said. "Go ahead, I'll be quiet while you speak."

"Thank you," he said sarcastically.

"You're welcome," I replied, just as sarcastically.

A snort or two later, the piece of scum began to talk.

"Originally, my plan was never to come for you, or even for Aideen, it's always been Kane that I've wanted. You can't catch someone like him off guard though. I created him, and I know firsthand what he is capable of doing when he's backed into a corner."

I gritted my teeth in anger. He was speaking of Kane like he was some animal he trained... I suppose for a time, he *was* that, but not anymore!

"Then I got to thinking," Big Phil continued. "Who would it hurt if I managed to kill Kane? None other than his brothers, and I don't want that, I want *him* to suffer. When I got here last year, I watched him for a while, to see if there was someone important in his life outside of his family, and that's when I came to know about Aideen, and her pregnancy. It was like God Himself was gifting me the lives I needed to end that would finally break Kane and force him to live with the pain I do."

Sickness swirled in my lower abdomen, and I fought with my

body not to heave.

"You're a ragin' fuckin' lunatic."

"My son was murdered, of *course* I'm a lunatic." Big Phil argued. "You think losing your child keeps you sane?"

Kane stumbled upon his 'precious son' violating a little girl; he deserved a medal for ending the waste of space's life, nothing less.

I shook my head. "Your son was a dirty paedophile who hurt children, it was justifiable what he got. I personally think he got off too eas—"

Big Phil cut me off with a bang to the face. It was so forceful, that the knock caused me to surge backwards, tipping the chair until it fell and hit the ground. I cried out in pain as fire spread across my cheek and pounding pain erupted at the back of my head.

"I'll kill you right now if you talk about my son like that again, do you hear me?"

Death—to just be gone from this Earth, was what I wanted, but I couldn't bring myself to ask for it. I didn't acknowledge Big Phil's warning, I only continued to whine in pain.

"That's why *you're* here," he pressed. "I can't have Aideen, and your sister is always with Nico. Alec and his woman are together constantly as well. That other girl in your group is single, and Damien has no one so that left *you*. I thought you would be as hard as the others to snatch, but I've come to learn a lot about Ryder's routine, and yours. He leaves you alone a lot with only Damien for protection when you aren't at the hospital. That was the weak link in your chain, and I took advantage of it."

It sent chills up my spine that a stranger knew so much about us. It was a feeling I couldn't describe—it made my already churned stomach twist once more.

"So that's the answer to *that* question," I said, curtly. "What's the answer to me other one?"

I yelped when the chair I was bound to was pulled back into an upright position, and the blindfold I wore was yanked from my face. My instant reaction was to close my eyes until they adjusted to the light. It didn't take long because the room I was in was dimly lit, and thanks to the window facing me, I could see through the net curtains that it was dark outside.

How long am I here?

I felt a presence to my left, so I turned and looked at the man who stood next to me. He was taller than the brothers with a normal build, but his face was severely scarred. He reminded me of *Freddie Kruger*, and that thought didn't bode well with me. I refused to show it though.

"Well, aren't you a sight for sore eyes."

He slapped me across the face, and then laughed.

"I think you're a bigger pain in the ass than Aideen was."

I scrunched up my face in pain before I turned my head back in his direction and glared up at him. "I'll take that as a compliment."

"You shouldn't," he countered. "Mouthy pieces of ass give me headaches, and you and Aideen are a cut above the rest. I don't understand what Ryder and Kane see in you both."

I wasn't fazed by the insult.

"You won't ever want to meet Bronagh or Keela then, they're *worse* than us."

Big Phil lips quirked before he walked away from me and moved over to a fireplace across the room. He opened up a small bag of coal, threw two or three pieces into the already lit fire along with some wooden sticks. He reached over and lifted a poker from its stand and used it to move around the fire contents.

I used his distraction to take in my surroundings. I was surprised at what I saw because for some reason, when he said he brought me to his apartment, I envisioned it as being small, dark, cold and dirty, but it was the complete opposite. The sitting room I was in was really spacious and even with the lights dimmed, you could see everything clearly—the decor was beautiful. I wasn't expecting such an evil scumbag to be living in such a nice place.

"Why'd you pick such a nice place to live?" I asked, still glancing around.

"Because I have standards," Big Phil replied in *duh* tone.

I rolled my eyes.

"It wasn't nice when I moved in," he continued. "I decorated it because once Kane is dead, I plan on ending my life too. My son is gone, and once his life is avenged, there is no reason for me to exist anymore. I want the place where I'm going to die to be comfortable... the condition it was in before didn't cut it."

If I didn't know what a scumbag he was, and what a monster his son was, I'd think him a pretty great father.

"I won't kill you," he suddenly said, regaining my attention.

He was still hunkered down in front of the fire, but the poker he had a few moments ago was still in the fire—the pointy end was anyway.

"Why not?" I asked, curious to know why.

I wasn't pleased with his answer because if he didn't kill me, it meant I would leave here and go back to my life of nothingness.

"If I didn't know any better, I'd say you were sad with my answer."

I shrugged. "I rather die than listen to you talk, but you can't blame me."

I wasn't letting him know a thing about my life, it would only give him more information about me, and he had enough of *that*.

Big Phil laughed. "Smartass."

I looked away from him and scanned the room once more. If I wasn't going to die here, then I needed to figure a way out. The door leading out of the sitting room was closed, and the only other exits were two windows in the room. I wasn't sure how high up the apartment was, and from my angle, the window I could see out of, there was no fire escape next to it so I had no way down even if I somehow managed to get free and get it open.

"If you aren't goin' to kill me," I said and returned my attention to Big Phil. "What are you goin' to do with me?"

He smiled at me but it didn't improve his face whatsoever, in fact, it only made him look creepier.

"You're the bait."

I blinked. "Lucky me."

"I'm goin' to contact Kane, tell him I have you, then set up an exchange. I'm not playing around anymore. He took a life, and I plan to reciprocate.by taking his."

I felt like I was in a very bad non-fantasy *Avengers* film with the crap this man was spewing.

"He won't leave his fiancée and son."

"Bullshit," Big Phil growled. "I know Kane, and he considers you family. He will come for you if I ask, he will know I hold your life in my hands."

I set my jaw. "Fine, let's say he comes, he won't be alone and you know that."

"I have more than one bullet, Branna. Kane *will* die tonight, and if another Slater brother or two being put down first gets that result, then so be it."

"You disgusting son of a bitch!" I bellowed and fear shot through me. "Stay the *hell* away from me family!"

He laughed at me then took out his phone. "Give me his number."

"Fuck you!"

He moved across the room to me in a couple of seconds and fisted his hand on my hair. He pulled my hair with such force that I felt him pulling clumps out at the root. I screamed and tried not to give into him, or the pain, but it hurt too much.

I cried out Kane's number so Big Phil released me, punched the numbers into his phone and put it to his ear. He stroked my face as I cried from the throbbing in my head. He remained in front of me when he began speaking.

"Guess who?" Big Phil sneered.

I closed my eyes and wished for a way to get free so I could push this waste of space into the burning fire across the room and finish the job Kane started all those years ago.

"You know why I'm calling you. You're missing someone from

your close knit group, are you not?" Big Phil chuckled after a couple of seconds. "You always were a smart cookie."

I heard shouting then.

"There is no need for that language, or for the yelling, I'm on the phone with you, not a thousand miles away. I can hear you perfectly."

He was *such* a dickhead.

I jumped and opened my eyes when the phone was pressed to my ear.

"Confirm you're here."

I licked my lips and said, "Kane?"

I heard sharp intakes of breath, then a whimper or two. Big Phil then pulled the phone away and put it on speaker so he could hear what was being said to me.

"I'm here," he said. "We all are."

I heard the echo on Kane's end—he had me on speakerphone, too.

My eyes instantly pooled with tears.

"Let 'im kill me, okay? Don't come for me, he plans to kill you all just to get to you Kane—"

Big Phil pulled the phone away from my ear and punched me in the stomach, which caused me wheeze, and choke on air as blinding pain consumed me. He hit me on the head once more but I barely felt that over the agony in my stomach. I felt a sharp tug as he fisted his hand in my hair one more time. It took a minute, but when I could focus on something other than my pain, I heard all sorts of screaming coming from the phone in Big Phil's hand.

"Stop," my sister pleaded. "Please, stop hurtin' her. She's done nothin' wrong! *Please*."

"I *will* kill you for this, Philip," Ryder cut in, his voice menacing. "What you do to her, consider it child's play compared to what I will do to you."

My heart jumped the second I heard his voice and was shocked at the instant anger I had towards him but still wanted nothing more than to be in his arms.

"You probably will, but I plan to put your brother down, too, boy. Let's see who can make good on their promise first."

Before Ryder could reply, Big Phil walked over to the fireplace, took something from the mantle piece, and then advanced back on me. I was whimpering in pain already, but when I saw what was in his hand I screamed.

"No!" I pleaded. "Stay away from me."

He had a blade of some sort in his hand, it was sharp, long and I knew it was going to be inside of some part of my body soon. I fought against my restraints with that knowledge. Without speaking to me, or acknowledging my pleas in any way, Big Phil kneeled before me and jammed the blade into my thigh and pulled, slicing my flesh open.

The scream that tore out of me was one you would hear in a horror film.

"Branna!" Ryder roared, but this time his voice sounded far away.

I heard Kane's shouts from the speakerphone, too, but everything blended together except the pain I felt. It consumed me, and with every pulse of my beating heart, it became more agonising.

Big Phil lied; he *was* going to kill me, because my body couldn't take much more.

I felt a sharp pain in my shoulder then, and when I looked to see what was causing it, I widened my eyes as I watched the blade that cut my thigh, being pulled from my shoulder. I stared at my now bleeding wound and felt lightheaded.

He stabbed me. Again.

"Omigod," I whispered and continued to stare at it.

Surprisingly, I didn't move a muscle; instead I sat still as I felt blood seep out of the hole that now marred my shoulder.

Things were quiet and eerily peaceful in that moment until suddenly the shock of what just happened wore off and the agony set in. I cried out when what felt like fire filled my shoulder, and thigh then quickly turned to a sickening throbbing. Each pain pulse reminding me that this was real, and not some sick nightmare.

I'm really somebody's captive, and he is really going to kill me.

"Stop your screaming," Big Phil hissed. "They're just flesh wounds, not deep enough for you to bleed out, so *stop*."

Oh, they were just flesh wounds. That made them not hurt.

"Ryder?" he suddenly said, tapping on the screen on his phone and placing it against his ear. "Are you still there?"

I held my breath when Big Phil spoke even though the throbbing in my shoulder and thigh demanded I scream to release some of the pain I felt.

"I'm going to cut to the chase, I want Kane for Branna."

Silence.

"You want to test me right now?" the sick fuck laughed. "I'm putting you back on speaker. I want you to *hear* her more clearly so you understand I'm *not* playing."

He put his phone down on the table close by and he advanced on me once more, his eyes locked on me with a sick smirk on his face.

"Get away from me," I pleaded then screamed bloody murder when he reached me and grabbed hold of my wounded shoulder, pressing his thumb into the wound.

"I'll kill you!" Ryder's voice screamed through the phone.

Big Phil laughed some more as he moved away from me and picked up the poker from the fire. I cried then, tears falling from my eyes in streams.

"Please," I sobbed. "*Please* don't do this. I'm *beggin'* you."

My pleas only fuelled him on, and in seconds he was standing before me holding the burning red head poker inches away from my skin. I could already feel the boiling heat from it, and I whimpered in fear.

"Tell Ryder what I have in my hand, Branna."

"A...a hot poker." I answered, my voice shaking.

Big Phil nodded. "And what am I going to do with it?"

I cried. "Please, don't."

"You're bleeding more than I'd like, so it has to be done." He said to me making it sound like he was doing me a favour.

"You shouldn't have stabbed me then!" I shouted.

Big Phil ignored me, and pressed the hot end of the poker against my wound and for a few seconds I was consumed by darkness. I came to just as the same blinding pain consumed my leg and I blacked out once more, my body falling to the side and hitting the floor with a loud thud.

"Branna?" Ryder's voice screamed. "BRANNA?"

"Shut up fucking screaming!" Big Phil snapped as he lifted the chair, and me, back to an upright position. "She's fine, just passed out for a second. I used the scalding poker end to burn her wounds to stop her bleeding. You're welcome."

"When I fucking get my hands on you," Ryder swore, "I'm going to kill you slowly. I'm going to make you beg for death!"

"I'm not afraid to die," Big Phil dryly replied. "It's only a heartbeat away."

I willed myself to stay awake, though my body pleaded desperately to succumb to the bliss that was darkness. I managed to open my eyes in time to see that the next thing Big Phil cut was the restraints on my ankles and wrists. I fell forward when my limbs fell free, but he caught me and hauled me over to the big sofa near the fire. He dropped me onto it, and it was the stupidest thing to think of considering the circumstances, but the sofa was like landing on a soft cloud and for a moment I felt like I was already in Heaven.

"If you move, you'll be sorry."

I didn't reply to Big Phil when he spoke to me because I was simply too weak to. I hurt all over, and felt like never moving again. I heard more talking and shouting coming from both parties on the phone, but I couldn't pay attention any longer and I allowed myself to fall into sweet, sweet darkness.

"Wake up."

Those two words were the first thing I heard, the second was my own heartbeat, and the third was my scream as it tore from my throat. *Pain.* So much fucking pain. It filled me from head to toe and it was constant.

I opened my eyes and whimpered when I realised I was still trapped in Hell.

"Please," I pleaded to no one. "Please, help me."

My voice sounded scratchy, and felt like it needed a big glass of water to soothe away the ache in my throat.

"They're in the building," Big Phil mumbled, making his presence known. "I just buzzed them in."

I had no idea who he was talking to; I looked at him and found him gazing out of the window with a gun in one hand, and a glass of brown liquid in the other. My eyes lingered on the gun for a few moments, and I prayed to God that he wouldn't use it.

"Wha-what are you sayin'?" I asked as I lifted my right arm and used my hand to press against my left wounded shoulder in an attempt to stop the pulsing sting.

"The Slaters," Big Phil replied. "I just buzzed them into the building, they'll be here soon. I unlocked the front door for them."

What?

"Why?" I asked, trying to control my sobs. "Why did they come?"

"For you," he replied and took a sip from his glass. "I told you they would."

"You can't hurt them, please, just—"

"Be. Quiet." He growled. "This isn't about you anymore. You can leave if you want to, you have served your purpose."

I made an attempt to sit up, but hot pain filled my leg keeping me from doing so. When I jerked in response to the pain, I fell to the side, off the sofa, and hit the floor with a sickening smack.

"Branna?"

Kane.

"No!" I cried. "Get away!

I heard quick paced footsteps, then a loud bang as the door to the sitting room was swung open and cracked against the wall.

"Oh, my God," I heard Kane rasp.

I tried to turn over to see him, but I couldn't. I was so weak, and hurting so much that even breathing was a struggle.

"Kane," I groaned. "Get out."

While you still can.

"What the *fuck* have you done to her?" he asked, his voice gruff.

"It looks worse than it is," Big Phil responded as he turned around. "She brought most of it on herself if I'm being honest."

"Kane," I rasped as I forced myself to roll onto my back. "Run, he has a gun!"

I reached up with my good arm, gripped onto the arm of the sofa and pulled myself into a sitting position. I blinked when I saw Kane standing mere metres away from me. He was dressed... odd. It looked like he had on hospital scrubs, and booties people wore over there shoes when then didn't want to get dirt or stain on a floor.

"He doesn't want to shoot me," Kane replied to me, but kept his eyes on Big Phil. "He wants me to suffer like I made his piece of shit kid suffer. A bullet will be too quick."

Fear gripped me when Big Phil dropped his glass to the ground and didn't flinch when it smashed to pieces. I screamed when he lifted his hand that contained the gun and pointed it directly at Kane's head.

"Where are the rest of your brothers'?" Big Phil asked, sounding eerily calm.

"At home... it took a lot of convincing, especially with my oldest brother who wants to tear you limb from limb for hurting his woman... but they know ending your miserable life is my task. Mine *alone*. I'll make you pay for everything."

Big Phil sneered. "The student has come to take out the master, huh?"

"Something like that," Kane growled through gritted teeth.

Big Phil gestured to Kane's cover-ups with the gun he still had trained on him.

"You want no trace of you ever being here, do you?" he humourlessly sniggered. "If you manage to kill me, you won't need to have gone to such extremes. This apartment may look nice because I did it up, but the rest of the place is a dive. No cameras, no security, and no paper trails. The son of a bitch who owns this place made the rooms sound proof too, he runs a brothel on the first five floors, and I'm pretty sure he runs a drug cocktail lab on the sixth."

"Is that why you picked here?" I asked, my voice sounding like sandpaper. "Killin' us, and then yourself, won't draw attention... not until your rent is due at least."

Big Phil sniggered, and I took his merriment as a big whopping yes.

"You're going to off yourself?" Kane probed Big Phil. "Really?"

"What's left for me once you're dead?" he grilled.

Kane didn't acknowledge the question, instead he asked, "Do you really want to shoot me, or do you just want me to hurt? All those times you hit me and stabbed me with needles to punish me, and now you switch to bullets? Have you lost your creativity? Does burying a hell-bound child do that to you?"

I wanted to tell Kane to stop, because with each verbal jab, Big Phil's face was getting redder and redder.

"This is for Johnny." Big Phil suddenly exclaimed then surprised me by *dropping* the gun to the floor. "This is for everything you have put me through."

"*You're* my last job, you son of a bitch!" Kane spat before he ran at Big Phil, and speared him to the ground.

The sickening sound of fists connecting with flesh would forever be seared into my brain. It was relentless, and I wanted it to end as quickly as it begun.

I could do nothing but watch Kane and Big Phil roll around on the floor, but I was delighted to see that Kane had the upper hand.

He was landing all the hits… it almost looked like Big Phil wasn't even trying to fight him back. I knew how much of a snake he could be though, so I used my good leg to push myself up into a standing position, and I hobbled over to where he dropped the handgun.

The pain I felt surged me on, and when I picked up the gun, I allowed my adrenaline to take over.

"Kane, move!" I ordered.

He turned his head so he could look at me, and his eyes widened almost instantly.

"Branna, no!" he shouted and hit Big Phil once more across the face so he could break free and jump to his feet.

With Kane out of the way I had a clear view of Big Phil and was shaking as I pointed the gun at him. I squinted my eyes to make sure my aim was precise.

"Branna, *no*!" Kane said again, but this time his voice was different, like he was pleading *without* having to beg.

My arms were trembling as I kept the gun aimed at Big Phil, my body was weakened and exhausted from the torture he had put me through. The gun was heavier than it looked and it caused my arms to ache from holding it up in the air for just a few short moments.

"Branna, this is not your call, okay? Look at me," Kane said, his voice firm but soothing at the same time. I flicked my eyes to his. He slowly came to my side, and carefully lifted his hand to mine, but I quickly stepped away when his intentions became clear. He wanted the gun.

"He isn't worth it, Bran."

Kane was right… Big Phil *wasn't* worth it, but that didn't mean he didn't have to die.

"Look what he has done to you." I snivelled. "To our family!"

"We're *still* a family," Kane assured me. "And he has no hold over me anymore. He has nothing. He *is* nothing."

I began to lower the gun, until finally it hung in my hand by my side.

"Good girl," Kane breathed in relief, his shoulders sagging. "It's all going to be—"

"Kane!" I screamed when Big Phil pushed himself from the floor, and charged at Kane. Every thing felt like it happened in slow motion. Big Phil grabbed the knife he used to hurt me from the table he rushed past, and sprinted at Kane with the knife-wielding arm raised.

Kane swung around, and grabbed hold of Big Phil's arm as he began to bring it down in his direction. They both struggled for the knife, and I saw the muscles and veins in Kane's are bulge as he used all his might to keep Big Phil's arm at bay. My arm was raised once more and the gun was pointed straight ahead, but I didn't pull the trigger because I didn't have a clear shot. I couldn't risk hitting Kane.

I tensed when the pair of them hit the floor, for a moment there was grunts, and fumbled movements, then the next there was a sharp intake of breath, and everything went still. Kane was on top of Big Phil, but neither of them were moving.

I heard my heartbeat in my ear as I approached them.

"Kane," I whispered.

Silence.

Oh, please, no.

"Kane," I said a little louder.

I heard a wheeze then and rasp of, "I'm okay."

Relief smacked into me like a tidal wave.

I watched as Kane rolled of Big Phil and groggily pushed himself to his feet. He stumbled for a second then steadied himself. He looked down at a still unmoving Big Phil then he turned and walked towards me. Before he could reach me, I dropped to the ground like a sack of potatoes when I saw the scene before me.

The blade that was used to stab my thigh and shoulder… it was lodged in the centre of Big Phil's chest.

"Oh, my God," I breathed.

"Branna, slow your breathing—"

"Is he dead?" I cut Kane off, my chest tight with fear. "Is he fuckin' *dead*?"

"Yeah," he replied, calmly. "He took his last breath, and I saw the life leave his eyes. I saw the moment he realised I was going to be the last thing he saw before he died, so I smiled."

Christ.

"Oh, my God," I rasped. "He is dead. Oh, we're goin' to prison. We're seriously goin'—"

"We're aren't going anywhere if you do *exactly* what I say."

What?

"Kane?" I whispered. "I'm scared."

He dropped to his knees next to me, and his eyes scanned over my body and grew dark when they landed on my stab wounds, spilled blood and other injuries. He carefully reached out and slipped an arm under my legs, and the other under my back.

"I'm sorry," he whispered.

Sorry?

"For wha—" I cut myself of with a moan of pain when he lifted me up into the air, and the movement caused my wounded limbs to burn in protest. He quickly moved me back to the sofa and gently lay me down.

"You have to call the cops," he quickly said. "I'm going to leave down the back entrance when you do. There are no cameras in this building, but to make sure I'm not picked up on surrounding business' cameras, I'll use the back exit. You have to call them and say you've been kidnapped."

I didn't have time to argue with him even if I wanted to because he thrust the phone Big Phil used to call Kane into my face, so I grabbed it and dialled 999 before I lost my nerve. Almost instantly someone replied.

"999, what is your emergency?"

"Please help me," I cried which was very easy to do considering everything that had happened to me. "A man has kidnapped me, I think I'm dyin'. He stabbed me twice and beat me."

"Ma'am, slow down. This man, is he still close by?"

"Yes!" I wailed and then quickly thought of a lie. "He's in the buildin', he left his phone here by mistake and I grabbed it. He said he would be right back though. Please send someone. *Please*."

"Stay on the line with me, ma'am. Where are you? Do you see anything that can give us a clue to your location?"

"Me location?" I repeated and looked at Kane with wild eyes.

He held up a matchbox that had the name of the building, but to play it dumb I said, "I'm in the new apartments across from The Plaza Hotel, I can see the buildin'!"

"Top floor," Kane whispered.

"I think I'm on the top floor, it's really high up!"

"Okay, ma'am we have a unit dispatched to your location. Stay on the line with me okay? What is your name?"

"Branna Murphy," I replied. "Please, hurry. Please—"

I was cut off when Kane grabbed the phone from my hand and threw it on the floor, smashing it.

"Why?" I asked staring at the now useless device.

"You gave them your location, and a unit is on the way. They'll get here soon."

I nodded.

"You're goin' to be okay," Kane said firmly. "I promise."

I hoped he was right.

He stood up and said, "I have to go."

Fear gripped me.

"Don't leave me, Kane." I begged and reached for him with my good arm. "Please."

A look of anguish passed over his face.

"The cops are coming, they'll arrest me if they catch me here."

I still didn't want him to leave me.

"Branna, they will call an ambulance right away. I promise."

I tried to move, but my body was drained, and I only managed a slight twitch.

"He is dead, he can't hurt you. I stabbed him in the chest, and I think it went straight through his heart. If the cops ask, say he came back and fought you for the phone and you were able to grab the blade and stab him when he came at you. Okay?"

I sucked in a breath.

"Okay," I rasped. "I'll say I killed 'im."

"It will be self-defence." He said then jumped to his feet. "I'm using the back stairs and exit, don't mention anything about me being here, can you do that?"

I nodded, and Kane looked like he had to force himself to walk away from me.

"I'll show up at the hospital with everyone else as soon as they call your sister. I promise."

He was gone then, and once more I was alone with Big Phil. The only thing that comforted me was this time, the piece of scum wasn't breathing. I sat up and stared at his body, mainly at his chest, just to make sure he was faking it. I wanted to make sure he was *really* dead. I didn't have to think twice about whether he was really gone or not when I saw the fast growing pool of blood gather around him. It was impossible to tell what colour his shirt originally was because it was soaked with dark red blood.

When I couldn't sit up any longer, I lay back on the sofa for so long that I felt myself begin to relax to the point where I could go asleep if I wanted to, the adrenaline I was feeling earlier now completely gone. I closed my eyes and when I opened them next it was because I heard a loud bang then an awful crunching sound.

"Oh, shite," I heard a male voice hiss. "It wasn't a prank call. Radio it in and get an ambulance here ASAP. Possible suspect is down, and the victim looks to be in bad shape."

"Copy that." Another male voice replied then moved away as he spoke using weird code words.

I flinched when I felt a hand on my forehead.

"You're goin' to be okay," the first man said. "An ambulance is on the way, ma'am."

I lifted one of my eyelids open, and for a moment everything was blurry, then my vision focused, and a handsome man was leaning over me. The first thing I noticed about him was his eyes—they were bright blue. The second thing was the uniform he had on.

"Garda?" I whispered.

The man nodded. "Yeah, I'm a Garda, sweetheart. You're safe, I won't let anyone hurt you."

I didn't think I had enough energy to even feel relief, but I did and it slammed into me at that moment.

"He stabbed me, and tried to kill me," I whispered, my eyes becoming blurry once more as tears filled them. They spilled over the brims, and slid down my temples and into my hair. "I stabbed him in the chest... I had no choice... he was goin' to kill me. He said so."

I felt a hand press against my shoulder, and I cried out in pain.

"I'm so sorry," the Garda said, "I need to slow the bleedin' until the paramedics get here."

That fucking hot poker didn't do its job.

"Am I goin' to die?" I asked.

"No," came the man's instant response. "You aren't goin' to die. Look at me, you *aren't* goin' to die."

I didn't know whether to believe him or not, because I felt like I was dying.

"I killed 'im," I whispered. "I *really* killed 'im."

"You had no choice, darlin'. It was your life or his, and I'm glad it was his."

I nodded. "Who is he?"

"No idea yet, did say why he abducted you?"

I forced more tears out. "He said he wanted to... to rape me, and keep me, but I fought back and he hurt me."

"Son of bitch," the Garda hissed.

He was lapping my story up like a starved dog.

"Don't let 'im get me," I mumbled and closed my eyes when they suddenly became too heavy. I wanted to continue with my act, but I couldn't, everything became too draining to keep up.

"Ms Murphy?" the man's voice shouted as I felt my body being shaken. "Branna? Fuck! Mikey, where is that ambulance?"

"On the way!"

I felt myself being pulled away from everything, and damn if it didn't feel good *not* to feel anything.

"Stay with me, Branna. Be strong."

Be strong.

Beep.

Beep.

Beep.

That's what woke me up. Not a loud piercing sound, just a steady beeping that would more than likely grate on my nerves if I had to endure listening to it for a long period of time.

What the hell was beeping?

It wasn't my phone alarm, I knew that much. I mentally groaned when I realised I was going to have to get up and go find the source of the unholy noise so I could put a stop to it. I quickly found that idea was out the window when I adjusted my body slightly, and tenderness caused me to whimper.

"Branna?" a familiar voice said at the same time a hand clasped mine. "It's Damien. I'm here, and you're okay."

Why is Damien in my bedroom?

I squeezed his hand, but the action was weakly executed. When I opened my eyes, it took a couple of blinks for anything to come into focus, but when I could see clearly, my little brother's face was leaning over me.

"Hey," he breathed, and if I didn't know any better, I would think he had tears in his eyes.

Why does he have tears in his eyes? I wondered. *Did I forget to make him breakfast again?*

"Dame—" I cut myself off when a pain in my throat caused my voice to sound raspy, and feel like sandpaper.

"Open up," Damien urged. "I have water."

I opened my mouth and gulped down the water offered to me. It felt like liquid heaven sliding down my throat. It hurt a little swallowing, but the ache wasn't as bad as before.

"Thanks," I said and cleared my throat.

I focused on Damien once more, and when I flicked my eyes beyond him, I took in my surroundings that were most definitely *not* my bedroom.

"What the hell?" I breathed. "Where am I?"

"The hospital," Damien said as he made himself my prime view. "You were brought here a few hours ago. We're all here; everyone is just down the hallway with the doctor. They all wanted to hear what he had to say, but I wanted to stay here with you in case you woke up, and you did. I'm so fucking happy you did, Mama Bear."

Damien did cry then.

"Dame," I said, panicked. "Don't cry, honey. I'm okay."

I had no idea what happened, but I was awake and I was talking so that must have meant I was okay. Or would be okay.

"Before they cleaned you up you had so much blood on you, we didn't know if—"

"Damien," I cut him off. "What happened to me?"

I felt a bit of pain, but mostly my body felt like it was floating on a cloud.

"Don't you remember?" he asked, wiping his eyes with the back of his hand. I shook my head and he continued, "Big Phil took you to lure Kane to his apartment."

As soon as he said the name Big Phil, I remembered everything. Everything I felt, every word I spoke and heard, and everything I saw.

Kane.

"Kane," I said then quickly lowered my voice. "Is he okay?"

Damien nodded. "He's perfect, not a hair out of place."

The relief that hit me caused my eyes to well up.

"It's okay," Damien crooned. "It's all over. He's gone and is never coming back."

The image of the blade used to hurt me sticking out of Big

Phil's chest was once I'd never forget.

"I'm glad it's over," I whispered..

"Me too."

I inhaled a deep breath. "I'm so tired, me eyes hurt to keep open."

"Get your rest, the doctor mentioned to Ryder before they left the room that you'd need plenty of it."

Ryder.

I lazily blinked as my eyelids became heavier.

"Where is he?"

"With the doctor," Damien answered. "Everyone else is too."

I nodded.

"He wanted to go and get you himself," he quickly added. "But if he did that then he wouldn't be able to finally be done with the Feds."

The who?

I furrowed my brows. "What are you talkin' about?"

"You know the thing Ryder and my brothers kept from us?" he asked, lifting his arm so he could scratch his neck.

I managed a nod.

"Yeah, well, let's just say it's a fucking *shit* storm."

I felt my eyelids droop.

"Can't be any worse than what's happenin' here," I mumbled.

"It's just as bad," Damien grunted.

That wasn't good.

"Tell me about it when I wake up."

My eyes closed just as my sister's voice could be heard, my friends, too.

"Oh, my God!" Bronagh cried. "Is she dead? She looks worse!"

"No," Damien replied instantly. "She was *just* talking to me. She's really weak from blood loss, and the nurse came in after you left to talk with the doctor and upped her morphine to manage her pain. With that combination it's no wonder she's out. I'm surprised she woke up so soon in the first place."

"What did she say?" Alannah's voice asked, nervousness sounding in her tone.

"She wanted water, so I gave her some. She wasn't really with it, but she knew who I was which is good. It means her memory isn't affected."

"Thank God," a few voices murmured.

"What did the doctors say to you about her?" Damien quizzed.

"He said it could have been a lot worse," Alec explained. "She has flesh wounds, but nothing serious now that the bleeding is stopped. A few of her ribs are bruised, her face, too, but that's it. No long term damage."

"It's not the physical damage I'm worried about," Keela said, her voice tight with what I think was emotion. "It's the mental. What that bastard did to her will haunt her."

"You all were exposed to evil like Branna was, and you have overcome it." Alec quickly stated. "She will, too. She's strong."

Be strong.

"Please," my sister whispered close to my ear. "Don't leave me. I love you so much, Branna."

I love you, too.

I wanted to verbally say it, but I couldn't. I couldn't speak or move. My senses were beginning to shut down.

"You got this, Bran," Aideen said, and I wanted to force myself to open my eyes when I could hear in her voice that she was about to cry. "You're too strong not be okay."

Be strong.

I heard quick paced footsteps, then a loud intake of breath.

"Oh, Christ, she looks even paler than before!"

Ryder.

"She's okay," everyone whisper-shouted in unison.

I heard more movement, and then I felt a hand on my chest, and a hand on the crown of my head then lips on my forehead.

"I'm so sorry," Ryder whispered. "I'm *so* sorry, baby."

"Ry," my sister sniffled. "She's goin' to be okay. She won't leave us, I know she won't."

I felt a droplet of liquid fall onto my cheek, then another one quickly landing on my nose. I didn't know what it was, until I heard sniffling right next to me.

Oh, please, no.

"I love you so much," Ryder said, his voice breaking. "Please, don't go anywhere."

He was crying. I heard his sobs perfectly as he pressed his face against mine, and I knew that everyone in the room heard him, too, because he wasn't trying to hide the fact that he was crying, he was wailing as if nobody was watching.

It was then that I fully shut down and silently drifted into darkness, even though inside, I was screaming.

CHAPTER FOURTEEN

Three weeks later...

"I'm goin' for a walk," I said to my sister. "I'm goin' batshit crazy being cooped up in here."

It had been three weeks since the attack and death of Big Phil, and my life had become a shit-storm. An even *bigger* one than before.

Health wise—I was on the mend and each day my pain became less and less. I got more movement out of my shoulder and leg without nagging discomfort as well which I was most thankful for because being bed ridden wasn't for me at all, I was used to being on my feet and suddenly being off them *sucked*.

Work wise—I was on paid leave. The Health Board was made aware of what happened to me, and they booked me with a therapist to talk about everything—when I was ready—before I could return to work. Ash was the only person in the hospital who knew what happened to me. He didn't know *everything*, just that I was attacked and taken to a dangerous man's apartment that ended in his death. He had been incredible, and even though I was sure it was very difficult for him to have heard my actual kidnapping over the phone. He was the one who called my family and told them what he heard; it's why they were all together as they awaited Big Phil's call. When he was told not to call the Gardaí, he listened and trusted Ryder and his brothers. He made sure to visit and call me as often as he usually would when I got home. The normality of it made me feel a little more like myself.

Law wise—Everything had gone perfectly. After I gave my detailed statement in the hospital of what happened with Big Phil—the lying version Kane coached me on—the Gardaí only came to see me a few more times to follow up on a few minor things. To them, it was obvious that what 'I' did was out of self-defence so there was no need for any trails of any kind. The suspect who harmed me was dead, and I was okay. Case closed.

Privacy wise—I had none. You would think being attacked, kidnapped and almost killed would be punishment enough, but according to the media, my story was everyone's business. My attack made front-page news in the papers, and even onto the evening news. It was a choppy story they were presenting because I refused permission for interviews, and the right for anyone to use my name and photo, and since the Gardaí couldn't find any trace of Big Phil's existence anywhere, they had no information on him either, just that he kidnapped a girl then was killed in self-defence. It was a mystery to the world, and that was the way we wanted it to remain.

Family wise—I was at my wits' end. My sister, the girls and Ryder's brothers all became mother hens, and while I greatly appreciated their help, it was driving me bloody insane. Someone was always with me, they never let me do anything for myself and if I winced or made any sound that showed my pain, they were right there trying to shove pain pills down my throat.

Relationship wise—mine was non-existent. I thought that when I saw Ryder for the first time after I woke up in the hospital that I would want nothing more than for him to hold me like I did when I heard his voice back in Big Phil's apartment. I didn't though. I demanded for him to be removed from the hospital and banned him from visiting me. When I saw him, his betrayal slapped me across the face with a force that shook my bones.

I only had to spend a few days in the hospital, and when I was let out, I chose to go to Dominic and Bronagh's house. I didn't want to see Ryder, speak to him, or to think of him at all. Bronagh went over and packed up some of my clothes for me so I wouldn't even have to step foot in the house.

I didn't want anything to do with him.

Of course, that meant nothing to him because he constantly tried to gain entry to my childhood home, shouting for me to 'let him explain'. I humourlessly laughed every time he said it, and every time I thought about him saying it. He wanted to explain himself now, but not the millions of times I asked him before I was kidnapped. I refused to 'hear him out' and his brothers respected that so they kept him at bay.

I knew it was only a matter of time before he got me alone, but I wasn't scared, I reached a point where I wasn't letting him walk all over me anymore. I was done with that bullshit. Being so vulnerable with Big Phil toughened me up.

When Bronagh and Keela went through their ordeal, they both suffered from night terrors and didn't want to be left on their own for ages. Luckily, that didn't happen to me; so far I was as well as could be expected. When I slept, I didn't dream, and when I was awake, it didn't scare me when I thought about what happened. I knew the person who harmed me was dead, and he couldn't hurt me any longer.

It was a *living* person who I was more concerned about causing me more pain.

My primary focus was on the being that brought me so much emotional agony. I was cold as ice when someone brought Ryder up, but I knew it was a defence mechanism to shield my crumbled heart. It was a front because when I thought about him in the comfort of my own mind, I became devastated and constantly fought back tears.

I was heart-broken that he cheated on me, I was destroyed that we were broken up, and I was completely torn apart that I couldn't call him mine anymore. Even when things were at there worst with us, he was still mine, but not anymore.

"I'll come with you," Bronagh said, cutting through my thoughts.

I firmly shook my head. "There is black ice on the roads and I don't want you out there walkin' on it. You could fall."

"So could you," Bronagh countered.

I loved her for loving me so much.

I grinned. "You're pregnant though, I'm not."

My sister opened her mouth to argue, but I lifted my hand and silenced her.

"I'm fine. Me leg is practically healed, and walkin' isn't painful anymore. I won't go far, I just need some time to meself to think," I explained. "I'm feelin' all kinds of fucked up, Bee. Being trapped in here isn't helpin'."

"Okay," she relented after a couple of seconds. "But *please* be careful, and don't stay out long. I'll worry otherwise."

We had somehow switched roles over the last few weeks. *She* was parenting *me* now.

"I won't," I assured her. "I'll be no more than ten minutes. I'm just goin' for a quick walk then I'll be back. I promise."

I kept my promise, I took a very short walk once around the block, and then I returned home, much to the relief of my sister. I didn't mind taking a quick walk; I just wanted some fresh air, and some space. When I assured Bronagh, again, that I was okay, I went up to the bedroom that was *still* my bedroom. I stripped naked, wrapped myself in a towel then went into the bathroom and took a shower. When I finished, I headed back into my room but froze when I walked through the door.

"Branna?"

My heart jumped in fear of the man who had broken it.

"I *told* your brothers that you weren't to come here." I said, gripping the towel around my body tightly.

"They told me what you said," he said, softly, "but I decided not to listen anymore."

I started to humourlessly laugh.

"Because everythin' has to be on *your* fuckin' terms, right?" I asked through my cold laughter.

"No," Ryder frowned, "because I *had* to see you."

I shook my head and turned from him and walked over to my wardrobe. I grabbed some knickers, a bra, a pair of black leggings and a baggy T-shirt. I looked over my shoulder and narrowed my eyes at Ryder who turned and put his back to me, giving me some privacy.

He had never turned away when I dressed, or undressed, before, but things were different because I was his then, and now I wasn't.

Don't think about it.

I quickly dried my body, mindful of the scabs on the stitches of closed wounds on my shoulder and thigh. The rest of me was still tender, but all of my bruises were a light mustard yellow colour now, and it wouldn't be long until they healed and faded completely.

"I'm decent," I said when I was dressed.

Ryder turned back to face me, and instead of giving me a once over like I expected him to, he kept his grey eyes locked on mine. I didn't know why, but I couldn't hold his gaze. I looked away then busied myself as I brushed my hair out then tied it up into a bun.

"You're beautiful."

The unexpected words slammed into my layered heart like a train.

I keep my gaze averted when I said, "Don't, Ryder. Don't try and butter me up. I look like shit—I know it and everyone else knows it, too. I'm still recoverin' so me appearance isn't on me list of priorities."

I felt him step towards me, so I took a quick step back.

"*Don't.*"

He stayed still.

"You're beautiful no matter what you look like, darling."

I lifted my eyes to his as I snorted. "I'm darlin' now, am I? I'm not just Branna anymore?"

He looked hurt.

"You've always been my darling, and you always will be."

My stomach roiled as sadness seeped into my bones.

"Stop it," I pleaded, feeling my tough demeanour crack. "Stop talkin' to me like the real you used to, just *stop*."

"I'm still me, Bran."

I furiously shook my head. "No, the real you would have *never* put me through what you did."

Ryder audibly swallowed. "You're right, I wouldn't have, but I took the coward's way out because I was too scared to rope you into things."

Rope me into things? I silently repeated. *What the hell is he talking about?*

"Just leave," I asked. "I can't listen to this."

"You have to."

"No," I snapped, looking at him. "I don't have to do a fuckin' *thing*. I did nothin' wrong, *you* did!"

"I know," he agreed, "and I'm trying to fix it."

I wanted to scream.

"You can't!" I bellowed. "You broke what we had."

"Don't say that, Bran," he pleaded. "Please."

I hated that his obvious pain was hurting me, too.

I balled my hands into fists. "I'm so angry at you... you've hurt me so much."

Ryder nodded in defeat. "I know, sweetheart, and I wish with all of my heart that I could take it back."

"You can never take it back. You don't understand the magnitude of what you did to me," I whispered. "I wanted 'im to kill me. When Big Phil had me, I was at the lowest point in me life, and death looked like the best possible outcome for me."

Pure horror overtook Ryder's expression.

"It was shortly after I woke up in his apartment that I wondered why I was so scared of 'im, and why I was so scared to die, when in reality, I died the moment you pulled away from me."

"Darling—"

"It was a moment of weakness," I cut Ryder off. "It was one moment of *many* over the last year and a half. I've been so focused on you changin', that it has changed me, too, and I hate it. I stepped on eggshells around you, I just accepted your refusal to tell me what you were up to, I fuckin' *saw* you with another *woman* and—"

"That wasn't what happened." Ryder cut across me as he reached for me.

I angrily pushed his hands away and shouted, "Let me finish! I saw you with another *woman* and I *walked away*. All because I wasn't strong enough to face you or me reality of how things were with you. I turned into a doormat, a coward, and for what? Fuckin' *nothin'*!"

I shook my head in disgust at myself.

"The moment I asked you where you were goin', and you blocked me out, I should have left you. No—I should have given you a chance or two to redeem yourself, but after *that*, I should have packed up and left you. I shouldn't have put up with it; I should have walked away and never looked back. I keep thinkin' about how different me life would be now if I had done that. Big Phil still would have probably kidnapped me because I'm tied to your family, but I wouldn't have been as weak as I was when I was alone with 'im. I would have fought for me life, not silently pleaded with 'im to take it."

"Branna, I hate myself."

Out of all the things I expected Ryder to say—that was *not* it.

"What?" I asked, not sure if I heard him correctly.

"I hate myself," he repeated, louder. "I knew that I was ruining us, but I kept telling myself that it'd be okay, and when the time came for me to be done with the bullshit that distracted me, I'd fix everything and we'd go back to normal." He shook his head and shoved his hands into the front pockets of his jeans. "I was naive to think that you would always stick by me when I was treating you so poorly."

"You aren't makin' any sense," I said, annoyed. "The 'bullshit that distracted you' was *another woman*. You can't fix us. The moment you decided to give yourself to another, we were doomed."

Ryder looked me dead in the eye and said, "I have *never* cheated on you. I have never *considered* cheating on you, and I have never, in all our time together, *wanted* to cheat on you."

"Don't treat me like I'm stupid, I'm *not* fuckin' stupid." I set my jaw. "I *saw* you. I followed you the night he took me, and I saw you with a woman in a white Range Rover."

Ryder nodded. "That was Lucy, she's my contact, not my mistress."

His contact?

I stared at him. "Are you hearin' yourself right now?"

"I know, none of this makes sense but if you let me explain, it will."

"No," I replied instantly. "I don't want to hear it, I wanted to hear it the first thousand times I asked, but not anymore. I am *done* with this conversation, and with you."

"You don't owe me anything, but darling, I owe *you* this explanation. Please let me give it to you."

I wanted to shut him down again, but I couldn't, it was like my body physically refused me to say the word 'no' again. I wanted to know what he had to say; I wanted to know the truth. He was right. I deserved that much.

"You'll tell me where you went every night if it wasn't to this Lucy?"

He sighed. "Yes, but it doesn't start there, I have to start from the beginning—"

"No, answer that first *then* start from the beginnin'."

"I can't, it won't make sense," he said and looked down.

"Look at me," I demanded.

He did. Ryder looked up at me, and when I saw unshed tears in his eyes; it broke through some of the protective ice that had layered itself around my heart.

"Branna," he whispered, his body trembling. "Please. I know how hard this is, but trust me."

No, I told myself. *He wasn't using that against me.*

I shook my head. "I can't do this anymore, Ryder. I can't handle the lies. The deceit has broken me, *you* have broken me more than Big Phil ever could."

Ryder visibly paled as he took a hesitant step towards me, but I held my ground.

"I don't give a shite if it confuses me, tell me where you went every night right now, or I swear I will *never* even look at you again. This is your *last* fuckin' chance to ever tell me the truth. The *whole* truth."

There it was—the ultimatum I should have given him a *long* fucking time ago.

"Every night I had to meet with my contact Lucy from the FBI, get wired up, and go to Darkness where I was a mole for information against Brandon Daley."

I stared at Ryder when he finished speaking; I stared at him for a long time before I said, "Get out."

"No, Branna—"

"Get fuckin' out!" I screamed. "Do you think this is funny? Do you think tearin' me apart then tryin' this bullshit on with me is fuckin' *funny*?"

"It's the truth!" Ryder shouted over me. "Just *listen*."

"No—"

"Branna?"

I looked to my doorway when my sister called my name. My eyes instantly dropped to her round belly, and I said, "Are you okay?"

She nodded. "I'm fine... I just... you have to listen to 'im."

I stared at Bronagh and couldn't believe what I was hearing, but before I had a chance to say anything, she pressed on.

"You have refused to be around Ryder since you got home from the hospital, but do you remember when I said Dominic agreed to a family meetin' so we could get all this shit out into the open?"

I managed a small nod.

"We had that meetin' last night when you were sleepin', and trust me, you have *got* to listen to what Ryder has to say. I know what pulled 'im from you, and it's *not* what you think. I promise."

My eyes pooled with tears as she closed my bedroom door.

"If you don't trust me, Bran, trust your sister. Listen to what I have to say. Please."

I looked back at Ryder and before I broke down I said, "Start from the beginnin', and don't leave *anythin'* out."

I couldn't even begin to form a clue as to what he said before Bronagh came in.

The FBI?

Wired up?

A mole?

Brandon Daley?

The only thing I could think of was, *what the fuck?*

Instead of speaking, Ryder removed his jacket and jumper then gripped the hem of his t-shirt and pulled it up to his chin. I raised my eyebrows at what I saw.

He... was wearing a wire.

I stared at the black cable that was stuck—with what looked like surgical tape—to his chest, then to the tiny black box that was taped at his lower abdomen. I flicked my eyes between the two then looked up to Ryder to find his eyes were drilled onto me watching him.

"You're wearin' a wire," I murmured.

"Yes," Ryder swallowed. "I am, this one is not active. I broke it, but I just wanted to show it to you so you know what it looked like."

"Why're you wearin' a wire?" I asked when he lowered his t-shirt.

"Sit down and I'll tell you *everything*."

An emotion I couldn't explain surged through me when I realised that he was, in fact, finally going to tell me the reason for our life together ending.

"Sit down," he prompted once more.

I looked at my bed and moved over to the end of it where I climbed up and sat down, letting my legs hang over the edge. Ryder grabbed the chair in front of my vanity desk and placed it in front of me. He sat down and leaned his elbows onto his knees leaving only a little bit of space between his knees knocking against mine.

I had to tense my entire body when his scent surrounded me and the familiarity of it caused my insides to flutter and come to life. The urge to reach out and touch him consumed me so I shoved my hands under my thighs to keep from doing so.

I focused on him when he began speaking.

"About a year and half ago I fell into a rut where I didn't know what I wanted to do with my life, and I didn't want to talk to you about it because I was embarrassed to admit I didn't have the skills to do anything."

I frowned, but didn't interrupt.

"Kane had his landlord and property developer thing going on, Dominic had his personal trainer thing, and Alec was always helping out at the animal shelter nearby. I wasn't qualified for anything." He scrubbed his face with both of his hands. "All I've ever known is drugs and weapons, and I felt like a failure because I wasn't made for working in your world. I *still* have no qualifications for anything... I didn't even finish high-school, Branna."

"I know that about you," I said, "and if you think I give a damn whether you're educated or not then you don't know me at all."

"I *know* you don't care, and to you it doesn't matter, but to *me*, it matters. I want to be the one taking care of you even though you're more than capable of doing it yourself. I just didn't feel like a man, and I'm not looking for sympathy, I'm just trying to explain where my head was at."

I nodded. "I get that, but I still don't know how everythin' else comes into play. I mean, the FBI, Ryder?"

"*That* is actually the easy part," he grunted. "It's unbelievable that it happened, but it wasn't like their heat wasn't warranted."

My head hurt. "Explain."

"I still haven't figured out the best way to explain it, but here goes nothing," he said and blew out a deep breath. "Pretty soon after I started to feel like shit, I wanted to do my part around the house to feel like I wasn't completely pathetic so I went down to B&Q to get some materials so I could paint the rooms, patch up any dents or holes in the walls... shit like that. I was leaving the store when two men in black tailored suits approached me at my car. At first I thought it was funny, they looked like the *Men in Black*, so they *had* to have the wrong person, but when they told me who they were and what they wanted from me, I honestly nearly fainted."

Fear gripped me.

"What did they want from you?"

"They told me a construction site up on the mountain side that was levelling out land discovered a mass grave site."

I felt the blood drain from my face.

"Trent?" I questioned. "Marco's men from that night in Darkness when he took Damien and hurt Bronagh?"

Five years ago, Marco Miles, Ryder's old boss, attacked my little sister and tried to use her life, and Damien's, as a bargaining chip to keep Ryder and his three other brothers under this thumb. It blew up in his face, and he paid for it with his life, his nephew's life, and a few of his thugs' lives.

Ryder nodded once. "They can't identify the bodies, but mine and Dominic's finger prints were on one of the plastic bags we used to wrap them up inside. We didn't clean them as well as we thought."

My heart was beating so fast I could hear it.

"There hasn't been a single mention of it in the news though, how could—"

"They're the Feds, Bran, they aren't your regular cops. These are the people that hunt you down and find out everything about you know matter where you are on the planet. They have a small team here and only that team and the commissioner of your police knows about this operation. If they want something kept under wraps, you won't know about it unless they *want* you to."

What operation?

"I can't believe this," I breathed and lifted my hand from under my leg so I could place it on my chest.

"This is as real as it gets, Branna." Ryder said, trepidation in his tone. "We were all arrested one time in the States... we did nothing wrong, but the cops arrested us one day just so they could get our finger prints and DNA on record. They knew who we ran with and I guess they didn't want to take any chances with us. When the cops here ran the prints, they found us through the system, and the FBI was flagged and immediately flew over here. Marco was well known to them, but they could never pin shit on him because his crew was so good at what they did. They wanted to know where he disappeared to, and they also knew we had something to do with it because a source told them Marco came to Ireland after us and that he never left."

I clasped my hands together, just so I had something to hold.

"Are they goin' to arrest you both for murder?" I asked, and then held my breath as I awaited his reply.

"If I didn't do what they wanted, then yes, they would have arrested us, but I did what they wanted so no, they won't. That was the deal they offered me, and I took it."

"They can do that?" I questioned with disbelief. "They will completely let you get away with *murder* if you help them?"

Ryder nodded. "They have our prints on the plastic, but that's their only evidence and while it's a crucial piece, there is so much more they *can't* get us on, but I didn't want to test them and actually make them dig for something else to convict us with. I did what they wanted and they let us off the hook."

"But *how?*" I pressed. "Does there not have to be a trial before a judge—"

"Not with these people, Branna. The Feds can be just as corrupt as gangsters. They can make everything disappear if they get what they want, and all they wanted was information on Brandon Daley's dealings. I never confirmed it, but they know Marco is dead, and that actually made them happy. Everyone hated him."

"Are you're sure what you did was the right thing?" I asked, worried sick this would blow up in his face.

"What choice did I have, Bran?"

My shoulders sagged. "None, I guess."

"I *know* it was risky, and that I can't trust them, but if I refused their deal, then they'd have arrested me and Dominic. They don't care about a couple of dead untraceable bodies because they know who they are without me having to say it. No one misses evil gangsters, Branna, *especially* the law."

"I understand that, scarcely, but what *exactly* were the terms of the deal?" I asked as a pounding took up residence in my temples. "What did they expect of you?"

"They wanted me to wear a wire, and get a job running shit for Brandon. He is squeaky clean, and is more private than Marco ever was, which made him a mystery to the Feds. They wanted to know who his contacts were, where he got his product from... they basically wanted to know everything about him."

"The FBI has been keeping tabs on Brandon?" I questioned with raised brows.

"Of course, everyone with power like him is on the Feds' radar."

That shouldn't have been a surprise, but it was.

"So the deal was for you to be a mole, pass on information and that's it?"

"Almost," Ryder said on a grunt. "Marco, the son of a bitch, had me listed as owner on a lot of fucked up properties where shit went down in the city. He had contacts everywhere, and filing the fake paperwork to make me look like a legit owner of somewhere wouldn't have been hard for him. Now, since I've been living here the last five years the Feds *know* I physically had no interaction with any of the properties, but because they were in my name, I was responsible for what was found during the busts."

Oh, my God.

"The Feds threw out the cases as part of the deal, but they refused to pick up the bill for 'damages'. They said they would clear me of any wrong doing if I paid it instead. I didn't have a choice, they could have deported me and tried me in the States for that. And when my sentence there was up, I could be brought back here to be tried and imprisoned for murder. I had to pay them a *lot* of fucking money to make *that* bullshit go away, but I didn't have enough so Dominic and Alec gave up their shares from what they earned over the years and helped me. Kane did too, but because he has his business, he wasn't broke like the rest of us. I told you that I got mixed up in a bad investment deal when you asked where the money went because I didn't want to tell you the truth, and to be honest, if I hadn't ruined everything and you never noticed the change in me, I would have n*ever* told you."

"You'd *keep* this from me?" I asked, shocked.

He'd really keep this from me?

Ryder nodded and without hesitation said, "I'd do anything to keep you safe from harm or worry. *Anything*."

I didn't know whether to be annoyed over that or appreciative.

"My brothers, bar Damien because we never want him involved in nightmares like this, helped me with my job. I had to look like a shiny diamond to Brandon so he'd learn to trust me. I had to run every shipment successfully, and turn him a sizeable profit. I didn't want to be at this for years, so I needed to fully invest myself back in the life to make it end faster. I had to be become close to him. But by bringing myself into his world, I pulled away from you. I didn't want to, I didn't even notice it at the beginning because I was so stressed out. I now know I was bringing my anger and resentment for the situation I was in back home to you, and you didn't deserve it."

I exhaled an unsteady breath. "How were your brothers involved?"

"As you know, Dominic got a job fighting for Brandon. With his money being gone, and being a personal trainer not making enough income, it was the perfect cover to Bronagh. He'd fight under Brandon, get paid, but also keep his ear to the ground to help me with any information he could find. That's why there'd be days here and there where I was out with him all the time. He was helping me. Kane and Alec too. Kane came with me on a few jobs to watch my back because I don't trust anyone in Brandon's crew—except Gavin, but he's only a small ranked solider, and he wouldn't have any information that I wouldn't already know."

Aideen's little brother was caught up in Brandon Daley's world *still*, and I hated it. The stubborn little bastard wouldn't bow out no matter how much Aideen and his brothers tried to force him to. Keela was working on having her uncle just kick him out of the gang, but he was proving to be just as difficult.

"Alec can charm a snake, and I was dealing with a *lot* of snakes, especially when I was trying to close deals on weapons. Once or twice I'd be dealing with a hard-ass woman, or a stuck up man, and that's when I needed Alec. I'd bring him along with me, and without making it obvious, he would do his thing—flirt, and effortlessly make people like him. He didn't even touch anyone; he just smiled and struck up conversations with them. Typical Alec style. It made closing those kinds of deals with greedy people a lot easier."

I lifted my hands to my face and rubbed my eyes. I lowered my arms, and shook my head, not being able to comprehend the depth of what I was hearing.

"This is a *lot* to take in."

"I know it is, but you need to know *everything* so you understand how tied my hands were."

I couldn't begin to imagine what he felt like, or went through, but... I understood that he had to do what he was *made* to do in order to remain prison free. I got that. It was so hard to believe it was real life, but I got it. My mind pieced together all the fall-outs, fights and the general break down of our relationship and concluded it was inevitable.

Ryder wasn't a God; there was only so much he could control. His experience with his past life made his task a familiar one, but this time the stakes were a lot higher, and by trying to protect me from it, he unwillingly subjected me to another kind of horror.

My mind understood all of that, but my heart didn't. I couldn't just erase the pain I felt, or get over what I saw. The most superficial and idiotic thing I could have said left my mouth when I thought about the night I was kidnapped.

"You really weren't cheatin' on me with that Lucy woman?" I whispered.

"No, I swear it." Ryder said without hesitation. "She was only my contact to the Feds. I'd meet her every night at a different location, get wired up, and find out what shit they wanted me to do."

Oh.

"I just thought… when I saw you lean into her car, and she laughed… I just thought the worst."

"She laughed and giggled like that every night in case I was followed by Brandon's men to make it *look* like I was meeting up with her for a hook up, but I swear, it's only ever been you, Branna. I have never touched another women since the night we met."

My hands were trembling.

"What was I supposed to think? I saw what I saw and came to a conclusion most people would come to as well," I said as my lower lip wobbled. "You pulled away from me, you left the house every night and showered before you would come near me. When I saw you with 'er, I started to piece all of that together and it just made everythin' worse inside me head."

Ryder frowned. "I felt dirty every time I walked through the front door of our home knowing the shit I came from. I didn't want to taint you with it. You're pure to me, and I didn't want any of what I've been doing to affect you."

"But it *has* affected me," I whispered. "You… you made me think you hated me."

"I *never* meant for it to go this far," he stressed as he leaned forward and took my hands in his, shocking me as the familiar feeling of his calloused hands instantly soothed me. "I meant to distance myself from you just until this was done, and when we started arguing, I couldn't stop the spiral. You, your sister, the other girls, you all mean everything to me, to my family. We agreed that keeping you in the dark was the best thing to do. Damien, too. We didn't tell him anything because we knew he'd want to help us, and it was decided a long time ago he would never be involved with what we had no choice in. If anything went wrong and me and Dominic *did* go to prison then none of you could be implicated. You wouldn't know about any of what was going on so they couldn't try you as an accessory."

I shook my head in disbelief. "This just doesn't feel real."

"I wish it wasn't."

Me too.

"You said you did want the FBI wanted, does that mean Brandon has been arrested?"

Ryder shook his head. "No, I got all the information I could, but they still don't know any of his contacts, sources and distributors. Brandon never directly gave me my orders either, it was another man who told me what to do and where to go, so even if there was a bust, it wouldn't trace back to him. Brandon was good to me, but he knew what I was doing in his gang, and why I was there. He was *very* careful during my time with him."

Fear gripped me.

I gasped. "He could kill you!"

Images of pure horror flashed through my mind.

Ryder snorted. "He won't, I think he found it amusing. He told me he doesn't like rats, and said he had a bad habit of standing on them. I agreed with him and said I hated cops more because they were snakes in the grass. When I said it, I adjusted my shirt to show the indent of my wire and looked him in the eye. He quickly picked up on what information I was offering."

I felt my jaw drop open. "You gave it away what you were there for? *Why?*"

"Because Brandon is fair... and I fucking *hate* cops, Branna. The Feds... they're a whole different level of scum, they'd throw you under a bus to get what they want."

"You eejit!" I snapped. "What if they *know* why you got shit information?"

"They're none the wiser, they called time on my part in the operation the night you were... attacked. They told me that evening that after forty-eight hours they'd be packed up and out of the country, and I could go back to my normal life. That's why I wanted to wait to tell you... in case they changed their minds."

"I don't know how to feel about all of this." I admitted. "It's too intense."

Ryder leaned forward and pressed his forehead to mine. "I'm so sorry, Branna," he whispered. "Having you in my life has ruined yours."

The touch of his skin against mine was like a jolt of electricity shooting through me.

I pulled back from him and looked into his eyes. "Don't you *ever* say anythin' like that to me again. You're still everythin' to me even though I'm furious with you. I'm angry and hurt, but it's only because the thought of losin' you *kills* me."

Ryder's face softened. "Why did you leave me if you don't want to lose me?"

My shoulders sagged. "You left me no other choice. Either you told me what you were up to, or I had to leave. It has destroyed me to be apart, but livin' the way I had been with you over the last year and a half has ruined me, too. *I* had no choice."

Ryder slightly smiled. "I'll fix what I've done."

"I feel like your smile is a beautiful lie," I whispered, "and that I can't trust it any more than I can trust you."

"But... but I just told you why I was the way I was."

I nodded. "And I understand, but that doesn't change anythin' right now. I need space."

"Don't leave me on my own, Branna." Ryder pleaded. "I'm begging you."

"You've left me on my own for months whilst being right here with me, and I understand why, but it still hurts." I countered. "Whatever we had faded to black."

"No," he hissed. "Nothing faded away because I still fucking love you more than life itself, and you love me, too. I know it."

"Lovin' you is easy, Ryder, but trustin' you isn't."

"I know, and I'll forever be sorry for causing you so much hurt."

I was silent for a few moments just gathering my thoughts.

"Can you ever forgive me?" Ryder asked, his voice so low I barely heard him. "Could you ever reach a point where you think you could do that?"

Could I? I asked myself.

"I don't know," I admitted. "I need time to think."

"I'll give you time and space. I'll give you whatever you need, I promise."

He was grabbing onto my words like a lifeline.

"This won't happen overnight, Ryder." I said firmly. "I can't just mend what's been broken with the snap of my fingers, so make sure you give me time, okay? I can't go back to the way things were before all this started just because I now know the truth; I have to do this slowly. We *both* do. I understand what you have told me, but me heart, it can't just forgive and forget so easily."

Ryder bobbed his head up and down. "I understand. I'll do anything you want."

I was relived he was going to do what I wanted without giving me hassle.

I blew out a breath. "Don't come around lookin' for me, okay? When I'm ready, I'll come to you."

"What... what if you never come to me?" he asked, fear laced in his tone.

"I can't answer that, and I'm sorry if I'm being cruel, but right now, I need to do what's best for *me*."

After a moment, Ryder nodded. "Okay, sweetheart."

He stood then, and it looked like he was going to lean down and either hug or kiss me, but he stopped himself and moved over to my bedroom door.

"I love you, Branna," he said. "I have a shit way of showing it, but I love you, sweetness."

He left then, and not long later, I burst into tears. I didn't know why I was crying when I was the one who asked him to give me time and space. The confusion was killing me.

My mind felt one way, and my heart another.

I *hated* how mysterious Ryder had been over the last year and a half, and now *I* had become an enigma. That was fucking irony for you.

CHAPTER FIFTEEN

Two weeks later…

It had been fourteen days since Ryder told me the truth, and I was still in my room where I confined myself to so I could *really* think. Unless it was to eat, use the toilet or take a shower, I stayed in my room. I wished I could return to work to busy myself, but I was only two sessions into my scheduled six with the therapist The Health Board assigned me to, and it was difficult actually opening up to her without revealing any secrets that weren't for her ears.

Even with her help, I was emotionally at a standstill because I didn't know how to get my heart on the same track as my mind. I knew what happened with Ryder in full detail, and I understood every aspect of it, but I still resented him for the hurt he brought me over the last year and a half, even though he didn't do it willingly.

While I felt anger, I didn't know if it was directed solely at Ryder himself, or how he made me feel when he pushed me away. It was an on-going mental battle for me because I couldn't make my mind up. It didn't help that I missed him terribly either. Being so unsure about how I truly felt after everything I learned was hard when all I wanted was to be with him so we could deal with this together.

On one hand, I wanted to go to him and make a go of things because even if we had a bad rough patch, it was five years of my life with someone who I truly loved, and I wasn't ready to just give up on that... but on the other hand, I was so emotionally destroyed that I wasn't sure if I could ever get back to a place where I fully trusted Ryder, and if there was no trust, there was no relationship.

I turned my head and looked over at my door when a soft knock sounded.

"Come in," I called.

The door creaked open, but instead of my sister checking up on me, it was Alec.

"Hey," I said and sat upright. "Is everythin' okay?"

He nodded and closed my door behind him. "Everything's fine ... Bronagh's just worried about you. I told her I'd come and talk to you and pull a smile or something from you."

"I just have to look at your ugly face and I smile."

"Fuck you, too."

I laughed, and it made Alec's lips twitch as he crossed the room. I moved over so he could sit on the bed with me, and I smiled wide when he kicked his shoes off before he climbed onto it and relaxed back against a few of my pillows. I leaned back too, and together, we both stared at the ceiling.

"If you stay in this room any longer," he began, "I'm afraid you're going to turn into a piece of furniture. *Beauty and the Beast* style minus the singing because you can't sing. At all."

Again, I laughed.

"I'll keep that in mind, *Beast*."

Alec snorted then after a period of silence between us he asked, "How are you? And don't say fine just to appease me. How are you... *really*?"

That question was constant, since the attack, and I still didn't have a solid answer for it when I was asked.

I swallowed. "One minute I'm okay, then the next I'm in pieces. I'm really confused about Ryder, I just don't know what to do and it's driving me *insane*."

"You know keeping things bottled up isn't good for you, look how sad you became because you kept your issues with Ryder to yourself."

He was right, but that didn't mean I could break character so easily.

"Old habits die hard, I guess."

"I can't imagine how hard it is to let someone be your shoulder to lie on, when all you've known is being the strong one." Alec reached over and took my hand in his. "You've always been strong for Bee, then for each of us when our individual bullshit came back to bite us in the ass. You're incredible, Bran, and we don't mean to pester you, we just want to show you that we're here for you like you're always there for us."

Tears pooled in my eyes.

"I have a thing about not cryin', but you're makin' not bawling me eyes out *very* hard."

"Listen to me," Alec then said as he stood up from the bed, pulling me along with him until we were standing facing one another. "You can cry for days if you want to, and that's okay. Before your night of evil, you suffered a year and a half of hell. If crying will help, then fucking *cry*."

I shook my head and wiped my eyes with the back of my hand.

"I'm sick of cryin', it changes nothin'."

"Then smile instead, it takes more effort to frown than it does to smile anyway."

My shoulders slumped. "I've nothin' to smile about."

"Sure you do," Alec quickly stated. "You survived a night of terror, you found out Ryder wasn't cheating on you, and that he wasn't pulling away from you because he doesn't love you anymore. You have a *lot* to smile for."

When he put it like that, I wanted to kick my own arse for feeling so miserable.

"It's hard," I admitted.

"Believe in yourself," Alec said. "In Ryder."

I sighed. "That's easier said than done."

He kept his eyes locked on mine as he said, "You believed in Santa Claus, the Easter Bunny, and the Tooth Fairy for years growing up. You can believe in yourself, your man, and what you both have, for five minutes, okay?"

I blinked, dumbly.

"What?" Alec questioned, shifting from foot to foot.

I cleared my throat. "I just forget that you're a very wise person. You joke around all the time and make everyone laugh and smile, but you're so real when it comes down to it. You give good advice."

A beautiful smile overtook Alec's face.

"I love you, Bran, I will do and say anything to help you and Ryder get through this." He reached out and tugged on my hair like I was a little girl. "You're both the reason I decided that someday I'd settle down, did you know that? Before I met Keela, I used to watch you both and I liked that Ryder could be happy and complete by just seeing you. At first I thought he was pathetic and pussy whipped, but the more I was around you both, the more I realised it was something real. I wanted it, and now I have it. It's hard work, but you and Ry have got this. Don't give up, okay?"

He laughed when I jumped forward, and wrapped my arms around his waist, pressing my face against his chest. He put his arms around me and squeezed me tightly. Tears flowed then, but for once they weren't sad tears, they were hopeful tears. That was what Alec just gave me.

Hope.

I hadn't experienced the feeling in a long time, but I couldn't deny that it felt incredible.

"Thanks, Alec," I murmured against his chest.

When I pulled back from our hug and looked up, I couldn't help but giggle. He was so different now compared to when I first met him in Darkness all those years ago.

"What?" he asked, grinning at my goofy expression.

I shook my head. "I was just thinking about the first time I met you *and* about the first thing you said to me."

Without warning, he reached around my body and smacked my behind making me yelp with surprise.

"You *still* have a great ass," his grin deepened. "But don't tell Keela I said that."

I laughed, and playfully swatted at him until he ducked out of reach.

"You're crazy."

"No one sane is *this* awesome," he said as he pointed a finger at himself.

I snickered. "I need you to do me a favour."

"Name it," he stated.

"Before I lose this bit of courage, I think I need to pay your big brother a visit. You have really straightened things out for me. If I don't believe in what me and Ryder had, and what we could have again, then I'm givin' up without a fight. I'm exhausted, but I've one more round in me to make this work. I have to try or I'll regret it for the rest of me life."

Alec lifted his hand in the air, and I clapped my palm into it, laughing. I was already dressed, so I grabbed a pair of shoes and walked downstairs with Alec.

"Where are you goin'?"

I looked at my sister in the doorway of the sitting room with Dominic behind her; both of them were looking at me expectantly.

"To talk to Ryder." I answered.

"Really?" Bronagh said, her eyes wide. "A good talk, or a bad talk?"

I shrugged. "My intentions are good, and I know Ryder will like what I have to say so I'm goin' to go with a good talk."

Being tackle hugged by a thirty week pregnant woman was not what I expected, and I know that if Alec hadn't been behind me when Bronagh rushed me, we would have both fallen to the floor.

I took it as a good omen though; hopefully it wouldn't be the only thing falling today. I hoped my heart would run and jump off a high dive board when I spoke to Ryder.

I *hoped.*

"You know, for this to work, you actually have to get *out* of my car."

I clasped my hands together over my trembling legs.

"What if he's changed his mind about us?" I asked Alec who took his keys out of the ignition of his car. "What if he got pissed off that I haven't contacted him in two weeks?"

"Branna," Alec laughed. "He is willing to wait the *rest of his life* for you. He's the one who is scared out of his mind that you won't come to him at all. We've been dealing with his bitchiness since he told you the truth."

I really hoped he wasn't saying that just to make me feel better.

I inhaled and exhaled a deep breath and said, "Fuck it. Let's do this."

"Atta girl," Alec whooped.

We both got out of his car, and walked up the cobbled pathway that led to my old house. It was strange that just seeing the house made me miss Ryder that much more. I decided it was because so many good things had happened there, so many things that outweighed the bad. There were memories from within the house that I would keep forever, and others I would never think of again.

When we entered the house, I had a quick flashback of being attacked in the kitchen, but I quickly shook it off. Big Phil was gone, and the twisted son of a bitch couldn't hurt me anymore. I wouldn't let him.

I'd never let *anyone* have the power to hurt me ever again.

I followed Alec down the hallway, and when he entered the kitchen, I hovered outside by the doorway.

"What's up, bro?" Alec asked Ryder.

I heard a sigh. "Nothing. I painted your old room to give me something to do. I'll probably patch up some of the holes in Dominic's old room if you want to stick around and help?"

"Can't bro, I'm just dropping her off."

"Who off?" Ryder questioned.

That's my cue.

I stepped into the kitchen with my head held high and when Ryder saw me, he jumped up to his feet and let the cup that was halfway raised to his mouth fall to the floor with surprise.

"Shit," he hissed when the cup smashed to pieces then cleared his throat. "Branna."

I lifted my hand and lightly waved. "Hey, Ry."

"Hi, hey," he said in rapid succession. "Hello."

"Bro, one greeting is enough," Alec mumbled.

Ryder didn't know what to do with his arms because he folded them across his chest, and then dropped them to his sides before folding them back across his chest. His obvious nervousness at seeing me made me feel less nervous about seeing him, and I was glad for it.

"Sorry for just droppin' in unannounced," I said, and gnawed on my lower lip.

Ryder shook his head. "No, no, it's more than fine. It's great actually. Really, really great."

"Ry," Alec said, and when I looked at him I saw him trying not to laugh. "You need to calm down."

"Calm? I am calm."

He *so* wasn't.

Ryder cleared his throat then, and scanned me from head to toe. "You look gorgeous, darling."

I felt my cheeks heat up as I looked down at my plain white t-shirt, black leggings, and grey slip on shoes. I was makeup free, and my hair was in a high ponytail. I mostly definitely did *not* look gorgeous, in fact, I felt like a hot mess.

"I wore this stuff to bed last night," I said and scratched the back of my neck. "I wasn't plannin' on comin' here, but then Alec had a talk with me, and here I am."

Ryder looked at Alec, and when I saw the gratitude in his eyes for his brother, a lump formed in my throat. "Thanks, bro," he said.

Alec winked. "Just doing my part. I'll catch both of you later, okay?"

Before any of us could respond, Alec was out of the house, and closed the front door behind him. Ryder and I were standing in the kitchen a couple of metres away from one another, and for some reason, I felt anxious.

"It's good to see you," I said nonchalantly.

Ryder blinked. "It is?"

I nodded. "Yeah, I've missed you, Ry."

His chest puffed up a bit.

"I've missed you, baby. A hell of a lot."

My lip twitched. "That much, huh?"

"Even more," he stressed. "A heaven *and* a hell of a lot."

I smiled then, and without warning Ryder crossed the space between us, cupped my face in his hands and stared down at me with his eyes glazed over.

"Honey," I breathed. "What's wrong?"

"You don't hate me," he whispered.

I lifted my hands and placed them on his waist.

"No," I said firmly, "I don't."

"I can see it in your smile," he murmured, "and the way you were just looking at me."

I gave him a little squeeze. "I've never hated you, hon. I was very angry with you, but hate was never an emotion that was directed at you, just about how you made me feel."

"*Was* angry, meaning you aren't anymore?"

I shook my head. "I'm more confused than anything. One minute I'm furious with you for lettin' everythin' run on so long without talkin' to me, then the next I'm so understandin' of the situation you were in and I get why you bottled it up and kept it a secret from me. My indecisiveness is drivin' me insane."

"But you're here... why?" he quizzed. "I mean I'm so glad you're here, but... why?"

I licked my lips. "Alec talked with me, and he was right, I have to believe in you, in us."

"And do you?" he asked, his voice now raspy. "Do you believe in us? In me?"

"Yeah, I do," I said with a firm nod. "I just won't be able to pick up where we left off. I think we should just ease back into everythin'. In time my worries, my fear, and my doubts will fade away if we do this at a slow pace."

"Yes," Ryder rasped. "Anything to have you as mine again."

"I'll always be yours."

"And I'll always be yours, sweetness."

Sweetness.

Hearing the term of endearment I loved so much caught my breath, and caused my heart to skip a beat.

"You're you again," I whispered. "I thought this Ryder would never come back to me."

"I never left, babe," he breathed, his skin flushed. "I thought I was protecting you by blocking you out, but now I see the damage I've caused. I've broken your heart, and I'll never forgive myself for that. I am so sorry, sweetheart. So fucking sorry."

"You can mend it," I said, my voice tight with emotion. "You can make me heart forget about everythin' and just revolve around you once more. I know you can."

Ryder leaned down to kiss me, but I was hesitant.

"What if kissin' leads to somethin' more?" I questioned. "Is it too soon for it?"

"For someone who wants to be swept away, you sure ask for a lot of directions."

I frowned. "I'm sorry, I'm tryin'."

Ryder gave me a small smile. "I know, darling. Just let it happen, you don't need to have control of this. Just feel."

Just feel.

"I'm... I'm scared." I whispered. "What if it's not the same as before?"

Ryder stepped closer to me and whispered, "What if it's better?"

My heart fluttered. "What if it's too much?"

"Too much?" Ryder repeated. "Branna, it's never enough. I can *never* get enough of you. Do you understand that? I'm addicted to you."

I sucked in a deep breath, and locked my knees together when my legs began to tremble.

"Everything about you is alluring to me." Ryder continued. "Your face, your body, your smile, your voice, your laugh, your hair, your scent, your personality. Fucking hell, sweetness, you're *it* for me. You have been since I laid my eyes on you five years ago."

My chest was rising and falling rapidly as my heart slammed into my ribcage.

Ryder stroked his thumbs over my cheeks, and with his alluring eyes he looked right through me and found my soul. "I. Love. You. Branna."

I forced down the lump of emotion that sat in my throat and whispered, "I love you, too, Ryder. So much it hurts."

He wasted no time in claiming my mouth with his, kissing me with a hunger I hadn't known from him in a long time, and unlike before, I didn't stop him. I kissed him back, and when he pulled away, I was delighted to find I didn't want him to.

"You're the light of my life," Ryder said, breathing heavily against my lips. "Without you everything was dark, and unappealing. I didn't want to live without you."

His honesty made me cry.

"Look at me," he demanded.

I opened my eyes and stared into his.

"I. Love. You." He said clearly. "I never want to be without you. Never."

I clung to him

"Marry me," Ryder said with his next breath. "I know we're going to take this slow, but say you *will* marry me. I will still move at a speed you are comfortable with, but I need you to agree to marry me."

I sniffled.

"We're already engaged," I said, confused.

"We were on the verge of ending things for good, I *need* to hear you say you still want to be with me for the rest of our lives. Please, darling, I need to hear you say it. I *need* to."

"Yes," I said without hesitation. "Yes, I still want to marry you. I want nothin' more. We're in this for the long haul."

Ryder lifted his hand and lifted his pinkie finger to me.

"Forever?" he said.

I hooked my finger tightly around his, and with my heart pumping with nothing but pure love I said, "Forever."

CHAPTER SIXTEEN

Three months later...

"Why are your eyebrows so nicely shaped?" Keela asked Dominic as we sat in the sitting room of her and Alec's house. All of us were together so when the lads laughed, Dominic's face turned red with embarrassment.

He avoided looking at his brothers as he said, "Bronagh cried because I wouldn't let her pluck them, and the only way to make her stop crying was to let her do them so I sucked it up. She's extremely pregnant and is touchy about *everything* so I let her do what she wants without argument if it means no tears."

Smart lad.

Bronagh, Alannah and Aideen were in the kitchen making food so they were out of earshot for this very interesting turn in our conversation.

"Hold the fucking phone," Alec laughed as he got up and walked over to Dominic and bent forward. He grabbed hold of his brother's head, and forced him to look at him. "Aw, how cute! You're a pretty little princess!"

Dominic shoved Alec's teasing self away and glared at Damien and Kane who were covering their mouths trying, and failing, to muffle their chuckles.

"I think you look great," I offered. "It's nice to see a man that grooms his eyebrows. They're *such* an important facial feature."

Alec, Damien and Kane looked at me like a vagina suddenly grew on the middle of my forehead.

Dominic blinked. "They are?"

"Of course," Keela answered for me. "Yours aren't perfectly shaped, but they're *very* nicely done, I'd say you're just even *more* attractive now. I never noticed that they were a little bushy before, but Bee did good. You look sexy."

Dominic smugly grinned at his brothers who were now eyeing him, and his eyebrows. Alec, on the other hand, was glaring at Keela who had done well to avoid catching his stare.

I snorted. "Leave her alone, it's not like she's lying, Dominic *is* sexy."

Dominic's grin deepened, and smugness radiated from him in waves as he clasped his hands together behind his head and he looked around the room. I laughed and shook my head at him.

I jumped when a finger sticking into my side startled me. I quickly looked at the poker and grinned, "I know, I know, I'm goin' to pay for talkin' up your little brother, and let me just say that I *can't wait*."

My Ryder's lip curved upward. "You're a hellcat."

"I know," I teased.

It had been three months since I made up with Ryder, and four months and one week since all hell broke loose. We were still taking things slow, and by that I mean *really* slow. We hadn't done much more than kiss one another, and it was the best decision we had *ever* made.

The first night we met, sex between us was almost instant. There was thick sexual tension from the moment we locked eyes on one another, but this time, we were trying a different approach. One where we listened to our minds, and hearts, instead of our libidos.

We knew that if the FBI hadn't uprooted our lives then we would have been perfectly fine continuing the way we were in our relationship, but since we were starting over fresh, we wanted to try taking a different path this time around. We switched up our tactics, and instead of doing everything arse backwards, we took things in baby steps.

That meant on date nights a chaste kiss on my front porch was the only outcome.

We spent time together, *lots* of time, and reintroduced ourselves to everything we loved about one another, and learned new things along the way. It sounded boring and it was anything but. When I knew I was going to see Ryder, my stomach fluttered with butterflies, my heart pounded with excitement and I couldn't remove the smile from my face for all the money in the world.

We were happy again. I was me, and Ryder was Ryder. We weren't our old selves anymore, we were new and improved versions. What we endured, not only over the last two years, but from the moment we met, made us better people. *Stronger* people. It solidified our bond and proved to me that we really could overcome anything.

I came to that realisation over a week ago, but I had yet to tell Ryder because I was a little afraid we would take our slow paced relationship and just run at a hundred kilometres an hour, and I didn't want that, I loved how we were progressing, but even I knew we couldn't stay the way we were forever, it's why I planned on seducing Ryder and making love to him for the first time in nearly a year.

There was one problem though, and it wasn't with Ryder, *or* me, it was with our little siblings.

As I was still living with Dominic and Bronagh, they both took our new outlook on our relationship *very* seriously, and wanted to help us as much as humanly possible... and that meant we had switched roles and they had become the parental figures. And let me say, they didn't hold back. Once the clock struck ten when Ryder was over, Bronagh was there giving him his marching orders. When we went up to my room, Dominic would make a point of leaving the door wide open.

I appreciated them, but I also wanted to strangle them.

It didn't help that Bronagh was thirteen days overdue on her sweet—and terribly lazy—baby girl. It added nerves and agitation to an *already* nervous and agitated person. The combination was not good.

It was one of the reasons why I was happy I was still living with them because I wanted to be there to help them with the baby if they needed it. Being a first time parent is hard enough, so if they needed me to help out with anything, I was on call.

Just call me Super Auntie.

I smiled at my thoughts then looked at Ryder when he poked me again.

"What're you smiling about?" he asked, staring at my mouth like he wanted to devour it.

An ache formed between my thighs, and I decided to play dirty.

"Just thinkin' about the plans I have for us later."

Ryder audibly swallowed.

"What plans?" he asked, his voice now a whisper.

I smirked in response, and his hold on me tightened.

"One little smirk, and I'm already hard for you."

"How hard?" I boldly asked, and placed my hand on his thigh, giving it a squeeze.

He gritted his teeth. "Stop, or I might succeed in traumatising my brothers *this* time."

I laughed at that, and thought back to our first night together, but quickly found it didn't bode well to think of our hot, sweaty bodies moving together as one when I was almost panting with need next to him.

"I don't think I can wait," I murmured.

Ryder's entire body tensed. "It's your call."

Yeah, it is.

"Now," I breathed. "I want to feel you. All of you."

"Fuck. Yes."

He kissed me then, and a few moments passed by before many throats were cleared.

"Uh, guys?" Alec mumbled. "I'm all for you both bumping uglies after such a long drought, but we're *still* here. Jax, too."

At the mentioned of Jax, Ryder and I broke apart in an instant.

"Sorry," I squeaked.

"What're you sorry for?"

I looked over my shoulder when my sister spoke, and smiled because she looked beautiful. She would disagree because she was convinced she was an undiscovered species of whale. Being a day shy of forty-two weeks pregnant was apparently no excuse either.

"Nothin'," I replied. "We're just talkin'."

"Is *that* what you call it?" Keela snickered.

I looked at her grinning face and narrowed my eyes before grinning right back at her.

"Keela said Dominic is sexy!" I quickly stated.

Keela gasped. "You agreed with me!"

Bronagh groaned. "Don't use any word around me that has sex in it. Sex does *this* to you"—she pointed at her large round stomach—"*and* gives you stretch marks!"

"Did you get many?" Keela asked, apprehension to her voice.

She and Alec were trying to get pregnant.

"Yes!" Bronagh almost cried. "On me stomach, boobs and even on me arse. Me fuckin' *arse!*"

Dominic opened his mouth to speak, but Bronagh pointed her finger dangerously at him. "Not now," she warned. "I don't want to hear it. I'm fat, I have stretch marks, I haven't seen me feet in *weeks,* and I forget what regular sex feels like. Don't annoy me more than I already am."

Alec looked like he was about to pass out.

"Pregnancy stops you from having sex?" he asked wide-eyed before looking to Keela and saying, "We're adopting."

We all laughed.

"It's only the last few weeks that it's stopped," Dominic grumbled. "It hurts her a little so we don't do it."

"Why would it hurt?" Kane questioned.

I've learned this about the brothers over the last few years—they have *no* limit on what we converse about, they don't mind talking about a lot stuff lads normally turn away from.

Everyone looked at me when Kane spoke, and I cleared my throat.

"Lots of different reasons, but there doesn't have to be a specific one. When a woman is pregnant, there is more blood flow to 'er entire pelvic region, and that engorgement is sometimes just too uncomfortable durin' sex. It goes away when the baby is born."

"Praise Jesus for that at least," Dominic said. "And for anal."

The women cringed while the lads snickered.

"Bronagh," I said. "Chill on the sofa."

"I can't, me body is currently experiencin' some technical difficulties."

With a raised brow I asked, "What does *that* mean?"

"It means her ass is sore and she can't sit down."

"Dominic!" my sister screeched, horrified.

Alec high-fived his younger brother and said, "My man."

Brothers.

"You might as well do all the kinky shit now," Kane mumbled. "After she has the baby all that stuff only happens on rare occasions… like when you get a babysitter."

I snorted. "Don't worry, I'm sure they'll find a way."

"Damn right we will," Dominic grinned and winked at Bronagh who was shaking her head good-naturedly.

"Change the subject," my sister said as she eased down onto the sofa next to Dominic who absentmindedly slung his arm over her shoulder.

"Oh," Keela chirped. "The let's play 'Ask Me Anythin'. It's a game for adults where all questions are appropriate. I'll start off simple, Alec, who is your celeb crush?"

"Mila Kunis," he replied almost instantly.

"Mine is Chris Evans," Keela chirped.

"I know which *male* celeb Alec fancies. It's Matt Bomer," Aideen grinned as she entered the room and sat down next to Kane with a sleeping Jax lying on her chest. "I asked him that *ages* ago."

Alec nodded. "It's true, my lust for him *was* strong."

Bronagh burst into sudden laughter.

"What's so funny?" I asked, amused by her outburst.

"When I first met Ryder," she laughed, placing a hand on her side, "I thought he looked just like Matt Bomer only he was heavily tattooed and now I learn Alec wants to have his dirty way with the lad. He wants to give it to someone who looks like his *big brother!*"

I laughed and so did everyone else.

"The joke's on you, Bronagh, because Keela already ruined Matt Bomer for me when she said the exact same thing in the Bahamas. So fuck you very much!"

I doubled over with laughter, while the other girls wheezed for air when their laughter amplified.

"Let's get off the topic of celeb crushes," Alec then grumbled.

"Branna," Keela rasped, calming herself. "Ask one of us a question."

I thought about it, and since I had a feeling all the questions would be related to sex, I made mine related to it, too.

"Bronagh," I said, grinning at my sister. "What is your favourite position in bed?"

Dominic looked at his lady, a smirk playing on his lips. Bronagh mulled my question over in her mind then after some serious consideration she said, "Near the wall, so I'm closest to me phone when it's chargin'."

I tittered at her answer, then looked to Dominic and burst into laughter. The look of hurt and betrayal was plastered all over his sculpted face.

"Kicking me in the nuts would have been less painful, Bronagh," he muttered as he stood up and practically dragged himself, and his wounded ego, out of the room.

Bronagh looked at his back then looked to me and frowned before she widened her eyes and asked, "You meant sexual position, didn't you?"

I nodded, still laughing.

She sighed and shouted, "Doggy style!"

Things were silent for a moment then there was a loud shout.

"I fucking *knew* it!"

My shoulders shook as I laughed.

"Why do you bait him like that?" Bronagh asked, a smile twitching at her lips.

I shrugged. "It amuses me."

"You're a sick woman," she growled. "Being on morphine when you were in the hospital has messed with your mind, it's wiped away all your niceness."

I continued to laugh.

"Dominic, come back," she called out, groaning. "Me back is still sore."

He re-entered the room as quickly as he left and fell back down next to Bronagh who leaned forward enough for Dominic to slip his hand back behind her so he could rub the base of her spine.

"Don't be afraid to do it harder," she grunted.

"That's what she said," Alec said earning a laugh from Keela and myself.

"Have you ever thought of givin' up sexual innuendos?" I asked him with my lip curled upward. "Because you should, you can be so disgustin' at times."

"I've tried," Alec sighed. "But it's hard, *so* hard."

I picked up the cushion next to me and threw it at his smirking face. He caught it before it could make contact though.

"Ryder, you go next," Damien said, as he stretched his arms over the back of Keela and Alec's sofa.

Ryder thought about it, then to Dominic he said, "What was the first thing about Bronagh that you found yourself attracted to?"

Dominic looked down at Bronagh and said, "Your eyes. I had

never seen eyes so emerald green before, they were, and still are, beautiful."

Bronagh's face flushed crimson, and it made Dominic smile.

"I thought you were goin' to say me arse," she mumbled.

His lip twitched. "You hadn't turned around at that point so I just got a frontal image of you. I didn't get a good look at my baby until we were in woodwork class and you were at the gluing station. I swear I instantly fell in love with you when I saw your ass."

I snorted.

"You're such a perv." Bronagh said, but I could tell she was pleased with his original answer.

Dominic shrugged. "I've always made my fondness for your ass known, don't act like it's a sudden surprise."

Ain't that the truth.

"Okay, next question," my sister said. "Alec, what won't Meatloaf do for love?"

"Anal," he replied. "It's definitely anal."

We all laughed.

"Are all these questions going to be about sex, or a sex act?" Alannah then questioned when she entered the room and leaned her arms on the back of the sofa beside Bronagh's head. "Because sex is overrated."

Every one of us snapped our attention to Alannah when she spoke. She rolled her eyes at us and said, "It is, just because you *all* have good sex lives doesn't mean everyone else does."

Meaning her?

Alec grinned. "I know someone who would be *more* than happy to rectify that problem for you, darling."

He didn't understand the term 'subtle'.

"I'm going to get some water," Damien said and shot up from his position on the sofa, and briskly walked into the kitchen.

Alannah focused on Alec. "I don't think I need a *someone* when I have a *somethin'*."

"Sex toys?" Keela questioned, with her eyebrows raised.

"You're filled with surprises."

I was surprised too, because Alannah was very timid compared to the rest of us, the fact that she was openly taking part in a conversation about sex was shocking in itself.

"It's 2016," she replied to Keela. "Vibrators are *perfectly* acceptable life partners."

Bronagh frowned. "We *need* to get you a boyfriend."

I second that.

Alannah laughed. "Trust me, as long as I recharge me double A batteries, I'll never need a man again."

Dominic blinked. "Right now, as a man, I feel cheap. We're more than sex machines, we have feelings too, you know?"

Alannah rolled her eyes. "*Please*, in school you fucked your way through the girls in our year for sport. Their hurt feelings never made you feel cheap, but I can guarantee your actions made them feel cheap."

The conversation took a turn from playful to serious in a spilt second.

Dominic frowned. "I was a kid…"

"That doesn't change anythin'." Alannah angrily cut him off. "You were old enough to know what you were doin' was hurtful, but you did it anyway. You broke hearts and didn't care about it. You were so horrible."

Shit. I thought. *What the hell was up with Lana?*

Dominic looked sullen as he said, "I'm not Damien, Alannah. I didn't do those things to you."

Alannah blinked her eyes then darted a scared look over her shoulder to make sure Damien wasn't in earshot. Her shoulders sagged with relief when she didn't see him. I looked over my shoulder too, and from my angle I saw he was leaning against the wall outside of the sitting room. There was no doubt from the expression on his face that he had heard *everything* she just said.

Fuck.

"I know," Alannah then mumbled to Dominic, "it's just hard for me to separate him from you sometimes. You have his face and when I see it, I hurt all over again."

"Lana—"

"Look, I'm sorry," she quickly stated. "I had a bad start to me day and I'm takin' it out on all of you and that's not fair."

"What happened?" Ryder asked, and I heard it in his tone that he was concerned.

Alannah may not be dating any of the brothers, but she was part of our family and we all loved her.

"Some arsehole rear ended me and I've to fork out a fortune to get me car fixed. It's the *last* thing I need. Shit has just been goin' from bad to worse for me lately. I just can't catch a break," she said and shrugged her shoulders.

I felt like a pretty shitty friend because I had no clue she was having problems, and from the look on my sister's face, she didn't either.

"Talk to me," she stood up and rounded the chair until she was in front of Alannah. "What's wrong?"

Alannah looked at Bronagh then out of nowhere she burst into tears.

"Me da," she cried. "He is havin' an affair and me ma has *no* clue about it."

"Oh, fuck," Alec whispered when Bronagh folded her arms around Alannah.

Oh fuck was right.

"What am I goin' to do, Bee?" she sobbed. "If I tell me ma it's goin' to break 'er heart, and if I don't, I'll be the worst daughter for keepin' it from 'er."

Bronagh hugged Alannah tightly.

"Are you *sure* he is havin' an affair?" she quizzed. "Maybe you're mistaken, babe."

"I'm not," Alannah sniffled. "I went into town yesterday evenin' to get some ink cartridges for me printer, and as I was passin' by a restaurant somethin' told me to look through the window. I did, and there he was, sittin' with a woman half his age at the table near the window where anyone could see them. I think she might be the same age as *me*! At first I didn't even consider anythin', then he reached out and took 'er hand in his. One-second they were holdin' hands, and the next he leaned over and they *kissed*!"

"*Double* fuck," Alec whispered.

"I didn't know what do," she said, her lower lip wobbling. "I was scared he would see me so I just ran back to me car and drove back to me apartment. I rang me ma to see what she was doin' and she said she was preparin' dinner for me da, his favourite because he had been workin' such long hours lately. She doesn't know, Bronagh... how could he do this to 'er? To our family? I hate 'im."

My heart broke for her, and for her unknowing mother.

"We'll figure this out," my sister said, consoling her friend.

I knew Bronagh was saying what she thought was necessary, but I could see from her face that she had no clue how she was going to help Alannah through this, but I knew she'd do everything possible to help her. We all would.

"About your car," Aideen added, shifting the attention onto her. "I'll ring me da and have 'im hook your car up at his garage. Me brothers love you. Dante thinks you're, and I quote 'im, a goddess, so I'm sure he will work on it free of charge."

Alannah pulled back from Bronagh's hold and looked at Aideen.

"I'll pay, I don't want them to help me with no charge, but if it could be in instalments, that'd be perfect."

Aideen said, "We'll work it out, just don't worry about it."

Alannah nodded, but she wore her heart on her sleeve, and I could see worrying was all she would be doing. When I looked at her, I saw myself only a few months ago. She knew her whole life was about to change, and she wasn't sure if she could handle it.

"Lana," I said and stood up, feeling Ryder's hand drop away from me. "Come with me, I want to talk to you."

We left the room then, and went outside to the front garden

where we could speak alone without being heard.

"Don't bottle it up," I said. "No good will come from holdin' it inside. Trust me."

Alannah's shoulders slumped. "I know that's why I told you lot."

"I'm proud of you for that."

She wiped her face with her hands. "I can't tell me ma, this will kill 'er."

I didn't want to tell her what to do so I just listened while she spoke.

"I think... I think I'm goin' to talk to me da. I don't know when, I'll figure it out, but I need to talk to 'im. Maybe... maybe I can make 'im stop the affair... I mean, this could have been their first date together, right?"

Her mother said he had been working long hours recently, so I doubted it.

"Lana—"

"I can make 'im stop," she continued. "He will pick me and me ma over some little *thing*. I know he will... he just... he just made a bad decision. That's all."

She was killing me.

"Alannah—"

"It's gettin' late, I have to get goin'," she cut me off. "I promised me ma I'd come by and help her bring her old clothes to a few charity shops. I'll talk to you tomorrow, say bye to everyone for me, will you?"

She gave me a quick hug, and before I could say a word, she was walking down the driveway then across the road to where her car was parked outside Ryder's house. I saw the damage to the back of her car and how smashed on her boot door was, and I hated that it was just another worry added to her list.

I watched her drive off, and when she was gone out of sight, I re-entered Alec and Keela's house and went into the sitting room.

"She's in denial," I said, getting everyone's attention. "She thinks she can make 'er da stop cheatin' on her ma. She is puttin' pressure on 'erself to keep her family together."

Bronagh rubbed her face with her hands. "What are we goin' to do?" she asked.

"All we can do," I replied. "Just be there for her. Tellin' her what to do will only result in a fight because right now, what she has decided is the only thing that makes sense to 'er."

Silence fell upon the room until Damien said, "I have to fix shit with her. I heard what she said to Dominic, and I need to fix it. I hate what I've done to her."

"I understand you better than anyone," Ryder said, "and my advice is baby steps. You've said you're sorry a million times, and you give her space whenever she is around, but what you need to do now is let her know you're here, you're staying, and that you will earn her trust back."

"How the fuck am I going to do that?" Damien asked on a groan. "She barely looks at me."

"I can't answer that, it's something you'll have to figure out for yourself, kid, but it's obvious you do like her, so just stick to your guns."

Damien nodded, then retreated into the company of his own mind so he could think. We spent the next few hours together and after Keela made us a big feast, we scattered around the house to digest our food.

Kane, Damien and Ryder went upstairs with Alec to look at a new weight set he bought. Dominic didn't leave Bronagh, which was standard protocol since she hit the thirty-eight week mark in pregnancy. He refused to be away from her side in case she went into labour. He didn't want her to be without him like Aideen went without Kane for the majority of her labour.

The conversation, as usual, switched back to sex.

"It's difficult with you sometimes though, babe," Dominic said to Bronagh. "I'm constantly torn between wanting to fucking *destroy* you, but I also want to bring you flowers and chocolates and treat you like a princess."

Bro, TMI!

Bronagh didn't bat an eyelid. "Why not do both?"

Sis, TMI!

"That right there," Dominic snapped his fingers, "that's why I love you."

I laughed and so did Bronagh as he lowered his head and kissed her. It was adorable.

"I can't believe you're both having a little human being." I said as I gazed at my sister's extremely swollen stomach.

Bronagh smiled against Dominic's mouth before turning her head in my direction.

"I know, I wish she'd hurry up. I'm goin' to be down at the hospital with you first thing in the mornin' to get induced if nothin' happens tonight. I'm pregnant nearly forty-two weeks. Enough is enough."

I knew she was miserable and wanted her baby in her arms, but I couldn't feel sorry for her when I was so bloody excited.

I clapped my hands together. "I'm goin' to be the coolest auntie *ever*."

"Technically," Dominic started, "you're the *only* auntie since I have no sisters…"

"Finish that sentence, Slater, and you won't be around long enough to see your child bein' born."

I didn't need to look at the door to know Aideen re-entered the sitting room, her voice was enough for me to move my legs, with a smile on my face, as she dropped down next to me with a still sleeping Jax bundled up against her chest.

The kid slept a lot—like father like son.

"I'm goin' to be her auntie, too," she stated crossly. "Keela and Alannah as well."

Without speaking, I reached my arms out for Jax, and Aideen gently lifted him from her chest, and passed him to me. I leaned back, and lay him across my chest. I couldn't resist smelling his head, and it almost caused me to gobble him up on the spot. I leaned my cheek carefully on his head, and sighed in delight.

I could get used to this.

"Yeah," Keela jumped into the conversation, regaining my attention. "Fuck you for suggestin' otherwise."

Dominic held up his hands when he realised he was outnumbered.

"My bad, I forgot."

He was such a wuss when it came to us, and it amused me greatly.

I closed my eyes as I heard footsteps as someone descended the stairs. I listened to my family converse while I gently stroked Jax's back, but opened my eyes when I felt like someone was watching me.

I locked my gaze on Ryder when I saw him leaning against the doorway of the sitting room; his arms were folded over his chest as he watched me with his nephew. I would have paid good money to know what was going through his mind, but I think I had a clue as to what he was thinking because I was thinking the same thing.

I wanted to come home and see him lying on our sofa with our baby on his chest. I *really* wanted that, and I knew in my heart that he did too.

With my gaze still on Ryder I said to Aideen, "Ado, take 'im, will you?"

She took her son then looked between Ryder and myself and said, "I've a feelin' the drought is about to come to an end, am I right?"

"Yeah, babe," I said as I stood up, still staring at Ryder. "There's about to be a fuckin' storm."

"Go get 'im, mama."

Without a second thought, I walked towards Ryder. His eyes flared with heat as he pushed away from the wall, and grabbed hold of my hand when I reached him. Without a word to anyone, he turned and together we almost sprinted out of the house.

"Don't break him, Branna!" I heard a voice shout from behind us then, "I *still* want to be Ryder when I grow up!"

Ryder and I laughed until we got into his—no, *our* house. As soon as the door closed I turned to face him.

"I'm movin' back in. Tonight."

"Okay."

"We aren't usin' a condom either, because I want us to have a baby."

"Okay."

"From this moment on, being a gentlemen is *over*. When we're alone you touch every part of me. Every. Single. Fucking. Part."

"Okay."

"And I want to get married. Soon. We can figure out a date."

"Okay."

Every time I spoke, I took a step backwards, and every time Ryder replied, he took a step towards me.

"Just okay?" I asked. "You agree with everythin' I've said?"

"Every. Single. Fucking. Word."

Oh.

I blinked. "Do you have anythin' else to say?"

"Yeah," he said and shot forward. "I'm going to make you scream."

My legs went weak, and before I submitted to him completely I said, "Promises, promises."

With a promising grin, Ryder grabbed hold of me. I yelped when he picked me up, put me over his shoulder and beelined up the stairs, taking the steps two at a time. Like the snap of my fingers we were in *our* bedroom, and he had me pressed against the bedroom door, pulling my clothes from my body as he dominated my mouth with his.

I matched his hunger and kissed him back, hard. My hands pulled at his shirt, and I heard some of the material rip. Ryder growled against my move, grabbed his shirt and continued what I started. He ripped the fabric from his body and tossed it behind him.

I placed my hands on his bare chest and groaned when I slid them around to his back and felt rippling muscles contract under my fingertips.

Damn.

"Now," I begged against his lips. "No foreplay, just you inside me. Please, Ryder."

I didn't have to ask him twice.

"I love you, sweetness" he said.

I hummed. "I know, and I love you too."

"I just wanted to tell you."

I licked my lips. "Why?"

"Because I'm going to fuck you like I don't."

My breath caught in my throat when he picked me up and moved us over to the bed. When he lay me down, he rid me of my shoes, socks, jeans and knickers. My top was thrown somewhere in the room, and so was my bra. He got himself naked then in record time and it made me laugh.

"You're so eager."

Ryder growled. "You have *no* fucking idea."

Oh, but I did.

I was starved of being imitate with him for a long time too, and I was beyond ready to bring that to an end and reintroduce myself to every part of his hard body.

To show *my* eagerness, I parted my thighs for him as he crawled up my body and hovered over me. I groaned when he balanced his weight on his left forearm and used his right hand to grip the base of his cock and rub the head back and forth over my throbbing clit.

"Ryder," I moaned and slid my hands from his waist around to his back.

"I'm here, sweetness," he replied. "And I'm not going anywhere. Ever."

I gasped as sensation filled me.

"I'm holdin' you to that," I moaned.

He slowly rubbed the head of his shaft down my pussy until it kissed my entrance. I burned to have him inside, but knowing he was a hair away from being inside me was *such* a turn on.

"Fuck," he breathed and shook his head. "I'm scared and I don't know why."

I pulled my hands from his back and placed them on either side of his face.

"You're nervous, but don't be. It's just us."

"Just us," he repeated.

I nodded. "Watch me as you enter me, you'll feel better. I promise."

With his eyes locked on mine, he slowly slid into my body. I saw his jaw set, and the muscles in his arms flex as he entered into me inch by agonising inch. It felt so good that I couldn't keep eye contact with Ryder; I allowed my eyes to roll back and for a groan to escape me.

"Beautiful," he murmured.

I felt his lips on mine then. The taste of his mouth was mixed with the pleasure in my core, and it caused me to become very vocal.

"I fit perfectly with you," he said against my mouth. "You're wrapped around me so tight, Bran... *fuck*."

I returned my hands to his back and gently grazed my nails against his skin, causing him to hiss and thrust into me harder. The urge to come was overwhelming so I took one hand and trailed it down my body until my fingertips grazed over the swollen bud that hurt so good.

"Yes," he rasped. "Rub that pretty clit of yours, baby. Show me what you've been doing when you didn't have me."

Yes, sir.

I bit down on my lower lip as I lifted my fingers to Ryder's mouth as I watched him lube them up with his saliva. I placed them back on my clit and began to rotate them.

"Holy fuck!"

Ryder drove into me harder, faster and a *hell* of a lot deeper. He switched up from slow and steady to fast and furious and had me almost screaming in pleasure.

"Did you pretend your fingers were my mouth, baby?" Ryder asked, his voice primal. "Did you fuck yourself and wish it was me?"

"Yes!" I panted. "Only you."

He picked up his pace. "Come on, baby. I'm so close."

Me too.

I rubbed my clit faster, and watched Ryder's face contorted with pleasure as he reminded my body, and me, just what we could do together. We could make fireworks.

My orgasm slammed into me just as hard as Ryder's did. It consumed me and flowed through my veins, pumping the feeling of ecstasy throughout my body. With my back arched, and my toes curled, I was thrust over the edge and into heaven.

I heard, and felt, the moment he let go too. He roared my name and slowed his hips to slight jerking motions as he spilled himself inside of me. I opened my eyes just as he fell forward, covering my body with his.

I laughed and moved my hands to his sides and began to tickle him. He twitched and jerked in response and rolled to the side, falling off me, and out of me, in one fluid motion.

"Oh, my God," he breathed.

I hummed. "My thoughts *exactly*."

Ryder reached his hand out, and before I closed my eyes, I threaded my fingers through his.

"Can we do that again?" he asked, his breathing still laboured. "Right now?"

I laughed, again. "After I take a power nap because that orgasm was... wow."

"I know how you feel," he chuckled. "It wasn't the longest sex we've ever had, but damn if it didn't feel like the best."

"All that built up foreplay and teasing over the last three months has finally found its release." I said, and yawned.

Ryder turned to his side and grabbed hold of me. He pulled me a few inches up the bed until my head rested on a pillow. He covered us with the bedcover, and snuggled his body against mine.

"I love you, darling."

I squeezed him. "I love you, too."

We both fell asleep quickly and when I woke up, the clock on my nightstand told me it was after nine pm. I only had a few hours of sleep, but I felt so rested. I turned in Ryder's arm and stared at him. He was sleeping, but thanks to our bedroom light still being on I could take my time and scan his features without worrying he would open his eyes and tease me about it.

His plump pink lips were parted, and he was lightly snoring. He hadn't shaved in a few days, and the scruff of hair on his face really suited him. I made a mental note to tell him that.

His mop of dark brown hair needed to be trimmed because it was long enough to fall into his eyes now. Aideen usually did it for all the brothers, she grew up with four of them and had learned how to trim hair without butchering it when she was in her teens.

I reached my hand up and gently brushed the hair back out of Ryder's face. I smiled and ran my fingertips down the side of his face, admiring the man I love so much. I was going to lean in and kiss him, but my phone rang from my bag and it caused Ryder to shift in his sleep.

He woke up when I had to move out of his arms so I could find my phone. I found my bag near the bedroom door, grabbed my phone then scurried back to the bed and under the warm covers. Ryder gathered me up in his arms almost instantly, his hand resting on my stomach.

I looked at my phone, saw Dominic's face on the screen, answered it then pressed it against my ear.

"What's up, buttercup?" I answered.

Ryder snorted from my side as he stroked my bare midriff.

"It's happening."

I gasped and shot into an upright position. "Bronagh's in labour?!"

Ryder sat up, too, staring at me as I listened to Dominic.

"Yes, her water broke an *hour* ago while I was bringing Tyson on a walk. She waited awhile to make sure the water had stopped coming out of her, then showered and dressed herself and made us fucking *dinner*. She said she didn't need to call me, you or anyone else because she was okay. She is so calm, Branna. What's wrong with her?" he said, clearly frustrated.

I couldn't help but laugh.

"Honey, women react in different ways. This is her reaction to her labour right now, her body is tellin' 'er to be calm, so that's what she's doin'."

I heard Dominic practice Bronagh's breathing tactics, and I wondered if I'd be taking care of him in the delivery ward as well as her.

"I feel like I'm about to pass out."

Yep, I'm definitely going to be looking after him.

"Keep breathing, you'll be fine," I assured him. "Where's me sister?"

"Why're you telling Dominic to breathe?' Ryder murmured.

"He's freakin' out," I whispered in response making him snicker.

"She's in the bathroom—oh, wait, here she is now."

I heard him ask my sister if she was okay.

"Shit, Branna, she's feeling contractions now, but they don't last long she said. They're hurting her though. What do we do?" Dominic asked, his voice raising a couple of octaves.

"Ask her does she want to head into the hospital now, or wait it out at home until the contractions get stronger, come quicker and last longer?"

Dominic relayed my question to Bronagh then to me he said, "She wants to go to the hospital. Is it normal that she is shaking? Because she is and I don't like it."

He was too bloody cute.

"Yes," I replied. "She nervous, that's *perfectly* normal."

"Okay, right." He breathed. "I'll grab her stuff, we have her bag packed and ready to go. We'll drive to the hospital, and you'll meet us there, right?"

"Try and keep me away." I stated.

I wasn't on shift tonight, but I was going to be the acting midwife for my sister throughout her labour, and I knew no one on the ward would object to that.

"Thanks, Branna." Dominic said, and I heard the gratitude in his voice.

"Of course, honey. We'll see you soon."

"Text everyone for me, tell them what's going on."

When I hung up with Dominic, I turned to Ryder and dove on him.

"It's happenin'!" I squealed. "Bronagh's waters have broken."

We hugged then we jumped up from our bed, and rushed to put our clothes on. Ryder grabbed his phone and texted everyone as we hauled arse out of the room. I knew rushing was pointless because this could take a long time. I would slow down when my sister was in front of me, but until then, all my cylinders were on full blast.

Before Ryder and I left the house, he stopped me at outside our front door and said, "My baby brother and your baby sister are about to have a baby, sweetness."

I smiled so wide it hurt my cheeks.

"They're all grown up," I said as my eyes welled with tears. "We done good with them, huh?"

"Yeah, darling, we done good."

When he kissed me, I felt it deep in my bones. My body reacted to his like none other, and my heart did, too. I knew then, without a doubt, that this beautifully imperfect person owned me body, heart and soul. And I never wanted them back. They were his to keep—forever.

Ryder truly kept his promise; he made me fall in love with him all over again.

CHAPTER SEVENTEEN

Three months later...

"Branna, she is *gorgeous*!"
"Look at 'er chubby cheeks!"
"And 'er mop of dark hair!"
"She is gettin' *so* big now!"

I beamed with pride as my co-workers gushed over pictures of my three-month-old niece—Georgie Branna Slater. I still got teary eyed when I thought of her name. My mother's name was Georgina, but she hated her name and only went by her nickname, which was Georgie. Her middle name was what surprised me the most. Bronagh and Dominic gave her *my* name, and it was a true gift. I was honoured.

My sister surprised me with the knowledge of her name shortly after she was born, and to say I was an emotional wreck was an understatement. I was already crying tears of joy for my little niece entering the world, and for her to be named after my mother, and me, caused a feeling of love and pride directed at my sister and Dominic, that I had never felt before.

It allowed me to feel nothing but happiness, which was an emotion I had experienced a *lot* over the last few months. Ryder and I were better than we had ever been in all our time together, and since we didn't want to be separated, he would stay with me every night in Dominic and Bronagh's house after Georgie was born.

We stayed with them the first month, and that was only because Dominic wouldn't let me leave. Bronagh was an amazing mammy, and Dominic was an incredible father... but he was so overprotective that he drove himself crazy. My sister's instincts took over the moment she laid eyes on her daughter, and she didn't need my help with anything once Georgie latched onto her nipple and began feeding about twenty minutes or so after she was born.

Dominic, on the other hand, needed me for everything. Every high-pitched cry my niece made and he was screaming for me because he thought something was wrong with her. When he couldn't wind her straight away he panicked that she would get tummy aches and would need to go to the hospital. When she didn't feed for very long, he was convinced she would starve. It was, quite possibly, the best month of my life because I got to experience everything with them, and watch them grow as parents.

Bronagh is so chilled and natural with everything, and now Dominic is more relaxed, but probably even *more* overprotective because if he thought Bronagh had him wrapped around her finger, Georgie entering his world knocked him on his arse.

He already foresaw himself going to prison because he was certain he would murder any lad who even looked at his precious little girl when she was older.

As I continued to look at pictures of my niece when everyone went back to work, my hand absentmindedly stroked my abdomen where my own baby was growing. My and Ryder's baby. And I couldn't wait to see how he took to fatherhood.

"When are you going to tell that lad of yours that you're knocked up?"

I jumped and dropped my arm to my side like I had been caught with my hand in the cookie jar.

"Excuse me?" I asked, pocketing my phone.

Ash was leaning over the station.

"You can't bullshit a midwife," he stated with a bright smile. "You have been puking for weeks, you're constantly smiling, *and* you keep touching your belly when you think nobody is looking. You're with child, my dear."

I glared at my friend. "Why are you so perceptive?"

"Because I'm brilliant."

Smartarse.

"Look," I said, lowering my voice. "I just found out a few days ago. I thought I was sick with the flu when me mornin' sickness hit, being pregnant never even entered me mind. I'm so happy, and I know Ryder will be happy too, but I keep chickenin' out when I try to tell 'im, and I don't know why."

"You've been through a hell of a lot together, and worked hard to get to where you're both at now after what happened to you. I know you're happy, but maybe you're scared of another big change?"

"Maybe," I said, chewing on my inner cheek. "I plan on tellin' 'im tonight for real though because I asked Taylor to give me a quick ultrasound this mornin' when we had some downtime. I wasn't sure how far along I was so she just gave me a regular scan to see if she saw anythin', and she did. The baby is measurin' at twelve weeks *exactly*."

With the dates, and measurements of the baby, it meant I conceived the first time Ryder and I were intimate since we were back together, and if *that* wasn't a sign that things were meant to be, then I didn't know what to believe.

"That's wicked," Ash said and bumped fists with me. "You're officially starting your second trimester!"

"I know," I beamed. "I'm so excited."

I can't believe I'm really pregnant.

Ash came around the station and gave me a big hug.

"I'm happy for you, kid, you deserve it."

I poked him in the ribs. "I'm older than you."

He jumped away from me. "How many times do I have to tell you that age is just a number?"

"At least once more." I teased.

"Fine," Ash grinned. "Age is just a number."

I swatted at him, making him laugh.

"How did your date with Taylor go last night?" I asked him, waggling my brows.

He snorted. "Why ask when I know you were both talking about it during your ultrasound."

I smirked. "Okay, she told me how *she* thinks it went, but how did *you* think it went?"

"We had a delicious dinner then I had her for dessert." Ash said, winking. "We had a fucking *incredible* first date."

I pointed my finger at him. "You'll call her, won't you?"

He nodded. "You think I'd sleep with her then never call her again... when we work at the same job? Really?"

I shrugged. "You've never mentioned that you wanted to start datin' so I wasn't sure."

Ash scratched his head. "I never thought about it, and I'm *still* not thinking that way because I don't want to label shit this early, but Taylor is a hell of girl. She's gorgeous, her arse is to die for, she's on fire in bed, and she can cook. Also, she supports Man United. I may eventually marry the woman."

That delighted me.

"I better be part of the weddin' party at your weddin'," I warned.

"Only if I can be part of yours." Ash countered, chuckling.

"It's happenin', we haven't picked a date yet, but it's happenin'. Eventually."

I looked to the switchboard when a call light flashed, and a small alert to it sounded. I turned it off, poked Ash once more then headed down around the corner and down the hallway to check in on the patient who called for assistance.

When I left the woman's room, it was ten minutes later, and I was yawning as I dragged my feet up the hallway. I checked my watched and was delighted to see it was ten to eight. It meant Ryder would be picking me up soon and bringing me home.

I thought about how I was going to tell him I was pregnant as I walked, but when I thought I heard his voice, I halted at the turn before I came to the nurses' station.

"You'll take care of this for me, won't you Ash?"

It *was* him.

"Yeah," Ash replied. "I'll make sure everything goes good on my end. You didn't need to remind me, I already have it sorted since last week."

"Thanks," Ryder exhaled. "I owe you one for this."

"Before you go, I want to talk to you."

I think Ryder chuckled. "Is this a big brother kind of speech?"

"She hasn't got a big brother, so yeah, I guess it is." Ash countered.

I imagine Ryder folded his thick arms across his broad chest as he said, "Shoot."

"I'm going to be blunt. Would you do anything for Branna? If you fought over the simplest of things, would you get on your knees if that would bring her home to you?" Ash asked Ryder.

What the hell was Ash doing?

"Why are you asking me this?" Ryder asked, his voice suddenly a growl.

"Because," Ash hissed, "I care about Branna and unless you're willing do *anything* to keep her *forever* then you don't deserve her."

I heard movement then a grunt.

"Go on, hit me," Ash urged. "It won't change anything, she'll still always be in my life and you can't change that so you might as well accept it."

Silence.

"Are you trying to take her from me?" Ryder asked a few moments later, his voice dangerously low. "Think *very* carefully before you answer."

"No, I'm not," Ash answered almost instantly. "I won't lie to you, I thought about it when I found out how bad things were between you both. She is incredible and I see that, even if *you* don't."

"I *do* see it," Ryder spat. "No one comes close to her, you think I'd ask this of you if I didn't know how amazing she is? I fucking *know!*"

What was he asking of Ash?

"Are you confident *she* knows that you think that of her?" Ash quizzed. "Because I'm not sure."

"She does know, things have changed between us, and if she doesn't know, I'll fucking remind her every damn day!" Ryder stated.

"Good," Ash quipped. "Because I want to see her happy, and she won't be unless she is with you. I don't know why, but that woman loves you something fierce and I think you're a fucking idiot for risking your relationship with her in the first place."

"I *was* a fucking idiot," Ryder agreed, "but that has changed, too. I love Branna, and that has never been a question for me, and I'll make sure it will *never* be a question for her ever again."

My lower lip wobbled.

"Look, Ash, you seem like a nice guy, and I respect your friendship with Branna, but if you *ever* over step the line I've drawn, I'll break you. Okay?"

I peeked around the corner and saw Ash blink at least ten times before he said, "Okay."

Ryder smiled and clapped him on the shoulder. "Great, happy we settled that."

Ash looked at Ryder with a what-the-fuck-is-happening look, and it made me want to burst into laughter.

"What's goin' on here?" I asked when I rounded the corner.

Both men turned their attention to me.

"Nothing," Ryder smiled and stepped away from my friend. "I was just introducing myself to Ash while I waited for you to finish up."

Liar.

"Oh, okay," I said, staring at them warily. "I'll get me stuff."

"Hey," Ryder said and caught my arm.

I smiled. "Hi."

"I love you," he said then kissed my cheek.

My heart did a summersault.

"I love you too, sweetheart."

He winked and let me go as I walked into the break room and put on my coat. I buttoned it up then hooked my bag over my shoulder. Ash entered the room and grabbed his stuff too, but he was stiff.

"What's wrong?" I asked.

"He just Rocky three'd me."

I raised my brows. "Excuse me?"

"Ryder," Ash clarified. "He said he'll break me, and Ivan says that to Rocky in Rocky III."

I tried and failed not to smile.

"He won't break you—"

"I know that because from now on I'm standing at *least* five feet away from you at all times."

With that said he took a few hefty steps backwards making me laugh.

"For the love of God it's never, and will never, be like that between us and you *know* that. We're friends."

Ash nodded in agreement. "I know that, you know that, but everyone else seems to doubt it. I don't know why though, I flirt with *everyone*. Sally has more chance of getting a seeing to by me than you do. You're like my very hot sister."

My laughter was loud, and joyous.

When we walked back out front, Sally and Jada walked down the hallway, greeted us then went and put their things in the break room before coming out and taking their seats behind the station.

They had just come on shift, which meant Ash and I could leave and go home.

"Where is Ryder?" I asked Ash.

When he didn't respond I looked at him and saw he held a cardboard box. I stared at it for a moment, then looked to his grinning face and eyed him.

"Is that what Ryder gave to you?" I asked Ash.

He instantly burst out laughing.

"You're *such* a nosey git, I'm not even surprised you eavesdropped!"

I fought off a smile and said, "Spit it out. He is gone when he is supposed to bring me home and he asked you to take care of somethin'? What?"

Ash continued to smile. "I'll tell you, and *give* this to you now to *hold*, but first I just want you to know that you're right."

I blinked. "About what?"

"When you told me you were giving Ryder another chance, I was hard on you. After you were attacked and put through your ordeal, I worried you were making a rash decision, but you haven't. I see what you see. He is loyal to you, and knows your worth."

"You really think so?"

"Of course,"Ash nodded. "You're his Adrian."

That was possibly the sweetest thing I have ever heard.

I shook my head. "I feel like your theme song should be Eye of the Tiger."

"It is now!"

I chuckled, but my eyes suddenly welled up with tears, but I quickly wiped them away before they fell.

"You're already a hormonal mess," Ash teased.

"Bite me," I quipped, but had a smile on my face when I said it.

Ash pushed the cardboard box towards me, and said, "Read the card that's stuck to the box, but *don't* open the box. If you try, I'll take it back from you."

"Uh, okay."

I placed the box on the nurses station, pulled the card off, opened it and began reading.

Don't cry.

I repeated the thought over and over as I read Ryder's note. I was so happy that I could have let myself cry for days, but I didn't want to do that. I didn't want to cry anymore, not even if it was happy tears. It was hard though, because his message made me giddy with excitement. I scanned my eyes over the words he wrote one more time, and did a little happy dance.

> Sweetness,
> I love you, and I'm going to prove it to you all over again. Ash is going to bring you to me so follow his every instruction. Don't give him a hard time, okay? He's helping me out.
> All my love,
> Ryder xxx

"What is goin' on?" I asked my friend."

Ash smiled as he said, "I have strict instructions for you to hold the box, but do *not* open it. You're to come with me. No questions and no talking, just follow me."

He turned around after he spoke and walked down the hallway. I looked from him to Sally when she laughed and said, "I'd hurry after 'im if I were you."

I looked back at Ash then grabbed the box and card and ran down the hallway after him, shouting for him to wait up. He didn't slow down his pace until we reached his car that was in the car park. By the time I caught up to him, I was panting for air, which he found amusing.

"Your legs are longer than mine," I panted. "That's not fair!"

He opened the passenger door for me, and gestured me into the car with his hand, but I stayed rooted to the spot.

"Talk to me," I pleaded.

"I said no questions."

"Ash."

"Branna."

I stomped my foot on the ground. "You're being horrible."

He laughed. "I know, but the faster you get in the car, the faster you get answers."

I glared at him for a few seconds before I turned and got into his car. I balanced my box on my knees as I buckled my seatbelt. Ash closed my door then walked around to his side of the car and slid into the driver's seat.

He turned to face me and when I saw he had a black piece of fabric in his hand, my heart almost stopped.

"What's that for?" I asked, warily.

"I have to blindfold you, it's part of the instructions... is that okay?"

He wanted to blindfold me?

I cleared my throat.

"Yeah," I said. "I trust you."

I did trust him. This was Ash, my friend. I trusted him with my life.

He tightened the fabric around my head and I listened as he buckled his seatbelt and stuck his key in the ignition and started his car.

"Are you ready?" he asked.

"How can I be ready when I don't know where we're goin'?" I replied.

"You're just going to have to trust me, Angel."

He was going to meet real angels if he didn't give me answers soon.

Ash pulled out of the car park, and pulled onto the main road. I tapped my fingertips on the box as we drove, and I worked really hard to be patient but it was very difficult. When twenty minutes had passed I came to the conclusion that I had no more patience and felt I was near my breaking point.

"Where are you bringin'—"

"Don't ask because I'm not telling you."

"Ash," I groaned. "Come on, mate, give me a break."

"Haven't you ever heard the phrase *don't distract the driver*?"

I wanted to thump him.

"You suck."

"Still not telling you."

I let go of my box and crossed my arms over my chest like a five year old who didn't get her way. Ash wasn't bothered though, he only laughed at my little tantrum.

"We'll be there in about one minute if these sets of lights stay green."

They did stay green because he didn't slow down. I sat very still as we pulled into an area that had very uneven ground if by the way Ash's car was jumping around was anything to go by. When we exited the car, I waited for him to come around my side and help me out. I held onto my box and Ash held my bag with one hand, and took my arm with his other as he instructed me to walk.

"It's bloody freezin'," I grumbled after Ash instructed me to take my time as we climbed a few steps.

I listened as a large door was opened and felt Ash's hand on my lower back as he nudged me forward. I jumped when Ash let the door go and it shut behind us with a little force.

"You could have done that gentler!" I chastised.

"Sorry, mum," he chuckled and took my arm once more.

He told me he brought me to a room and that I was to take a seat. I sat down when he told me it was safe to do so and almost instantly I heard a door open.

"Ah, right on time." The voice belonged to a female that I had never heard before.

"Branna, listen to me carefully, okay?" Ash began. "This lady, Sandy, is going to remove your blindfold and do your make-up and hair for you. You're not to open your eyes, not even once. Sandy won't speak to you, so don't try and get any info from her. Got it?"

"You're a right bloody arsehole, do you know that?" I grumbled.

Ash tittered. "I'm aware of it, yep."

I sighed. "You're obviously goin' through a lot of trouble to surprise me with Ryder so I'll bite. I'll do what you ask, okay?"

Ash was satisfied with my answer because I felt my blindfold being removed and I listened to Sandy when she spoke only to tell me what she was going to do while I was in her care. I wasn't good at keeping track of time, but I think I was in the room Ash brought me to for forty minutes or so while she applied makeup to my face, and curled my hair with a curling iron then pinned it up and plated some kind of braid, too.

I broke a rule and tried to get some information out of Sandy, but she took whatever vow of silence Ash made her take *very* seriously.

When she asked me to stand up I did. She gently put the blindfold back around my eyes, but it was much looser that before so it would smudge my makeup. After Sandy left the room, I jumped with fright when I heard familiar female voices.

"Bronagh?" I questioned. "Ado, Keela, Lana? Is that you four?"

"Yep," my sister chirped.

I sighed with relief. "What the hell is goin' on?"

"It's a surprise," Aideen stated. "And don't say Hell here."

"What? Why?" I asked.

"No questions!" she quipped.

"Mate, come on!" I pleaded.

"You aren't gettin' any information from us, Bran, so zip it." Keela chuckled, making me groan.

"Okay, fine," I grumbled. "What're you four doin' in here?"

"We've to help you get dressed," my sister said and I think she was about to cry from her tone of voice.

"Bronagh?" I pressed. "Are you okay?"

"She's fine," Alannah chirped. "Now, let's get you out of your work uniform and dressed."

I knew better than to ask another question so I gestured with my hand for them to get it over with. They took my blindfold off once more and I forgot about it altogether because I was bloody mortified when I was stripped down to my birthday suit and used my hands to try and retain some modesty. Apparently wearing new under garments that was bought for me was *very* important.

When I got my underwear on Aideen put something around my thigh that had me asking all kind of questions, but she said I'd find out soon enough if I *stopped* asking questions.

I was quiet until they made me put on heels, then opened my box—I bloody *heard* them open it—and put on a dress that I'm pretty sure was inside of it.

"It didn't crease," my sister said in a relieved breath. "Thank God."

They put the dress on me and it was a snug fit and floor length. It felt like a very elegant dress, so I ran my hands over it and asked, "Is this lace?"

"Most of it is," Alannah replied.

I shivered when my sister clipped a necklace around my neck, but I smiled when she kissed my cheek. She removed the blindfold after I promised not to open my eyes, but it was very hard they I heard everyone's sniffles.

"Okay, *why're* you all bloody cryin'?" I asked, impatiently. "What's goin' on?"

"You look beautiful," Bronagh whispered. "Just like ma."

Like our mother?

"Bronagh, what is—"

"Come with us," she cut me off. "It's time."

Time for what?

"I'm about to blow a fuse," I said as I grabbed onto the hands that took hold of my forearms.

We only walked a maximum of twenty steps when I was brought to a halt and my sister said, "We're going inside now, and when you hear the sound of a door shutting, I want you to open your eyes then when you're ready, I know you'll follow us."

"Follow you *where*?" I asked my sister.

I heard the *clip clop* of heels then the sound of a door shutting. I sighed and shook my head before I slowly opened my eyes. I almost jumped out of my skin when in front of me was a floor length mirror, and in the reflection was... me.

"Oh, my God," I whispered and covered my mouth with my hand.

I looked down at myself and touched the dress I wore and the necklace that dangled from my neck, too. My *mother's* necklace. I would know it anywhere. It was silver with diamonds set in an intricate pattern. I remember admiring it as a young girl and always begging her to let me wear it.

"*One day, sweetheart.*" She told me with a breath taking smile. "*One day when you're old enough to understand the significance of diamonds and forever you can wear it.*"

"I think that day has come, ma," I said aloud, knowing she was right beside me.

I *felt* her. My father, too.

With a lump in my throat, I looked back into the mirror, and roamed my eyes over my dress. I was wearing was the most beautiful, delicately laced white sheath gown I had ever laid my eyes upon. The bodice had a deep v-neck with straps that went over my shoulders. It was simple but elegant and perfect.

It was the dress I showed my sister weeks ago when we were looking at bridal magazines for fun. It was even more beautiful than it looked on the model in the photos.

"Me weddin' dress," I whispered.

I'm wearing a bloody wedding dress.

My heart began to pound against my chest as I reached up and touched my beautiful hair that was clipped up into a stylish updo of curls with a French braid plated across the front of my head acting as a hairband.

My makeup was done beautifully too. It matched my light skin tone perfectly.

I managed to tear my gaze away from myself when I noticed next to the full length mirror that was clearly put in the hallway just for me was a side table with a few items on it. I walked up to it and picked up a card that had a message for me.

> Branna,
> Your dress is something new, your gartar is something blue, your necklace is something old and borrowed, but not quite as sweet as you. Meet me at the altar. I'm waiting for you,
> Ry x

I sucked in a deep breath, and had to re-read the message on the card a couple of times before I could think clearly. Ryder wanted me to meet him at the altar, in a wedding dress with something old, something new, something borrowed and something blue.

I carefully pulled up my dress until I saw the blue gartar that I felt Aideen put on me before I realised what it was.

"They're all in on it," I gasped as I lowered my dress back down to the floor.

My sister and my friends, they got me ready for my *wedding*. That was why they were crying, and my sister said I looked like my mother.

Oh, my God!

"If you cry and ruin your makeup, I'm not taking the heat for it."

I spun around when Ash's voice broke through my thoughts and I stared at him with my mouth agape, while he stared right back with me with the same expression.

"Branna," he breathed. "Wow!"

I looked down at my dress then back up to him.

"I can't believe any of this."

My friend smiled a big toothy smile. "I can, you told me how brilliant Ryder is to you, and how much he adores you. This proves it."

I quickly fanned my face with the card with his message on it to keep my tears at bay. And I had to fan faster when music began to play inside what I now knew was a church hall. Ash walked over to me and picked up the beautiful bouquet of peach and white roses from the table and handed them to me.

"That's our cue, Angel," he said as I touched the stunning arrangment.

"Our cue?" I repeated.

"It'd be my honour if you'd allow me to give you away, Bran," he said, his eyes a little glassy.

"Oh, Ash," I whispered. "Yes. Yes, I would *love* for you to give me away. I love *you*!"

"And I love you," he said, his voice breaking. "You're my best friend and you deserve every bit of happiness in life. No one deserves it more, Bran."

"Don't cry," I said to myself. "Don't cry, don't cry."

"Are you ready?" Ash asked and wiped his eyes with his free hand.

"You have no idea how ready," I replied, still not wrapping my head around what was happening.

Ash and I began to walk forward, and I gasped when the huge double doors that lead to the stunning church hall opened wide automatically. We stepped forward into the hall, and the first thing I saw were flowers that matched my bouquet were tied in the same stunning arrangement on the end of each bench I passed by as I walked down the aisle.

The next thing I noticed was Bronagh, Aideen, Keela and Alannah were standing to the left of the church altar in matching floor length peach dresses. Bronagh was holding Georgie who was wearing a tiny version of the dress, too.

I shifted my eyes to the right and saw Kane, Alec, Dominic and Damien standing to the right of the altar in matching black suits with peach ties, and Kane was holding Jax who matched the lads with a tiny tailored suit.

Sally, who was sitting on the front row of benches next to her husband, twisted in my direction with a smile in place. All eyes were on me. Especially *his*. I could feel my skin tingling as his gaze lingered on me. Ryder was in the middle of the altar, wearing a black suit and peach tie like his brothers, as he stood next to the current Parish priest.

"Nanananana!" Jax suddenly shouted.

Without hesitation I said, "Heya, darlin'."

He was seven months old now, and I claimed he was saying my name because he said it often, probably because there were a lot of N and A letters that he had fun with. The rest of the time he blew spit bubbles, and murmured gibberish.

He was a delight.

"You ready to become Mrs Slater?" Ash murmured to me as we walked.

I sucked in a breath before I said, "Hell *yes*."

That made him chuckle under his breath.

We neared the end of the aisle, and for the life of me I couldn't look away from Ryder. His eyes were trained on me too, and I felt every flick of his gaze caress me.

When we reached the altar, the priest asked Ash a question, and he replied, but I missed it because I was too focused on Ryder. I snapped out of it when he stepped forward and took my hand that Ash was offering him.

"Thanks, Ash," Ryder said, gratitude in his voice.

"Take care of her," my friend replied then winked at me before he took a seat on the front bench next to Sally and her husband.

How the hell had she gotten here with Doctor Harris, and how she was dressed up in pretty clothes when I literally saw her an hour ago was beyond me.

I turned my attention to Ryder when he squeezed my hand.

"Ry," I whispered.

He had tears in his eyes as he said, "You look so beautiful, sweetness."

Warmth filled my pounding heart when he suddenly dropped to his knee and reached for my left hand, which I gave to him freely.

"What're doin'?" I asked, my heart pounding against my chest.

"I didn't do it correctly the first time around, but I want to start off by doing it the right way now."

Oh, my God.

"There's no one but you, Bran," Ryder began, his chest puffed out. "I never thought I'd be the type to settle down and get married until you, quite literally, fell into my life. I never thought I'd want a wife, a family, and someone to love me as much as you do until you smiled in my direction and took my breath away. I never thought, after everything I've been through in my life, that someone as beautiful, smart and selfless as you would stick by my side through thick and thin, but you have. I'm not perfect, and I have my flaws, but you love me in spite of that. You have changed me, and my entire life for the better. You love my brothers, like they are your own, and you made us part of your family. You've given me purpose. Will you do me the greatest of honour of being my wife?"

It took the might of God and willpower I never knew I had not to burst into tears there and then. I squeezed his hand to the point of pain and said, "*Yes!*"

Ryder's shoulders sagged with relief, and I heard practically everyone release a shaky breath. I looked to my family and friends and raised a brow, "You all thought after six years I was lettin' him out of this church *without* puttin' a ring on me finger, *really*?"

Everyone laughed, even the priest.

"We were hoping you'd say that," Ryder chuckled as he got to his feet.

"You don't need to hope anymore." I took his other hand in mine and said, "I'm ready."

"Really ready?" he asked.

I nodded, forcing back the tears that gathered when he told me how much I meant to him. "I've never been more ready for anythin' in me entire life. I *need* to be your wife, honey."

He leaned his forehead down, and rubbed the tip of his nose against mine. With his voice, and body, trembling he said, "You're my everything, sweetness."

"And you're mine."

His lip twitched. "Have I surprised you?"

I closed my eyes and breathed him in. I bathed in his scent, touch, and the love he offered me in waves. I re-opened my eyes, and looked up into his shining ones.

"Surprised me?" I repeated. "I don't think I'll ever feel like this is real. You have given me everything I didn't know I wanted in a weddin'. Thank you so much."

Ryder hugged me tightly before we separated, held hands and looked at the priest.

With a smile he began to read prayers, and I'm sorry to say that it all became background noise because my entire focus was on the man before me. He clouded all of my senses, and I had zero problems with that.

I was pulled from my Ryder clouded thoughts when the priest asked me if I wanted to recite the standard vows to take Ryder as my husband, but I told him I wanted to go with my own. I stuck to the original first line then spoke from my heart.

"I, Branna Fiadh Murphy, take you, Ryder James Slater, to be my husband. I promise to never leave you. I promise to *always* be there to say good night. I promise to never go to bed angry. I promise to always take care of you, to love you, to cherish you. I promise my heart, body and soul to you—forever. I love you so much, darlin'."

I held my breath when Ryder began to speak.

"I, Ryder James Slater, take you, Branna Fiadh Murphy, to be my wife." I beamed when he decided to do the same with his vows to me, and repeat it back to me what I said instead of sticking to the original one.

I looked to my right when my sister stepped up with Georgie and together—with a little more take than give from Georgie—they gave me a beautiful silver band that I slipped onto Ryder's ring finger, and Kane stepped up and gave him the matching ring that he slipped onto mine.

It was magic.

And if I thought it was a dream before, it most definitely was when Ryder surprised me again. He turned and took a beautiful candle with lace tied around the middle with names engraved on it in gold from Kane.

My *parents'* names.

A sob tore from me before Ryder even spoke, and he smiled at me when he saw how touched I was.

"Branna," he began, "I know that if your parents were here today they would be so proud of the woman you have become. We light this candle today in remembrance of them. In honour of them. They raised the woman who I love more than life itself and I wish so much that they could be sitting with us today."

My sister joined me in crying tears of love for Ryder, and our dearly missed parents.

Together, we both lit the candle as the priest read the final prayer of the ceremony. We placed the candle on a stand next to us, then took one another's hands once more.

"I now pronounce you husband and wife," the priest joyfully announced, his voice echoing around the hall. "You may kiss your bride, Mr Slater."

"Thank God," Ryder breathed.

I cried and laughed as he came at me, grabbed hold of my face and covered his mouth with mine. I thought I saw a flash, but I wasn't sure if I did, or if Ryder was just blowing my mind.

My sister and friends cheered, and my *brothers in law* whooped and whistled.

We broke apart, hugged everyone, and then had to sign our names onto our marriage license that I had no knowledge of Ryder ever obtaining. I got a fright when a strange man took a picture of us signing the document, and Ryder filled me in that he was a professional wedding photographer.

He had been out of sight when I came into the church, but Ryder said he took pictures from the moment I began to walk down the aisle, he had tripods set up around the hall, too, with cameras recording the wedding at different angles that he would later edit and send to us.

After we signed the official document binding us together as husband and wife, the photographer snapped several pictures of Ryder and me. When he got what he needed of us, he took pictures of just me and my bridesmaids, then Ryder and his groomsmen, the kids with me and Ryder, then all of us together and finally us with Ash, Sally, and Doctor Harris.

By the time picture time was over my cheeks felt like they were about to split in two, but the slight pain was overshadowed by the warmth that filled my heart when I turned and looked up at Ryder.

"You're me *husband*," I whispered in awe.

He smiled with pride. "And you're my *wife*."

Holy. Shite.

"We're *so* grown up," I replied making him laugh.

"We've *so* much to look forward to together," he beamed.

I nodded. "I know, and I can't wait to spend every second of me life with you."

Ryder growled as he lowered his head to mine. "Right now, I'm thinking of a week in a secluded cabin, and you naked day and night in my bed."

A week in a secluded cabin?

"What do you mean?" I asked, confused.

Ryder's eyes gleamed. "You think we'd get married and not have a honeymoon?"

"A honeymoon?" I gasped.

Ryder nodded. "Yes, you and me. A week away. Sex, relaxing, sex, sleeping with no alarms, sex, peace, sex, nature—"

"You said sex four times," I cut him off, laughing.

His lip twitched. "Well, we need to have a *lot* of sex for two reasons. One, I love being inside of you and two, I need to put a baby in you."

My heart stopped.

"Really?" I whispered. "A baby, Ryder?"

Say yes.

"Really, really," he smiled.

I stared up at him in disbelief. "You *want* us to have a baby?"

"I want us to have a baby." He nodded.

When I had the confirmation I needed, I silently lifted his left hand that I just put a ring on binding him to me forever, and placed it over my stomach. Ryder stared down at his hand for a few seconds, then he looked back and forth from his hand to me and back again.

"Branna."

I smiled. "I found out a few days ago and was waitin' for the perfect moment to tell you, and this was it."

"You're *pregnant*?" he asked, the shock he felt was obvious in his tone.

I nodded. "I'm twelve weeks exactly."

He sucked in a huge breath before he encased me in his arms and hugged me like his life depended on it. When he pulled back, he stared at me then looked around and shouted, "She's pregnant!"

Gasps and excited squeals filled the church and even a "No fucking way" followed by a quick "Sorry, Jesus" was heard.

"Branna!"

I turned my attention to my sister. Bronagh was right next to me, with my beautiful niece in her arms. I hugged both of them and smiled.

"This little chubster is gettin' *another* cousin," I gushed.

Bronagh began to jump up and down and scream. Georgie laughed at the movement, but because she was still very young, Dominic came over and took his daughter so Bronagh could continue her jumping and screaming.

She all but dove on Ryder and me when she was baby free.

"Can you believe all this?" she asked.

"No," I replied. "I really can't. I had no clue what the hell was happenin', Ash would barely talk to me on the way here."

"This has been in motion for *weeks*, I helped get your dress." My sister beamed.

"You sneaky bitch!" I laughed and hugged her.

Georgie began to cry so Bronagh moved over to Dominic who was soothing her and swaying her from side to side.

"Here's mama," he said when Bronagh approached.

I looked from them with a smile and turned my focus back on Ryder.

"While you were in work, we spent the day putting up a white tent out in the back yard. We decorated it, too."

"You mean... like a reception too?"

"Yeah. We put up twinkling lights, more flower arrangements, and I have that restaurant from the village that you love so much catering."

My lower lip wobbled, and I lifted my fingers to my eyes, and carefully wiped under them.

"You have made me so happy, honey."

Ryder smiled. "Are you ready to go home?"

"I don't care where I am as long as it's with you," I replied honestly.

He squeezed my body against his and said, "I feel the same way.... *Mrs Slater.*"

Oh. My. God.

I gasped, and it made Ryder snort.

"What?" he asked, amused.

I blinked up at him. "I'm somebody's wife."

"Not just somebody's," his lip curled upward, "*mine.*"

Shivers raced up and down my spine. "Yours," I whispered and pressed my face against his chest, breathing him in. "Forever."

"It's only forever," he murmured, "that's not long at all."

He just quoted the late and great David Bowie and it only caused me to fall in love with him that much more.

I closed my eyes and thought about how things have changed. A few months ago I dreaded every waking day, but now? Now I couldn't wait for the rest of my life by Ryder's side. By my *husband's* side. I had a fecking husband. Emotion filled me, and for the first time in a long time I felt nothing but delight. Everything was how it should be. I had my family, my friends, my husband, and my whole life with him ahead of me.

My eyes welled up with tears and I smiled. For months I willed myself never to cry because I was afraid it would show as a weakness, but now I knew it was another way to express pure happiness.

It's okay, I told myself, *you can cry.*

ABOUT THE AUTHOR

L.A. Casey is a *New York Times* and *USA Today* best-selling author who juggles her time between her mini-me and writing. She was born, raised and currently resides in Dublin, Ireland. She enjoys chatting with her readers, who love her humour and Irish accent as much as her books.

Casey's first book, *DOMINIC*, was independently published in 2014 and became an instant success on Amazon. She is both traditionally and independently published and is represented by Mark Gottlieb from Trident Media Group.

To read more about this author, visit her website at
www.lacaseyauthor.com

ACKNOWLEDGEMENTS

This is one of my favourite parts of writing a book. This section is where I get to thank my team of people who make my books possible. Without this team there would be no *Slater Brothers* series, or L.A. Casey in general. Without these people, I wouldn't be me.

My daughter – everything I do is for you, I love you.

My sister – thank you for always been there, and allowing me to use you as a scratchboard to bounce the craziest of ideas off of. I love you.

Jill Sava – you're more than a brilliant PA, you're a true friend who I am so happy to have by my side. You. Rock.

Yessi Smith and Mary Johnson – you both are what keep me sane when I'm sure I'm about to dive off a board straight into Crazyville. Thanks for keeping my feet on the ground, and for giving me some much needed laughter in my insane life.

JaVa Editing – Jen, you're superwoman. *RYDER* has been a very trying book to write, but you stuck by my side and arranged your schedule to accommodate mine. I'll forever be grateful to you. You saved my arse. Thank you.

Mayhem Cover Creations – LJ, your covers are the bomb diggity. Just when I think I can't love another cover, you create one and prove me wrong.

JT Formatting – Jules, you're a life-saver. Thank you for making the inside of my books look beautiful time and time again.

My readers – we're eight books into this series, and you guys are still by my side and wanting more. That blows me away every single day. This book is for all of you. Thank you all for allowing me write stories for the characters that dominate my heart. <3

Made in the USA
Charleston, SC
08 May 2016